CU00406155

Cover design by: https://www.SelfPubBookCovers.com/Ravenborn

To MH, thank you for believing in me.

CONTENTS

CHAPTER ONE

Catch a Falling Star

Monday 5 March 2001.
Washington DC.

The warm breath lingered over the tear-smeared cheek, becoming an instant paralytic as the disembodied voice whispered. "Scream for me."

Carla Simmons obliged until her lungs burned. Her only release was slipping in to unconsciousness as the maniacal laughter continued its mocking. On awaking, it was with sudden alarm to find leather restraints pinning her limbs to the icy surface of a steel table. Her predicament fuelled her breathing, becoming erratic as she felt powerless to influence the blade she felt resting on her bare skin. Offered little time to react as the proceeding cut released precious blood, snaking the contours of her trembling limbs. The brutality forced a rapid rush of adrenaline hindering the dulling cocktail of sedatives still flooding her body. Carla's response was to contort her back and through clenched teeth stem her building scream. Her vision blurred, becoming lost to the distressing reality of a sedated mind. A mind refusing to concentrate on the simplest of tasks, a reluctant witness to her own anguish, incapable of mustering resistance as her tormentor mutilated her flesh. Her ordeal became an endeavour to block the mounting pain, a scream once again her only surrender. The pitiful effort echoed the confines of her prison until once again she slipped into an unconscious darkness. Her next sentient thought was that her breathing felt shallow and strained. Her body remained a personal prison, almost unresponsive as the simplest effort became a struggle as she sought to swallow against the dryness of her throat. Clouded senses hindered by disorientating flashes of colour crossing her vision. Carla craved to push past, closing tear-stained eyes in a battle for control. Then, with reluctance, she opened to search her unfamiliar surroundings, ever fearful of her returning tormentor. "Why is this happening to me?" She asked, twisting in the restraints, searching for answers.

All around, her prison remained in ominous shadow but for a single fluorescent strip light suspended from the ceiling. The light cast an unfiltered flicker in harmonic buzz to stay lit. Its effect added flashes of disorienting colour behind her once again closed eyes as she turned away. The simplest effort to move sent a spasm of discomfort contributing to a mother of all headaches. It also released an immediate wash of nausea and need to retch. The resulting anxiety pressed against her breast, forcing her racked body back to the ice-chilled table with a final cough. Once again in forced solitude, she tried to calculate how long since the start of her ordeal, a futile task, as she considered having passed out many times. The only certainty was as her nausea dissipated it exposed an expanding list of abuse fuelling an internal fight for control of her fragile mind. She tried to cope by prioritising her thoughts, desperately finding reason to be living an unimaginable nightmare and make sense of the cascading memories flooding back. One of which was the ominous hooded figure gripping her flailing limbs. The image fuelled an increasing uncertainty to perhaps becoming a casualty to her own stressed imagination of an obviously drug induced state. The details of her tormentor fleeting as Carla focused on her current predicament. She gave a reluctant tug against her shackled restraints, confirming the nightmare all too real and offering little chance of freedom. In her anguish, she despaired to the isolation and the growing possibility of her fate. Time passed, becoming incalculable as she once again slipped in and out of consciousness. During a lucid moment, she felt her ordeal took an alarming toll on her physical and mental state. Most alarming was a warm irritation emanating from her right thigh, starting as an itch swelling to an uncomfortable burn. A sudden spasm of pain sprang up her entire side, her reaction forcing her to release a held breath until the sensation subsided. Then cautiously she gently eased her arched body back to the table. Further spasms continued in varying degrees, becoming manageable for the moment as she returned to her constrictive isolation. Carla dreaded the uncomfortable truth; she wished to awaken from this disturbing nightmare and find herself in the safety of her apartment. Her wish fleeting as the truth was more than a tortured dream, concluding her circumstances were far from safe. Eyes shut, she pushed past welling tears, threatening to cascade her already tear-stained features. Her nightmare becoming a battle to focus as the room fuelled heightened fears to what lurked within its walls. Including the possibility her tormentor watched and revelled in her flailing discomfort. Carla concluded her prison was a sub-basement of a much larger complex.

The room's white-walls in disrepair, with grime tarnished tiles covering every surface. From the ceiling hung chains and pulleys of ominous intent, almost obscuring the only hope of escape, which was the rust scared door at the far end of the room.

Not that it mattered, as Carla's restrained predicament hindered any chance to flee. "I just want to go home?" she sobbed, as her mind travelled a roller-coaster of emotions, but returning nausea caused a further need to retch. She clutched the table, a violent cough a fitting response to having little in the way of content in her stomach. The result made her gasp for breath, overwhelmed by the pungent stale odours of death that stoked a craving for cleaner air. Her predicament made the hairs of her neck bristle to consider the possibility to not being the first to share such a grizzly fate. That frightening realisation caused her chest to tighten again, increasing her breathing to an alarming rate. Her world spiralled as she lost control to hyperventilating stress. Hysteria threatened, tensing her body as an internal battle raged to stop her going frantic. She pulled against her restraints, hindering her ability to clutch her chest as the leather went taut, cutting flesh. With her heart racing, sweat soaked the creases of her skin, matting her hair that fell across her stained face. The resulting struggle made her crave a calmer place and in her haste almost missing the faint sound hidden within the turmoil of her frantic mind. Her subconscious filtered its rhythmic simplicity, pushing past her building hysteria. The sound brought a smile of recognition, almost laughable under the seriousness of her predicament, and in her distress she gripped on the source of normality emitting from the darkness. The familiar sound was a leaking pipe, long forgotten in the decay, becoming a catalyst of calm in Carla's ongoing battle to regain focus within the chaos. She needed to slow her erratic breathing to match its rhythm, and soon enough her breathing dissipated to a more manageable rate. As time passed, her heart rate normalised, the tightness ebbing with her released lingering breath. The panic attack diminished to leave Carla motionless with exhaustion but thankful for a temporary reprieve from her torment. Slowly twisting dried lips to the remaining pains of her awakening body, her immediate need was releasing the building tension emanating throughout her tired limbs. She sought a change of position, arching her back to brace against the restrictive restraints and surface of the table. Once again, sweat soaked flesh pressed against the grime-stained fabric of what remained of her underclothes. She ignored the discomfort and inevitable disappointment as the leather held, adding to another failure, forcing her back in frustrated exhaustion. Further attempts of resistance followed with similar outcomes, and before long she returned with reluctance to her forced solitude.

Carla felt a sudden desperation to return to a happier time, a safer time, but her fading sanity conspired against her. Her mind returned to the ill-fated morning of her abduction, the day starting like any other sun-drenched morning and reminiscent of any normal workday shared by millions. She had left her apartment to walk the short distance to the private parking bays situated underneath her single bedroom apartment complex, a quiet little rental in picturesque Washington Heights. Her morning routine completed countless times as she fumbled for the elusive car keys in her shoulder bag as she approached her reserved space. She felt a sense of satisfaction to the central locking flashing with an echoing response from the recovered keys. That moment unfortunately signified the end of any normality as a stinging pain to her neck brought spiralling darkness and beginning of a frightful nightmare. Soon her mind shifted back to the present, swallowing a silent curse to being so predictable to her choices. If only she had changed her routine that morning, perhaps started later, taken the bus or worked from home, the list endless and all not involving entering that parking garage. Once again left to find a reason for someone to harm her, let alone strap her semi-naked to a metal table, subjecting her mind and body to agonising brutality. "I'm a personnel assistant from New Hampshire, for Christ's sake," she cried out. "What can you possibly need from me?" The outburst ignored as the shadows again refused to surrender any secrets, fuelling a blaze of anger as she clasped her hands into fists, beating the table in frustration.

The metallic thud echoed the narrow confines of the room.

With frustration Carla slumped back as forced paralysis continued to fade to the point she felt a growing list of injuries emanating throughout her body. She needed to see for herself so adjusted her position, the exertion made her wince as her breathing became restricted. Cautiously she inched her hand down her right side to reach a smear of warm blood coating her fingertips. Undeterred, she traced the inflamed wound, a deep painful cut. Through curled lips, she braced. Then slowly retraced the outline of the wound again, but the slightest touch increased the pain and added to her fading health and exposing her immortality and fears. Her injuries also explained the increasing dizziness increasing to include an overwhelming urge to sleep. Taking another deep breath, she filled her lungs to release a strained scream of frustration, a futile gesture, taking little solace in the inevitable outcome, but she needed to vent.

Somewhere in the deep shadows of the room, a sadistic laughter echoed to replace Carla's dying screaming.

Fear replaced pain in the desperate search for the source, taking morbid pleasure in her suffering. Again, Carla's restricted confines and limited light proved a hindrance to uncovering what lurked. A shocked thought entered her mind to the possibility she imagined the laughter, amplifying earlier doubts to what was reality or becoming a victim of her own mocking imagination. Under the circumstances, there was a possibility, but her more pressing concern was her latest injuries. In her search, she opened the skin around her restraints, adding to her continuing blood loss. Her only release left was opening the emotional flood gates, of which she did with a pitiful sob as stressed emotions took hold. She floundered, helpless, as throughout her confines the chilling laughter continued its echoing mock.

Emerging from her latest blackout, Carla was at once aware of her increased, weakened state. Light-headiness contributed to unable to concentrate, fuelling an effort to stay awake. Even raising her head to glance at the lower half of her torso was a challenge. With breathing shallow and chest heavy, she sensed sweat navigating the curves of her face and neck. Pushing through the exhaustion and increasing desperation, she mustered what little strength remained, her situation proving difficult as eyes rolled back and she fell deeper into her closing mind. Returning to consciousness, she no longer cared about her physical or mental state, only craving the suffering to be over, even if it meant death to achieve it. The parts of her body not numb were a surge of increasing pain. She struggled to study the latest additions of violations as fraught senses lay open from cuts in half a dozen fresh places. The scale of brutality inflicted registering on her fractured mind and threatened to overwhelm her, but she forced herself to focus on her surroundings. She noted similarities between her inflicted wounds, and the symbols now adorning her prison's tiled walls. Not that understanding their meaning helped her predicament, only stoking an increasing fear of the unknown.

Sudden movement alerted attention to the far side of the room, chilling her entire body on hearing the distinct rustle of heavy fabric trailing the tiled floor. Her body's response was releasing adrenaline, allowing Carla to find the strength to glimpse a slow-moving shadow stalking the darkness. Through red strained eyes, she pressed past the tightness of her dry throat to speak. "Why are you doing this?" She asked in an inaudible, strained whisper. "Who are you?" Her questions unanswered as the figure circled, resulting in a flash of anger, and Carla took that rage to flex, pulling on her restraints. "What do you want with me?" she screamed.

The ominous figure inched closer, staying in the shadows, continuing to circle. "Who is who is unimportant," answered a chilling disembodied voice.

Carla flinched at the sudden response, eyes wide.

"You are an abomination, a whore that darkens His light. I'm an instrument of His anger to purify that light. Your guilt is spreading false prophecies by claiming to speak in His name." With those chilling words, a gloved hand appeared from beneath a brown sleeve to point in Carla's direction. "Evil lingers within you, speaking through you and using you as a defiled vessel to spread lies. To the eyes of our true God, you are a heretic. So repent your sins, and together we will defeat this evil, and send it back to hell from where it came."

Carla struggled to understand the cryptic conversation. The limited, strained light hindered any chance of identifying her tormentor at first until catching movement as a robed figure stepped into the light, their features masked by a hood. Carla caught her breath to the realisation of her imagination had not played tricks, and she had seen the same figure earlier in her ordeal. Her eyes fixed in terror, sensing her body unable to move as she became an unwilling observer to her torment. She watched as from under the folds of the figure's robes a glint of metal appeared, at once recognising the instrument of her torture, combining precision and cruelty of design.

The blade's slim length began with saw-like teeth emanating from its polished handle, narrowing to a delicate fine honed edge and razor-sharp tip.

The mere sight and slightest touch drew an instant response of fear. "You needn't do this," Carla pleaded. "You have the wrong person, I swear, as God is my witness, I didn't do what you say I did."

"If true, let the true God be your witness as He too can be your salvation." The figure restrained Carla's ankle in a tight gloved grip, followed by a shallow chanted whisper, reciting unrecognised words.

In response, Carla thrashed against the table; drawing blood from her lower lip that filled her mouth with a coppery taste as she reacted to what came next. The blade's gentle pressure inched forward, resting against her bare flesh of her inner thigh. Her body reacted with the piercing by arching her back and twisting as her jaw locked tight.

"You are a host to evil, a heretic and a witch. Your words speak against the one true God, and in His name I shall release you of this affliction." The robed figure sliced again into her reeling body, continuing to recite the unrecognisable words.

Turning to her uncontrollable screaming, Carla uttered the name she hoped would bring her salvation. "SIMON!"

Saturday 17 July 2027.
Sufferance, MO.

In the beginning, as life set forth across God's creation, there have been many questions about that journey. Do our choices in life define us come judgement and can we become a better person to ourselves and to one another before that time comes? Perhaps the choices are a willingness to sacrifice everything we have for the greater good or simple understanding the difference between good and evil in its many forms? Maybe it's denying temptation to follow the simple path rather than working hard in reaching those same goals, but it all leads to further questions...

The pen paused as Father George Peters reread his latest paragraph of unfinished dinner sermon. He offered a heavy sigh, considering the words in a hunt for the intended message without risk of sending the captive congregation of hungry and homeless to sleep. The words faded, mind wondering to a fond childhood memory back in Edinburgh of an adolescent boy accompanying parents to their local Sunday morning service. Forced to sit in reluctance and listen to the same message filled sermons from his hometown parish priest. Back in those days and being from a respected Catholic family, his first experiences with religion were that small draughty church.

The building's stone lined dreary interior flooded by cascading shafts of coloured light from ornate glass windows provided by occasional breaks in otherwise dull greying Scottish mornings.

The youngster's interests fast evaporated in forced captivity with a wish to be anywhere but within these four walls. His further frustration came by the harsh wooden pews, causing a constant need to shuffle feet to his parent's growing annoyance. Another reprimand from his mother and the boy's posture sank to a needed search of the surrounding congregation. Obvious to note, most shared the same blank, bored expressions as attention remained on the priest elevated behind the carved altar as he continued his sermon.

That priest's name was Father Donald, a tall stoic man of impeccable morals. His ever-watchful gaze expelled welcoming warmth over thick-rimmed glasses.

Thinking back to those days, hard to imagine the young Father Peters ever considering the priesthood for boredom could never fully describe those earlier experiences. *Did you experience the same doubts, old friend, when preparing your own sermons?* The thought lingered as the Father pressed his pen to his lips. *Guess helps to believe in the message you were trying to deliver.* The fleeting recollection of his friend, who Father Donald would become to that young boy, brought the thinnest of smiles to an otherwise sombre mood. With a scratch of unshaven cheek, his mind returned to searching for the words in conveying his own unfinished message. Time passed in silent contemplation at the half finished sermon until pushing a strained back into the comfort of his high-backed chair. The chair's leather and aged frame responded with a groan of resistance to his movement. It's worn out condition symbolised his own circumstances since arriving at the Refuge of Lost Souls. He too considered himself threadbare and beaten, but for now welcomed the relief to an aching back. Pushing the scratched frame of his glasses against his misshapen nose, an unintentional result of a former boxing youth, he felt the discomfort of heavy, tired eyes. With a quick rub of relief, his mind returned to memories of childhood and of his friend Father Donald. Longing to hear once again the old priest's distinctive gruff voice, offering wisdom filled advice so needed.

"It's never easy understanding Gods message," the aged priest would explain. "To properly understand, you must feel the power of the message you're seeking to invoke. Without that feeling, there's nothing to nurture, to grow."

No truer words spoken, perhaps why those same words fail me, my old friend. Perhaps I've lost their true meaning? As the concerned filled thoughts passed, Father Peters considered his shortage of spiritual fulfilment these past few months. The void he felt replaced with a darkening depression, becoming harder to move past with each day. Perhaps that explains why he kept turning to the fond recollections of that bored, irritable child so many years ago. Seeking to recollect how those chilly Sunday mornings ever led to his calling to joining the priesthood. It was clear he missed the old priest; always a force of inspiration, helped no doubt by his tough Gaelic tone looming from the man's giant-like persona. Fuelling impassioned love for the church and the community he served.

Father Peters features flushed with embarrassment, a sentiment to being a fraud compared to his old friend and wishing he had the same resolve.

Nothing appeared to fluster Father Donald, not even when interrupting local teenagers forcing their way into the church office one late evening. The culprits caught and paraded in his office to circle the group in menacing judgement, striking the correct amount of fear in each shamed face. Not they needed to worry, for Father Donald was always a man of compassion, never holding a grudge as he recognised the good in all. Then applying the correct intimidation through long silent disapproving glares, the group's punishment was a casual wave of hand and an invoking verse on the sins of stealing. The only applied threat was of informed parents. Back in those days scaring any respectful Catholic child back onto the correct path of which it did for Father Peters. Thinking back, it was natural to laugh about that night, but for months the youngster feared his strict parent's wrath if ever they found out. Spending each Sunday service that followed low in his seat, believing Father Donald would mention his crime to the entire congregation and to his parent's embarrassment.

The elderly priest explained years later his reason for not informing on those responsible. "Simple," he had answered with a mischievous grin. "I noticed potential in one scared lad that night and understood the great deeds he would achieve in the world if given the chance."

Hope you were right, Father, Father Peters thought with fond recollection. Still, the young Father Peters repaid for his crime by volunteering around the church during his summer break. Not knowing it was the start of a growing friendship that would last decades. The next few years Father Donald watched as the youngster grew into a young adult. He always encouraged his achievements in various career paths, but somehow knowing he would return to that small church with a passion to don the robes of the priesthood himself. Father Donald even sponsored his young protégé's doctrine, making the lengthy journey from Scotland to Rome, to attend the ordination in person. Where he reached to embrace the new priest in enormous arms afterwards, visible tears rolling his face and helpless to mask his pride.

The next years, Father Peter's career included various assignments around the country. But without fail, his friend's written correspondence arrived to keep the young priest updated with news of home. On one particular occasion choosing to visit in person, understandable under circumstances as he brought grave news of Father Peter's mother's sad passing so soon after his fathers. Even now, her loss contributed to a deeper sadness, for he had been close to her and had taken the news hard.

Father Donald had consoled his friend as best he could. "Nothing prepares a person for losing a loved one, leaving us with our memories and to always know they loved us."

Father Peters thanked for his friend's kind words, agreeing to have had more time, a lie in part, as he had wished for more time. But even to this day he struggled with the guilt that he hid behind church commitments as an excuse for missing many visits back home during her illness. Unable to face her failing health and unwilling to witness her withering away from the matriarch she had once been. It had been easy to leave the responsibility to Father Donald, who gave her the spiritual support needed in her last weeks and never judged his young friend. Father Peters drew a deep, pained breath to the returning guilt, adding it to an expanding list of regret over the years. With a gentle rub at his temple, he regarded the other choices made and what had happened to that eager, energy filled young priest. The same priest accepting the challenge to manage one of the much sought after New American refuge centres? A position sought by many within the diocese, answering the humanitarian appeal after the civil breakdown of the then United States.

A time when the country suffered the greatest economic crash in its history, resulting in the federal government invoking an international call for support. Charitable and religious organisations heard that call worldwide and rushed much needed aid for the displaced, losing everything in the economic collapse and unrest that followed.

During the days leading up to taking his new position, Father Donald had rung to offer congratulation. Unable to hide surprise to a young priest granted such a prestigious position. That night they had talked for hours, Father Donald continuing to wish all the best for the future, knowing his friend would achieve so much by doing God's wonderful work.

The following years Father Peters immersed himself into his work and the new undertaking. Further exchanges with his old mentor were brief and all infrequent. Perhaps explaining how he had missed the warning signs to his friend's failing health, the lengthy pauses and shortage of breath when speaking on the phone.

Father Donald hid the facts with not wanting to burden others with what he considered a trivial matter.

Then, a little over seven months since their last conversation, Father Peters received a letter enclosing what would be the last correspondence from Father Donald. The cover letter was from his friend's housekeeper, informing him of his sad passing from colon cancer. A condition suffered for many years, and towards the end he had been in tremendous pain but never wanted to impose or burden anyone with his own problems. That selflessness another fine quality Father Peters admired and gave him something to aspire to become, perhaps making him a better person. With sombre reflection, he closed his eyes on remembering the father figure his old friend had become. Then, with a push of emotion, he released a throaty growl to hide his embarrassment and again turned to the sermon. *Old friend, I'm so in need of your wisdom tonight. Your no-nonsense approach so full of confidence and when all else failed, resorting to the threat of a swift kick up the arse.* Once again, Father Peter's cheeks flushed with fond memories before forcing to focus, mind becoming a pit of self-doubts and constant tiredness threatening the unfinished sermon. His lack of concentration was a constant struggle against a loss of purpose, culminating in the past few weeks often becoming detached from himself and those around him. He found it easy to wallow in his lack of commitment to the priesthood, including considering continuing as manager of the refuge. Once again the darkening mood chipped away at him, to form a constant pressure. With an annoyed frown, he pushed past the growing negativity. The challenge was finding a path to the normal day-to-day reality, ignoring the questions to where it all had gone wrong. Not helped by the shabby individual staring back from the large mirror on the far wall. A far cry from the youthful priest who's once thick locks now thinned and flecked with grey and exposing lined, solemn features framed behind temporarily taped glasses. The once toned figure replaced by middle age of little exercise, a dangerous smoking habit, and the whiskey hidden from inquisitive eyes in his desk draw. "You're looking older than your years, Peters, my boy," he confessed, puffing out his cheeks and patting the solid mass of stomach under the threadbare green cardigan. Another scratch of unshaven cheek, considering his change of mood stemmed from the pressures of managing the refuge. With a mute nod, he dismissed the theories, attempting to clear his mind. So returning glasses further down his crooked nose, he concentrated on the still hall-filled page.

The briefest of time passed and once again the words became a blur, the pen reluctant to write as thoughts transpired against him. His mind returned to considering the declining state of the refuge from its once prosperous beginnings, trying to note the time the rot had set in to it all changing. Perhaps as far back as when the diocese suffered a major scandal, rocking the church to its foundations. That scandal culminated in further revelations, including a well-publicised investigation and trial involving arrests of clergy at the highest positions. An uncovered trail of secrecy implicated even his Holiness and senior clergy, hiding the truth for decades. It became a precursor to further shocks that included a financial mismanagement investigation escalating from the global banking collapse. The church became broke overnight with financial losses and mounting compensation payments totalling in the hundreds of millions. It was inevitable they would never amass the financing resources needed to support interests and commitments outside of Rome. This left the refuge centres and overseas charities forgotten, struggling to fend for themselves as many faced closure. If not for the support of the remaining local businesses and small public donations each month, the refuge would have closed years ago. Though, the priest's personal and refuge troubles paled in comparison after Christmas 2022. A day pivotal to hastening his struggles with faith and the increasing disenchantment towards his own belief and loyalty to a religion he so loved. Even now, the memory invoked emotions to the horror and loss of life, a day becoming synonymous as 9/11 and the Paris chemical attacks of 2024. The investigation that followed uncovered a large commercial transport plane had diverted from its permitted flight plan. The alternative path put it on a course for Rome and Vatican City. It was unknown to authorities the plane packed with explosives and intentionally headed to the crowds attending that year's Christmas mass. Over four and a half thousand pilgrims died, many thousands injured, and the death toll included his Holiness himself and a large proportion of senior clergy.

Father Peters had collapsed to his knees on watching the live coverage of the devastation. With tear-filled face he wailed in anger to a God forsaking his most devoted and thinking back. Perhaps that moment was the catalyst to him questioning his faith. To fuel doubts, including a rising sense of hypocrisy to face his congregation week after week and trying to inspire trust in a God willing to sacrifice so many.

Then in silent contemplation Father Peters' attention came back to the words etched on his notepad and with reluctance ripped the top pages as he struggled to his feet. The leather chair scraped resistance across the wood floor as he rose, and an involuntary tug at the hem of his cardigan a failed response to his unkempt appearance. On glancing up, he saw the wall clock above the door, making a quick calculation. His presence needed downstairs soon enough. So with a stretch of back he started for the door, but a forgetful mind made him turn and sweep up the glass and half-empty bottle of neat whisky. He deposited his secret indulgence back to their hiding place of the large oak desk drawer. Locked from prying eyes and certain to have forgotten nothing else, Father Peters left his private office.

The Refuge of Lost souls was a modest two storey red brick early ninetieth century build in what was once the business district of Sufferance. It offered, on the second floor, a small office and half-dozen bedrooms, occupied by the occasional guests and staff living on site. The ground floor was storage and a spacious kitchen that led to the main dining hall, allowing the refuge to cater for the needy passing through its doors each day.

Father Peters took the long narrow panelled hallway running the full length of the building. Its windowless dated interior never more emphasised by the moulded twined light fittings, throwing a pale yellow gloom throughout as he went on his journey. The priest's footsteps crossed faded flowered carpet, his passage conveying groans of resistance from the hardwood floor with each step. From the floor below noises of preparations from the kitchen resonated, as familiar odours of cooking permeated the air. Those same odours antagonised the lurching hunger from a missed lunch, but forgetting his own needs, he continued to memorise the short sermon. On reaching the stairs, his concern went to a door he knew gave access to the roof. The door ajar, where a narrow shaft of light highlighted the dust filled confines of the hallway. It was common knowledge that the volunteers often used the roof for the occasional unauthorised cigarette break. Well aware of the penalty Sister Angela would inflict if caught doing so on the premises. With guarded apprehension Father Peters approached, flinching to the haunting whistle emanating from the slight gap as he pulled on the door handle.

The staircase shared the interior's dated panelling and ascended well-worn steps to a half opened heavy fire exit.

With care Father Peters pulled himself up each step using the bannisters for support and reached the door where the metal-framed door gave brief resistance on rusted hinges. As he stepped out, he became suddenly consumed in an overwhelming light and forced to shield his eyes. With hesitation, he allowed his senses to adjust to an abrupt change of environment.

From the street circling below came the distinct sounds of everyday life, merging with the half-dozen vents and air conditioning units. The nearest with a shudder and clatter disgorged heated contents into the evening air.

Father Peters, though struggling with the sunlight, continued his exploration for the culprit who had left open the doors. Realising he was alone; he stopped to appreciate the cooling remnant of a breeze that brought instant relief from the building's sticky interior. A glimpse of his scratched watch, grateful there was still time until required downstairs. He fumbled at his shirt breast pocket under the frayed cardigan to retrieve the crumpled packet of cigarettes. Then, crouching from the breeze, he sheltered the flickering flame of the plastic disposable lighter. With eyes closed, he took the first intake of the slender cigarette, bringing a welcoming calmness and immediate change to his mood as the intoxication flooded his system. An immediate respite from self-inflicted gloom, allowing enjoyment in the peace the rooftop offered. With a slow release of breath, the smoke dissipating as he paced the gravel-strewn roof in continued contemplation.

The surrounding neighbourhood expanded on all sides of the refuge, which stood in an elevated position offering a vantage to recognise what remained of the original town of Sufferance. The town's distinct dark dated grey tenements included dilapidated shop fronts of nineteen forties architecture. All stood in poor contrast to the vast modern city of New Eden to the east. It's continuing erosion of the once sizeable town of Sufferance's boundary with each passing year. That realisation brought a sudden pang of sadness to the knowledge Sufferance would give way to the never ending industrial and residential construction projects of New Eden.

Father Peters took another slow draw of the cigarette, contemplating how long until the refuge was to close its doors. It too deemed no longer necessary in the modern city or to the masses of the unfortunates pushed out. Not long before the refuge, like Sufferance, became a forgotten footnote in the history books. With cigarette fast depleting, he continued his pacing, kicking a stone under foot until a reflective glimmer broke his concentration.

In the distance hovered an advertising drone, its enormous screens rotating through various advertisements of the latest must have products. Its programmed route brought it past the high-walled security of Paradise Valley Estates. Sways of plush green lawns circled rows of luxurious white clad homes housing the wealthy and influential of New Eden. Its residents safe behind high-floodlit protection granting a piece of the New American dream, far enough from the masses of the forgotten, scraping miserable existence a few miles away.

Father Peters studied the estate, lips twisting in bubbling anger to the vast vanity project, causing a sudden need to shift his attention. A stroll around the rooftop, he recognised New Eden's business district to the north. The skyline filled with large factories manufacturing everything from cheap plastics to high-end luxury goods. All sold in the latest multi-floored shopping malls where exteriors bristled in the dying light with glaring media advertisements for items only the privileged could afford. But all of that dwarfed compared to the monumental project in its centre and dominating even the largest of businesses. The vast rising constructions resembled monolithic headstones forced from the ground. The three state-of-the-art high rise constructions known as the Reformation Towers and coming to represent New Eden's vast wealth and opulence.

Father Peters continued his observation, incapable to stem a need to shake his head in annoyance at remembering the infomercials advertising the project.

Each tower stood one hundred and thirty levels of glass and reinforced polished steel. When completed housing the multinational global entity known as the Order of Light. The Order's opened hands emblem already embossed the nearest tower to signify its dominance to the surrounding area. The Order had weathered the worldwide economic collapse almost unscathed. They took advantage of the chaos to buy competitors and bankrupt America as though it were any other acquisition and merger. The result was their corporate logo branded almost every item sold in New America.

Father Peters shielded his eyes again to fixate on the closest of the constructions. He noted huge cranes positioned steel support frames into place to complete the last levels. Soon becoming another example of the Order's increasing need for power and wealth disguised as religious belief and enlightenment. *Who would have thought their idea of God was the same as running the world's biggest corporate entity?* With that thought, he sensed his mood darkening again and flicked the growing ash from his cigarette. He felt desperate to change his current train of thought, but it was not to be. His disappointment and bitterness continued to swell as he became caught in the Order's rhetoric's and way of doing business.

The sound of a siren offered a reprieve, forcing attention back to the present. Observing an ambulance, green and blue flashes highlighted its position as it sped up the freeway off ramp leading to the older parts of town.

"What a surprise, it's heading for Slumville." A derogatory street term so despised by the priest chastising himself even though it best described the older and less desirable parts of Sufferance.

The town's decaying streets turning into the home for the unwanted pushed out to the fringes of the ever-expanding city. All deemed irrelevant suffering in the name of progress as Sufferance's once prospering businesses and industries moved to the more modern city. That left those unlucky to not move with the work, to become the unfortunate scraping a meagre existence in the rundown parts of the familiar town. A situation mirrored throughout the entire country.

Father Peters contemplated what the country had become since the troubles. Maybe historians would say it began with the worldwide debt crisis caused by complacent banks. Those same institutions gambling other people's money and found that the money was not infinite as losses stacked one after another. It took just one major bank to hide a massive mortgage debt. Starting the dominoes falling, the situation sped up with a run on the banks again, turning to the government for a bailout. This time the price was too high, the federal government incapable of helping, and this triggered a panic in the markets. The impact was for larger industries and corporations short of capital, unable to raise funds. Soon those companies could not make loan repayments or pay wages, drowning in a debt of their own making and causing a cascade. The once glorious America, a beacon to the world, now bankrupt after one inept administration after another, mishandled the situation. Their federal spending soon outweighed the diminishing revenue from the tens of millions now losing their jobs. The situation became global, as world economies so dependent on the mighty dollar crashed, escalating to civil unrest in most major cities worldwide. The only hope rising from the despair was developments like New Eden, somehow untouched by the world's economic downturn. Positioned to offer a lifeline to so many as opportunities rose to fill the positions being offered in its growing infrastructure. The by-product was moving the unwanted elements to areas vacated in and around Sufferance, where they turned to the seedier side of society, shunned and ignored.

Father Peters, in silent thought, kicked a stone and flinched as it echoed off the closest vent with a violent clatter to break his train of thought. With a flick of ash, he took another needed intake of the cigarette, its contents fast extinguishing the spark of bitterness threatening his mood. It became a temporary euphoria as he slipped a spare hand into his cardigan pocket and resumed his pacing. He soon reached a low wall that snaked the entire edge of the roof, wide enough for a person to sit, if brave enough. A cautious peer over the ledge brought a flood of nausea that made him take a step back to a more comfortable distance. With the cigarette still smouldering and gripped in the corner of his month, he rocked on his heels. A curious glance skyward, he observed the slight changes of colours from yellow to orange in the filtered gathering sky. "May be rain later," he mused, almost jumping at the sound of his own voice.

Through the low clouds, a rhythmic flash caught his eye of a distinct shape. The helicopter navigated the gathering clouds towards its intended destination, an immense complex visible off the shores of Lake Solace to the west. Even from the refuge, Father Peters could make out the towers of columned white, protected by high walls soaking the heat of the dying day. The effect made for a mystical shimmer of the surrounding air. Almost hiding the extensive high facade of intersecting steel and glass linked walkways above distinctive stain-glassed windows. The looming complex inspired by Gothic trappings included modern architecture of glass domed rooftops. A design completed by spires of multiple security towers bristling with digital communication arrays and satellite receivers in paranoid surveillance of the immediate area. The building symbolised the genuine power of New Eden and known worldwide as The Monastery of Light. The religious element of the Order of Light and it seated his Eminence Cardinal Vladislav Ambrozij and his clerics.

With a begrudging snort, Father Peters admitted to being impressed on seeing the huge monastery on his arrival in the city. The priest joined other visitors, in awe, to walk the Pilgrim Path for the first time. Watching groups of visitors weaving the well-manicured park, flanked by ornamental fruit and blossom filled trees. Canopies of bright colour ending at an ornate archway, topped by giant marbled hands opening to mimic the emblem of the Order. As they passed through, the path led to an impressive red timbered entrance hall, arched in smooth white stone. The gathering crowds ushered inside, finding the interior as impressive as the exterior. White marbled carvings decorated the walls and ceilings, depicting scripture from the Book of Enlightenment.

Father Peters noted nothing in history came close to its grandeur. Not even Europe's cathedrals or the Vatican's own Sistine Chapel. Never had one place imposed such spiritual and religious imagery on the masses as the Monastery of Light. On that same visit he attended the nightly mass, to stand surrounded by thousands of the Order's faithful, waiting to witness the lighting ceremony. The immense crowds gathered on the pilgrim path, clutching small white candles flickering in the evening light. It was impressive as their attention concentrated on the observation gallery protruding high above the main entranceway, not waiting long as the crowds erupted in response to the figures appearing.

Cardinal Ambrozij emerged, flanked by his most trusted bishops. The frail cardinal, swathed in full ceremonial white, raised a hand to silence the crowds before addressing them with the verse of the Enlightened Flame.

In unison, the crowd recited the same passage, their attention focused on the marbled archway Father Peters had passed through earlier in the day. There was a flash of blue flame that leapt up the arch, converging in a solid flame cupped between two marbled hands to represent the Light of the True God. The marbled hands remained lit as followers and visitors moved under the arch on to the grand hall for the last service of the evening. Four huge floodlights flanked the arch and beamed sky wards, symbolising the touching of heaven of the true God.

Father Peters could not resist an annoyed grunt to the fact the Order gave a belief, a hope of a fresh start in spiritual enlightenment. The fact not lost on him to the same purpose, lacking his own church for many years. *Wish we had marketing like that.* The thought flared his nostrils. *Our damn church wouldn't be in such a bloody mess.*

The prior history of the Order had started as a small community, encouraging many to flock to teachings by the Order's clerics and inspirational leader. Within as little as ten years that small backward community grew, investing its growing resources in vast building projects. Also including housing for its followers willing to work in its many industries, funding it all.

"Order of Light my arse," Father Peters spat, drawing on the cigarette's last remaining morsel, extinguishing the remnants against a kitchen vent. With attention once again drawn to the darkening skyline of massing clouds, he considered again that rain always brought in more for the dinner service. With a tug of cardigan, he was about to leave, when noting a single bright flare breaking the gathering clouds. Stood in puzzlement, the object flickered between blues and yellows, expelling a fiery tail expanding in its wake. Father Peters remained transfixed as the spectacle unfolded, analysing what he was seeing. The night sky had always fascinated him from an early age. He had often studied the stars through an old beaten telescope, but never saw something so… beautiful? "Too fiery a tail for a shooting star," he considered. "Possibly debris burning up in the lower atmosphere, or" With speculation the hairs rose on the back of his neck on realising the mysterious object continued to grow. Sensing unease in the pit of his stomach, he remained wide eyed with surprise to note the object appeared to change direction mid-flight. In shock and disbelief he took a step back, concluding the fiery spectacle now headed for Sufferance, including the refuge. He calculated the estimated speed and size, concluding the impending impact would level an enormous part of the old town within a matter of moments. With no place to hide, he threw himself to the ground and curled tight, awaiting the inevitable. The air above became heated, tensing every muscle in his body and with eyes shut tight, breath forced from his lungs as he tried to scream. "Oh, sweet Mary, Joseph and all the saints in Heaven," he shouted, pushing his head deeper into his chest, reciting a prayer and then silence. On opening one eye, Father Peters was very much alive. There had been no sudden moment of bright light, no crashing force of power ripping him from his hiding place. So with caution, he lifted his head before rising to his feet. A quick brush down from the dust and dirt of his impromptu dive for cover, he resumed his search as an eerie silence descended the entire area. With a flash of confusion, he questioned his sanity. *Had my mind played tricks, imagining what I had seen?* He thought. A curious inspection to the contents of his cigarette packet confirmed what he had smoked. Then with a dismissal of the idea with a shake of head it was then he spied a familiar figure.

A middle-aged vendor appeared distracted until hearing a repeated shout of his name snapping him from his forced shock. He recognised Father Peters trying to gain his attention as he offered his own cautious wave. "What was that, Father?"

"Blakey, tell me you saw what I just saw a few minutes ago, a fiery light?"

With a rub of unshaven chin, the vendor pondered the question before pointing. "I did, Father would guess it be heading towards the old tenements off thirty-third?"

With a wave of acknowledgement, Father Peters hurried to the other side of the rooftop and with his knowledge of Sufferance recognised the area in question.

Four square blocks dominated by three large twined

towered tenements built with distinctive red tiled rooftops, but nothing appeared out of the ordinary. There was no smoke, fire or residents screaming in panic as expected from an object the size of a small pickup hitting a built up area. In fact, there was a distinct lack of response, including emergency services to the entire spectacle. His curiosity would have to wait. With a silent curse, Father Peters in his haste for answers had lost track of the time. Now late for dinner service, he considered the consequences of taking a major impact event over facing the wrath of Sister Angela for a tardy attendance. He rushed for the door, answers having to wait as he made a mental note to catch the next news vids. With a shrug of disappointment he reached the stairs, remembering to close the door, oblivious to the far-reaching consequences of what he had seen. The consequences of which were to test his belief in ways he could never imagine. For unknown to the priest, his long awaited sign of faith had arrived, and it trailed flames in its wake.

The track ahead was a dust-laden labyrinth of well-used pathways of broken curves and dips. Part of an area stretching two full blocks, it was now a derelict landfill of what had been the Harold Jacobs Recycle Plant. Flourishing amongst the concrete slabs and brick waste rose islands of rough straw grass, broken by crisscrossing protruding roof struts of twisting fingers snaring the unsuspecting. A desolate, dangerous landscape, but to the youngsters racing its well-warn tracks had become a challenge testing the symbiosis of rider and bike.

The same challenge pushing one particular racer to battle those perilous curves. Jake Selby, a typical eleven-year-old kid whose thick curling mop of dark hair lashed his flushed features as he held his breath to power through the last lap. With eyes tightened in determination, pushing forward to gain on the rider ahead. Timing was the key, a touch of a brake, a controlled slide passing into the corner with a flurry of dirt and grit. Now on the inside, the end in sight, it was with the last push of momentum he urged tired muscles for more power in desperation to peddle faster. Being such a young age, everything fuelled an internal struggle of approval and acceptance by those around him. One of his personal insecurities as he was short for his age and not quite lost the baby fat filled features that made him appear younger than his years. But what he lost in height, he gained in energy and enthusiasm to push the threshold, often resulting in a weekend grounded when his mother found out. Regardless, she would be the first to describe him as rough around the edges, but deep down she knew he was a decent kid at heart. Just thankful he was not following others his age, more disadvantaged. Many left to roam the streets, caught up in drugs, abuse, or joining the gangers in darker parts of the city. Rather, a surprise considering Jake's early start in life could have put him on a much different path. Jake was smart and often quick to ask questions, but lacked concentration towards his overall studies. Lost to a world of his own imagination, that same imagination his mother encouraged, nurtured, in less troublesome ways if possible as he grew older. Those troublesome days increased with the summer months spent exploring the neighbourhood rather than stuck in the refuge, under the keen eyed supervision of his mother when not working. The time spent together cherished by both but often limited, especially as his mother, Lisa Shelby, worked long hours in the Refuge of Lost Souls kitchen. She prepared the two daily servings, often starting at five in the morning and finishing well into the night. It was gruelling work, even with volunteer support when available. Forever thankful the opportunity provided a roof over their heads, which was more important. Besides, it enabled her to squirrel a little savings away towards a place they could call their own, well away from Sufferance and New Eden.

Jake accepted the arrangement, for it left him to his own thoughts and inquisitive curiosity. Also, never admitting to anyone since their arrival at the refuge, he had never been happier. Facts being they were local to school, where he was making friends for once. Including, it was longest time spent in one place, since he could recall. Their life before comprised escaping one rundown apartment after another, always unable to put down roots before having to move on again. A routine of woken in the early hours by his mother, hurrying to gather the continuously packed bags of their few cherished belongings and back on the road. Making their way to a new city where another flea pit apartment awaited before months or even weeks passed and the vicious circle started again. With age, Jake questioned why, but his mother's response remained a wall of upsetting silence. Though Jake was a smart kid, recognising her shield of silence hid a darker truth. That truth being his father had been a drunk, violent, and deadbeat. What memories he had of him were vague and frightening, remembering that their last night together, listening to the heated argument, one of many the past few nights. Anger filled voices silenced with the cries of his mother and finally slamming of doors. The experience left a young Jake cowering under his covers, waiting in silence and unable to sleep until disturbed by a soft sound of movement entering his room. A shape caught in the dim illumination of his night light. Jake tensed to the intrusion until recognising the shape come to sit on the side of his bed.

Ever cautious to stay silent, Lisa wiped the remaining tears lining her flushed cheeks, before gentle leaning in to kiss her son's forehead. Her reassuring touch in the ambient light, insufficient to hide dark bruising or the latest swollen lip as she offered a forced smile. Her explanation was always not to worry, and he should sleep. Then in silent observation she needed to protect him as she pushed back his hair to uncover the soft features as he faked slumber. Unable to resist the temptation, she would sweep him up in her arms in an embrace, unable to hide the released emotions. Becoming a pivotal moment starting a chain of events that became a nomad life of late night escapes and years of desperate struggle. But no matter how hard they tried to escape that old life, the vicious torment returned as Jake's father would track them to their next apartment. In the beginning Lisa fell for the apologies, the charm and heartfelt explanations of how he had changed, wanting to be a family again. Those lies over time became tiring until seeing through them to the real man underneath of false pleasantries as he fell back to his former drink fuelled violent ways. Another escape brought them to New Eden, promising fresh opportunities for all. But what awaited them was homelessness and desperation until a chance meeting at a rundown refuge. Both huddled against the cold, fighting a lingering hunger, just hoping for a few hours' rest under a warm roof and grateful of an offer of a hot meal.

Father Peters recognised their plight, coming to sit and listen to their story. The night ended with the offer of a spare room, a few nights' rest until getting back on their feet.

Lisa reluctant to accept unless she repaid the generosity by working in the kitchen, an arrangement that became permanent and was a turning point for the young family. As time passed, they hoped their old life was behind them. But fate had other arrangements with the sudden reappearance of Jake's father once again, this time appearing sober and dressed as a man of means. His explanation was to be working again and getting his life back together, including needing to reconnect with his family without causing further trouble. For Lisa, feeling conflicted, recognising the same stories. But Jake was older and at an age to make his own choices, understanding a child's need to connect with their father. Against her better judgement and reluctance, she allowed supervised visits in the hall if Jake agreed.

Since Jake could remember, he had struggled with memories of his father. Now confronted with the bogyman the man had become, he spent their first meeting fidgeting, clutching his mother's side, observing the stranger stood before them. Two years had passed and to his father's credit the arrangement continued without incident, but far from proving he was an exemplary father. But it was a start. It also proved to be a fresh beginning for Lisa and Jake. For whatever the outcome they refused to move again, supported by Father Peters explaining that whatever happened they would always have a home at the refuge. The situation uncovered a softer side to the old priest, later admitting to enjoying laughter and a sense of family around the place. Never more felt than last Christmas. Still half asleep, they ushered Jake downstairs.

At one corner of the hall stood an enormous Christmas tree, brightly decorated with paper ribbons and lit in coloured lights flickering in unison. At its base lay stacks of wrapped items of varying sizes, the largest of which a brown paper covered item.

Jake had never experienced a Christmas like it, pushed forward and encouraged to read the tag with his name written in bright red pen.

Everyone gathered, including Father Peters and Sister Angela, watching Lisa entice Jake to unwrap the gift. Emotions ran high as he tore at the wrapping, releasing a small gasp of excitement as he uncovered the dark blue bike.

The bike was far from new. It had been a reclaimed frame found in a storeroom. Father Peters had searched for parts through barter and exchange until restoration was complete with a new paint scheme of metallic blue.

Unable to suppress his joy, Jake leaped at Father Peters to wrap arms around the priest. Still laughing, Father Peters crouched to return the hug whilst trying to keep his own emotion filled composure. A last flurry at the remaining paper had Jake pull the bike out with a wide grin lighting his face. Lisa came to offer her own hug of gratitude to Father Peters, incapable to resist her own emotion at seeing her little boy so happy.

Christmas was several months ago and Jake cherished his gift as he raced, testing his knowledge of the track for any advantage over the competition. With a decisive push of speed, the finish line passed with a close second. The bike's momentum pushing Jake to the top of the largest of three earth mounds dominating the site. From here he could oversee the whole unofficial track as he caught his breath. Adrenaline continued to flood his system, heart thumping as he checked the remaining rider's pass as a huge grin exemplified his satisfaction of his triumph. Worth the pained response from arms and legs, but his enthusiasm would not wane as he searched for his next challenge.

A steep descent ended at a barrel and plank jump packed against a mound of dry earth.

The front wheel now rested at the edge of the drop, hands gripped white in preparation as Jake sensed perspiration run down his neck and back. His remaining focus remained on the drop before him.

To his right a small group of riders stopped to watch, a feat few would try themselves.

Jake lived for the moment and the rush, slowing his breathing, focusing on the silent countdown.

Below, Jake's audience of spectators scattered.

His focus broken, Jakes expression flipped to confusion in the search for the cause to their sudden flight. High above, a rush of heated air overcame Jake, forcing him to the ground. Any exposed skin tingled with heat as he recoiled at the trailing flames of dark greys and orange. Eyes wide and mouth open were suddenly awash of grit and dust as the fiery spectacle rushed overhead. All Jake could do was to roll onto his stomach, coughing violently as the dust cloud enveloped the whole site. "Cool," he spluttered in complete amazement.

The flamed object rocketed overhead, continuing on a low trajectory before dissipating towards the populated area of the old town where towering tenements stood in the distance.

Without hesitation, Jake untangled from the bike, pushing off in desperate pursuit of the fiery object. The last sight his friends had was of his blue and white backpack bobbing on his back as he rode across the waste ground in pursuit. Jake covered the site in haste, taking jumps and dips like a professional. A glance of oversized watch showed impending curfew was fast approaching. With priorities changed and frantic peddling, the collapsed section in the boundary chain fence fast approached. With little time to slow, he pulled hard on the handlebars to clear the gap and hit the pavement with a screech of brakes and tyre. Startled pedestrians shouted alarm to his sudden appearance, but he was already down the street. In the back of Jake's mind, he feared a mother's wrath. But even with the impending threat of being grounded, curiosity got the best of him as he focused on the fast disappearing object, proving more important. Turning on to the main expressway flyover, he weaved grid locked drivers, leaving their vehicles to join other shocked onlookers at the spectacle overhead. All attention remained on the object, ignoring the kid speeding further into the old town, back pack bobbing in his wake.

Slowing on entering the interchange, Jake turned at Mario's Coffee house where Sufferance changed from run down businesses to a more built up residential district. It was the prime route in to the city and so the traffic grew heavier, hindering Jake's ability to keep up his speed without risk to himself. He had also lost sight of the object, forcing him to work on instinct and awareness of the area. Then, taking various shortcuts through alleyways and side streets, he exited into a large communal area. The open ground adjoined residential gardens backing on to a large tenement. A frantic exploration of the actual area uncovered no evidence of what had happened to the object, no smoke or debris, nothing. With disappointment, Jake dismounted, choosing to push his bike over the uneven ground.

As the tenements loomed over him, sounds of the neighbourhood resonated. Televisions blurted out the latest mind numbing shows, drowned out by the distinctive voice of Mrs Basilio arguing with her oversized waste of a husband. His shirtless frame sat lounging in his favourite recliner, oblivious to his wife's gesticulating rant as he watched the game. Mrs Basilio screamed a last insult, explaining how he sucked the life out of her and she was moving in with her mother.

Jake ignored it all, pushing his bike further into the residential gardens separated by a high chain fence, decorated with coloured plastic strips fluttering in the breeze. Those same strips directed towards a few smallholdings and gardens cared for by local tenants growing what few fresh vegetables and fruit they could. It was also the site of the occasional block party in the warm summer evenings. Today deserted as distant sirens brought Jake's attention to a few blocks away. Sensing they were getting closer caused a sudden need for urgency, understanding that witnesses to the object's flaming spectacle by now must have reported to the authorities.

Just then, there grew a strong pungent stench of rotten eggs mixed with petrol, almost causing a need to retch. Quickly composing himself, Jake continued through the gardens, opening to a larger open green space reclaimed with weeds and wildflower. He remembered a worn path that led to a block of garages at the rear. Soon, pushing through the wildgrass and onto the pathway, he came across six lockup garages, weathered concrete construction roofed with corrugated sheeting. Years back, they offered secure parking for many residents of the tenements. Now, like most living in Sufferance, those same residents could neither afford the basics regardless have means to own the luxury of a car. So now the garages lay abandoned to the elements, and in the past Jake and friends had spent many an hour exploring those left open. Suddenly a not too pleasant memory returned, bringing on a sudden pang of guilt. He remembered a time caught trespassing and brought home in the rear of a police cruiser to face his mother's wrath. Pushing the memory to the far reaches of his mind, he came to pass rows of slatted doors in various degrees of ill repair. Jake stopped at one set of double doors that had seen better days. Large patches of flaking paint air brushed by ganger tags highlighted local rivalry daubed on both doors. With curiosity, he noted the light plumes of greying smoke protruding from between the cracks. Quickly searching the immediate area, he uncovered rusting railings hidden in the long grass. Tugging on the straps of his backpack, he removed it to retrieve a bike lock. A reassuring click fastened the lock around the railings, and with his bike secured, his attention shifted back to the doors. He kept a tight grip of the handles, still resisting. Then bracing his legs, he pulled until the doors gave way just enough to enable him to push his upper body inside to explore. A sudden rush of smoke greeted him, filling lungs with an acidic taste that made him cough. He spat to rid the taste as he backed out with need of fresher air. His eyes stung red, needing to blink past the irritation before a final cough cleared his throat. Unperturbed and with a wipe of eyes, he tried again. This time the smoke appeared less dense, continuing to disperse through the open space made with his body as he pushed inside to investigate. What he found was a windowless, unlit space, unable to search further. Undeterred, he came back to his bike, reaching for the battery lamp hooked on the front. With a stubborn pull, it sprang from its cradle. Jake smiled with satisfaction at finding a reason to have the large lamp after all this time. Another of his mother's safety measures if ever caught out in the neighbourhood after dark. As he examined the lamp, the irony not lost on him as his curfew did not allow him out after dark to even use it. The switch appeared stiff, but with a firm metallic click switching on to Jake's relief. Then, with the lamp in hand, returned to the garage where he noted smoke hung in patches close to the ceiling. With eyes narrowed, he became accustomed to the darkness, now making out the far side. He remained low and under the thinning smoke, greeted with a familiar stench smelt earlier down at the tenements. The light flickered as he swept the room to uncover more colourful graffiti, and further ganger tags adoring the walls. There was also a patch of green mould covering the far corners, showing rainwater had crept through the gaps in the corrugated roofing, making the floor conditions slippery underfoot. Jake continued to recoil from the stench that grew as he made his way further in, his free hand over his nose as he panned the light around the space. It was then a loud crash from behind made him jump.

The double doors slammed shut, enclosing the room in complete darkness but for the wavering light of the lamp in Jake's shaking hand. With a nervous swallow, fears amplified with what might lurk in the darkness and also an unfortunate moment for his light to struggle to stay lit. It added to the creepy atmosphere, and Jake's increasing agitation. With a frantic shake, he stabilised the flicker to illuminate the far wall where he noticed a wood stained door. He assumed it lead to another room adjoining the garage. A quick examination uncovered the age battered door had swollen shut on rusted hinges as smoke passed through broken panes in its panelled window. With a trembling hand, Jake gripped the round door handle. Even in the obvious poor state, it remained anchored tight into the frame, resisting movement. In need of leverage, Jake hooked the lamp to his trouser belt, grasping the handle in both hands. With a brace of legs and arch of back, he put his full strength into the effort.

The door fought before budging with a crack of splintering wood, followed by a harder jolt as the full frame gave way, shattering glass across the floor.

Jake fumbled backwards and off his feet, hitting the ground hard if not for his backpack cushioning his fall. Recovering from having the wind knocked from his chest, he sat sprawled with the handle still in his grip. In a state of confusion, his gaze went from handle to the opened door resting sideways on its remaining rusted hinge. With a twinge of a bruised ego and embarrassment, Jake picked himself off the floor, discarding the useless handle to rub his bruised backside. A last check confirmed to have suffered no other injuries, and so retrieved the lamp from his belt and entered.

The room was slightly smaller than the main garage. Someone had piled discarded tyres against one wall, still smouldering, answering the question for the pungent odour hanging heavy in the air.

Moving further in, Jake noted collapsed crates and twisted corrugated sheeting littered the centre of the space. He passed the light to the roof, uncovering a large opening the size of a compact car where overhanging branches of the mature ferns outside now blocked the space. A rhythmic sound of small stones striking metal started, and a single droplet of water hit his hand. The rain increased, soon trickling a course through the thick branches to smother the small patches of smouldering debris hissing in protest. A fresh scent of damp pine filled the air, a refreshing change from the otherwise pungent odour.

Pushing aside cardboard boxes and more sheeting, Jake uncovered the remnants of an old car. Its body a patch work of peeling paint and rust, half hidden by a green tarpaulin stained in dust and grime. Its roof and left side mangled, twisted metal, and crushed no doubt by an object smashing through the ceiling. Edging around the wreckage, Jake was careful not to become snared on any sharp metal protruding fragments.

It was then came sudden voices from outside, getting closer.

Jake froze, heart lurching in fear at the possibility of being caught. Time slowed in a desperate wait, until the voices grew fainter, the threat passing. Not until he was sure of his safety did he release his held breath, but his anxiety flared again at movement from further in the room. He was not alone.

A scraping rustle of hard fabric emanated from under a wooden workbench.

Passing the light found a large rusting drum oozing black tar contents from a gash down its side, oil congealed around its base before spreading across the floor. Further movement brought Jake's attention to the remains of a heavily used tarpaulin. Crouching for a closer inspection, he tugged on the material and made something move further under the desk. Jake was not taking chances, keeping his distance and using the lamp light to uncover what was hiding. "Hello," he asked.

"Somebody need help?"

The response was a muffled groan.

Jake flinched, the lamp choosing to flicker in protest before a hurried slap against his palm in hope for enough power to uncover what might linger. To his surprise, it remained lit once again, and he aimed it under the workbench. "Hello, do you want me to get my ma or Father Peters?" Jake took a step closer, hesitating as the lamp flickered again before tugging at the tarpaulin.

A pain-filled scream filled the compact space, making Jake lurch backwards, as he offered his own scream of surprise. On losing his footing, he sat spread legged with the echo of his own heartbeat filling his ears. His breath constricting his chest as he noticed what had made him scream.

Oil covered arms flailed to obscure a startled half naked man.

In Jake's panic, he still shone the lamp towards the discovered stranger, causing further distress. "Sorry, mister," he apologised, lowering the lamp to risk as little light as possible. Easy to notice the stranger was young, not Jake's own age but perhaps the same as his mother. The tarpaulin covered the man's modesty, but what flesh showed was blistered red with painful burns and blooded gashes. The most serious of which was across the forehead, above a swollen closed eye. A thin layer of oil covered him, making for a ghastly sight.

"My... my name is Jake," said Jake, stumbling for words.

The stranger remained silent, his uninjured eye wide as his breathing remained heavy from obvious pain showing on his strained features. "Didn't mean to hurt you, you know, with the light or nothing."

The stranger groaned and rolled on to his side. Matted hair clung to his face as he appeared to slip into sleep.

Jake studied the half-comatose stranger, having seen hundreds of homeless since living at the refuge, but never one as desperate and helpless as this one. Time passed, and he continued to study the man with comforting reassurance as he poised no harm. Instinct was to involve the emergency services, but felt a sudden urge for secrecy.

Involve no one.

The peculiar words came from deep within an inner voice as Jake navigated the pooling oil. A quick rub of the grime across his top resulted in making it worse, and so retrieving the lamp he made the scant distance back to his bike. Once outside, Jake searched for observing eyes. The continuing light rain appeared to keep prying eyes from the tenement, as did the increasing darkening grey sky reducing visibility further.

Several blocks away sirens sounded and the familiar sight of searchlights from police drones patrolling street by street.

Jake glanced back, considering what to do next.

The stranger is secret. Knowledge is dangerous.

The strange words ebbed as Jake considered his options, mouth twisting in thought. A battle started in his mind about how to help and keep the stranger safe, keep him a secret.

Tell no one.

Jake entered the garage, mindful to close the doors, and came back to the adjoining room.

The stranger still lay unconscious under the tarpaulin.

As Jake observed, he continued his nervous habit of biting his thumbnail when stressed, wrestling with his decision. *What would Father Peters do?* He thought. Clipping the bike lamp to his belt again, he pulled on his backpack. A quick search of its contents uncovered a juice box and sandwich prepared earlier. The retrieved items placed within reach, leaving the lit lamp on a hook protruding from under the bench. "I will be back in the morning, Mr, before morning service if that okay?" Jake pulled on the tarpaulin, trying to make the stranger more comfortable. "Tomorrow I will bring you something to eat and clean clothes, so you don't catch a chill or nothing. Don't worry Mr, I will keep our secret." He checked the supplies remained in reach and then left the stranger bathed in the flickering light for comfort. Once outside, he pulled up his hood, adjusting the backpack over his shoulders.

The rain was dissipating.

As he knelt to unlock the bike, he turned to confirm the doors secured and no further need for investigation from those curious to the garage's contents. He was soon on the worn path, made to a soup consistency by the brief shower. The entire time his mind a struggle with secrecy, and the impending punishment for missing curfew. Even that prospect did not dampen his mood or wipe the grin etched his oil-splattered face. For unknowing to Jake, keeping the secret would affect everyone he loved, in ways a young child could never imagine.

CHAPTER TWO
Message from Heaven

The doors of the elevator closed to encase its latest occupant. A chime of warning preceded the distinct low hydraulic hum as it started its decent.

With irritated posture, Bishop Alexander Nikolaos stood dressed in full ceremonial robes. The purple embossed insignia indicting office of First Bishop of the Order of Light. He fidgeted at the clasp holding the draped garment, becoming more constricted than his combat armour worn as commander of the Guard Cleric Legions. After so many years, he should have become accustomed to such garments for official ceremonies, often willing to suffer long arduous hours wearing the restrictive garment. Today, he had suffered a three-hour ceremony conducted, virtually stood, and now needed to relieve the burden. So it was through clenched jaw, his decreasing mood fluctuating from mild annoyance to danger of physical harm to those unaware, as he waited for the doors to open. Nikolaos had earned a well-deserved reputation for lack of patience, ever noticeable with his subordinates on his rise to First Bishop. Perhaps a trait no doubt inherited from a less than tolerant father, often expressing his own lack of self-control by bringing up his siblings in a rundown part of Pittsburgh. A hard start in life for any child to endure, leading to an uncertain future plaguing the United States in the early twenty-first century. No one imagining the situation could get any worse as the country entered an economic downturn unseen since the great depression. With no job prospects, his choices on leaving high school were long term unemployment or the military. So choosing the latter, he embarked on a career most suited. It was during an extinguished military service he gained decorations for tours of the Middle East, the European insurgencies of Greece, and the expanding conflict in Eastern Europe. On his discharge, he came back to Pittsburgh to find his city had become a more desolate place from the one he had left. It had been during his last tour abroad picking up on rumours of the civil unrest back home, but the controlled news media quashed most indications to the troubles. Nothing had prepared him for what he found for himself. The country appeared bankrupt, with various foreign wars and a floundering, non-existent economy. After decades of overspending, it created enormous debts with no way of paying back. That financial debt bubble burst, its catastrophic impact felt worldwide as banks and large corporations without financial support collapsed. With a bankrupt government unable to intervene, vast amounts of workers were unemployed in a brief span of time. Food bank lines became a normal sight in major population centres. People could not afford necessities or pay mortgages, making many homeless. Then small, localised disturbances and black market corruption sparked unrest, whilst independent news organisations still operating reported major riots in Denver and Seattle. The troubles flared to other cities, resulting in marshal law being enforced and emergency crackdown enacted on the general population.

Nikolaos, once proud of the country he had served with pride and distinction, felt frustrated to watch it spiral into chaos first-hand. He was one of thousands swept up at the Pittsburgh food riots. To watch twenty-two desperate people die and hundreds injured during five nights of running battles with police and the National Guard. Open disobedience engulfed entire parts of the country as a weak federal government collapsed to a temporary administration of low-level bureaucrats in its place. A grass roots movement swept to the forefront on a wave of anger. Anger directed at the established elite who had suppressed the voices of the masses. Soon this movement gained support from those sympathetic to a need of a common government of the common people. A snap election brought a unique way of government and a fresh way of thinking. Gone were the major parties of career politicians, under control of those with their own personal agendas and backed by big money. It was those same individuals and organisations that were the principal cause of the country's failings. So the responsibility for a shattered country passed to a Congress of the People, and their first act was to raise the state militia to bolster a weakened emergency service.

With Nikolaos's earlier military background, he volunteered for the 12th Pittsburgh Volunteers. Their first deployment was restoring order to the streets, to patrol the mass refugee camps emerging to house the displaced and desperate, and those who had lost everything. It was in these camps he heard rumours of mysterious clergy moving amongst the crowds; talking of a new church. They offered a fresh beginning and a path of enlightenment for those willing to listen. Many of the camp's inhabitants flocked in hope and belief of salvation from the despair plaguing so many. Nikolaos came upon such a gathering conducted by a robed cleric whose new teachings were finding a growing faith amongst many. The large tent appeared crowded to capacity as Nikolaos, sensing his own apprehension, sat listening to the white-robed cleric, reading passages of scripture. After the service, he received his own copy of The Book of Enlightenment to the Wisdom of the Second Reformation. He turned the small red leather bound pages in his hand, tracing the embossed lettering on the cover. Just holding the book brought a sudden change. On returning to his tent that night, he read until sensing clarity and understanding in the words and towards life and those around him. In the next months he considered the teachings, attending further meetings and encouraging others to join and listen. It brought a need to do more, resulting in his resignation of his military commission and begin his dedication to becoming a cleric in the Order. He enrolled at the fledging construction that would grow into the Monastery of Light and expanded out to become the city of New Eden. The next few years he was to become one of many clerics to live in the new housing complexes constructed for the growing followers. His dedication and willingness to the Order made him a prime candidate to become an apprentice to the priesthood. He soon earned his robes and inducted into in a new sect of the Order, as a commander of one of the first Guard Cleric cohorts. The group's purpose was protecting the religious clerics, teaching the gospel to the masses. In those years, Nikolaos could never imagine he was nurturing the establishment that would become the formidable Cohort Legions. As was with his earlier military experience, he rose in the ranks, soon coming to the interest of the cardinal himself. In the following years, under the cardinal's personal tutelage, Nikolaos took the mantel of bishop and given the responsibility to command the Order's growing security division.

Many years had passed since then and now Nikolaos waited for the lift to complete its journey, shifting the robe over his shoulder so not hindered on his exit.

With a final chime, the doors parted to a pristine white walled corridor and greeted by a group of nervous administration clerics.

Nikolaos took a perverse pleasure at frustrating the clerics as he kept a quick pace once striding from the lift. They were desperate to not become entangled in their own robes and keep in step. Once ready, he pointed to the nearest cleric, a short, portly man who, with hesitation, passed a small device for his attention.

The lightweight secpad was compact, and the slightest brush of a finger across the screen displayed the evening's official reports. The first highlighted choices required immediate review and authority.

Nikolaos kept up the quick pace, still browsing the details

as the attending clerics dared not interrupt as the group continued on to their destination.

The corridor ahead expanded into an observation walkway, glass walled windows viewing the spiralling complex that was the Monastery of Light far below, spreading out on both sides. There was no time to admire the breath-taking view before entering the far corridor. The interior's climate control environment was a modest temperature, imitating a cool summer's day, whatever the time of year, catering to everyone's comfort in the ultramodern environment.

As the group maintained its pace, the clerics still struggling as most by now appeared dishevelled with perspiration and breathless as one by one Nikolaos signalled them. Without hesitation, they would pass over their own listings of further mundane requisitions and inventory requirements, nothing of significant importance but the usual day-to-day bureaucracy.

"Sign off and pass to logistics, that equipment has to be on site no later than Friday," Nikolaos ordered, breaking the imposing silence.

An ashen-faced cleric scurried to his side, retrieving the secpad before breaking from the group with a hurried bow, then paused for breath before exiting through a side room. No sooner had he left another cleric replaced him, this one older and whose narrow thin features squinted as he offered another secpad.

The screen requested a thumb print verification, which Nikolaos pressed against the screen. A flash of green confirmed his authority and a brief read of the contents and authorisation resulted in Nikolaos waiving the device back to the cleric.

"Good evening, Sir," a Guard Cleric offered in greeting to their approach, his statuesque white and red-piped armoured uniform blending with the impressive white pristine walls. "Bishop Nikolaos on route, passing cleric station one twenty-six."

"Acknowledged," returned the computerised response as two chestnut doors parted.

The room beyond led to the inner chambers and Nikolaos's private offices. These rooms differed from the pristine white of the corridor. The walls painted in warmer hues and hung with paintings of early eightieth century landscapes and smaller works of art breaking the usually sterile decor.

Two female priests rose from their desks in greeting, dressed in more modern stylish business suits rather than the traditional robes favoured by the administration order.

"Bishop Nikolaos," they greeted in unison.

Nikolaos passed back the last secpad to the remaining cleric, scurrying backwards through the doors before they closed.

The room fell silent but for the background tone of the temperature-controlled ceiling vents.

"What have you for me this evening, Sister?" Nikolaos asked, removing the ceremonial robe which he handed to the youngest and more petite of the two waiting assistants.

Nikolaos felt relieved to lose such a restrictive weight and rolled out his shoulders.

The remaining priest, her blond hair tied to give an un-flinching expression as she adjusted her pencil thin glasses highlighting her slim nose. She approached with the bishop's personal secpad in one hand and a glass of his favourite malt in the other.

With a nod of gratitude, he took both before walking to his office. With a sip of drink, he read the waiting messages and went to stand behind the regal oak table in front of a bay window. His office was less ornate than the other rooms, the only luxuries being bookcases displaying old literature, religious manuscripts and historical texts dating back centuries. Nikolaos pushed back the black leather executive chair, placing the glass on the desk. His attention remained on the secpad as he scrolled through the list of routine incident reports and emails. Then flagged the most interesting for future reading and passed non-critical reports to the waiting assistant's personal secpad. The first report titled 'Government positions for financial incentives for Congress, priority two.' The following titles were 'Subversive intervention of New America and the Pacific zone, priority two' and the 'Pacification of lesser souls, priority one.'

Nikolaos continued to read, pausing at the highest priority incidents first, double tapping one in particular, and opening it for further details. He studied the short briefing flagging items before continuing to scroll down the screen. 'Meteorological initiative and global observation, priority one' and 'Insurgent infiltration of Italy and northern France, priority two' and the last heading read 'Second-generation weapons manufacturing and testing, priority one'.

Nikolaos paused again, returning to a heading dismissed at first glance. "This entry from the meteorological division, I'm unfamiliar with this division." The question aimed at the blond priest waiting in the doorway. "Are there any further details?"

With a slight tilt of head, she manipulated her own device to retrieve the information. "Marked for your own and cardinal level only," she answered, eyes not leaving her screen. "No project leader assigned, so this may be a cardinal pet project?" She concluded her analysis and pushed her glasses further up her nose. "No further information at my security level, Sir."

Nikolaos nodded, going back to his own screen to select the entry. The automated warning appeared, seeking retina scan authority before proceeding. Nikolaos accepted the scan and a green light pulsed across his face. The warning changed to a detailed map of New Eden's downtown district and Sufferance. The following pages of information included trajectory data of an object entering the atmosphere and triggering the city's early warning protection grid. First indications were that it had been nothing but a meteor shower triggering the antimissile protocols. *Damn systems so sensitive, it happens far too often.* He amused to himself. The last paragraph of the report surprised him, describing the object's descent into the lower orbit on a straight trajectory until decelerating and changing course mid-flight to the ground. Guard surveillance towers reported a glowing light, but no secondary explosion or reported impact site. Emergency security personnel were on the scene with routine security drones sweeping the same area, but nothing reported yet as an ongoing investigation was still underway. Collaborating eyewitnesses reported the object, but no details of any crash site. Standard media lock down was in place, including a cover story of space debris throughout normal news sources. Nikolaos placed the secpad on his desk, clasping hands behind his back before turning to the window to consider the details as he took in the view. On a cloudless day, he could see between the monastery's large white towers towards the panoramic view of New Eden city and Sufferance in the distance. Tonight, rain lashed down to distort his view to a distant blur of lights a hundred feet away. His thoughts came back to the report details. They were basic, none-descriptive, that in its self-increased his curiosity. *Why assign this incident with a top clearance level?* He walked to his desk and picked up the secpad. "Why had the meteorological division access to our protection grid?"

The assistant searched for details. "Inconclusive, no official authority given," she responded.

I know as I'm that official authority; he thought to himself. He stifled his irritation, reading over the details again. "It mentions the object's changed trajectory mid-flight, is this possible?"

"Findings make it impossible for a free-falling object to decelerate speed and change course mid-flight. This would rule out meteorite or space debris," she offered.

Nikolaos nodded agreement. "That leaves human control, would it not?"

"Yes, sir," confirmed the expressionless priest.

"That would make it a security threat which comes under

my jurisdiction."

"Also correct, sir, but without details you could not make an acceptable threat assessment. Do you wish me to flag it for investigation and assign it to a priest?" She typed again at her screen.

Nikolaos stood at the main window to watch the cityscape, masked in a grey veil, considering his next actions. "Not yet," he responded. "I need more details, to be certain." His face was a mask of concentration. The report was basic on purpose, the threat of the object ignored. It changed speed and trajectory mid-flight with no trace of landing or crash site discovered. Most of the witness's statements collaborate on the object flight path lead to the more populated parts of city limits. *That is where we shall continue our search.* Nikolaos paused. *Why flagged top priority if it's not deemed important enough?* His face distorted in thought. *Did someone not want the incident investigating or gaining unwanted attention so kept it within a small circle of individuals? If it was a cardinal project, why wasn't I informed? Am I not one of his most trusted?* Nikolaos attention went back to the priest, still waiting. "Is the cardinal aware of these developments?"

"All reports sent to his Eminence's Private Secretary, Father Jozafat. So I took the liberty to contact him on your behalf, but his Eminence is not contactable. He is conducting a closed session with no interruptions," she replied. "His diary is free at 5.30am tomorrow at the earliest. Would you like me to seek a meeting for then?"

Nikolaos turned back to the window, grinding his jaw at the mention of the cardinal's private secretary. No secret, both men loathed each other. "Please inform Jozafat I will be down in ten minutes, like it or not, it's imperative I disturb his Eminence."

The priest bowed before returning to her desk.

Nikolaos could but stew in his own thoughts. *Pompous prick that Jozafat. How dare he dictate when I can see his Eminence?* His attention returned to the secpad, trying to understand why a mundane incident worried him so much. He needed answers, and they awaited him with the cardinal himself.

Another brief elevator ride brought Bishop Nikolaos to a vast garden atrium. One of three built within the Monastery of Light, these lavish spaces housed a vast array of flora and fauna from around the world. All inside their own climate-controlled eco system were high glass-domed ceilings filtered natural sunlight to feed the mini habitats. Stood in their centre were two redwood trees, towering the full height of the open space. The largest of its appendages branched out to create living walkways of greenery, offering vast canopies to envelop the atrium in a colourful scene for clergy and visitors alike. Situated amongst the grounds were immaculate, well-kept gardens populated with ornate seating for quiet meditation and contemplation. The created tranquillity finished with free flowing pools of clear blue water, adding to the whole calming effect.

Nikolaos inhaled the scented jasmine on the air, enjoying the peacefulness the garden offered, remembering many an hour spent meditating amongst its beauty. He noted, high above, clerics sauntered across the sky bridge, disturbing small birds nesting in the canopy. With graceful flight they plunged amongst the lower branches, hurrying in a continuing search for food before returning to their roosts. The tranquillity of the gardens was not to last, as Nikolaos recognised the waiting, agitated figure of the cardinal's Private Secretary pacing the far side of the atrium.

Father Amnandeusz Jozafat wore plain white clerical robes. The only sign to his authority was the thin golden piping of a priest of the Custodians of the Word. A small secretive sect within the Order of Light, their prime responsibility was serving as the cardinal's personal religious advisers. The short man was half-blind without the thick-rimmed glasses perched his hooked nose and, as Nikolaos approached, his features wrinkled into a weasel like frown as he struggled to focus.

A viper in priest's robes, Nikolaos thought, taking the quickest path linking the main grassed areas to where Jozafat waited. As he approached, a sudden urge to be cautious overcame him as he straightened his posture and fixed his own emotionless gaze upon the priest.

Jozafat gave a courteous but less than enthusiastic bow, but behind his glasses the priest's expression betrayed an icy contempt for his superior. No secret; both men despised each other, but they shared a fanatical devotion in service to the Order and the cardinal. Never more so was Jozafat's responsibility overseeing the intricate intelligence gathering of the Monastery Bureau of Intelligence known colloquially as the MBI. When needed, he had senior authority over all ranking personnel, including Nikolaos, to complete his role of High Inquisitor. This position gave him a well-earned reputation as a man dangerous to underestimate. As High Inquisitor, he had access to vast resources of information, and many a tragic secret. Well-known within the high-ranking officials of the Order, the MBI gathered detailed information on those deemed influential in political, public, and corporate top office across the globe.

Nikolaos knew Jozafat had many resources at his disposal. The man never afraid to achieve his ambitious goals, including confronting him when the situation arouses. With little time for pleasantries, Nikolaos glared upon the short priest as he passed.

Jozafat tried to match his pace, hurrying in his protest. "This is most irregular, bishop. To disturb his Eminence is unacceptable under the circumstances."

Nikolaos halted, turning on the hounding Jozafat.

The priest staggered, tripping over his robes with little agility and almost crashing into the bishop's sizeable frame.

"Has the cardinal seen today's priority one reports?" He

asked.

Jozafat straightened his glasses, struggling to regain his posture. "His Eminence is inducting two new clerics and is not available for mundane matters, so I'm sorry bishop, but I..."

Nikolaos cut the secretary off mid-sentence, striding away to leave Jozafat stewing in his growing anger.

"That's not what I asked Jozafat, I'm convinced his Eminence might want to see me about this matter."

The secretary stopped Nikolaos just short of two impressively carved closed doors. "I must protest, bishop." He had pushed his way, so now blocked any further chance of proceeding.

Nikolaos flexed his fingers, resisting the urge to dispose of the irritable obstruction through the nearest window.

Jozafat caught his breath, recovering his secpad from beneath his robe, tapping the screen to activate. "Bishop, as mentioned, he is teaching with clerics and doesn't like to be disturbed. At his Eminence's earliest convenience we can reschedule a meeting for the morning."

Nikolaos became agitated. "A priority one report came in this evening, of which I must discuss the details with his Eminence as it concerns the meteorological division."

"Yes, yes, bishop." It was Jozafat's turn to interrupt the conversation. "I'm well aware about the monitoring alert from tonight's reports." A narrow smile etched his lined face. "The strange object broke up and fell in the old town. I've received similar reports from reliable sources suggesting no further concern for the security division. I have taken the liberty to flag the incident as an intelligence concern for my people to investigate."

Nikolaos felt his jaw tighten, noticing the casual smugness on Jozafat's face as he tried to dismiss him.

Both men starred in silent contempt.

Nikolaos saw no fear in Jozafat's face, which unnerved him. *You are a brave man, Jozafat, anyone else, and I would have split you in two for just being in my way.*

The small cleric ignored the disdainful stare, returning to his device. "My sources, bishop, inform me the object burnt up harmlessly in the atmosphere without even contacting with the ground. So I'd rather we didn't interrupt his Eminence with such a trivial matter. Don't you agree?"

"Let his Eminence decide." Nikolaos lent in closer. "But tell me Jozafat what would happen to the individual who thought it unimportant in disturbing his Eminence about a certain detail. Since certain ill-informed sources had led them to believe it warranted no further urgent investigation on the matter."

Jozafat frowned. "What detail would that be?"

"Did your sources inform you the object observed changing speed and direction mid-fight?" It was brief, but Nikolaos caught the flicker of doubt behind the thick lenses. "From this we speculate the object was under controlled decent. Not a supposed free fall as first thought, a major development, would you not say?" Nikolaos could not hide his satisfaction, and a thin smile formed as he let the words sink in that Jozafat might be wrong.

Jozafat glanced up with suspicion. "I've heard of no development of which you describe."

"But it's in the same report you mentioned to have read yourself." He offered, pointing to the priest's secpad.

Jozafat let out a scant breath before keying his screen in obvious announce. "I have sent a message to his Eminence, please wait."

Nikolaos expression showed that his patience with Jozafat was evaporating and instead folded his arms to wait.

Jozafat smiled his weasel smile, adjusting glasses back up his nose as his attention turned to finding something more urgent on his secpad.

Time passed with Nikolaos relaxing, his attention on his surroundings. In all the years of service, passing through these rooms on numinous occasions, he had never stopped to notice the office next to the cardinal's private residence. Often in the past it had been a fleeting visit to see the cardinal, but as he waited he could appreciate the elaborate decorations scattered throughout the room. In fact, the office was three separate offices. Glass panelled double doors partitioned each space. Two were cleric offices where several clerics continued to undertake their many mundane duties. The office Nikolaos stood in was larger and was Jozafat's personal office. Various paintings and tapestries adorned the walls, out-of-place by the modern trappings of large video screens feeding live world news and financial statistics. Older male clerics typing on virtual keyboards projected to their desk surface staffed two tables, oblivious of the two men waiting. Other clerics appeared and disappeared through the side doors, hidden within a mural depicting a scene from the Order's formation.

Nikolaos recognised a well-known depiction called 'Reverence of Enlightenment'. The image depicted the cardinal enveloped in a bright light, gaining his gift from the true God, before becoming His voice as he received the first teachings. He remembered the cardinal describing the event, downplaying the bright lights and theatrics given to the masses. He remembered being enveloped in warmth never felt since and having crystal clarity to his purpose. With the fading thought, Nikolaos's attention returned to Jozafat, occupied with his secpad. "After all these years, do you enjoy your role as High Inquisitor, knowing everyone's secrets?"

Jozafat appeared to consider the question before answering. "Well bishop, I serve his Eminence and the true God, as do we all. I serve by shining light in the darker world outside these walls, always in secret as we can't all be war heroes like you bishop."

"I've been in many a darkened place, I can assure you," Nikolaos responded.

"That might be so, but I'm just an instrument of the true God, diligent in duties that need a unique and surgical resolution. For you my dear bishop is best described as a hammer, blunt, unfocused, and content to put faith in guns, bullets and tanks. I pride myself of being a scalpel, intricate and precise as information and intelligence are the weapons of the age. For a single image or line of text has toppled many a government or brought down the deadliest of adversaries than any bomb or bullet."

Nikolaos was about to answer when the secretary's secpad chimed.

"You may go in now, bishop." The contempt remained etched in the cold thin smile and never faulted as he offered a well-rehearsed bow, gesturing towards the double doors now parting.

Nikolaos ignored the gesture, glad to be getting away and not having to look upon the venomous smile any longer.

The doors now parting stood taller than a man and documented to be originally Venetian in age. Both cut from solid oak, handcrafted to a polished dark reddish hue, there was a dark rumour salvaged from the ruins of the Vatican bombing. They parted with ease and grace, making no sound from the eight ornate hinges.

Bishop Nikolaos stepped into a curtain of crimson drapes hung from decorated ropes, all suspended from a high carved ceiling. A glance back, he watched as Father Jozafat remained outside waiting for the doors to close.

The darkened room divulged little at first, but the sweet scents filled the air.

Nikolaos made out the distinct sounds of chimes echoing from the darkness as he disturbed the drapes.

"Enter bishop," spoke a strained, aged, filled voice.

Nikolaos's eyes, accustomed to the brightness of the secretary's office, reacted to the darkened interior, until recognising various handcrafted furnishings. Sparse trappings of luxury fitting to the period design of the apartment, including a large veiled four poster bed positioned against the far wall. The light offered was by dim wall lights situated around the room, casting a red hue to illuminate the distinctive silhouette of a man. As the figure rose from the covers of the bed, he retrieved a robe draped over the arm of an adjacent chair. Then slipped the garment over naked shoulders and raised the hood to shroud his features. The man's movements appeared strained, old, frail, and with caution, as he edged to a half table at the foot of the bed. "Youth is so wasted on the young, don't you agree, bishop?" queried the figure. A crystal decanter of red wine sat waiting on the table. Retrieving a glass, he poured a more than adequate measure.

Nikolaos glanced to the grand bed, observing the naked forms of an unresponsive man and woman entwined in the velvet red purple sheets.

"Experience over youth your Eminence," Nikolaos replied to the cryptic question, detached at what he was witnessing.

Cardinal Ambrozij nodded to the response. "May I ask the reason my loyal bishop needs to disturb me this evening?"

"My apologies you're Eminence, but it's about a priority one message received this evening on a classified project, of which I was unaware existed."

The cardinal remained shrouded under the hood, sipping at the wine until returning the glass to the table. He gestured towards the waiting bishop. "Let me see." A fragile hand took the device Nikolaos had brought with him and was soon passing a thin, bony, gnarled finger over the screen. "I see," the cardinal mumbled under the hood, leaving Nikolaos at attention.

Cardinal Vladislav Ambrozij, spiritual religious leader of the Order of Light, private to the point of secretive. His most trusted advisers, even Jozafat, were not privy to everything about the reclusive cardinal. He shaped the Order from a backwoods Missouri convent, to the most dominant religious entity since the Holy Roman Catholic Church. Now in his senior years, he still attended the daily masses in the grand hall, courted by corporate, political, and celebrity's seeking private audiences. The faithful felt his guidance and influence daily, and millions loved him. "You sent the relevant personnel to bring back what crashed?" The cardinal asked, retrieving his drink and making his way to sit behind a writing table.

The sudden question brought Nikolaos back from his own thoughts, clearing his throat before answering. "Emergency services attended, with a complement of Order security, but nothing as yet recovered. There also appears to be no visible crash site, but we are optimistic further searches will uncover something. The surveillance data has been inconclusive to what happened, primary evidence suggests the object burnt up in the lower atmosphere before contact with the ground."

"But you're sceptical to this conclusion, bishop?"

"I have my doubts and so added further personnel to sweep the immediate area, extending drone searches to the surrounding district and re-interview witnesses. Most corroborate seeing an object and that it might have landed in Sufferance. The local authorities, as always, are reluctant to cooperate with our own personnel in searching old town, but we dispatched further units as a precaution, your Eminence."

The cardinal studied the details, nodding whilst continuing to scroll the information.

Nikolaos felt uncomfortable in the silence, so pressed by the urgency. "As mentioned, the project flagged as highest priority even though I was uninformed of such a project being..." His words interrupted by the cardinal with a raised hand for silence, continuing to read the report. With a grind of jaw, Nikolaos's face flushed.

The cardinal rose from his table, his pace shuffling as the slightest movement was an effort. The hood of the robe half obscured the old man's features but for his dry, chapped lips and yellowing teeth as he came to face the bishop. "I was not aware I had to inform you of everything bishop." The last of his sentence conveyed a hint of menace. "Understand when I say, I pride myself with 'need to know' arrangements with my subordinates. You, my loyal bishop, need not know about this matter until I see fit to do so."

Restrained anger flashed Nikolaos's face as he straightened

to his full height, keeping his statuesque pose.

The cardinal let slip a slight glimmer of a smile, replaced by a more concerned expression to the secpad's contents. "It states they observed the object changing direction mid-flight before heading towards a less populated part of the old town. What do you surmise from that?"

The small hairs on the back of Nikolaos's neck rose as he caught the gentle aroma of the cardinal's wine tinted breath. He calculated his response to not exacerbate the situation. "It is most irregular for an object to be at first observed free falling before deviating course and decelerating. This suggests a man-made object under direct control, hence the urgency and why the disturbance Eminence?"

The cardinal's features remained hidden beneath the hood, but Nikolaos knew he was being scrutinised on his response, for the slightest doubt or hint of suspicion in his words. "A surveillance operation, as the report states, was tracking objects entering our atmosphere, but there was no mention about what objects or the threats they posed."

The cardinal remained silent.

Nikolaos hoped the explanation was enough. "If I was to understand the threat, then I may divert Order assets if so needed," he added.

The shrouded head turned, exposing the cardinal's lower features again as his lips drew tight, considering the explanation. Anxious moments passed until he took another sip of wine and pointed a bony finger towards the bishop. "You are as cunning as Father Jozafat. Pray it does not get you into trouble one day."

"Thank you, your Eminence." Nikolaos felt the tension evaporate from the room, so released his clenched fists to relax.

"That wasn't a compliment, bishop," the cardinal continued.

It was then a knocking emanated from the bed.

Both men turned to the disturbance, to see a small door

had opened, uncovering a hidden entrance within a large wall painting. Two hooded clerics emerged, offering a courteous bow, before removing the naked male from the bed, carrying the unresponsive body back through the secret door. Moments later they reappeared to remove the female.

Alone once more, the two men continued their conversation, thoughts of the interruption a minor inconvenience of little importance.

The cardinal gave a thin smile, swilling the remaining contents of the wineglass. "Tell me, bishop of what knowledge do you have about Seers or Chosen, and the truth surrounding the myth?"

Nikolaos, being well versed in major religious histories and folklore, considered the question. "There are various stories, your Eminence, all going back to early recorded histories, but Catholic Rome suppressed much of the documentation."

"So do you believe an individual can gain the ability to predict future events?"

"I pay little attention to the old practises and folklore."

The cardinal, moving easier than before, less stooped, sat against the writing table taking another mouthful of wine. "Would you believe their existence if I was to show you authenticated evidence that these so called Chosen had foreseen significant changes in world events? That throughout history the Catholic Church detailed hundreds of witness statements going back centuries, documented by clergy approached by those seeking help for those they considered afflicted. I've studied these documents, deducing that for every generation three individuals have awoken to convey of the word of God. The Chosen are from various backgrounds and are unaware of each other's existence or understanding of the gifts they have." The cardinal swilled the wine around the glass in silent contemplation before continuing. "Well, true or not, it comes to my knowledge that certain fringe groups, who do not share our vision, have discovered details on the Chosen. These same groups now state that the documented predictions are the foretelling destruction of everything we have built here in New Eden."

Nikolaos stared at the cardinal in disbelieve, unable to hide his shock. "You're Eminence, we cannot allow such heresy to spread or tolerated."

The cardinal raised a hand. "Don't worry. As you say, perhaps just rumours and unfounded documentation. But would I be foolish to dismiss these Chosen and naïve to consider they don't exist? Even a rumour can spark a movement to gain support throughout our enemies, galvanising them under one purpose."

"You have details, evidence of these predictions?" Nikolaos asked.

"They're somewhat vague, but pertain to speak of future events," the cardinal answered. "If these fringe groups believe these predictions relate to our own fate and that of our Order, should we not take them to be threats, untrue or not? Perhaps our lack of actions and our apathy results in the events becoming true." The cardinal rose to return to the leather chair again. A computer screen stood at the end of the desk. With a few keystrokes, he navigated through files to find a particular folder. The screen requested retinal scan authorisation and so the cardinal lent forward, allowing the scanner to pass across his face. With access granted, the required folder opened to list sub folders. Selecting a file which opened in a separate window, the cardinal moved so as not to obstruct Nikolaos from reading the contents. "See for yourself, documented throughout time, individuals sharing the same unique gift of prediction or foresight. You are familiar with the Greeks and the legend of the Oracles of Olympus?"

Nikolaos nodded.

"For centuries the Catholic Church quashed knowledge of these Chosen, seen as a risk to the security and authority of the church. They took those suspected into church care, never seen by family or loved ones again. That was the fear they posed if their predictions ever became true. Many were branded heretics and witches as inquisitions rooted out these individuals."

The screen flipped through various images, drawings and documents.

"Others not routed out went through life unaware of their gift. Modern medical developments dismissed the symptoms as mental disorders, controllable with medication, whilst those trying to live with the condition remained fearful of persecution."

Nikolaos watched as the cardinal scrolled pages of scanned documents and manuscripts dating back centuries.

"As I mentioned, certain groups might own details about the most recent predictions and be willing to use the words to fit to their own plan against the Order. Over the years I have undertaken my own investigations and gained details of three people with matching symptoms, including nausea and visions. These individuals came to the knowledge of their respected religious leaders or medical practitioners. Early analysis stated they suffered from stress or mental fatigue. So their cases passed through normal chains of authority, with further investigations deemed lacking in any credible evidence." The cardinal paused, his voice strained in thought. "If these same authorities had taken the time for further investigation, they would have discovered all three cases shared details which form part of a much bigger event."

The screen changed to show images of three individuals.

"Elizabeth Otobba was a mother of two West African national. Malcolm Dawber, a post office worker from West Kansas and last was Carla Simmons, a personal assistant from Washington DC."

Nikolaos leaned closer to read the details before stepping back. "It also reports dozens of other incidents with individuals proclaiming to have the same precognitive gifts. It also states they suffered from attention deficit or were opportunists trying to cash in after the fact. What makes these three so special?"

"I too share your scepticism, bishop, but the evidence is in the details. These three named, having no affiliation with each other, living in different continents and states and all reciting the same sections of text, word for word."

Nikolaos, unconvinced, shook his head. "The deranged dreams of a few individuals, how do we take the ramblings of dubious individuals as threats to us?"

Three small paragraphs of text appeared on the screen.

The cardinal closed his eyes and recited the memorised words.

"It will be on the turning of a new century when the arrival will bring forth the fall of a false light. To form a rebirth of admiration for God in heaven, for he shall dwell in the hearts of the man once more, they shall love him as once they did." The cardinal paused and then recited the second paragraph. "Falling from the stars, a child of heaven and earth, who will herald the end of false prophets. Silencing a spread of a corrupt message whilst burning the corrupted in a fire of their making, for man shall look upon God's fresh light and they shall embrace it." The cardinal appeared lost in the words as he continued. "With this light, God's wrath shall fall onto New Eden. All shall tremble and the ground shall take back that built by false prophets and the greed of man and beast." Finished, the cardinal took a deep breath as his attention returned to Nikolaos, who himself remained deep in thought to what the passages of the text could mean.

"As you can see bishop, the second verse is of most significance after tonight's incident. It presses the demand for secrecy if our enemies misinterpreted something as harmless as ordinary debris flaming over New Eden to be a sign and used against us. So we need evidence to the contrary."

From the far side of the room a pair of large curtains parted to show a large stained-glass window, its centre bearing the emblem of the Hand of God. The dying light of the evening bathed the room in a multitude of coloured rays, as the cardinal studied Nikolaos, awaiting his response.

"Words are vague and lack substance to their proper meaning, your Eminence. Words of the delirious and misguided, who knows their true meaning," he answered, head shaking in doubt.

"Perhaps, but what if our enemies had sight of these documents? To turn them into an advantage to undermine the good we have achieved here, that is the reason these words shall not leave this room, do you understand?"

Nikolaos nodded in agreement.

"Arrangements are already underway to purge the matter. There's no truth to them, but you can understand why we regard this matter with the highest importance and the need for the covert monitoring. We watch for situations deemed as omens to these so-called predictions." The cardinal stood, his movement appearing confident, more agile than before the meeting, and as he returned to face Nikolaos, he placed a hand on his shoulder. "Treat these words as threats to our Order, bishop."

"That was why you sanctioned a covert operation as a safeguard."

Cardinal Ambrozij offered a slim smile. "Sometimes it's prudent in being cautious than ignorant. The Greeks valued the Oracles, and besides, words can be weapons in the right hands. There are many who regard our Order as an enemy to their own deities and beliefs. Others think we have become too powerful and too influential in the world today and pose a threat to their own agenda and liberties."

The cardinal took Nikolaos's arm for support, as both men moved over to the large stain-glassed window.

"All I have mentioned is in confidence, and I ask you prioritise your duties to the Order and this monastery during the coming days. I implore you; make certain no one impedes those duties. Those working against us shall never use these vile words against us, promise me, bishop."

Nikolaos straightened, a clenched fist pressed against his chest in salute.

The cardinal lowered his head in response. "We have much to discuss, to plan bishop. Organise the fight ahead and the challenges we must overcome."

Both looked upon the emblem adorning the great window, both pledging protection of what it represented.

CHAPTER THREE

Lies and Secrets

For the dedicated staff and volunteers of the Refuge of Lost Souls, a normal weekday started at six in the morning. The daily routine comprised preparing breakfast for over ninety plus hungry mouths. This increased daily. The limited choice was a thick porridge or vegetable broth with baked bread. An unusual breakfast choice but offered a filling, warm and nutritious alternative to scrounging for scraps on the streets. Each day the same familiar faces returned, young and old and sometimes entire families grateful for a warm meal and the respite from the streets.

Never more so dedicated was Lisa Shelby, working five full days a week, sometimes six if the volunteers were not available. The days long and tiring to complete the two full sittings offered, and today were no different. Lisa slid the cutting board over to the two waiting, smouldering pots. She split the sliced ingredients between the contents already bubbling on the industrial cast iron hobs before moving to the ovens, checking the trays of baking bread rolls. The huge preparations added to the accumulating heat and stifling air encasing the confined kitchen. She was suffering as she released a heavy sigh. The inadequate and dated ventilation struggled to cope, including every window and door open, and still the mugginess of the early morning was taking its toll. With a wipe of her brow, she released a wayward strand of hair that clung to her cheek, adding to her annoyance. With her little finger, she eased the strand back behind her ear and continued to chop the next batch of waiting ingredients. The tasks were mundane, often offering the same limited menu, day after day. Lisa coped with the boredom by reminiscing on memories of life back in hometown Cleveland. To remember that teenager girl, knowing everything about everything at that argumentative age, never contemplating how lucky she had been. She had come from a wealthy family weathering the financial troubles unscathed compared to other unfortunate families sharing the exclusive neighbourhood. It had been a rich life. She had a promising future mapped out by controlling parents, but that changed with the introduction to high school. It began with a chance meeting with a boy of many a parent's nightmares, meeting during a late night party. Lisa becoming lost to the charm and devilish smile of an older boy named Brian Shelby. She had found a pivotal excuse to rebel against her strict parents. The next few years became a blur in ways no one expected, least of all Lisa. Her biggest change was falling pregnant just before her seventieth birthday. The resulting scandal and her parent's determination to end the pregnancy brought pressure from all sides. Then, with the threat of being banned from seeing the child's father, it pushed Lisa to embark on a fresh life far from Cleveland. They eloped and found a small chapel willing to make their love official. The long honeymoon was travelling from city to city down the east coast until Jake arrived. In Lisa's world she had found the perfect life, and that included a love she felt for Jake's father that no one had ever felt for another person. But it was not to last as the pressures of supporting a baby and isolated from her generous trust fund. Their squirrelled savings evaporated and forced cracks in their relationship. The culmination was seeing Jake's father for what he was, the dead loss chancer her parents had warned about so many times. Her husband's darker side became fuelled by lengthy periods of unemployment and alcohol, all spiralling into a tentative relationship of abuse. With her money gone, all interest in Lisa and their child evaporated, replaced with increasing abuse, until unable to take any more. She escaped with her son with nothing more than the clothes on their backs. The following years became a struggle. Whilst still cut off from her family, Lisa had nowhere else to go. Her life was falling into one low-paid job after another to just keep the damp roof over their heads. It was during one of those low-paid jobs Lisa overheard stories of better-paid employment in another city. So with little to lose, they were on a journey to New Eden, but the expected promises proved hollow as Lisa struggled to find even a rundown apartment in Sufferance. Any hope of a fresh start evaporated as the growing businesses were not interested in a high school drop out with a five-year-old to support. As the years passed, their life was a constant struggle. Made worse with the sweat soaked advances of her overweight building manager losing patience with the weekly rent being overdue. Every Friday brought the distinctive rap on the door she so dreaded. The man's overweight gut greeted her by crushing her against the door as he pushed his way into the apartment. With no chance to escape, an icy shiver ran down her back as his lecherous eyes flitted over her body. Their brief conversation ended with a creepy proposition to pay her debts in another way. The repugnant threat resulted in another midnight escape with what they could carry. Seeking shelter on a rain soaked night at an all-night diner. A kind hearted waitress took pity on their plight, passing the occasional leftover and free refill their way when not observed by the eagle eyed manager. Every grateful Lisa nursed the free coffee as Jake slept, his head resting her lap as she considered their predicament could not get any worse.

The following day their luck appeared to change for the better. They came across the steps of a little refuge offering warm food and shelter for a few hours, and the rest was history. The wintry night had been four years ago and Lisa still worked the kitchen and together they called the refuge their home.

Lisa moved to the large ceramic sinks with a small hand

basin at the side. She flicked the tap to leave the water running, splashing her face. The refreshing spray gave a brief reprieve from the kitchen's heated discomfort. She towelled dry with the hem of her piny, then glanced across the kitchen to the open serving hatch adjoining to the hall.

Sister Angela stood by the serving tables, busily separating stacks of plates and cutlery into more manageable piles whilst singing an Irish hymn. The scene brought a thin smile at the Sister's contentment.

Back to her own job, Lisa craved a cooling breeze, so pushed at the windows, but the relief was not to be. She turned to the chopping board to gather the potato waste for the recycle unit. A flip of a switch resulted in a satisfying grind as it mulched its contents. It was then came the familiar thumping footsteps of her little bundle of joy, Jake bounding through the kitchen doors with a crash. "Hi ma, bye ma," he offered, making a beeline for the back door, struggling with his backpack in haste.

"Stop right there. Where are you going so early?" Lisa gave her best authoritarian parental voice.

Jake froze, turning to offer a smile. "Just out, you know places."

With the cloth of her piny, Lisa dried her hands and came to block Jake's path. "Is that so?" she asked with suspicion.

Jake's smile faltered as his mother knelt before him, trying to flatten a clump of errant hair.

"Were you not helping with the morning service for Father Peters?" She lifted his head so to see his face. "He likes it when you help pass out the hymn books. You missed last Sunday, disappearing on your adventures first thing, so you did."

With his best hound dog expression, Jake hoped to win over his mother with the sullen look. "Oh, ma, I'm just going on my bike, not far."

"Don't you give me that sad face, not this time? Go help put the books out and then ask Sister Angela if she needs anything else doing whilst you're at it. Not until we complete chores, then you can go out, so go on scoot." With a twist she shoved him towards the hall, taking his backpack, which she returned to the coat-stand by the door.

"Oh, ma." Jake resisted as he headed towards the swing doors.

"Don't oh ma me, go," she chuckled, giving him a last push. "If you're quick, I will make you something for your trip out." She observed Jake pass back through the large double doors, where Father Peters was putting out folding chairs.

Later in the day, the breakfast service completed, all that remained were the piles of used plates stacked on the kitchen table.

Lisa contemplated the task ahead as she rolled her sleeves, making a start. Soon the water taps flowed, filling the two large sinks as Jake returned with the last of the dirty cutlery from the hall.

He placed them in the bucket on the kitchen counter with the others and came to stand next to his mother, to watch fascinated in the bubbles filling one sink. "Can I go out on my bike?" he asked, taking a handful of soapsuds, blowing with a smile as they floated around to his amusement.

Lisa gave him a gentle smile. "Are your chores done?"

A thin smile and nod answered the question as he blew again on the latest handful of suds.

"Oh, I can't resist those puppy eyes, go on, and play out."

Jake offered a last grin, rushing to grab his backpack, and ran out of the door to his waiting and padlocked bike.

"Made you a sandwich for later and it's in your pack. Don't forget to be back for tea, okay?"

Just then, Father Peters entered, engrossed in various pieces of paperwork heading for the table and an empty chair.

Lisa was still smiling as she twisted to greet him. "He's a hand full." she offered.

"Hmm... yes much so," he replied still concentrating on the latest bills in his hand attempting to add columns of figures in his head. Then, realising his mind had not been on the question, he peered over the rim of his glasses to see Jake unlock his bike.

Lisa had turned to the dirty plates, her mind lost in thought until turning back to Father Peters seated at the table. "Where do you think he goes in such a hurry each morning?"

"Wouldn't know, dear," the Father responded, though only half listening.

"This past week he leaves early, comes back just before curfew with no explanation to what he's been up to all day. Has he mentioned anything to you, Father?"

"Has he what lass?"

"Mentioned, where he has been going?"

The priest mulled over the query. "You asked him?"

"Don't want it to appear that I don't trust him. It's so damned strange he's out so much, you know what I mean?"

Father Peters sat back in the chair, welcoming a brief distraction from the pile of bills. "Perhaps he's just with friends, or he likes to be out on his bike when the weather is so nice?"

Lisa scrubbed a plate with the brush, rinsing in the second sink, and then put the plate on to the draining board before drying her hands on her piny. "Father, could I borrow the car, please?"

Father Peters looked up, confused at the sudden change in conversation. "Borrow the car? Well yes, can't see, why not?"

Lisa untied her piny and retrieved her bag from under the kitchen table and taking the car keys from the hook by the back door. She hurried out. "Thank you, Father."

"Second gear sticks a little, don't forget," he shouted, but Lisa was already unlocking the little red Ford parked in the backyard.

She offered a polite wave of acknowledgement before getting in to the driver's seat. The engine started with a throaty cough of protest and grinding of gears.

"Splendid idea Lisa, don't ask the lad but stalk him instead." The Father muttered as his mind returned to the paperwork.

Outside, Lisa pulled out of the yard in search for a sign of the direction her secretive son had taken. Nothing appeared out of the ordinary as the slow afternoon traffic passed with locals continuing their daily business. It was then she recognised a familiar face, so leaning out of the window she sought to get his attention with a wave. "Hey! Blakey, any chance you saw Jake today?"

The short, stocky vendor startled to hear his name before seeing Lisa waving him over from the car. On reaching the car, he lent through the open window. "How's goes it, Lisa?"

A wave of cooking fat and cigarettes filled the compact car, and Lisa wrinkled her nose in response to the pungent odour. "Not bad, I was looking for Jake. Have you seen him?"

With a frown and scratch of unshaven chin, he considered the question for a moment. "Can't say I have, not this morning, but you might try the tenements lock-ups off thirty third, been seeing his bike there the past week."

"What would he want to do there?" She asked.

"They're not used by the tenants, but the local kids use them."

"Thirty-third you say." Lisa made a mental note of the most direct route. "Will try there, thanks Blakey, and say hi to Marie and the kids for me?"

With a flick of the indicator, Lisa was pulling into traffic and heading towards town. She left Blakey waving goodbye.

As the trip continued, the gears protesting as the small Ford filtered its way through the slower traffic. The journey lasted until pulling up in front of the tenements where Blakey had seen Jake's bike. She parked and retrieved her handbag, pulling the strap over her shoulder before heading for the garages at the rear.

Few residents were in the gardens, or sitting out on the metal fire walkways enjoying the weather. None took any notice to the woman cutting through, trying not to lose her footing on the uneven ground. In the distance, fern trees shaded the shantytown looking garages, and as Lisa approached, there was little evidence Jake was here. As she reached the first of the garages, she found the doors unlocked. With a brief resistance and a creek of rusted hinges, she entered. A search found nothing but rubbish and colourful ganger graffiti adoring the walls. Lisa continued on up the trail, checking each garage. It was not long before finding a familiar item in the undergrowth. A bike locked to a street lamp by a large bike lock. "Jake," Lisa shouted. "Jake." Movement from behind made her turn, finding Jake stood puzzled at finding his mother shouting his name.

"Ma, what you doing here?" he asked.

"What I am I doing here? Well, I could ask you the same question."

Jake's entire posture changed as he scraped a foot at the ground, unable to return his mother's gaze.

It was then Lisa realised in her haste to find out the truth about Jake's mysterious coming and goings the past week. She had not given him a chance to explain for himself. She never considered the possibility he would not lie, but by following him she was showing she had no trust in her own son. Her mind went blank to what plausible excuse had she for not trusting him? She remained open-mouthed, fighting for words. *I'm I being an awful mother in not letting him explain in his own time?* She considered as there had been no proof he had lied or kept secrets from her. That brought a sudden stab of guilt to flush her face. Why had she not allowed him to give his side of the story? She felt her mouth go dry, wrestling with an internal struggle as she watched Jake continue to push at a stone with his foot. "Damn it, Jake, I'm your mother and I need to know what you have been up to these past few days." Her hand covered her mouth as she closed her eyes in disbelieve to her sudden reaction. *Well done Lisa, use the 'I'm your parent and I know best defence', that's so going to make you feel less guilty.*

Jake did not speak, instead shrugged and turned back into the garage. "I'd have told you earlier ma but knew you wouldn't understand. You would have called the police or something." Jake offered an open hand to lead Lisa through into the dark, damp garage, careful to close the doors behind them. There came a distinctive click as a bike lamp flickered to lead them towards the joining door at the far end. Nothing appeared any different from the other garages. Rubbish and old packing boxes littered the floor. On entering, Lisa noticed a sizeable hole in the roof and the remains of an old mangled car covered in dirt and oil. The whole situation was now conjuring frightening thoughts that raced Lisa's struggling mind to find a reason for him to want to spend time in such a disgusting environment? "You play in here, sweetie?" she asked, cautious of her footing. Noting pieces of cardboard placed across the floor to soak most of the pooling oil.

"Ma now don't get mad at me, okay. I was trying to help a friend. God says we help our fellow man and to never leave someone in need." With the sincerity of the moment, he pulled her lower until she crouched and both were at eye level. Jake's face was a mask of concern.

Lisa tried to suppress the images of horror befalling a small boy in such a frightening secluded place. "It's okay, sweetie. Now I won't be mad. Tell me why you've been playing in here." She was unconvinced anything sinister was not happening.

"Do you swear? Not to tell anyone?"

Lisa looked hesitant. "I swear."

"Pinky swears," Jake asked, offering his finger.

"Jake, please tell me what's going on here."

"Ma, meet my friend." Jake moved aside to let his mother see the figure propped up against the back wall, half hidden under a workbench.

Lisa frowned, eyes adjusting to the low light until seeing the dirty, oil covered mess sat staring back. At first, she believed she was seeing a discarded store dummy until it blinked. Oil thick hair fell in clumps across the stranger's scared face, hindered by a child's smiling daisy plaster that covered a deep gash above a still closed bruised eye. Dressed in a ghastly coloured Hawaiian shirt, he sat eating the sandwich prepared for Jake earlier that morning.

Lisa stared, rooted to the spot and unable to speak but for a small pitiful squeak emerging from the back of her throat.

Jake broke the silence, tugging on the sleeve of her jacket to get her attention. "Ma, he's okay, he needs to rest and get his strength back after his accident. I've been bringing him food and water, books to read so he's not bored and…"

Lisa's eyes widened as she gripped Jake's arm, dragging him back towards the main doors. The light from the bike lamp strobed the interior in their haste, Jake continuing to resist his mother's grip until anger made Lisa spin and she grabbed his shoulders. With the slightest of shakes, she looked him straight in the face to stem his protest. "It's irresponsible for you to hang around homeless people like that without an adult present. You know better than that, Jake." Her words came thick and fast. "God, how many times have we told you that?"

"He is not homeless, ma. He dropped from the sky," Jake protested.

With a grunt, Lisa stifled her anger before getting her bearings outside, still clutching Jake with one hand. She shouldered her handbag, navigating the worn route to the car.

Jake continued to resist her grasp, trying to pull away. "But ma, he isn't homeless." He continued to defend his actions the whole time until struggling out of her grip.

Lisa was having no explanation from him, so stopping she turned to face the protesting eleven-year-old. "He lives in an abandoned garage, Jake, what would you call him?" Enforcing the fact, she pointed back up the path to the old garages, but Jake interrupted.

"But he isn't…" Jake offered.

"But nothing we are going home." Without a thought and abandoning Jake's bike for later, they headed across the waste ground. Once outside the tenements, Lisa fumbled for the keys in her bag.

Jake took his chance to make his stand. "No, he isn't homeless ma, he's a shooting star. I saw it and he's an astronaut."

Lisa pushed a hand through her fringe, catching her thoughts. "In the car, now, please Jake. We will talk about this when we are home." She opened the door, pulling on the handle to release the seat forward.

Jake accepted his mother was not willing to listen, so with reluctance squeezed into the backseat to sit, stony faced and arms across his chest.

"You can put that bottom lip away, as we haven't finished this conversation." Lisa returned the driver's seat into its position, getting in and pulling over her own seat belt. A quick pause observing her son in the rear-view mirror, she then turned on the ignition.

The car groaned at manoeuvring out of the space, and soon they were heading back to the refuge.

As the journey continued, Lisa shook her head, trying to understand what had been happening. A glance in the mirror showed Jake still sulking in the backseat. *What was he thinking, harbouring a stranger from the streets like that?* She thought. "He knew nothing about the guy; for God's sake, he could be a murderer or worse."

"He isn't a murderer," answered a voice from the backseat.

Lisa cursed, for her last thought said out loud. Her eyes flickered to the mirror. "I'm not saying he is Jake, it's that you have to be careful these days. There are so many dangerous people out there willing to hurt youngsters your age. It worries me. Please understand this."

Jake remained silent, thoughts on the passing scenery as his mother tried to reach third gear. *What in hell, Jake? What have you got yourself into now?* Her latest thought considered in the privacy of her own mind, whilst the car slipped through the traffic home.

The journey back home was in mutual silence, as the occupants of the little red Ford stewed in their own frustrations at what had taken place back at the garages.

For Lisa, her mind had become a swirl of anger and guilt, remembering the dark garage and creepy stranger hidden by Jake. "Bloody irresponsible," she mumbled, making sure her passenger did not overhear her vent of frustration. *It's bloody irresponsible for a child his age… when I get him home, he's not leaving his room until he's thirty.* The thought passed as she changed lanes on the last stretch of the journey.

Soon enough, they were entering the yard at the back of the refuge, disturbing a dust cloud that dissipated around the now stationary car.

Lisa released her seat belt, letting it slip back, taking another glance at the rear-view mirror to watch Jake sat with a forlorn expression in the back seat. She shifted to say something but paused, turning back to grip the steering wheel, frustrated. The words failed her, but she did not want to make the situation worse than it already was by saying something she would regret. So with reluctance she exited the car, releasing the seat catch that sprang the driver's seat forward. This allowed the sulking Jake to release his own seat belt and push himself out. Lisa held the door open to see her son with reluctance lift his gaze to meet hers as he headed for the refuge. "Too right I'm still mad at you."

Making his way to the kitchen door, Jake dragged his feet, backpack trailing in his wake.

Father Peters appeared to meet the two arrivals, wiping a glass lens with the inside pocket of his trousers before letting Jake enter, noticing the less than enthusiastic greeting. "A sad face if ever saw one," he remarked but receiving no response so his attention turned to Lisa who offered an unconvincing smile.

"Please don't ask, Father." She dropped the car keys into his hand.

"That bad, was it?"

Lisa could but offer a grunt of suppressed anger as she followed Jake through the door. "Come here please," she asked, placing her hands on her hips, waiting for Jake to face her.

With reluctance, he did as requested, still unable to meet her gaze.

"Did you not realise how dangerous it was, a child of your age, to explore those garages and keep a secret to harbouring a vagrant all this time?"

Jake did not answer, as his attention remained on his shuffling feet.

Lisa in need of answers prompted a response. "Well?" she asked but getting no answer, so tried a different tactic by kneeling before him, gentle touching his face. She kept her voice soft. "Jake, I'm worried. Can you see how much you scared me today? Do you understand why I would be angry and upset?" With a reassuring smile, she lifted his chin so to see his face.

His eyes were red, welling with tears that on seeing his mother cascaded his face. "I'm sorry ma," he sobbed, burrowing his head into her shoulder and throwing his arms around her neck.

Deep in embrace, Lisa rocked the tearful youngster in her arms, fighting back her own tears.

Father Peters observed the entire scene from the kitchen doorway, not wishing to interrupt with his own questions, willing to wait.

After a few minutes, Lisa pulled away and wiped her face. She retrieved a bountiful supply of tissue from her cardigan sleeve. A mother's trait for moments like this, as she let Jake blow his nose on the tissue and wipe at his eyes with the cuff of his jumper.

"Okay, upstairs to your room. Change out of your oil stained clothes and get cleaned up before tea."

A sliver of a forced smile broke through the tears as he nodded. Another wipe with the used tissue before turning to continue for the stairs that led to his room. But before reaching the double doors, he turned back. "What about my friend?"

"Your friend... well?" Lisa asked, confused. "Oh, your

friend, don't you worry about him? I will talk to the Father to get him the support he needs."

Satisfied, Jake nodded and continued to his room.

"Is everything okay with Jake?" Father Peters queried, coming to stand beside Lisa as she rose to her feet.

Both watched Jake make his way upstairs through the closing doors.

Then Lisa headed to the double sink where the dirty washing-up still waited. She let the stagnant water drain before running the taps to refill the sinks. "Well, it would seem Jake's been out making friends."

"What's wrong with new a friend, that's good for a lad his age?" the Father responded. "It's been a while since we have seen him playing with someone." He retrieved a chair to sit at the table.

Lisa scrubbed at a stubborn stain on a plate, her mind on other things as she pressed on hard with the brush. With a snort, she turned off the taps, pausing. "If only it was a friend from school, someone his own age."

The Father sensed the story of Jake's latest exploits was not as simple, curiosity getting the better of him. "An older local kid, is it?"

With placing the latest clean plate on the side, Lisa stared out the window at nothing in particular, before returning his gaze. "No, Father. His friend is not one of the local kids. God knows those kids are bad enough." She felt agitated, scrubbing a pan as the Father glanced over the rim of his glasses. The Father was waiting for an explanation to what had happened on her search for Jake.

"Did you know he had been sheltering and feeding a homeless man, who sleeps rough in the garages by the tenements?"

"Oh, you don't say," he offered, understanding Lisa's agitation.

The last of the pans finished, she started on the cutlery. "He's been taking food and donation clothing. The state of him, covered in his own filth and dirt and…"

Father Peters came to stand next to the sink, stopping her from interpreting her words with the hand full of sharp cutlery which he returned to the soapy water.

For a moment Lisa stared towards the old priest. "I'm sorry, but it was so scary finding him among that mess." She teared up again. "Anything could have happened. You hear such horror stories." The pent-up emotions flooded out.

Father Peters put his arm around her shoulder until she gave into the tears, patting her back until she pulled away.

With a wipe of her cheeks, Lisa composed her emotions and tried to hide her embarrassment. "I'm so sorry to become a mess like this."

The Father smiled from behind the thick glasses. "Nothing to say sorry for," he replied. "It's good to cry. Get it all out, don't let it bottle up inside as it eats away at you if you do."

She gave a slight laugh and nod as the priest comforted her and went to the coffee peculator, pouring two cups, offering one to Lisa.

She accepted the still warm, well stewed drink with thanks. "I'm sorry, Father, but sometimes it's so hard, bringing a child up on my own, trying to do the right thing for him. They don't come with instruction manuals."

"I can imagine," he smiled, sitting back in a chair as Lisa sat opposite to stir her drink, lost in thought again. The priesthood had taught him to be a patient man. It was almost impossible to make a person talk about anything until they're ready. So taking a sip of his drink, he waited for Lisa to continue.

Time passed in silence until Lisa composed herself, focusing on her cup and its undrained contents. "I followed Jake and before you say anything about that little nugget, yes, I should have trusted him, but the fact being he was coming and going without explanation. I needed to know why so secretive? Well, I..." She gripped tight the cup with both hands. Unable to return the Father's gaze, imagining a disapproving scowl from over his glasses and so remained transfixed on her coffee cup. "He's only just eleven and well, I'm his mother and I have to consider his safety when out on the streets, you see don't you?" A thin explanation for her reasoning for doing what she had done, but deep down she knew she could have handled it better.

Father Peters remained silent, as it was not his place to judge the actions of a concerned parent. His face softened, and he placed a hand upon hers. "What did he do?"

With a deep breath, Lisa explained how she found Jake in the old garages. Dark, damp, an unpleasant place for anyone to shelter regardless how desperate the situation. She continued her explanation, going into detail about the stranger. "Dirt and oil covered with horrific burns," she explained. "Then there were the cuts to his body, Father. It was horrible."

The priest listened, not wanting to interrupt until it was prudent to give his own advice.

Lisa continued. "The story Jake gave was he fell from the sky, like an astronaut from space or something."

"Saturday before last?" the Father asked.

Lisa paused, curious to his question. "Yes could have been, why?"

"Maybe a coincidence, but Jake could have seen the reported damaged satellite re-entering over the city. It was on the news links, even saw for myself as it buzzed the refuge. The news reported the object burnt up and was quite a sight. Not surprised if it flew over the tenements. Perhaps with a youngster's imagination and finding a homeless guy as you described, Jake has his spaceman."

Lisa frowned, considering the alternate explanation to Jakes. "You think it's possible it's just imagination?"

"Not surprised, imagining what he wanted to think had happened." Father Peters stood, retrieving the car keys by the back door.

"Where are you going, Father," Lisa asked.

"I'd better make sure this stranger gets the medical attention he requires. The way you describe him, it sounds like he requires help and the free clinic will be open."

"Do you need any help with him?"

"No, I'll be okay. He's trying to stay warm, dry. He's just grateful of Jakes help. If I have any problems, I will ring." With that, he checked the power on his battered mobile before heading for the door. "Don't worry about me lass, Keep that lad of yours safe and I will try not to be too late."

Watching the priest leave, Lisa threw the dregs of her now lukewarm coffee into the spare sink and added the cup to the pile of still waiting washing. The morning had been tiring; and the stress catching up with her. She felt so tired, pushing past the need to rest, for soon she must start on the preparations of the evening meal. She turned to the sinks and took another dirty plate to the waiting water, unaware of the repercussions of events unfolding.

The twin-towered tenements were distinctive to the surrounding area, looming as monuments behind the faded facade of a seven eleven. The store's dilapidated signage clung to the last illuminated letters in defiance as Father Peters pulled up, parking in the rear car park. A cursory pull on the door handle confirmed locked before heading for the far side, to find a well-used break in the link fencing. The gap led to a worn path leading to the first of three tenements, epitomising the desolate rundown neighbourhood they dominated. A vanity project of early nineties architecture for a bankrupt town, its construction marketed to the community as a beacon of future investment that did not materialise. What they got was shoddy built twenty-four story twin complexes of cheap accommodation and community shopping on the ground floor, at the time offering modern amenities for its residents. Now four decades ago and its long closed shops remained boarded. The one time pristine grey whitewashed exterior, now a checker board of cracked glass and graffiti tagged walkways.

Father Peters approached as the midmorning sun broke between its twin towers to highlight his route. As a regular visitor to the area, one of a few remaining community clergy left in Sufferance who still followed the old faiths. He had visited the tenements and its residents and knew of the garages Lisa had described to have found Jake. The tall summer grass hindered his passage, so he kept to the dirt track, thankful for a light cooling breeze of comfort from what was another warm day. With attention on his destination, silhouetted by tall fern trees, he came to the first of the garages with hope to still find the homeless stranger Jake had befriended. A little further on and he came across Jake's padlocked bike in the long undergrowth. *This has to be the place?* He thought, turning to pull on the handles of the nearest garage, offering a gloomy interior to include pungent odours of decay and burnt rubber. "Hello, I'm Father Peters." His announcement went unchallenged. "Young Jake Selby sent me to see if you needed help." He kept his tone light and friendly, so as not to make the stranger feel threatened by his presence. With doors closed behind, the limited light became an issue. So unclasping the bundle of keys suspended from his belt, he retrieved a small pen torch. With a twist, a narrow light illuminated the compact space, allowing a quick search to uncover a door hung on one remaining hinge. Still cautious, he eased forward, greeted by junk and debris left to the elements. He pushed past a piece of broken corrugated panelling from the sizeable hole in the roof, providing fractured natural light through the dense green foliage filling the gap. The Father continued his search, the ground a mixture of cardboard, pooling oil and the remnants of an earlier rainfall making him mindful to bypass the worst. "Hello," he asked. "Is there anyone still here?"

A sudden rustle of movement brought his concern to an old workbench fixed to the far wall. He paused, and listened before continuing to shine the small light, soon uncovering the crude patching of parcel tape to stem a leaking oil drum. An obvious temporary fix appearing to have worked, but conditions remained treacherous under foot as he made his way. It was then Father Peters heard the noise again, the scraping of coarse fabric. Then, crouching, he noted a faint light emanating from a small camping lamp hooked under the workbench. The dim light offered minor comfort and security from the darkness to the huddled figure he found underneath the oil-stained blankets and torn remnants of a tarpaulin.

In silence, the stranger stared back, flinching in apprehension as the priest leant forward to assess his condition. The layers of oil and dirt could not hide the fact the stranger was young, early twenties. His undamaged eye darkened in suspicion to the priest's curiosity, his face half hidden under oil thick hair that draped in clumps against his pale white features.

Father Peters surmised Jake had tried to clean him, the results uncovering varying injuries. So remaining crouched, he considered his options, eager to not appear threatening or cause a sudden movement which may cause further injury for the stranger. Content to continue his visual assessment from a distance, his light panned over the stranger's exposed body, proving inconclusive to the actual injuries under the mass of bruising.

The stranger appeared alert, calm if remaining suspicious under the circumstances. A patch of dried blood covered one side of the man's face. Various degrees of burns, deep cuts and darkening bruises were visible under the layers of grime.

With a pensive frown, Father Peters surmised the full extent of the serious injuries were under the flowered shirt and blankets covering the man's modesty. *I need a closer inspection, but if I go nearer, he might try to bolt or worse, try to defend himself from me.* The Father's lip twisted in thought, needing the stranger to allow him to remove the blankets without a struggle. *I need to get his trust, show him I'm a friend offering to help.* With a reassuring smile, he removed his glasses and took a curious moment to glance around at the surroundings that had been the stranger's shelter. "It's a miracle you're not suffering from infection from being here." With glasses returned, and his attention back on the stranger still watching wide eyed. "I'm to help you, lad. Didn't mean to startle you, but my name is Father George Peters and I'm priest at the Refuge of Lost Souls."

The stranger remained silent.

"You need treatment and medical help for your injuries. Do you understand?" The Father kept his voice low, friendly, and raised opened hands.

The stranger's defensive demeanour lessened, but a narrowed, suspicious gaze remained.

"I'm a friend of young Jake and he sent me here to help you. I'm not here to hurt you or cause you any trouble, okay?" Cramp set into Father Peter's legs as he remained crouched. So in need to sit and release the stress off his legs, he pulled at an old car tyre lodged under a pile of broken boxes. The improvised seat was a reprieve for his ageing limbs and allowed for his attention to return to the stranger. "Bit more comfy for an old man. Now then, I've told you my name, how about telling me yours?"

The question answered with silence.

Undeterred, the priest continued to break through the wall of distrust. "Can you speak, lad? Maybe tell me how you got those nasty burns on your head?" He imitated by pointing at his own forehead. "We have an excellent doctor in town, offers free treatment, so no worries about cost. Get you back on your feet, what do you say?" He reached over to ease back the top blanket.

The stranger at first did not resist, allowing the Father to peel back the material clinging to the oiled shirt. The stained material fell open to show further burns and cuts that stretched across his chest. "Dear God lad, what happened to you?"

The stranger snatched the blanket from the priest's grip.

Father Peters taking the hint backed off, holding up his hands again to show he meant no harm. "No problem, lad. That's all for now." With a quick scratch of stubble, he considered what to do before retrieving his battered mobile from his pocket and scrolling his contact list. He paused, returning the stranger's stare. Moments passed, and he returned his mobile to his cardigan pocket. "Right lad, you're in no obvious mood to answer questions, that's fine, they can wait. What's important is getting you medical care for those burns." As he stood, he offered his outstretched hand. "Come on lad, let me help you." He inched closer, still offering his hand. "I don't bite, but we have to get you checked for those injuries, and that means I can't let you stay here." Soon enough his patience paid off as the stranger's expression of doubt and suspicion softened as he grasped the offered arm.

Emanating up Father Peter's arm, an instant jolt of electricity convulsed every nerve in his body. The sensation forcing the priest to his knees, his right side numb to the stranger's grip and then nothing but a residual tingle spreading between his fingertips.

The stranger's expression showed to have had shared the same sensation.

Father Peters flexed his hands in confusion, all pain gone, including the pain from his often stiffened joints. His entire body became rejuvenated, stronger as the years of strains and pains of middle age no longer affected him. Even his damaged shoulder injury from weekend rugby in his youth and an ongoing back pain no longer plagued him. He remained perched on the makeshift seat, struggling to come to terms for an explanation, speechless as the two men studied each other in silence. Time passed, wrestling with questions, mouth open, trying to find the words that failed him.

It was then the stranger offered his arm out again, expressionless to his intentions.

Father Peters stretched with guarded fingers, still indifferent to the earlier effects of their last touch. Then deep within a part of his mind, there appeared a solitary voice, scratching, as it grew louder and whispered. *Help him, protect him.*

Their arms gripped with newfound vigour as the Father pulled him towards him.

The stranger unable to support his own weight slumped forward, the strain registering across pained features, as both men clung to each other.

The Father tried to take the full weight at first to navigate the pooled oil, keeping a tight grasp on the blankets that wrapped the stranger's body.

Both made it to the main doors where they rested.

The priest's breathing had become heavy, and sweat saturated his neck to soak the thin shirt under his cardigan.

The stranger had slipped into a comatose state as soon as making it to his feet. Not surprising from the pain he was experiencing, from the varying degrees of injuries wracking his body and then being man-handled.

A quick analysis found his pulse to be erratic but strong. *Help him care for him.* Father Peters struggled to shake the words. "Okay lad, my refuge isn't far from here where we have a spare room. How about we have you cleaned up, what you say?"

The stranger stirred, eyes rolling into his head before his body collapsed, limp again.

"You will see young Jake again," he offered.

The mention of the name brought a glimmer of recognition, eyes flickering open, but with a slight groan he was unconscious again.

"What you say lad, we get you back to my car." Father Peters closed his eyes, reciting a small prayer. It was his last source of encouragement left open to him. "Oh Lord, please grant me the strength and ability to help this unfortunate son of yours in his moment of need."

A quick peek outside showed the bright sunny morning when entering the garage had changed to a bleak overcast grey. Large ominous rain-filled clouds gathered across the sky with the increased breeze that blew through the overgrown boundary, whipping up dirt and dust around his feet. It was then a single drop of rain splashed the Father's cheek, followed by others striking all around them. A quick calculation of the distance back to the car made the priest hesitate and watch the stranger cradled in his arm. "That's a lot of open space, lad. It may prove suspicious for someone to see a priest carrying an unconscious semi-naked man from a disused garage." Panic grew towards what to do next.

All around, the rain grew heavier. The sky increasing from light blue to darkened greys as further clouds gathered in increasing threat. Within minutes visibility reduced to a few yards as swathes of rain crisscrossed the waste ground, screening unwanted attention from the tenements. With confidence that no prying eyes were watching, the Father adjusted his grip on the motionless stranger and asked a last brief prayer. "God give me strength."

The huddled pair lurched into the lashing storm, the path a slick torrent of mud pulling strength from legs and proving treacherous as they hurried down the path. It was a constant strain on overworked muscles. The urge to stop and rest increased with each step, but the priest persevered, refusing to falter. A tremor of electricity invigorated his strained body, muscles releasing hidden strength to carry them on the final distance. With one fluid movement, the Father holstered the stranger over his shoulder, taking a last glimpse at the tenement blanketed in a shroud of heavy rain. The stranger's weight evaporating as adrenaline powered him to clear the open ground. "Come on, lad, and stay with me," he shouted through gritted teeth. It was not long before pushing through the chain-link fence towards the waiting car, now in sight. With the car keys retrieved from his pocket, Father Peters unlocked the door. He released the handle that slide the seat forward, so able to lay the unconscious stranger out over the backseat. A check of his pulse found it remained faint but steady. So the Father returned the seat to the driving position before getting in, finally resting his exhausted body. Now able to catch his breath, the adrenaline of the effort ebbed, resulting in a strain to even reach to adjust the mirror. The muscles of his forearm were tight, unused to such stress. He applied pressure to nurse the joint as he watched the still comatose stranger under piled blankets on the backseat. Through a long deep breath, the Father caught his own reflection in the mirror. The whole effort had taken its toll, leaving him soaked with dark-ringed eyes peering back from behind rain lashed glasses. He gave a lingering glance at his hands, flexing fingers that still lingered with the effects of the tingling sensation. *What had given him the strength, had it been a spiritual response to his prayer? What other explanation was there?* His mind was a struggle of thoughts. How else did it explain the flash of sheer focus and determination in helping the stranger? It was then he remembered the inner voice, calming, willing him to complete the task. He sat in silence, water from his drenched clothes welling at his feet as he continued to struggle to understand what had happened. The experience had not only drained his body but also his mind, never experiencing a moment of such crystal clarity and calmness to get the stranger to safety. With a deep breath, Father Peters reached into the backseat to touch the stranger's arm. The skin appeared damp and clammy, normal under the circumstances, but nothing like he experienced back at the garage. With a tinge of disappointment, he turned back to grip the steering wheel and turned the ignition to start the engine. He left the engine to tick over as wipers cleared the windscreen.

The rain outside slackened to patchy blue streaks across the sky.

Father Peters cleared his mind of the chaotic questions he could not answer, continuing to stare out of the windscreen. *Adrenaline rush?* The thought came to him as he shook his head, trying to understand. *Surly has to be more than that?*

The car shuddered as he found reverse, and soon they were leaving the car park. "What makes him so special? Why have I broken my own rules with the need to shelter him at the refuge?" The last questions asked out loud, as though hearing the words would give him the answers.

Because you must, for he is the answer you seek. The disembodied voice faded to a remnant of his mind's darkest recesses, resulting in a stifled laugh as he shook his head and attention returned to the road ahead.

As the little car turned into the main flow of traffic, one question lingered. That question brought a sense of dread that remained for the rest of the journey home. *What happens next?*

CHAPTER FOUR

Stranger Amongst Us

The preparations for the evening meal were already well underway.

Lisa and Sister Angela were busily checking the stoves bubbling with various cooking pots, engulfing the kitchen in varied aromas.

Those same aromas made young Jake regret skipping breakfast. With a rumble of discomfort, he patted his stomach to stem its emptiness before pushing his way through the double swing doors from the hall.

Lisa noticed her forlorn son, offering a sympathetic smile before returning to the sliced potatoes on the chopping board. To then share the board's contents across large trays of meat pies before gentle adding the rolled pastry topping to finish.

Jake wondered over to stand and watch as his mother once again offered an encouraging smile, hoping to break her son's self-imposed gloom filled mood. It was not to happen. So with reluctance, she picked up a wooden serving spoon to scoop a sample of the vegetable broth. She leant forward, blowing over the steaming contents before sampling the latest batch. With an encouraging smack of lips, she confirmed approval before turning back to Jake. "Maybe a dash more seasoning for taste," she said with a wink, rummaging through the contents of a cupboard in search of the ingredient. "Perhaps you could make yourself useful instead of standing there all day?" The muffled question emanated from inside the cupboard.

Jake, hands in pockets, shuffled his feet. "Suppose."

Lisa reappeared with a jar of the allusive ingredient and added a pinch to the bubbling mix. "Be useful and help Sister Angela with those?" she asked with a nod towards a table stacked with clean plates. "They need taking through for the serving table."

With a frustrated sigh, Jake gathered the first of the stacks, struggling for a solid grip before moving to the hall, stopping at the door. "I'm hungry, ma. Can't I have something to eat soon?"

"We eat last sweetie, always have done but help the Sister and I will make you a sandwich to put you on until later, okay?"

It was then Sister Angela moved over from her own preparations. With a quick wipe of hands on her apron, she placed a bony hand on Jake's head to guide the youngster towards the hall doors, plates and all. "Let's get the tables set up for serving," she offered.

Jake, now ushered through into the hall, left the kitchen doors swinging back on their hinges.

It left Lisa to continue stirring the broth in silent contemplation, fighting the pang of guilt she felt towards Jake. She hoped to have put enough fear in him, to make him understand how dangerous it was for a child his age to hide such a secret. She knew Jake was a bright kid, and he understood the limitations and rules of helping the homeless and needy. Still, dark thoughts of the possibilities that might have befallen him scared her. *What if something had gone wrong?* She thought, continuing to stir the cooking pot, wrestling with how to make things better.

It was then came a familiar sound of a car entering the yard, announcing the return of Father Peters.

Glad for the interruption, Lisa turned down the cookers, washing her hands and drying them on the dishcloth draped over her shoulder before walking to the opened back door.

Father Peters was out of the driver's side and pulling forward the seat to lean into the back of the car.

"Are you okay their Father?" Lisa queried, arms crossed in curiosity. A warm breeze caught errant strands of long hair, crisscrossing her face before she teased them back behind her ear. Still curious, she moved forward as the priest struggled with something from the backseat. "Did you get help for Jake's homeless friend?" The view of the car became blocked by the priest appearing to pull a large bundle of dirty blankets from the rear seat.

"Help me with him, Lisa, there's a good lass." The Father's voice appeared strained, pulling what emerged to be a comatose man out from the back seat. At first struggling with the weight, then looping an arm underneath, he kept both of them balanced on the uneven ground.

Lisa checked her shock at the scene unfolding and rushed to offer support. She took the stranger's other arm, sharing the strain in carrying the dirty bundle to the back door. "Father, you're both drenched, what happened for you both to be in such a state?"

The stranger's unconscious head lopped from side to side as they manhandled him across the yard.

"It rained… a lot," he offered with a vague expression.

"I thought you were taking him to the free clinic?"

"Change of plan, lass. At the moment it's hard explaining the reasons just now."

Unknown to Lisa, Father Peters still struggled with a genuine reason. The entire journey back, he was trying to understand why he was doing what he was doing. Why not involve the authorities or get the stranger the proper care he so needed? "I had no choice. But for now, it's important we keep this a secret. So please, lass, I promise to answer questions later, but priority is getting the lad inside and for us to prep the spare room. Our friend is staying with us for a while."

The group made it to the kitchen door, resting to catch their breaths.

Lisa became concerned for the priest, noticed sweat race a path down his flushed red face.

Father Peters returned that concern, nodding to the stranger braced between them.

"You will get an ear full from Sister Angela, Father. The Sister doesn't enjoy letting strangers stop here," offered Lisa.

The Father frowned, peering around the door to the kitchen. "Let me worry about the good Sister and her objections. We need the spare room ready as this lad needs help and that over rules any objections the Sister may have."

"I hope she sees it that way," answered Lisa, adjusting her grip.

"She will understand." The Father gave an unconvincing narrow smile to Lisa's expression of scepticism before pushing into the kitchen. They shared the unconscious weight, heading for the double doors leading to the hall and the stairs to the next level.

"I won't leave someone in need, not this one."

"What's so special about him from the others passing our doors each day?"

Father Peters adjusted his grip on the blankets as Lisa waited for an answer. "Hard to explain, lass, it's a feeling. What is right is keeping him safe because it's important no one finds out?"

"What in all the saints are you doing, Father?" the question asked from Sister Angela, arms crossed with stern disapproval, blocking the stairs as they entered.

Jake, curious to the commotion, paused from sorting out cutlery and keeping his distance, strained to see past Sister Angela. What he saw was Father Peters and his mother carrying something between them.

"No explanation just now. We need to help him Sister so please get the towels, spare blankets, and the bandage kit from the kitchen and then meet us upstairs. I would appreciate your cooperation in this matter."

The Sister's glare went between priest, nervous Lisa, and the oil-stained stranger draped between them. Back to Father Peter's strained expression, she considered maybe now was not the time or place to argue her concerns. She offered a gurgled grunt and stepped aside to let them pass.

"Come on, Lisa, the sooner we get him up these stairs, the less chance of me rupturing something."

It was an effort to climb the narrow staircase, leaving Sister Angela to stew in controlled anger as they ascended the steps. The nun looked on, and then mumbled her displeasure in her native Gaelic at being overruled, before hurrying to retrieve the items requested.

Jake remained silent, edging his way to the bottom of the stairs to catch sight of his mother and Father Peters disappear at the top. His face broke out with excitement. In knowledge his newfound friend was under the care of Father Peters and they had brought him back to the safety of the refuge.

Upstairs, Father Peters, Lisa, and the stranger arrived at the spare room to face a faded, varnished door. It resisted at first, but with a firm nudge they pushed past its opposition. The room beyond released a distinct musty dampness. It was one of two rooms at the rear of the refuge, in the past reserved for visiting dignitaries, but had remained unused for years. A quick inspection showed it would take more than a coat of paint to make it liveable long term as damp stained the faded walls in one corner. For the moment it would have to wait, for now they needed the bed, stripped to its frame, the mattress rolled against the headboard.

Father Peters took the full weight of the stranger across his own shoulders. "Get the bed ready, would you, lass," he nodded. "Open the curtains too and get fresh air in here." A quick change of his stance made for a better hold of the still unconscious stranger as he waited for Lisa to make the bed usable.

She hurried to slide the curtains open and let in light to an otherwise gloom filled interior, then headed to the metal framed bed and unfurled the mattress. A small linen cupboard offered clean sheets and blankets, a little musty from years of storage.

The stranger stirred in the priest's arms, letting out a slight groan as his head rolled, and then fell back against his chest.

"Almost done, lad," the Father reassured.

Lisa finished preparing the bed before rushing back to help take the strain and carry the stranger to the mattress.

Not until released of the heavy burden could the Father sigh with relief, catching Lisa's concerned filled stare. "All will be well soon," he offered, catching his breath. "Please pass me the small aid kit from the top draw over there." He pointed to a cabinet by the bed where Lisa found the green kit and folded it out across the bed.

Father Peters took out two pairs of latex gloves, passing a pair to Lisa.

"Okay, first job is to peel back the dirty clothes and blankets so to get a look at his injuries."

The stranger moaned in response as they peeled away the material using a pair of scissors from the kit. Soon the man's injuries uncovered from underneath the soiled blankets and clothes he had worn. What they uncovered was a frightful sight, for the stranger's body appeared covered in burns and cuts, his skin patched by painful bruising.

Lisa hesitated, the back of a latex hand to her mouth in shock at the sight. "I've never seen such injuries. How's he even alive?" All she could do was shake her head in disbelief. "How did this happen, Father?"

"It's uncertain I've not seen so many wounds on one person before, and as you say, one still alive. Could you get me the water and clean towels, we can make a start and remove this dirt and oil, and then tackle the cuts and burns."

Leaving him to peel away the last pieces of clothing, Lisa rushed out, almost knocking in to Sister Angela in the corridor.

"Steady there, girl," the Sister protested, offering blankets and a large medical kit. With curiosity, she peered over the Father's shoulder at the stranger laid out. "He's a mess, this one, Father."

He did not reply, choosing to concentrate on not inflicting

any unnecessary pain by removing material that had some- how bonded with the scorched flesh in places.

It took well over an hour to clean and prepare the stran- ger's upper body. With most of the oil and dirt removed, they gripped the edges of the blanket, rolling him over so to make a start on his back. The stranger remained unconsciousness the whole time, being a blessing as he must have been under tre- mendous pain.

Lisa had left her kitchen duties to the volunteers to con- tinue helping Father Peters, careful not to mention what they were doing. She handed over a clean cotton pad; the Father applying it to a patch of oil and gentle wiping as he uncovered further cuts. "Did he tell you anything about what happened?" she asked, soaking a hand towel and gentle applying to an- other patch of oil on the stranger's shoulder.

The Father was looking over the rim of his glasses, cleaning a larger gash at the stranger's side. "Nothing, he was awake when I found him, but reluctant or unable to speak. He's been unconscious since I moved him." It was then he paused, mov- ing closer to examine another injury. "What in everything holy!"

Everyone in the room stopped, noticing with interest as the Father pushed harder at a patch of grime with a clean pad. He uncovered what appeared to be bone fragments protruding under the surface of the skin. Below the shoulder blade, three to four inches and parallel to an exact protrusion under his other shoulder.

"What are those?" Lisa queried, leaning forward for a closer look.

"My first thought would be bone below the skin," the Father replied. "I don't think they're from his injuries. My money says he was born with them." A gentle press of a gloved finger un- covered a solid mass. "A birth defect, perhaps."

"Poor soul," Sister Angela remarked, her interest fading in her need to gather the used towels for washing. "Inflicted with a disfigurement and thrown out on to the streets, poor boy."

With a final frown towards the stranger, she headed out of the room.

Father Peters ignored her comments. "Well, let's get him finished and get those bandages ready if you would Lisa. We will have plenty of time for answers once he is awake." The Father handed over another oiled towel to put with the growing pile.

"Yes, Father," Lisa confirmed.

Hours later, they finished cleaning and treating the wounds as best they could. They bandaged with the limited contents of the supplies of the large medical kit Sister Angela had retrieved from the kitchen. It was lucky the stranger's injuries had been no more serious. The Father had relied on his limited medical knowledge, mastered over the years, and Lisa's first year nursing night course, taken before the college closed. They had done what they could.

The Father removed his latex gloves to wash his hands in a bowl of clean water. He studied the stranger, drying hands on a clean towel. "We will need strong antibiotics from the clinic, treat any infection. If you could change the bandages at least twice a day for the next few days and keep a check on his temperature for any sign of fever." His face furrowed. "The odds are in his favour, God willing. You will need to keep him hydrated and check on him every hour if possible." He checked his watch. "If I set off now to collect the needed meds from the clinic, two hours tops. Can I ask you to take the first shift to watch over him?"

Lisa sat on the side of the bed, watching the strangers breathing under the bandaged chest. "He's young for the streets?"

The Father nodded agreement. "Suppose he is, yes." He removed his glasses for cleaning. "Many far younger than him travel to the city. Same old story, money runs out and so they end up living on the street." With glasses returned, he noted Lisa wipe perspiration from the stranger's brow with a clean cloth.

"Is it something to do with drugs?" she asked.

The Father considered the question before dismissing the idea with the evidence gathered so far. "There is no sign of track marks or usual signs of drug use. My guess, just another lost youngster this city throws out every year."

Lisa's eyes welled at the thought. "You didn't explain why you brought him to the refuge, Father? In the past you informed the free clinic, not set them up in our spare room."

Father Peters appeared lost in his own thoughts, crossing the room to the window. Then, with a heavy sigh, he turned to Lisa, who continued to tend to the stranger. "Truth is, lass. I can't give you an explanation, just had a powerful urge to bring him here, to protect him."

"Protect him from what you think someone did this to him?" She adjusted the bandage covering the strangers left eye. Getting no answer, she turned to the window, but Father Peters had already left. With a sigh and shrug to his reluctance to answer her concerns, her attention returned to her patient. With a gentle stroke of his face, she smiled at his peaceful slumber. "Strange one our Father Peters, you know, guess we wait to hear your story later." Lisa retrieved the dirty towels and headed for the door herself. She left the youthful man to rest in peaceful sleep, unaware of the changes his presence would have to the refuge and all their lives.

The room enjoyed the morning sun, and today was no exception. Warming rays of light pierced the half-drawn curtains, caught by the cooling breeze of the opened window. The effect a pleasant relief and the first sensation to the strangers stressed senses as he awoke to a binding tightness throughout his body. The slightest movement felt uncomfortable, including raising his head from the pillow. A sudden wave of nausea forced him onto his side as he grappled for a more comfortable position. But the light offered through the thin curtains spiked his impaired vision to over-stimulate an already brutal headache. He returned to his back, with an unwanted pressure against his chest, affecting his breathing. Despondent from achieving no relief, he could but lay nursing the dull thumping nausea clouding any recollection to the unfamiliar surroundings. The masked tightness around his skull appeared to hamper his vision, so with a trembling hand, he touched the bandaged side of his face. It brought an immediate flash of panic as he sought to recollect the circumstances for his predicament. What followed was a flurry of jumbled flashes, all too brief, causing a struggle to breathe. In his panic, he felt as though a weight pressed into his chest as he clawed at the bedsheets. He found his chest bandaged as he cautiously pressed his side to confirm to have bruised if not broken ribs. So with reluctance he conceded that the slightest change to his bandages would bring further pain, so resisted the temptation. He settled back into his reluctant mind, struggling to piece together a reason for his present state and why to have awoken in a strange bed. Images of a man returned, older in years, his unkempt beard and dark-rimmed glasses framing concerned eyes. The man offered an outstretched hand, resulting in sudden darkness. Further splintered flashes returned, of being supported by the same man as rain lashed their faces. Then an image of a dark haired woman, her slim features broke into a caring smile as she sat beside him. *She took care of my injuries;* he thought as further fragments returned, her soft soothing voice consoling him as he fell in and out of consciousness. As he remained in silent contemplation, the stranger experienced the slight sensation of strength returning to his limbs. He attempted to lift his bandaged arms to flex out his fingers. A sudden pain struck his lower half as he then tried to push himself up from the bed. With resistance to the pain, he sat up, peering under the covers again to note he wore a pair of brown pyjama bottoms to protect his modesty. A slight change to the tight dressing strapped around his chest eased the pressure of being sat in his elevated position. The nausea remained and the modest headache was becoming a constant dull thump at the base of his skull. Tiredness overwhelmed him as he rested his rebelling broken body and tried not to aggravate his injuries any further.

When he awoke again it was with alarm, realising he had fallen asleep, and in his anxiety searched the room for threats. He found he was alone, the sun still probing the break in the curtains, calculating little time had passed. He licked his dry lips, calming his anxiety as he lent his head against the headboard. Any movement forced a groan of resistance from the springs of the bed. With nothing else to do, he continued to familiarise himself with his new surroundings.

A pair of worn throw rugs crisscrossed the stained wood floor. The rest of the room littered with aged beaten furniture, including a two door wardrobe, and a single dresser stood against the far wall. Everything appeared dated and threadbare, matching the room's drab green patterned wallpaper, peeling in patches, highlighting the discoloured paintwork from years of neglect. The stranger could not complain or judge as it still was a vast improvement from the damp ridden darkness of the garage. His half bandaged face furrowed with the recollection of his earliest memory after the painful flame and deepening darkness. He put the images to the deep recesses of his mind, trying to calculate how long it had been since those first memories, days, weeks, or months even. A rub of chin showed thickening coarse stubble from the possibility of weeks since his accident. The sudden dry cough made him need to retch, bringing a striking cold pain from his ribs as he lurched forward, clutching his chest.

To the side of the bed was a small battered bedside table offering a jug of water on a wooden tray accompanied by an empty glass.

Another wince of pain as he tried to retrieve the jug, not helped by the tightness of the bandages across his chest pulling against injured ribs. Through gritted teeth and tear-filled eyes, he fought against the urge to scream and sit upright again.

"Steady there." The voice came from the doorway. Stood, silhouetted in the frame was a youthful woman, dressed in a thin floral dress, her hands bracing slender hips and eyes filled with concern. "Don't want you ending on the floor again do we." Her smile was captivating and at once reassured the stranger's apprehension as she neared the bed. Small bangs of brown hair framed her soft features, falling around her shoulders where it took a slight red tint with the morning sunlight. The slightly darkened rings of obvious tiredness around her eyes did not diminish his sudden infatuation. She brought a powerful sense of familiarity, brief memories of closeness, as though she was important to him. His effort to speak returned a painful series of groans and gurgles from his throat. He reeled from the dry tightness, mouth remaining open in confused frustration as the woman came to sit at his bedside.

"You're letting the air out, you know?" Lisa teased a playful glint as she adjusted the blankets by tucking the edges back around the bed. A periodic glance confirmed the continuing gaze of the stranger.

Now aware of his struggle to speak, the stranger's face flushed as he closed his mouth.

With a wrinkled brow, Lisa queried the attention. "Is everything okay?"

The stranger remained transfixed, even more so as a shaft of sunlight enveloped the room to emphasise her slim frame and the curvature of her back and shoulders. He remained mesmerised in her natural beauty, and the spark of familiarity quickened his breath as he struggled to understand the flood of unfamiliar emotions.

Perplexed by the silent scrutiny, Lisa eased a strand of loose hair back behind her ear and reached for the water to fill the empty glass. "You must keep drinking plenty of fluids," she said, offering the glass to his lips. "That's it, small sips at first."

The liquid eased his immediate thirst, stemming the coarse pain as the stranger licked the last drop from his lips, nodding his gratitude.

Lisa returned the glass to the tray in easy reach before adjusting the pillows supporting him.

The intimacy of the moment, inches apart, sent a wash of Lisa's sweetly scented perfume towards him before she pulled away. They shared a brief glance, a moment's spark neither ignored.

Lisa hid her embarrassment, finding urgency in rearranging the bed sheets for the umpteenth time. "Rest and sleep is what you need," she said, flustered. "If you're cold, I can shut the window."

The stranger tried to answer, the resulting gurgled groan followed by the inevitable pang of pain etching his discomfort.

"I'm sorry, what was I thinking," Lisa offered through a tight smile. "Easy with the talking, the Father mentioned you have burn scaring inside your throat." She gentle took and squeezed his hand. "You need to rest, so try not to stress it and make it worse." With her other palm, she pushed out the creases of her flowered dress and sat on the side of the bed. "Introductions are in order, don't you think. I'm Lisa... Lisa Shelby and you are my patient," she smiled, ever intoxicating. "So do as you're told." She gave a playful wag of a finger in mock jest.

The stranger returned a strained smile and continued to watch as Lisa went to collect the used towels to add to a growing pile next to the door.

A sudden flash of memory forced him from his complacency. The scene was of Lisa stood over him shouting, the words silent, but her expression conveyed concern and panic. Her features twisted, morphing into the features of another woman. This time the image was fleeting, leaving an emotion of grief and loss. It welled from the pit of his stomach. The entire experience forced the stranger to retreat into his thoughts, bringing with it the nausea and tiredness, threatening another blackout. It was a pointless battle as the image of the other woman returned to the dark recesses of his fractured mind.

Lisa saw the stranger's sudden anguish rushing to the bed, the adrenaline not enough to steam days of lost sleep. She reached for support against the chair arm next to her, forced to pause and wrestle with the strain his recovery had put upon her. She had slept a little over ten hours in the past three days, so pushing past the fatigue she stretched her back, pulling aching muscles to recover her composure. With a deep breath, she returned the smile and returned to sit back with her patient. "You will experience a lot of pain, even with the medication."

The stranger acknowledged the concern with a modest nod of a bandaged head.

"Do you recall anything about what happened to you?" she asked.

A shrug was the response.

"We spent many an hour wiping away the oil and grease before even treating your injuries, you were such a mess." Her hand moved up his arm, the lightest of touches. She then had to stifle a sudden yarn. "Not getting much rest, sorry," she offered, apologising. "Understandable as you were in so much pain, the Father had to knock you out with the strongest medication he could get."

The stranger's face softened under the dressing, revealing a thin smile.

"Under your beard it's easy to mistake how young... I mean from the grimy wild homeless figure that frightened me so much back at the garage." Lisa gave a subdued laugh in remembering his state and to find Jake had been helping him. "Do you remember anything about the accident, the fire?"

The mere mention of fire made the stranger tense.

Lisa squeezed again his hand to reassure him, an instant calming effect as both sat in silence.

There came heavy footsteps from the corridor, announcing Father Peter's arrival in the room.

Lisa leaped from the bed, straitening her dress in flustered reaction to the abrupt interruption that went unnoticed as the Father came over to the bed.

"Good morning, Lisa, and how is our young friend this morning?" He was swabbing his glasses with a spare cloth and returned them to his nose for a clearer inspection of the patient.

"Fine Father, as you can see, more responsive today."

Father Peters ignored her agitation, removing the top blanket to uncover the stranger's bandaged chest. "Time to change these bandages, now let's get started." He eased forward, unravelling the dressing protecting the stranger's chest and shoulders. "Okay, it's been a few days, but we have to look at how you're healing." With Lisa's support, another few twists uncovered the injuries.

The Father pressed two fingers against the skin of the worst of the burns to probe for signs of infection, relieved to find none. "Remarkable, a miracle you're healing so well." With a nod of confidence, he pointed a finger. "You, my friend, are a resilient lad."

Lisa waiting for any pleasant news was awash with relief as he continued.

"In all my years, I have never seen someone heal as fast as this youthful man." He removed his glasses, placing them on his head, then continued prognosis with a press around the ribcage, a deep blue bruising the only sign of injury.

The stranger winced with each touch.

"Sworn there were more ribs broken, if not cracked, but skin shows only light bruising now, remarkable." The Father's fingers moved up the body, continuing to check. "The burns to your shoulders and chest are healing fast and appear much smaller than when we last changed these dressings. Yesterday was it!"

Lisa nodded in agreement.

"How's his food and water intake, any problems?"

"None, Father, had been feeding him liquid supplements as suggested. His water intake is good but his throat continues to give him issues, seems he still cannot speak as you expected."

The Father retrieved a pen torch from his breast pocket, peering into the strangers' mouth, where the redness of the burns lined the throat. "It will be the scaring, I guess. We will wait a little longer for those answers." With a reassuring smile, he clicked off the torch to take a seat by the bed. It was then he noticed the brief connection of glances between Lisa and the stranger. With a raised eyebrow to their fleeting gaze, the priest suppressed a smile under the unkempt beard. A throaty cough cleared his throat before rising from the chair to tap the stranger's leg. "Remarkable your recovery, you know." He turned to Lisa. "No doubt to Lisa here and her tireless dedication to your care these past few days. She changed your dressings and watched over you every spare hour."

The words of praise made Lisa flush with embarrassment.

"Okay then." He clapped his hands together. "Last job is to check your head injury, so please lean forward again." The Father found the edge of the dressing and unwrapped. "Light will seem bright, at first."

More dressing came away.

"When you came to us, you had a nasty gash and burn across your forehead above the eye. We need to make certain there's no long lasting damage to your eye."

Another layer of bandage fell away.

"The way you've healed so far, I can't see any problems." Untying the last piece of dressing uncovered the cotton gauze underneath which Lisa held in place whilst the Father removed the last of the dressing. "Remember, this may hurt at first, but you need to get used to the light. Also, you might suffer slight dizziness so best to close both eyes at first."

The stranger did as instructed as the gauze slipped away and the Father stood back.

A tense, sharp twist of pain hit the back of the stranger's eyes. It was a savage response to the sudden glare of the room, followed by sparks of coloured light darting from behind his closed eyes. The experience lessened as he became accustomed to the room's bright harshness and having use of both eyes again. With a hesitant blink they opened to a flash of discomfort which increased the dull headache sensation. Two grey blurs appeared to form into darker shapes, and then became solid with detail, illuminated in vivid colour until he could recognise Father Peters and Lisa waiting.

"How does that feel?" the Father asked, peering over the top of his glasses. A quick pass of the pen torch light back and forth, watching the eyes react and follow the light.

Through a pained smile, the stranger nodded his response and gratitude.

The Father raised a hand. "That's okay, lad, the least we could do to help."

Lisa reached over, tidying the uncovered blond fringe to see the stranger for the first time. The fine narrow features took on a soft calmness of vulnerability.

"Was right about him being young...." Her voice trailed off with a slight tilt of head.

"Is there a problem, lass?"

"Yesterday, I could have sworn he had hazel brown eyes, now they appear a soft blue."

The Father lent in for a closure inspection over his glasses. "Maybe the light or having the dressing on, they look blue."

"Perhaps," Lisa answered with a twist of lip as she dismissed her confusion, and patted down the corner of the blanket. "Maybe later, perhaps a nice shave but for now rest, okay." She refilled his water glass, leaving it in reach. "It's here if needed."

Both Lisa and Father Peters, their jobs done for the moment, turned to leave.

Lisa, unable to resist a glance back, gave a last smile as she headed out the door.

Left with muffled sounds of the outside world through the open window, the stranger's head sank back into the softness of the pillow. Soon drifting as the tiredness overtook him, his last thought was for a peaceful dreamless sleep, but it was not to be.

The stranger's mind passed into deeper realms of sleep until a picturesque park surrounded him and the brightness of a sweltering summer's day warmed his face. The pain of his recovery and racked body opened to lethargic contentment, eyes flickering to the emerging peacefulness of lush green tranquillity of the unfamiliar park.

Rows of summer green trees flanked the perimeter, lining swathes of grassed space broken by a curved tarmacked pathway running the full-length of the grassed area. Large lush beds of floral displays broke up the space, their colourful contents bending in a cooling breeze as did the tall willows which formed the much-needed shade. Sounds of nature resonated with insects hurrying in haste, hopping from plant to plant in a frantic search.

With a tilt of head, the stranger content to soak up the sun's rays, warming his skin, and for the first time his body was pain free. A surreal moment in a surreal world as everything around him moved forward at a gentle pace, oblivious to the man seated observing it all in quiet contemplation.

The sound of conversation carried from a well-dressed man walking his dogs. A calming command to their agitated yapping as a group of children ran past to cross the well-manicured lawns, giggling in their chase.

The entire scene was a refreshing change to the four walled enclosure of his room. He was well aware and under no delusion that he was witnessing a world of his making, that would soon fade back to real pain filled reality. For the past few nights he had lapsed to the park, taken to a perfect, restful place, the story unchanging but all too brief. Each time the entire experience cut short and pulled out to a life he did not recognise. He tensed, taking a deep breath to savour the all too fleeting moment. As the point of his awakening fast approached, he sat back with eyes closed only for the moment to pass. *This is new,* he thought, unconcerned, content to witness the extended visit of his unconscious mind.

A skinny middle-aged man in unflattering cycling apparel raced past, disappearing out of sight. Then replaced by a blond-haired boy, supervised by parents watching him release a stringed balloon into the cloudless sky, all to their amusement.

The stranger had become somewhat bewildered by the sudden change of his nightly escape, searching for an explanation until interrupted by a polite voice that startled him. "May I sit?"

The newcomer, dressed in a pristine white pressed suit, waited to share the bench. With a courteous lift of the Panama hat, he released wisps of grey thinning hair. The newcomer took a slight bow of introduction, offering a warm smile of perfect teeth. He was in his later years, a pair of dated thin framed glasses bridging his hooked nose.

"Please do," the stranger replied, a pang of surprise at hearing his own voice as he caressed his throat.

The old man shuffled, aided by a silver-tipped cane, and sat down on the bench. "Thank you." Once comfortable, he turned to continue the conversation. "I so enjoy sitting here, to spend many an hour feeding birds whilst taking in the splendour of a beautiful garden, so relaxing." The old man unfurled a brown paper bag.

The nearest birds, sensing the impending feast, flocked around their feet, pecking and cooing in competition as the first scattered handful of seed, all eager for more.

"I think so," the stranger answered, a frown appearing to the interruption as further birds flocked for more offerings.

The old man nodded. "Are you visiting?"

"I guess you could say so."

"You look familiar; perhaps I have seen you around here. I'm excellent for remembering faces." The man cooed, scattering bird seed.

"Tell you the truth," the stranger responded. "Up to a few minutes ago I thought to be dreaming, but everything has changed, it's so different."

Another hand full of seed scattered the ground.

"You're saying I'm in a dream?" The old man made a slight chuckle.

"I thought it was, I mean... I'm not sure." The stranger stared at his feet, pushing a hand through hair in a struggle to comprehend what it all meant.

The old man recognised his struggle. "I once read that dreams are parts of a person's subconscious, making sense of one's search for answers." He crossed his arms, watching with curiosity. "You seek answers?"

Two pigeons fought over the same bird seed, as the stranger considered the question. "I wouldn't know where to start."

"At the beginning is best. One finds starting there helps get a clearer picture of a problem, the mind is no different."

"I woke up not knowing who I was. Something violent happened to me, and I'm unable to remember my life before the accident."

The old man remained silent, and with a slow nod appeared enthralled with the explanation. "Your story sounds fascinating," he said with a chuckle. "Tell me, may I enquire, how did you come to forget?"

"The accident left me injured and unable to speak or remember anything."

The man nodded as he spread more seed for the increasing hungry birds. "You can speak now."

"Because this place isn't real, it's inside my head."

The old man chuckled to the explanation. "Wouldn't that make me a figment of your imagination? Yet here I sit, well aware of my own surroundings. Also able to recollect the many times I've sat scattering seed, recognising the same park users who go about their day." His head tilted underneath the white brimmed hat. "Perhaps you, my peculiar friend, are a figment of my imagination."

The stranger sat back, confusion etched his face at the riddle like conversation.

"Perhaps I can help." The old man gave a thin smile. "Look around the park. Tell me anything familiar." Once again, pointing with the cane. "Look around at the trees, and at this park, and even the bench you sit, it's in the details. If you're correct and we are figments of your subconscious, then those details come from somewhere."

The stranger stood to take in the view, but nothing appeared familiar.

"Still nothing?" The old man understood his disappointment. "Okay, say you are correct and you are dreaming. Perhaps the connection is in a particular memory." He pointed with his cane again. "That business suited man, the one with the small dogs. Perhaps your paths crossed?"

The stranger's posture slackened, answering again with disappointment in his voice. "Nothing comes back, never seen him before today."

From the top of the park two women pushed prams, deep in conversation as they made their way down the pathway.

"How about these two attractive ladies walking past, why would they be in this park if not from your memory?"

Still concentrating, the stranger racked his mind for recollection.

Out on the open green, two children were catching a Frisbee. It flew high and came close to hitting a dark-haired woman sat eating her lunch. She composed herself after the near miss, brushing away the crumbs from her lap, her long hair caught on the breeze to obscure any chance of noting her features.

"Anything," the aged man asked.

"Nothing comes to mind."

"Come now, son, you must recognise someone if this entire place is your mind," he chuckled. "Did you know during periods of intense stress, or in your case injury, the mind's subconscious can struggle to create a sense of all that data stored? It copes by creating a whole another world to compensate, hence the park." He half turned, spinning the cane as its silver tip caught the light. "Your accident resulted in memory loss, you say, everything becoming blurred, and nothing but jumbled pieces."

The stranger rubbed his chin. "I suppose so, yes."

The old man's attention returned to the birds still agitated around their feet.

"May I ask who you are?" the stranger asked.

A slight smile appeared under the brim of the Panama. "Oh, that's unimportant, my boy. Perhaps a question for another time, once you're ready." His expression became quizzical. "Think of me as... a pivotal player. Here to help you understand everything locked in that fuddled mind. Then perhaps I'm just an old man who spends his time feeding the birds."

Tired and frustrated, the stranger put his head in his hands.

"It's fascinating that you remember nothing from before your accident." The old man considered. "So wonderful how the human brain works, how something so complex is so... fragile. Take you for example, you feel you're in a library without books, but what if I said you still have books, but your shelves are in the wrong order?" He turned, keeping his features hidden under his Panama. "Okay, let us start with something simple, like what is your name?"

The stranger became suspicious, annoyed at the dismissal of his own questions for the ramblings of this old man. *Okay, I will play your games,* he thought. "I don't remember."

"Okay, what would you say if I told your name is Simon? That I also know the reason you find yourself pulled back to this park, reliving this same day."

The revelation hit like a bolt of energy, a light illuminating a darkened room.

His reaction brought a pencil thin grin to the old man's face.

"You called me Simon, how would you know to call me that?"

"As you said, we live a dream; perhaps I'm a figment of that muddled mind, a part desperate for you to remember." He appeared to wave off the comment as an unimportant explanation, his attention returning to the gathering birds. "Besides, it's your name, isn't it? Does it not sound familiar?" With a cooing sound, he scattered more seed.

"It does. How could I have forgotten?" He continued to repeat the name. "Simon."

The old man continued scattering more seed.

It left Simon to struggle with the realisation of his own name. Forcing a sudden need to rub the base of his neck at the stressed knot he felt. "Who are you and how do you know my name?"

The old man paused before answering. "You continue to ask unimportant questions, just be thankful to have remembered your name. That was your first task."

More pigeons flew in for the scattered seed.

"When remembering the minor things, the bigger picture shall fall into place. So embrace that first and you will find your true self."

"Oh, great, more riddles." Simon pushed a hand through his hair, struggling to make sense of it all, frustrated from the entire conversation as anger built. "You give me riddles, old man, not answers."

With the last of the seed consumed. The old man folded the paper bag until small enough to place into the inside pocket of his white suit jacket.

"I don't understand," Simon confessed. "Who are you? Tell me what you know?" There came a sudden thought to being treated like a piece of an elaborate game, manipulated between reality and fragmented mind. The thoughts kept coming as he rose to his feet, scattering the pigeons under foot, still scratching for further morsels.

The white-suited man remained seated, hands cradling the silver tipped cane as he returned Simon's gaze with a sideways glance. "Do you remember how to fly Simon?"

"What? Is that another riddle I'm supposed to understand?"

"Not a riddle nor a question, but a statement. Your life may depend on it. So I ask again, can you fly Simon?"

"On course I can't fly. What question is that to ask?"

The old man did not answer, removing his glasses to clean the lenses on a cloth taken from his glasses case. Still cleaning the round lenses, he raised his head, revealing the age lined lower half of his face under the Panama. The once pleasant smile replaced with a crooked menacing smirk of contempt as he returned the glasses to the bridge of his nose.

A sudden coldness to the air made Simon take a step backwards, his attention remaining on the round-rimmed glasses and mousy expression, a chilling expression. "Who the hell are you?" Simon asked.

The feeding birds became more agitated around his feet.

"I have gone by many names, but if it helps, you may call me Samuel," he replied. "I helped you with the first piece, now the rest is up to you. For the game must resume, so I need you to recognise your true self, Simon." His tone took a dark coldness.

Simon pushed away the birds continuing to flock around his feet, and they struck out in protest to being disturbed. He defended himself by raising his arms to protect his face as they continued to flock around him, a mass of screeching and crowing. That was when the solidity of the ground gave way under his feet, and Simon was free falling.

The once calm safety of the park transformed to an open blue sky. Air rushed past to fill his lungs, hindering his scream. His body gained speed, buffeted and twisting, turning in desperation to slow his descent. A huge pressure built around his flailing body as tremendous heat ran across his exposed flesh, blistering red. The sleeves of his jacket smouldered and then caught fire. This time Simon could scream, trying to stem the flames with his bare hands, the ground continuing its fast approach. It did not matter, for Simon's entire body was in flame, streaking across the sky, lost in his own screams as every inch of him burned.

The desperate scream echoed throughout the refuge and then came a chilling silence.

Father Peters and Lisa shared a dreaded concern before rushing the stairs to the spare room, finding Simon flailing under the covers in obvious distress. Rushing to the bed, Father Peters pointed. "Grab his legs for Christ's sake, hold him." He pushed on his shoulders to force him to the mattress.

"I'm trying," Lisa replied, struggling with the twisting body. "He's dreaming again."

"More like a bloody nightmare," the Father grimaced, fighting the resistance until resting back on the bed, skin drenched in sweat, but his breathing appeared calmer and more regular pace.

Both exhausted, the Father picking up an overturned chair to sit by the bed.

Lisa retrieved a fresh towel to mop the beaded sweat from his face, smoothing back the matted hair, exposing a calmer expression in silent sleep. Then she touched his chest with her palm, a reassuring contact as it rose and fell, her own sudden adrenaline rush ebbing as she released her held breath.

Father Peters shared her concern. "It's the second time tonight, a sure sign he's remembering more." He reached for a clean towel from a pile stacked on top of the dresser, mopping his brow. "I've heard incidents where accident victims relived the trauma as dreams, many lashing out without realising."

Lisa took Simon's hand in a gentle grip, taking care not to disturb his sleep.

The Father lost in thought until remembering a similar situation. "I once knew a veteran who relived his experience in combat night after night, his last tour being his most traumatic. The poor guy broke his wife's nose one night, had no recollection he was doing it. Night terrors they called them."

"What would stop these... night terrors?" she asked.

The Father shrugged. "Not sure, lass, but it's a waiting game,

I suppose. Once he comes around and gains the strength to talk again, maybe telling us what happened will help, but until then we wait and see."

Both watched him sleep in silence until Father Peters rose from the chair. "A busy night ahead, so recommend fresh coffee as we can't risk him being on his own."

Lisa agreed with the slightest of nods, still needing to watch her patient sleep.

Sometime later, Simon awoke to the curtains drawn. The room shrouded in darkness but for a small child's night light on the dressing table casting a faint, comforting glow. With hesitant massage, his sleep-filled eyes adjusted to the silhouetted room. Over recent days, his health improving beyond what Father Peters could have hoped to have achieved. With most of the bandages removed, allowing movement with no serious pain. As he sat up, senses became heightened to another presence. He made a cautious search of the dark surroundings, focusing on a leather chair. Where he recognised a sleeping shape draped under blankets bringing an instant release to his tension on noting Lisa sleeping?

Her hair lay across her face as she slept, unable to mask a picture of peace and contentment.

Simon's thin smile wavered, overcome with peculiar emotions in struggling to understand why he had become so enchanted with Lisa's familiarity and her potential connection to his lost memories.

Across the room, somehow sensing the observation, Lisa stirred, stretching her arms and unfurling the fatigue in her limbs. On seeing her patient awake, she pulled back the blanket covering her legs and moved over, providing a tired smile through half-opened eyes. "Hello you, how are you doing?" The strain in her voice was a product of long sleepless nights. As was the weariness etched in her expression, but her warm smile flushed her cheeks with colour. "You gave us quite a few scares tonight."

Bad dreams, he thought, adjusting the pillows behind his head, and then twisting to retrieve the glass of water on the nightstand.

Lisa lurched for the same glass in need to help.

Their hands touched with the briefest of connections, sharing a glance of an unspoken bond that had formed during his recuperation.

Simon struggled to speak, offering a gentle nod of gratitude, accepting the glass and sipping the refreshing contents, giving slight release from his throat's tightness.

Lisa returned the glass to the side table, tidying the bed covers, filling the silence and slight tension when they found themselves alone together. "Wish you could tell us your name, seems so silly calling you Jake's unknown friend or the stranger upstairs. That reminds me, he says hello."

Another pause as Simon returned her smile.

It was then Lisa remembered an earlier conversation with Father Peters. "The Father mentioned Jake could come to see you soon. What with the worst of your injuries healed and on the mend, he thinks having a familiar face might help your recovery. How does that sound? I was hoping you wouldn't mind. He keeps asking about you."

Simon could but give a nod of acceptance to the idea, releasing a slight whine as he struggled to talk through a pained smile as he returned her gaze.

During his recovery, Lisa had become fascinated in the man now propped against the headboard. His bandages removed and first shave completed during his clean up, they had uncovered a handsome man. White blond hair shaped strong features, falling into the deep blue eyes sparkling as he continued to share her gaze. "You remind me of a small collie we had growing up in Cleveland." Lisa offered. "He would sit and stare, waiting for attention, and followed me everywhere." Her admission made her blush. "Not that I'm saying you resemble a little dog, no, what I'm trying to…" She became flustered, struggling in hiding her nervousness. "It's not that I don't like the attention, I do, its." Lisa took a breath. "God, I'm waffling." She gave a slight laugh to ease her tension. "Sometimes it's like we are on the awkward first date. Hoping to have the other person interested in hope for a second date..." Her mouth closed with eyes wide to her confession. Her cheeks flushed as she backtracked to explain what she was trying to say. "God, not you and I are... Not that it's a date, what I meant was it's like a date between two consenting..." Her shoulders slumped. "I will stop talking now." Lisa turned away, sucking on her lower lip. *"Oh my God, Lisa,"* she mouthed with a roll of eyes. She leapt from the bed to pace the floor until returning, noting his bemusement. So Lisa pushed away the fringe of her hair to compose herself. "Look." She offered a stifled laugh before continuing. "I might have mentioned in the past, I have this issue where... I don't always sound out my thoughts in my head before blurting them out." Her brow wrinkled. "Hope I've not shocked you. Forgive me?"

To her relief, Simon reached out to squeeze her hand. She stared at their entwined fingers, lost in the warm calming effect of his touch. Then she released another slight laugh of relief as she caught her breath. It was then she realised he tried to mouth something. She lent closer, making out the garbled words.

A soft scent of honeysuckle perfume carried on the air, electrifying Simon as he stuttered, gripped by the dryness of his throat. The words were a gurgled rasp of discomfort, forcing out the single sound. "Simon."

It had been moments, but feeling a lifetime as Lisa held her breathing the entire time. Her expression a mask of sympathy as the word left his lips and could not suppress her excitement. Her face lit up, clutching his hand in hers. "Simon. Your name is Simon," she responded in glee.

With a relieved nod, eyes red from the strain, Simon clutched at his raw throat. He also forced a smile, watching Lisa clap in excitement and rewarding him with a wide smile of her own.

"Well hello Simon, my name is Lisa Shelby, but you already know that. I'm I waffling again? Well, it's nice to meet you."

Both gave a slight laugh, and for the rest of the evening neither wanted to sleep, pushing past the fatigue they shared. This sudden change gave both renewed energy that took them long into the morning.

As daylight broke, Lisa wrapped in a blanket as she sat at the bottom of the bed, legs tucked against her chest. She had revelled in the latest development, finding out the name of her mysterious patient. She needed to keep the conversation well into the early hours, going into detail about life at the refuge.

Simon remained propped by pillows, enjoying the stories and nodding with a smile of agreement when the right moment arose. It was a strain to speak, but still struggled to string together a reply when possible.

Lisa understood, still days for a full conversation, so took it upon herself to describe how Father Peters had started the refuge for the church. She warned how Sister Angela ruled the place with a grip of iron and let nothing get past her without her meddling. Well, almost nothing she had chuckled.

Simon hung on her every word, becoming lost in her soft-spoken voice. Time passed, and he picked up on the subtle changes of expression, including the glint of happiness and then regret when describing her home back in Cleveland. A stark contrast to when hiding the mask of sadness when the discussion changed to her failed marriage. Whenever the topic came up, Lisa would glance over the details, changing the discussion by asking him a question of which his only reply was to shrug.

The latest lull in conversation fell to silence, Lisa offering a subtle sideways glance to her patient, confirming she still had his attention. Now left to their own thoughts, she returned the few strands of errant hair back behind her ear, a subconscious tell when nervous.

Simon's response was to give her time, lingering for her to

come back with a thin smile and continue. He also filled the time with his own concerns, returning to why he found Lisa so captivating, torn between an attraction and a growing guilt that something felt wrong. Those same strange feelings contributed to the confused flashes of memory returning over the past couple of nights, remembering another life, perhaps the one before the accident. He could not shake the deep sense of familiarity in the way she smiled, wore her hair, and the perfume that lingered even when she had left the room. As he lay listening to the latest story, his brow creased at the growing doubts and what they might mean. A sudden yawn caught up to him as he pushed further back into the pillows. The night had taken its toll.

The abrupt change had not gone unnoticed, Lisa tried to hide her disappointment with a shocked gasp at realising the time. "I'm supposed to be starting breakfast in twenty minutes. Guess time flies when you're having fun." She removed the blanket from around her shoulders, keeping the morning chill at bay. With a quick fold, she returned it to a pile on the table. "Will bring you something to eat later, if you are up to it?" She gentle brushed a hand against his face. "Try to get more rest." She asked, heading for the door, turning to give a last smile. "I'll be back in a few hours when I'm finished, okay?"

"Thank you," replied Simon, his voice still tinged with strain.

"Rest silly, we will chat later and thank you for letting me prattle." Soon her footsteps echoed down the corridor, with almost a spring in her step.

Simon, now alone, stretched the muscles of his neck to ease the pressure from his back. He then rolled onto his side to face the early morning light, clearing the gloom from the room. At first resisting the tiredness, fearful sleep would return him to the perplexing dream and the man in white. He lay still, considering the possibility the park did in deed represent his subconscious. *If true, how deep were those memories buried?* Eyes shut in tense expectation to once again wake in the park. In a twist to his already shattered mind, he slipped into a scene not visited until now. To find he stood in a rain-lashed street, hidden in a dark recess of an alley beside a coffee house, unnoticed by the faceless passers-by fleeing the heavy rain. A quick investigation of the surroundings found nothing familiar, forcing the forgotten memory to the remembering the street's name, which remained out of his reach. Then no sooner had the scene appeared, his vision blurred back to the park. Finding Samuel once again sat scattering seed for the waiting birds, oblivious to Simon's reappearance. With a need to release his frustration, Simon screamed into open hands. The anger ebbed before he turned to the white suited Samuel, reluctant to engage in another cryptic conversation. He observed with suspicion, growing thoughts, that the old man knew more about his past and the details of his accident. His next conscious thought brought him back to his bed, wide awake. A glance at the wall clock had minutes had passed, as he clawed at the tightness still gripping his throat. He craved the ability to settle further into the soft pillows and drift into a dreamless, undisturbed sleep for once, but for now left with his darkening thoughts.

The dated shelving braced all four walls, straining with the clutter of long-forgotten dust lined books, of faded trophies of a once promising boxing career. It was a lifetime ago. Hard to remember when Father Peters last considered the contents horded within the small office. Today's attention was organising the increasing pile of paperwork littering the desk, an impossible and fruitless task. He prioritised the most important, the latest bill for payment or a letter from pleading parishioners requesting non-existing donations. The demands grew daily, all requiring immediate attention. So he reread one highlighted 'final notice' in bold red. It forced a wish to push his aching back in to the well-used leather chair, pulling at his glasses, mindful of their temporary taped condition. He rubbed at the building pressure behind the bridge of his nose. Through a tired glance, the clock showed thirty minutes had passed since starting the dreaded task and already had enough. With eyes shut, he took a slow intake of breath and succumbed to temptation. He retrieved his keys to unlock the large draw of the desk, fuelling eagerness on hearing a distinctive clink of glass. He placed the cherished bottle of Brogan's Finest malt on the desk, the last of a grateful gift from a prominent figure of the community. The gentleman in question had the miss fortune of being recognised one dark night. Father Peters witnessing a heated pay dispute with a girl called Amber, threatening to cut off something important unless paid in full. A quick intervention to both sides satisfaction resulted in the delivery of a dozen bottles to the refuge with a note asking for discretion. All unnecessary, for what happens on the strip stays on the strip. But never one to refuse a grateful donation and unwilling to cause offence, he hid the bottles for occasions like today. The memory raised a smile. *Let God be their judge,* he thought. A gentle finger pressed down the faded label as the remaining contents swilled the glass. Father Peters savoured the moment as he unscrewed the top. The fermented textured odour escaped, increasing the anticipation as he drained the dark contents to the waiting glass. He was forever careful not to spill a drop of the last remaining bottle. The moment was important, as he manoeuvred for comfort and raised the glass in a mock salute before taking the first sip. In an instant, all troubles evaporating as he took comfort in the warm texture of the liquid, the smoothness coating his throat. "God loves a Scotsman, so he does," he whispered.

A sudden knock at the office door interrupted the brief indulgence. With the moment ruined, Father Peters muttered a small curse before swallowing the remaining contents of the glass. With haste, he returned the bottle and glass to their hiding place, followed by a quick wipe of his mouth with the back of his hand. He tried to compose himself before replying to the intrusion. "Yes, come in, please."

The door opened halfway, and Sister Angela appeared, her narrow eyes blinking from behind thick-framed glasses dominating her age lined face. "Excuse me, Father, but can I have a quiet word on a most pressing and troubling matter?" Her entire demeanour was suspect as she glanced back, expecting to catch someone in the corridor, loitering to overhear their meeting.

Father Peters frowned, unable to hide his agitation as the Sister closed the door.

Her attention turned to him whilst cautious in keeping her voice low as she approached his desk. "It's about our guest staying with us." She appeared hesitant, almost apologetic.

Over time Father Peters recognised the Sister's tells to what resulted in a hidden agenda with the simplest of queries. When taking over the refuge, he had inherited her services from the earlier administration. The arrangement caused friction from the start, making it clear of her objections as regards a young priest, with no genuine experience, receiving such a prestige position. Corresponding with the Diocese that they had passed over clergy and church administrators, she considered better suited to the position. *She would jump in my seat before it became cold if I ever left and over the years. Not through her lack of trying either.* The thought raised his expectation of trouble, so Father Peters straightened in his chair, bracing for the inevitable confrontation. "What about him, Sister?"

"It's been well over a week," she answered, playing with her rosary, voice remaining low. "Have you considered how long his stay might be?" The Sister not known for expressing a cheerful outlook to most situations, her weathered features a constant dower frown at the best of times. So when she smiled, her expression appeared more sinister than pleasant. "You mentioned yourself he's improving with each passing day and all under your dedication and the Lords' guidance, Father."

Up to this point, Father Peters had feigned interest in the

paperwork scattered around his desk, but now raised his head to meet her gaze. "True Sister and he will continue to improve but still have weeks of rest for a complete recovery." *Now say what you want to say, Sister, stop this probing crap.*

As though sensing his thoughts, she stepped closer. "Would it be more prudent to have him moved to the clinic or hospital? Where he would receive more... should we say... professional care?" She hesitated. "Not that I doubt your limited medical knowledge, but we do not equip the refuge for a long-term stay of full round-the-clock care. Please understand I only bring this up because it's affecting the everyday running of our primary obligations to the community."

The Father caught the insult within a compliment and allowed it to go unchallenged. The cat-and-mouse conversation was already grating on him, so removing his glasses he brushed at the side of his temple. "What impact may that be?"

The aged nun shuffled, still fumbling with her beads, considering the answer. "Well, there's the daily preparation in the kitchen, Father... and there's the whispering within the volunteers. What with the time devoted by Lisa... and I'm not one to gossip. I all too well understand you wanting to aid his recovery, but..." Her words went unfinished, noticing the colour drain from the priest's face. That made her tense, twisting out her bottom lip as the room fell into a tense silence. Her response was a stoic blink as she watched Father Peters sit back, studying her over his glasses.

It was never an effort to see through the thin veil of the Sister's supposed concern, deciphering her actual purpose, and today was no different. "So the reason for your visit is about the time spent by Lisa in Simon's recovery."

Her bloodshot eyes narrowed, releasing a shallow snort as though challenged to her true motives. "No... no, not at all," she blustered. "It would be amiss to not bring to your attention that her kitchen duties have lapsed of late. May I also make you aware, it has always been my responsibility running the kitchen, including management of the daily servings? Isn't it important we complete them with no distractions? I'm well within my position to query if her other duties are becoming a more long-term obligation."

Father Peters suppressed the building irritation and the urge to say what he wanted to say, watching as she stewed in her own irritation. "Is that so?"

"When you took up the mantle at the refuge, it was to the understanding the original responsibilities were to continue. That being, I was to stay in charge of the daily activities of the kitchen and its staff?" Her posture timid and reluctant since the start of conversation changed to a more defiant stance as she held his glare. "I wanted to bring these developments to your consideration before intervening as my role dictates."

The Father's frown dissipated, taking the time to clean a lens of his glasses before answering, keeping his voice low and calm. "Lisa has done nothing wrong and continues to deal with the kitchen preparations and servings at mealtimes with the help of the volunteers, when required. As to her other responsibilities, as always she completes them in her own time, including caring for Simon and we're grateful of the fact, wouldn't you agree?"

That brought no response from the Sister, who continued to fumble with her rosary.

"Nothing inappropriate has occurred with this arrangement," the Father continued. The words made him clear his throat. A silent admission to the changes over the past few days not going unnoticed, including seeing Lisa never happier in a long time. That was no doubt attributed to Simon's presence, and he would not impede the blossoming friendship or something more between two consenting adults. His attention came back to the Sister in seeking to find common ground, ones that all parties could agree. So releasing a held breath, he answered the waiting Sister. "Sister, it's been a joint effort in helping Simon's recovery. In a brief time too, regardless of the injuries suffered, he has made a miraculous improvement, well beyond expectations, would you not agree?"

With a roll of eyes, Sister Angela sighed, offering a slight shake of head before answering. "Father, you must be blind to have not seen the unhealthy attraction growing between them. A girl her age should know better. Still married in the eyes of the church, plus having a young impressionable child to consider. Instead, she acts like a love-struck teenager, it's disrespectful and a gross insubordination to your management."

Father Peters ground his jaw once again stemming his original response for diplomatic reasons.

The darkening mood of the room became noticeable to both parties.

So Sister Angela changed her tactics, still hoping to get her point across without further irritation if possible. An unconvincing smile reappeared. "Perhaps allowing him living here sets a bad precedence to others in the same predicament, Father. News already spreads about him staying here?"

"These others being who?" he asked.

"Why the unfortunates each day passing through our doors, Father? Already rumours spread, that we offer a warm bed and medical care. In the long-term this will cause problems if not dealt with soon, then there's the question of the medical visits and ongoing expenses. We have so little to cover the running of this refuge, and I ask where it stops." By now, Sister Angela was loath to return his stare, sensing she might have gone too far. So taking a step back, she found increase interest in her rosary before continuing. "Would it be prudent to find a more permanent establishment that caters for his needs, perhaps the homeless shelter on twenty fourth? With your permission I could enquire availability with Father Masterson, not giving details of course, but I'm sure he will have room…"

Father Peters raised his hand. "I have heard enough, Sister."

With a flash of anger, she sucked in her lip to the sudden interruption in making in her mind a valid case.

Father Peters placed both hands on the table, leaning forward. "Can I remind you Sister we never refuse help to those in need? The founding principles of this refuge that God himself gave us a duty to feed, clothe, and shelter, do I make myself clear?"

With mouth open, Sister Angela remained silent before offering a begrudging nod.

Feeling the tension leave his body, Father Peter's expression mellowed as he returned to the comfort of the leather chair. "About the matter of Lisa and Simon, under the circumstances I neither encourage nor discourage whatever is happening between them." He pondered the next words. "They are both consenting adults and capable of making their own decisions. What I witness is nothing but youthful infatuation and nothing to worry ourselves with, but I will take your concerns under advisement."

She tried to inject her own opinion, but he continued. "Then about the medical expenses and doctor's visits, the doctor is from the free clinic and owes me a favour, so we are incurring no costs. Also, I can insure you to funding the medications from my pocket and not from the small dwindling refuge budget." To emphasise the fact, he pushed the scattered unpaid bills around the table.

The Sister could not hide her frustrated anger, jaw twisting as though chewing something unpleasant. She gave another begrudging sigh, the fight evaporating, and was reluctant to continue her objection. "I meant no disrespect, felt a need to query how long our guest would be with us, that's all. Sorry for disturbing you and if you don't mind I have a few errands to finish down stairs." With a quick turn she scuttled for the door, leaving the distinct soft sound of footsteps dissipating down the corridor.

With a sigh of relief, Father Peters sat back in the chair. He went to recover the bottle of whisky, dispensing a needed tall measure compared to his normal ritual amount. In one fluid motion the contents were slipping down his throat with a satisfying lick of lips as he poured a second equal measure, the confusing conversation replaying his mind. Somewhat reluctant to conclude, Sister Angela had a point on one of her concerns. Not that he was rushing to admit the fact. How long could they allow Simon to stay at the refuge and what happens once he makes a full recovery and regains his memories? There are still unanswered questions, including being found in such a state, so if others are asking about him, what happens if someone asks the wrong questions? His mind returned to earlier that morning, overhearing two volunteers discussing Simon and Lisa's time spent in his room. They needed a cover story so as not to raise suspicions, but he was fast running out of time. If he did not act soon, everything could unravel and people could get hurt. With a rub of unshaven chin, he pushed past the growing doubts, trying to work out a solution. The whispering needed to stop, as there was Jake to consider. Simon had brought a significant change in him, and it was obvious both enjoyed each other's company. A surrogate big brother, or dare he say, a potential father figure, so needed for a growing child. Lisa had sworn Jake to secrecy, but any chance of secrecy was evaporating with every passing day. They needed more time to allow Simon to regain his full health and his memories. *Then what?* The doubt lingered. *What if Simon's past makes me regret my actions today? Could I risk putting everyone in danger?* With a silent curse, he considered what to do next. "God, I hate it when the Sister might be right," he said, rubbing at his forehead at the constant nagging pressure. He finished his drink, attention returning to the paperwork spread out. The problem of Simon preyed on his mind as he pushed his glasses back up the slope of his nose, trying to focus on the paperwork. Solve one problem at a time, for these bills would not pay themselves.

CHAPTER FIVE

Rise of the Fallen

The days fell into a routine of rest and nothing strenuous but light exercise working weakened muscles. In that time, Simon made remarkable progress regardless of the seriousness of his condition when first brought to the refuge. Much of it attributed no doubt to the diligent care of Lisa sat cross-legged at the foot of the bed.

She battled fatigue behind tired eyes, spending gruelling shifts in the kitchen only to return to take care of Simon and caught periods of sleep when she could. Not that she minded obvious to everyone that the two of them shared a special bond and both enjoyed each other's company. They talked often long into the night and tonight no different. Her patient hung on her every word, captivated as she recounted another funny story or described the mundane day Jake had spent at school. The hours fleeting until needed for another shift or tiredness overtook them both. The moments fuelled an enthusiasm to be together, once again lost in conversation. It was one of those moments as Lisa's cheeks flushed crimson to Simon's infectious smile of agreement as she ended the latest story.

Simon grateful to have regained mobility without too much pain, unaided he manoeuvred to a more comfortable position.

Under the watchful eye of Lisa, she noted his once tired gaunt features replaced by a healthier and leaner glow. Also, the gash above his eye appeared a faint reddish scar hidden by a mop of blond hair, which he pushed back when ever deep in thought. She felt herself lost in his blue eyes, making her lose her train of thought; the sudden tingles of excitement quickened her pulse but dissipated on noting a sudden change in Simon.

Unknown to Lisa, Simon struggled in an internal battle of doubt about his life before the accident. Over the past few days, further images had returned to fuel the growing apprehension and consequences of his past would have on his present circumstances. The images crowded his mind with unanswered questions, weighing on him, but for now he had to force past the growing doubts. So pushing them deeper into the recesses of his troubled mind, his attention turned to Lisa sat at the end of the bed. There was a seductive glint of excitement behind her eyes, encouraging smiles of response as their glances met. In an instant, lost to the soft curves of her features and how those same curves flowed to thin lips when she spoke. The returning emotions were all too fleeting, bringing about a sudden twinge of sadness in remembering a decision made earlier that morning. Could he live with the repercussions of once regaining his past and what impact would it have on his friends? His mind filled with interpreted memories, vague flashes of fleeting faces and places in which names failed him.

"Where did you go this time?" Lisa asked concerned, continuing to squeeze his hand to get his attention.

"Sorry, I was... thinking." Simon fought for the words, trying to cover the fact his mind had drifted.

"Don't worry, it's normal to struggle with your emotions as the memories come back," she offered, somehow understanding. "The confusion and frustration to not knowing, I'm hoping you will piece it all together." She gave him a reassuring smile. "Soon get your old life back." With her last words, it was Lisa's turn to frown.

Simon offered a smile, noting their entwined hands and the softness of her skin against his. "If it wasn't for you, I wouldn't have recovered."

"You're welcome, as long as I'm not boring you with endless stories. I've detected the last few days you haven't been yourself, somewhat more troubled than normal, and thought I was becoming a nuisance."

Simon's brow creased, still playing with her fingers. "Never Lisa, I'm just frustrated with how slow the memories are coming back."

The room fell silent as both were reluctant to share their thoughts.

Simon recognised Lisa's relief, increasing the internal torment behind his own expression, so wanting to be honest with her, to describe the memories that had come back so far. He secretly feared what the others would say if knowing the truth. The details were far from pleasant, often taking a darker and disturbing nature with each passing day. One had Simon awaking in an icy sweat, reliving the eternal fire of his flailing body, the details so traumatic and vivid.

"Lost you again?" Lisa asked.

"It was so real," he explained, voice strained.

Lisa edged closer, concern in her voice. "What was? Your accident and the fire dream, the one in which your falling through the sky?" She took the glass of water from the nightstand, offering its contents.

With thanks, Simon sipped at the refreshing liquid, quenching his thirst. "The outcome's always the same," he continued. "It's as though I'm plagued to relive the event, and it's all so real." A slow push through his fringe forced recollection of the fading images.

"The fire and flames, you mean?" Lisa asked, taking back the glass to return to the nightstand. She so wanted to press the questions in hope it helped, but was reluctant to stress him any further. "It's understandable after suffering such injuries. Then add the trauma of the experience, and perhaps it's your mind's way of processing with a need to understand what happened to you."

Simon recognised her worry, grateful that she cared so much, compassion being one of the exceptional qualities that attracted him. The swell of emotion and closeness sparked an abrupt sense of familiarity again. As their hands remained entwined, he observed Lisa became absorbed in her own thoughts. *What if I'm already involved with someone married even? Could there be a family searching, worried?* More growing questions brought a wash of nausea to his already conflicting thoughts in a constant need to make the correct decision. Simon decided it was important to limit the damage for all involved, to get answers before acting on anything else. So with a heavy sigh and hesitant shake of head he yielded to his scared mind.

Lisa left him to dwell in silence, tidying the few items around the room, curiosity and concern filling her glances. Then, with a straightening of her piny, she pulled over the wheeled trolley brought from the kitchen. A quick sort through of the items, a shaving stone and razor placed next to a bowl of lukewarm water. "Thought you'd like a quick shave, if you're up to it, that is?" she asked. "You could do with a haircut sometime soon too?" The last question asked with an encouraging smile as she ran fingers through his fringe.

Simon rubbed a hand against a coarse chin. "Guess I could do with a tidy up, thank you."

Lisa retrieved the first items, mixing the soap and water in a cup with the shaving brush before manoeuvring closer to apply the mix to Simon's face.

Inches apart, Simon noted every part of Lisa's olive features as she brushed in slow, small sweeps. He made a silent count of the small cluster of freckles below her left eye. Retracing the slightest of scares across the bridge of her nose, she sought to hide with a dab of concealer, unnoticeable until now.

Lisa met his gaze, both becoming embarrassed, as she applied the foam. "Okay, now for the shave." She returned the brush and cup to the trolley and unfolded the shaving blade to sharpen on the wet stone. "I'm sorry about Jake visiting you after school yesterday, he so enjoys having you here."

"Sorry, what for?" Simon asked, half listening. "No, it's fine and besides I enjoy having him around too, it's not a problem."

"He's not the only one loving having you here." The words confessed in afterthought and brought a deathly hush over the room. Lisa froze, wide eyed, to what she was saying, her embarrassment clear. She went to pick up a towel to dry the blade with a quick relish. With cheeks flushed, she tried to hide her admission, chastising herself under her breath.

Simon covered for her embarrassment with fake ignorance, thankful for the layer of foam hiding his amusement.

Lisa, now composed, moved the trolley closer to the bed before tilting Simon's head back a little to concentrate on the shave. "Okay, just like last time, stay still. The blade's sharp and you don't wish me to cut you, okay?" With one hand, she held Simon's foamed chin and brought up the opened blade.

Nothing prepared for Simon's reaction as light caught the blade edge, triggering a physical and emotion response of fear. The result was to lash out, contorting his body across the bed in a spasm of pain as he arched his back. One moment he was in the comfort and safety of his room, the next a shadowed filled apartment dazed and confused. He sat shocked to be cradling the unresponsive body of a dark haired woman. The situation brought a grasp of fear, a stabbing sense of loss as tears filled his eyes. With caution he eased back her long matted hair to uncover her soft, blood-covered features. Caught in a swell of emotions, he released an urge to scream and pull away. He needed to clutch his racing chest as he realised to have returned to his own bed. A hurried search found the surrounding floor littered with the trolley's contents, including the still shaking figure of Lisa.

Her face a picture of shocked bewilderment as her foamed hand clasped her mouth, tears forming.

The realisation of his actions struck Simon, and in desperation he offered a reassuring hand. "I'm so sorry Lisa, forgive me and understand I'd never harm you, never."

At first, Lisa struggled to answer, hesitating to retrieve a cloth to wipe her face and hands, still shaken.

Simon manoeuvred to the edge of the bed, continuing his apologies. "I didn't mean to scare you." He was desperate to explain. "The light, the blade... forced a relapse of memory, sorry." His face expressed anguish as he battled to hold on to the details. "So vivid, you could smell the..." He sat staring at his open hands, the woman's image fading.

Lisa kept her distance, her anger building. "What in hell's name made you lash out?" She struggled to compose herself as she rose to her feet, ignoring the offered hand.

"Lisa, please, please understand when I say I'm sorry and it won't happen again. Perhaps we should leave the shave until later?" Simon retrieved another towel from the side cabinet, wiping off the shaving foam as Lisa collected the scattered items. "I never meant to scare you like that, please understand." Simon continued.

The slightest movement from Simon made Lisa flinch and step away.

She appeared tense as she went about picking up the scattered contents of the trolley. Her demeanour remained sheepish and reluctant to answer at first. "You didn't scare me," she responded with a shaky voice. "The suddenness, it brought back a time..." Somewhat hesitant to explain, with reluctance she returned Simon's concerned gaze. "Brian... my husband." Her voice filled with emotion.

Simon could not apologise enough. "I'm sorry, I didn't realise."

In their entire time together, Lisa often glossed over any details of her turbulent marriage. Simon understood there were reasons for her tension when the topic came up in conversation. The regrets of that relationship etched behind her frown as she returned the last item to the trolley.

"You always hope it would be different. But I found out the hard way he wasn't the man I fell in love with in the beginning." She paused, lost to her dark thoughts. Tears crossing her cheeks, and in her embarrassment she wiped them with her sleeve, trying to force a smile. "Look at me, getting all emotional again."

"You know I'd never hurt you, please believe me," Simon continued.

With a nod, Lisa composed herself. "It was the suddenness. But I will be okay. Now if you don't mind, I have jobs to finish down stairs." With a half-hearted smile, she pushed the trolley towards the door, continuing to wipe away at the puffiness of her reddened eyes.

In frustration Simon let out a held breath, the faint memory of the blood stained woman lingering, still sensing her warm blood against his own skin. Overcome with sudden loss and bereavement, he retired to the familiarity of his bed.

When he awoke later, it was to the rhythmic tick of the clock. The room felt restrictive, as though he needed to escape its confines, to be anywhere but between these four walls. Simon knew everyone would be busy with the evening's preparations. So took a chance, as he pushed at the covers to cradle his weight on his arms. He pushed his aching body further up the bed, flinching from a stab of pain emanating from his lower back and unused muscles. The last few weeks of bed rest and occasional physical exercise had taken its toll. So propping himself on the bed's edge, the pain manageable when shifting his weight. He lowered himself over the side, before noting a large upright mirror stood in the room's corner. As he struggled, he caught his reflection of a remarkably unfamiliar man from the burnt creature he had seen a few weeks earlier. With a twist, he sought to trace the outline of the raised scaring visible just under his shoulders. Father Peters had mentioned the parallel scaring in an earlier conversation, speculating they were reminders of a life forgotten. Simon traced a finger across one scar, sensing a mass underneath the skin. No recollection of how he had received them as he tried to stand. A brief recollection returned of an earlier try that resulted in Lisa finding him floundering to claw his way back.

Today though he found strength, surprised his legs took his weight. The headboard gave support against trembling limbs as he manoeuvred to face the far window. With the focal point to his determination, he shuffled in slight steps, using outstretched arms to counter balance and push reluctant muscles. His mind was full of conflicting thoughts as he concentrated on stopping his body from shaking with the strain. He tried to ignore it all in his determination to reach his goal, which came closer with each step.

The cooling breeze from the opened window brought relief as the curtains parted, allowing Simon to view the world outside for the first time. Beads of sweat raced his back as he endeavoured to control his breathing. He stood to bask in the sun's glow, rejuvenating in new found strength. Then, using the window frame and bolstered by his new found strength, Simon focused on the next goal. A quick flex stretched burning muscles, the pain still manageable as he forced past a growing thumping headache caused by dizziness and nausea. With a push against the wall, he reclaimed his balance; the faint sounds from the kitchen echoing from downstairs. With a grip of the door frame, Simon peered into the gloom to see a corridor of faded patterned walls and tarnished panelling. A well-worn carpet under foot gave little insulation from the coldness of the wood floor. Simon retrieved his dressing gown from behind the door, slipping it over his shoulders, and wrapped its cord around his waist before continuing his journey. The smells of cooking filled the enclosed space, inflaming his own hunger as he glanced back to his room. There was no turning back, pushing himself on with his goal being the stairs at the far end of the corridor. A thin ledge stretched the full length of the corridor, broken by intersecting doorways of which he considered were the other rooms sharing this floor. So using the ledge for support he pressed forward, the pain and nausea increasing as each step was an effort, but he made it to the end. The entire ordeal of reaching this far had taken a toll, including a cold sweat soaking his body, making skin clammy to the touch. An increasing nausea continuing to make him want to retch, but he took solace in making it this far.

The slightest of breezes emanated from an open side door.

With curiosity, Simon pulled on the handle, finding a panelled staircase leading to the roof. The light of the day encased the space as Simon braced between the railings, taking one step at a time. A brightness of warming light rewarded his effort in sharp contrast to the dingy darkness of the refuge.

The rolling breeze lifted handfuls of dust in swirls to dance between various metallic vents positioned around the rooftop. The building's ageing air-con spurting plums of heated air out across the scene.

As Simon edged further out, the shingled floor stung his bare feet as he approached the nearest ledge. The air continued to cool his sweat stained body, so he stood with arms open, allowing the dressing gown to flutter behind him in the breeze. Lost to his euphoria, he balanced on the balls of his feet with eyes closed. He was unaware of the hurried footsteps emanating from behind, before being gripped and pulled from the ledge. The interruption broke his intoxicating trance as he twisted to fall on to his back. A jarring shock followed by the sudden weight of his assailant straddling his chest, pinning his arms above his head. With a blink of recollection, Simon looked upon the wide eyed, frightened expression of Lisa staring down at him.

"You should still be in bed, resting, and I find you wondering at the roof edge." She cradled his face in her hands, concerned he had hurt himself as she waited for an explanation. "You scared the hell out of me when I saw you on the ledge. I thought you would jump."

Simon glanced down at his pinned body, raising an eyebrow to their predicament. He then offered a wide grin as he looked upon Lisa's brown curls framing her face and emphasised in golden light. "Anyone ever told you, you have the most beautiful eyes," he smiled.

"What?" Lisa cried, shocked to the cryptic question. "Don't

change the..." Her cheeks flushed red. "Wait what... I have beautiful eyes? You think so?" Her own beaming smile vanished as she remembered what had happened, and with a roll of eyes she dropped his head onto the shingle floor with a thump. Then moved to sit beside him and stare out across the town.

Simon propped himself up on one arm, rubbing the growing lump on the back of his head. "Guess I deserved that and I have to get used to saying sorry, but wanted to surprise you and show how well I was doing."

Lisa gave a small irritated grunt, continuing in her interest in the view.

"When I found the door open, it was a chance for fresh air," he continued.

Both remained silent, nothing but the usual noises of the streets below echoing across the rooftop.

Simon waited for a sign she was listening and for a trace of forgiveness.

"It's beautiful up here," she responded, turning to return Simon's stare. "I enjoy coming up here at night, when the city lights are so beautiful, like candles flickering in the night sky."

"It would be a beautiful sight," Simon answered, stretching out and closing his eyes to enjoy the warmth on his skin.

Lisa observed him relax, all anger towards him ebbing away as her attention returned to the peacefulness of the view. She understood the need to be outside in fresh air, but that led to Simon making a full recovery and leaving the refuge. With selfish hope for more time, enjoying their time together and surprised at how much she would miss him.

Sensing Lisa's thoughts, Simon opened his eyes and again propped himself onto his arms so he could look at her better. "I've said this a few times today, but I'm sorry about everything."

"Stop apologising, it's not that," she replied, trying to hide her sadness.

Simon sat up, turning her head so he could see she was still upset. "Hey, what's the matter?"

Lisa's apprehension melted on seeing his blue eyes. "With your recovery, you will leave soon."

"You will miss me," Simon smiled.

"No!" Lisa protested, not wanting to show her genuine feelings. "What I mean is that Jake has become attached to having you around, that's all. It will be hard on him."

Still smiling, Simon rose to his feet, offering his hand.

Both stood to dust off their clothes before Simon took Lisa's hands, watching her struggle with her emotions, uncertain what was to come next. "It's hard to explain the reasons, but I would miss you too."

Lisa's face erupted with a smile, eyes glossing over with a teasing glint again. "You would miss me?"

Simon nodded. "Why would you think I wouldn't?"

She giggled.

The breeze caught a few strands of her hair that Simon moved from her face, still looking into her gaze. As he held her, Simon understood he was breaking his promise to keep his distance. "Always remember I..."

Father Peters rushed through the door with a crash, out of breath and blinking, oblivious to the scene before him. "You found him well done, lass."

"NO!" Lisa screamed in frustration, turning on the surprised priest who stood confused at the sudden outburst.

Closed mouthed, the Father glanced between the two before daring to ask. "Is he okay?"

"No, no, no," Lisa continued, a last glance towards Simon before barging on past the priest, continuing her protest to the interruption as she went. "He was saying such pleasant things," she muttered, heading out of sight.

"About what lass," Father Peters shouted, but she ignored the question.

A few strained and tiring minutes later and Simon was back to the safety of his bed, tiredness wracking his body as he slipped back under the blankets.

From the doorway, arms folded, Father Peters kept a watchful eye.

"I'm sorry." Simon winced at his still recovering voice.

The priest peered over his glasses, letting Simon get comfortable. "You scared us, lad. We thought the worst, and it was lucky Lisa saw the roof door open. In the future, I wouldn't recommend going off on your own without help."

Simon gave a begrudging nod.

"What was your talk about upstairs, anyway?"

Now Simon felt embarrassed. "It's nothing," he answered.

The Father, unable to stifle the chuckle at the aloof answer, smiled. "Looked rather cosy, lad." He raised a hand. "That's between two people. All I ask you take it steady. People get hurt in these situations. Lisa's vulnerable and I don't think you realise how deep down it goes." He cleaned a lens of his glasses. "I urge you both understand the facts about each other, before finding something neither is ready to face. Okay?"

"Okay Father, I understand." Simon had more or less come to the same conclusion.

Father Peters, satisfied his words had sunk in, nodded. "That's great, lad." He crossed to the window to watch nothing in particular, considering his next topic of discussion. "Well then, have you decided what you will do once you're back on your feet?"

"Haven't considered it, I'm still coming to terms with things and to know what happened first."

With a slight nod, Father Peters moved from the window to retrieve a chair and sat by the bed. "I understand, but what until then?"

Both men remained silent.

"Your body might have mended, but it's that fractured noggin of yours that will take time." Father Peters removed his glasses again to rub his forehead. "I will admit that Sister Angela has concerns and wants you gone as soon as possible. Under the circumstances and in her position, I can't argue she has a point as the situation sets a dangerous precedent to others."

A look of hurt and disappointment crossed Simon's face.

The Father tried to reassure him with a raised hand, leaning forward in the chair. He used the arm of his glasses to enforce his point. "She means no malice, but the good Sister has an uncanny knack of seeing the bigger picture whilst running things here. I would be amiss not to take on board her concerns and to understand her point of view. Meantime, she agrees to wait and give us more time, but how long, that's up to you." With a pause, he let information sink in and waited for a reaction. He received none, so continued. "There's also the matter of Jake and Lisa."

That got a reaction as Simon straightened, somewhat uncomfortable.

"Jake looks to you as an older brother or dare I say a parental figure of sorts. God knows his actual father is the last person you would want as a child's role model."

"I wasn't aware. Lisa never shared that part of her life."

"She has reason not to, lad. But she realises how he is around you."

"Lisa mentions he enjoys having me around the place."

"Well, that brings me to the other matter we should discuss." With a sigh, Father Peters sat back in the chair. "Lisa has cared for you these past weeks without complaint. I would have to be blind not to see what's happening between you two." He held up both hands. "Now, I was young once, hard to imagine but true."

"You want me to leave, Father?" Simon asked.

The priest's face frowned. "Heaven's sake, no lad, what I'm trying to say is we don't want you to leave. Not unless you wish to go." He removed his glasses to clean them again.

"I don't want to go either, Father, but if my presence causes problems then I have no choice."

Father Peters shook his head. "You always have a choice. All we ask is that you keep a low profile and take a few days until you find your land legs and don't go wondering off on your own again." The priest paused, not sure how to approach the next question. "About the situation growing between the two of you, now I don't need details but please be careful of gossip and all that, lad." He returned his glasses and slapped the top of his legs. "Don't want people getting hurt if we find out you're married with a posse of kids. I ask you to wait until you're sure. No surprises." The Father stood to push away his chair and headed for the door before turning back. "I've been looking through the refuge finances and it will be a push, but I wanted to offer you a job if you're interested? Don't pay well but there's food and lodgings thrown in and it will tide you over until you decide."

"You want to offer me a job?"

Sensing hesitation, the Father continued. "Once rested, lad, the refuge needs a few repairs." To illustrate the point, he pulled a piece of flaking paint from the door frame, examining it between his fingers as it splintered in his grip. "Yep, the place needs a lick of paint... new windows, doors, bloody new roof... Don't give me an answer straight away. Maybe sleep on it and mull it over for the next few days." With a farewell wave, he left to leave Simon alone to ponder the offer.

There was a lot to consider as Simon settled under the covers. Facing the opened window, he lay still until a chill made him retreat further under the covers. The Father was right until regaining his memories; he could not decide what to do. So pushing past the thoughts, the tiredness flooding behind his eyes, he slipped into unconscious sleep and released to his subconscious.

Simon found himself in the small apartment from his brief, disturbing memory earlier in the day. Once again sat on the floor where he searched the modest apartment.

The details clearer than before, including noting a pair of tall book shelves filled with books and prized photos. A dresser and mirror stood under the window with various personal items confirming a woman's apartment.

He remained hesitant to move as attention drew to a forming glimmer of light in the middle of the room.

The light appeared to twist and grow suspended above the floor and invoked no fear or surprise, just mesmerising curiosity.

Simon watched as it became fluid in movement and solid in appearance, continuing to twist and sway in silent rhythm. He remained transfixed as it morphed into the distinct shape of a slim figured woman.

Her athletic legs stretched from under the fabric of her dress as she maintained her dance. The room's dim light reflecting from her waist length hair, mimicking her movements and uncovering soft dark shoulders under a short strapless blue dress. Its thin material extenuated her delicate frame as she moved closer.

For a moment Simon swore to be watching Lisa. The similarities were uncanny and all he could do was watch bewitched and motionless.

The woman continued to sway with hypnotic grace and let out an intoxicating laughter as she spun. Moving closure, she held out her arms in beckoning jest whilst continuing her dance. Her flowing hair continued to obscure any chance of recognition.

It was then Simon found momentum to move, lurching forward to slip a hand around her waist, pulling her closer and stopping the hypnotic routine.

Still, her hair masked any chance of identity as her breathing became heavy under his grip.

"You failed her," spoke a chilling, unemotional voice, filling the room.

Simon flinched, noticing a warm sensation slick against the tips of his fingers. On retrieving his hand, he found blood. With his entire body tensed as the woman's head fell against his shoulder, her body limp through the dress's thin material and her breathing grew faint and shallow. Simon tried easing away the matted, unkempt hair that ran thick with blood. Soon he was staring into her ashen white features, face slashed deep as cynical eyes flickered open.

She gave a tentative smile of recognition as dried, chapped lips spoke. "Simon, you came back for me," she said. "I had faith you would, even though he said you wouldn't, but I knew you wouldn't abandon me."

"Who did this?" Simon's voice broke with emotion.

The woman's eyes flickered before she gave a final rasp. The tension left her, leaving Simon cradling her motionless body in his arms. A search for a pulse returned nothing, and as Simon closed her lifeless eyes, grief overtook him. Then without warning her body vanished, leaving the dark coldness of his mind as Simon awoke in a panic. With a desperate breath, he clutched his beating chest, taking a moment to compose himself as he rolled on to his side. A glance at the wall clock noting minutes had passed since closing his eyes. His heart continued to race as images of the woman lingered, but the recent development raised further questions as to her identity and reason for her demise. He sensed an unnerving apprehension and responsibility, and those final thoughts assured the remaining evening would be as sleepless as any other.

It was not long before Simon moved around the refuge unaided, grateful, and no longer confined in his room. The others had given him space to continue his recovery. They knew it would be a slow process as he came to terms with the trauma of his accident, including memories of a life he did not recognise. He spent hours convalescing sat by the kitchen doorstep under Lisa's watchful supervision, but often sort solitude on the refuge's secluded rooftop. Where he sat in silent observation of the neighbourhood, thankful for the alone time whilst lost in reluctant thought. At first it had been a struggle to reassure his friends that all was fine, what with the misinterpretation of his intentions during his first visit to the roof. So they left him to interrupt the varying degrees of returning memories, often disturbing to include that of the blood-stained woman. Her name still eluded him, but her image became so vivid that he still often felt her cradled body in his arms, her dying last words haunting him. The experience made Simon become withdrawn, unwilling to share with the others, fearing their reaction or outcome if he did. So, again he sat crouched at the roof edge, fixated on the view and welcomed the sanctuary the rooftop had become.

It was also the first place Father Peters searched as he stepped out into the bright daylight to offer an intentional cough of interruption. On receiving no response to his intrusion and not wanting to waste an opportunity, the priest retrieved a cigarette from the crumpled packet from his shirt pocket. The reluctant lighter lit the much-needed fix, allowing the priest to exhale to watch the smoke taken on the breeze. He then leant against a vent in the silent study of his friend, who perched birdlike on the narrow roof edge. Gone were the unflattering nightwear and threadbare dressing gown, replaced by the welcomed pickings from the clothing donation bins. Of which choices had been a pair of worn jeans and a baggy grey sweater, all peculiar choices for the unusual sultry August days of Sufferance. The whole casual urban attire finished with a pair of scuffed combat boots and a full length brown weathered duster jacket. Father Peters had chuckled at his resemblance to the lone gunmen from old westerns, watched as a child during many a Saturday morning matinee back home. As he continued his observation, taking another intake of the cigarette, curious to what had his friend's interest so captivated. "It's a massive city, and she gets bigger every day," he offered.

Still no response as Simon's gaze remained transfixed on something in the distance.

With the cigarette relegated to the corner of his mouth, Father Peters peered over the side. "Hope you're not thinking of jumping, would make a hell a mess of Luca's suburban down there."

"It's a beautiful city," Simon replied.

The Father took a step back, nodding in agreement, happy to have a response. "It helps to have a cloudless day like today, you can see for miles."

"Don't think you came here to give me talk about the weather or the view, Father."

"No... no lad, guess I didn't," he confessed. "Haven't seen you since yesterday and was wondering how you were doing. We've noticed you've been quiet of late." He held up his palms. "Now, we promised to give you time alone to come to terms with your returning memories, but there's something more than usual bothering you?"

"There's nothing to worry about, Father," he answered, still not sharing the Father's glance.

"Want to talk about it?"

Simon's expression did not change, "Not today, if you don't mind."

With a sigh, Father Peters considered pushing the issue with a need to help. Instead, he released another stream of cigarette smoke before pointing at nothing in particular. "Sufferance used to be such a friendly town before the country turned to shit and New Eden expanded in all directions. You know, before the Order changed everything." He nodded towards the enormous towers of the Monastery of Light, looming out of the summer haze far off in the distance. "Did you know this neighbourhood was part of the town's business district, filled with shops and restaurants of good honest family businesses? Generations provided for the community. Then the Order arrived to build multi malls and high-rise complexes to price out the locals. The old town left to suffer a slow death." His attention back to Simon with hope he was still listening. With the slightest of head shakes, he realised most likely he was speaking to himself. He let the rooftop fall into silence, struggling to find a reason for Simon's fixation on the monastery. He was lucky to just about make out black shapes moving the walkways and towers. With lip curled in curious thought, he guessed at what had his friend so enthralled. "They call it the Hand of God," he offered, pointing. "Symbolises the link to their true God, or something like that."

The explanation got a response. "Why do I recognise that symbol in particular and to those hands engulfing flame?" Simon asked.

Father Peters shrugged, tapping ash across the floor. "Fire comes up a lot in your dreams, lad, justifiable under the circumstances, I suppose." He leant forward, placing a reassuring hand on Simon's shoulder. "Easy to forget just how injured you were when we found you. It's a mystery you recovered so fast, a genuine miracle you lived at all."

Simon's gaze lowered. "Flames aren't the only fear I have to keep me awake at night." The confession brought discomfort as he relived hounded images of blooded hands, the woman's tortured features, and not forgetting the strange old man stalking his subconscious with sinister intent. "Last night I saw that symbol of two hands cupping a flame, accompanied by a two faced man robed in white and red robes."

"Two faced man, you say." Father Peters sought to sympathise with what his friend was going through in trying to decipher the latest dream's meaning. "Can you describe the two faced man?"

Simon's fingers pressed against temples, forcing the memory to return. "It's all too brief, but I remember robes and a black hood concealing a blurring face changing from old to young. Then there's the laughter as I burn."

The tip of Father Peter's cigarette turned red as he inhaled, considering the details. "Well, the old man you describe dressed in robes. Could be Order senior clergy, they wear robes like that, so maybe you had a run in with a priest or the Order?"

"Can't remember, just the robed man appearing and that he felt important... powerful," Simon continued.

Father Peters chuckled. "It's like you're describing the cardinal lad, him being the most important person in the Order."

The priest's laugh died on noticing his friend did not share his humour, understandable, he guessed, continuing his explanation. "Cardinal Vladislav Ambrozij is the religious leader of the Order of Light, the genuine power in the organisation." Unable to hide surprise at Simon's quizzical expression to whom he was describing. "There isn't a place on this damned planet without that branding somewhere or anybody who doesn't recognise the cardinal." He gave a silent curse and crossed himself at the thought of the Order. "Sorry lad, I can't give you the answers you want to hear. What I know is if your past involves the Order and the cardinal, we must tread with care." So offering a final reassuring pat on the shoulder again, he turned to leave. "I've got a mountain of paperwork in my office so if you want to continue this talk you will find me there, for the bloody paperwork never ends." With the cigarette finished and extinguished, the Father headed for the door.

"Thank you, Father," Simon responded.

The priest gave a last wave before closing the door to the roof behind him.

"A man filled with questions and no answers will forever chase his own tail."

The voice made Simon spin in search, finding he was still alone. "Who's there, show yourself."

A black shape separated from the shadows of the doorway, stepping in to the light. The man was tall, taller than Simon and not local judging by the expensive navy suit screaming money. As he approached, he adjusted his sleek crafted sunglasses and broke out into a beaming smile.

Simon's body tensed in expectation to the newcomers' motives and noted he had blocked his exit. The man's demeanour expressed quizzical curiosity, as though studying Simon. Everything about him spoke wealth and status, from the expensive jewellery, to the white tipped, handcrafted leather shoes. Jet black hair slicked back to define dark ebony features as the man's attention remained intrigued with Simon as much as he was with him. Then the unwavering white smile reappeared, and in a blink of an eye he was mere inches from Simon's face.

That forced Simon to take a step back by the suddenness, but held his ground.

With a tilt of head, the man continued studying every detail from behind his glasses. A few tense moments passed until stepping back to give a courteous bow, the wry smile stretching his face again. He removed his sunglasses to stand with a casual thumb pressed into the tailored pocket of a matching waistcoat.

The entire experience had become bizarre with each passing moment as both studied each other.

Simon then noted the man's solid black eyes, not a hint of white as though soulless but intelligent, much like a shark.

"Let me guess, no memory, right?" the newcomer asked.

Simon felt uncertainty to how to answer.

"Let me introduce myself, my card." He retrieved a concealed business card from the inside pocket of the tailed suit jacket.

Simon took the card, turning over to read the embossed gold lettering.

Malach D HaMavet CEO, Bereavement, and Funerals

Deliver Earth Angels to Heaven Est. B.E. (Before Everything).

"I don't understand, Mr HaMavet, is it?" Simon asked, puzzled by the sudden appearance.

"Call me D, everyone who knows me calls me D," he returned the glasses and paced the roof. "Listen, friend, can I tell you a funny story? It was a bright sunny day, this very day, and they I was minding one's own business. Then suddenly my little spider sense tingled and whoosh brought me here." As he spoke, D turned and retraced his steps, offering a disapproving glance towards the surroundings. "To this rather piss poor looking death trap if ever I saw one." He paused, pulling down his glasses. "Believe me when I say I have seen my share of death traps in my time." With a wink he headed to the roof edge, to release a slow drawn out whistle whilst glancing over the edge.

With curiosity, Simon peered over too to see nothing but the empty yard below with Father Peter's red Ford parked in its usual place. Then finding nothing of interest turned back.

D approached to stand his full height over Simon. The ever present grin had a creeping effect of its own. "So what's your story?" He asked with a quizzical frown, watching Simon with intense interest. "You're a lost soul from nowhere and with no memory of his past, correct?" There was no pause for an answer. "Such a classic loving Hallmark moment, I so could cry." With folded arms, D circled Simon, continuing his scrutinising gaze.

"Who are you anyway, and what are you doing here?" Simon asked.

D waved away the questions. "What can I say? I find a loner overcome with the pressures of modern life. Stood forlorn on a roof edge and the Good Samaritan in me springs into action. Selfish I know, so full of compassion offering help in a time of need."

"But how did..." Simon's question cut short as he found himself spun around and gripped by his shoulders before being marched across the rooftop.

"The names on the card, bro, please keep up with the program." D tapped the card still grasped in Simon's hands. "How I got here is unimportant. What's needed is for you to remember the important stuff, to get you back in the game." He gave an enthusiastic nod to his own answer, as though it told Simon all he needed to understand.

"My name is Simon... Simon Alksey," he answered, remembering the name Father Peters had chosen for his cover story. "I'm the handyman here."

"Well, hello Simon Alksey." D confirmed, taking his hand to shake with vigour. "Can I call you Si? No, I digress but pleased to meet you." Still grinning, he backed off to give a slight bow again. "You have read my card but what it doesn't tell you, I'm a collector of lists and names. Do you know the power in a name, Simon?"

Simon felt confused to the line of questioning as he shook his head. "I'm not sure what you mean?"

"Well, take yours, for instance, Simon Alksey. Are you aware it means 'He who's heard and defends humanity'? A peculiar choice, don't you agree?" He thrust a finger into Simon's chest to emphasise the point. "But once again I digress, lists! Every one's entire life is on a list, explaining their life from birth to death and everyone who is and will be, everyone." D took a small secpad from his inside pocket, tapping the display with a well-manicured finger. The device chimed as he input his notes.

Simon tried to steal a look at the screen.

D pulled away with a guarded glare before continuing to scroll through the device's contents. "So perhaps you can tell me, my newfound friend, why you appear to be absent from my lists? You're an abnormality which pricks my curiosity and I need to find out why."

Simon replied with nothing but a shrug.

With a snap of fingers D closed the secpad, returning it to his inside pocket, throwing an arm over Simon's shoulder to lead him on a slow walk of the rooftop. "What is your story, huh?"

Simon could not answer as D spun him around and walked him in the opposite direction.

"Simon, you sure I can't call you Si? Still no, okay. I have a hunch, a thought even. Do you trust me?" He clutched Simon's shoulders, manoeuvring him so both faced each other, continuing to squeeze tight as he waited for an answer.

"Well, I don't even know who you are," Simon responded, glancing at the business card. "So why should I trust you?"

That was the last unanswered question as Simon's world became a jumbled swirl of flashes as everything rushed past as he plummeted from the rooftop. The kitchen dumpster broke his fall with a backbreaking crunch. The pain racked his lower back and hip to form a wash of coloured lights passing across his vision. An intense taste of blood filled his mouth; further pain raced his chest as he fought to stay conscious, blinking through reddened eyes back to the roof.

D stood relishing with interest the outcome, a wide grin still on his face as he watched with interest. "Wow, fantastic," he cheered, clapping with glee. "It's an age since getting one of you down here. Welcome to the party bro, it all goes to shit from here." Still clapping, D turned to disappear from view, cackling laughter resonating as he left.

With a groan, Simon turned, rolling off the dumpster onto all fours. Another cough splattered blood across the floor. Moments passed until, forcing himself to his feet, a pulse of pain hit his back again as he staggered forward. *What maniac throws a complete stranger off a roof of a two storied building and laughs about it?* Simon cleared his throat, spitting more blood, wiping the remnants on the back of his hand. He clutched his ribs, making the slow journey for the kitchen back door.

Sat at the kitchen table, Lisa and Father Peters finished the last of the brewed coffee. Both jumped at the unexpected thump of something heavy hitting the door before opening.

With a gasp, Lisa recognised a dishevelled Simon, covered in dirt and blood.

Father Peters was the first to reach him, supporting him to a spare chair by the table. "What in all things holy? Last time I saw you, you were on the roof. How, in Christ's name, did you end up in the yard?" Not wanting to add to the obvious pain, he lowered him into a waiting chair. "Oh, dear God you didn't jump did you?"

Horrified, Lisa shook her head at the priest's query, hoping it was not to be true. She rushed to the sink to run water over a tea towel before returning to kneel and apply to Simon's blooded face.

Simon's anger building as he pushed away any form of help,

wincing as he did. "Where is he? Where did he go?"

Both Father Peters and Lisa shared a glance before Father Peters answered. "There are only us three here. Jake is out, and the Sister is completing errands."

Simon pulled an arm up against his ribs, heading for the swing doors leading into the hall.

Father Peters tried to support him, recommending he sat back down and rested.

"Who are you looking for, Simon?" Lisa asked, struggling to get him to focus on her and stop fighting them from helping.

"The guy on the roof called himself D."

"D, who in their right mind calls themselves D?" the Father queried. "There was nobody else up on the roof when I left, and nobody passed us in the kitchen. The main doors locked, so he has to be still upstairs."

"You have been under a lot of stress, including the nightmares and lack of sleep." Lisa added, trying to get Simon to sit still.

"You don't understand. He was real, and he gave me this," Simon interrupted, offering the crumpled business card still clutched in his hand.

Father Peters took the card, reading it over the rim of his glasses before passing it to Lisa to inspect. "I recognise the name from the infomercials, the biggest funeral business in the country. They have outlets all over since legalising suicide," the Father explained. "It states he's the company CEO, which still doesn't explain why he would want to be on our roof.

"Or need to throw you off," Lisa added, offering the card back.

Father Peters nodded in agreement. "Could be their latest marketing campaign?" The priest stifled a laugh at his own joke, stopping when recognising Lisa's glare of disapproval. Not the time for jokes.

She grasped Simon's hands, a gentle reassuring squeeze as she watched him struggle. "You have been under tremendous stress and medication, Simon. They can have adverse effects on making you imagine things, or it's a relapse involving one of those dreams of yours."

"Yes, Lisa may be on to something. You lost your bearings and fell over the ledge?" the Father added.

"I was not asleep or imagining it," Simon protested.

"Are you sure you could have slipped and fallen, you were close to the ledge when I left you."

"Then explain the business card."

Both fell silent, unable to offer any explanation.

Simon sat back in the chair, pushing past the tension in his back, examining the card again. "The guy was there, I tell you, and it wasn't a delusion or a dream."

"Okay, so explain this, why push you?" Father Peters was trying to understand and humour Simon.

"It was like he wanted to test me." Simon rose from the chair, heading with care for the double doors.

"Perhaps he wanted to see if you could fly," the Father joked, still trying to make light and break the tension in the room.

That resulted in a firm elbow to his side from Lisa.

Simon turned with a flash of anger. "What did you say? Why did you use those exact words?"

The Father put up his hands. "It was a joke lad, sorry, meant nothing by it. Your story is well... strange."

Simon pressed on, clutching the railings as he pulled himself up the stairs. He needed to rest with each step, as his mind recounted the macabre conversion with the lavishly suited D, his cryptic questions and references to lists. *What did he mean by one of you?* He thought. It made little sense, but one thing was certain, he would find this stranger. The business card was a start. Just as soon as his entire body stopped hurting.

There was no better example of a New American family than Georgina Appleby and her family. The demographic was a marketing executive's dream. Soccer mom to eight-year-old Robert, devoted wife to Marcus, together sharing the responsibility for their modest apartment provided by the Order of Light off Pailberry Plaza. Their bills paid on time, never overdrawn, trusted, and liked as true pillars of the community. They attend the local Order church each weekend, and Georgina volunteered at her son's school's after-school club when she could. They wanted for nothing, healthy and content, a warm picture perfect life now thrust in to a frightening nightmare of unmanageable horror as Georgina opened her drug fuelled eyes. The place she found herself remained in darkness but for the dimmest of light, invoking desperation as she fought to recollect how she had got here. Her heart rate spiralled, reacting to her fear of the unknown. Disorientation ebbed with the sense of muscles burning from the stress as she found her limbs shackled by leather restraints. Thick chains suspended her from grime stained tiled wall. She was semi naked but for underwear and slip covering her modesty and giving little protection from the cold harshness of a decaying windowless room. Her situation fuelled adrenaline stocked panic as her scream echoed with tortured intent, but it was in vain as no rescue came. Alone and silent tears flowed as she collapsed, pulling on her already strained muscles. Any resistance had opened the soft skin around wrists and ankles, releasing blood to run down the contours of her slim limbs. The increasing pain and strain continued to exhaust her with an alarming rate. "Why am I here?" she sobbed, fighting for a moment of clarity from the drug induced restrictions of her dulled mind. In an instant, her own predicament becoming secondary as she remembered her ordeal had occurred during a weekday morning school run. "Oh, my god, no," she cried in horrifying thought for the safety of her son, Robert. The striking fear made Georgina flail, ignoring the stressed muscles in the struggle to remember the last moments of their regular morning routine. Overcome with the terrifying thought no parent should face, the possibility of her child sharing the same fate whilst powerless to intervene. Not knowing brought on nausea, including a sickening tightness to grip her chest, considering her little boy locked away, alone and frightened. Georgina's emotion turned to anger, thrashing in her restraints. "Bobby!" she shouted. "Speak to me baby, momma's here. Say something, are you here?" With tears tracking cheeks, eyes closed to the silence. "Bobby, I love you baby," her voice hushed in fighting the impending darkness of a closing mind. "Momma loves you." The chains tightened in reply to her body, relaxing, leaving her slumped and despondent in not knowing what was happening to her child.

Time passed in silence, until Georgina stirred to raise her head, but her strength was failing, forcing her chin to slump back against her chest. From deep inside she freed a stifled laugh, a forced reaction of surprise at a curious response to her delusional state. Her thoughts, drifting to her childhood, sat, crossed legged at the feet of her grandmother, occupying her favourite blue porch rocker. The light of a dying day faded as she sat listening. Those cherished old days of a simpler, happier time, of days filled with joyous beliefs and understanding of God in Heaven. Georgina's grandmother was a spiritual woman, faith an enormous part of her life. She sat in the rocker quoting scripture, offering guidance during the pleasant times and the bad. So in Georgina's darkest moment, she took solace in those same words, the sweet image of her grandmother as she craved her protection more than ever. Georgina fought to cling to that memory, the old woman's warm smile as she leant forward to place a weathered hand upon Georgina's head. Milky white eyes closing as the old woman recited the words of her God, reassuring all would be fine if they shared the faith. Georgina clung to those words, moistening dry lips to repeat the same passages of old scripture. "Our Father, who art in heaven, hallowed be thy name; thy kingdom come; thy will be done; on earth, as in heaven." She spoke the words out loud, which brought on a sudden need to cough, urging her to clean her parched throat before continuing the words. "Give us this day, our daily bread. And forgive us our trespasses, as we forgive those who trespass against us…"

"You seek comfort in words of the false Gods in a hope of salvation, but will receive none. For they judge you on how you lived your full life, not repenting in your last hours."

The sinister disembodied voice chilled Georgina to the bone. She fell silent, searching the shadows, forcing strained eyes to detect the slightest detail of her tormentor.

"You're a heretic, guilty of blasphemy and reciting false prophecies. Together we shall cast out the demon walking amongst us and then judged for your sins."

Georgina, fatigued from her struggle, focused on movement appearing at the far end of the room. Her body saturated with adrenaline to the sudden development, as she observed the room's only exit open and close. With senses alerted to the slightest change in the room, she crouched, straining to see anything in the gloom.

A shape slipped through the shadows, hidden for any chance of recognition as a distinct chilling sound of metal scraping metal echoed the confined walls.

The sound sent a frigid chill down Georgina's spine, filling her with dread in an internal battle against drug fuelled fatigue. With a twist in restraints, she gripped the chain tight, pulling backwards until the cold tiled wall pressed her back. All her senses opened to the room, focusing to find whoever had entered, and the threat they represented. With the exertion on her limbs, her breathing becoming rapid to the point she heard her own blood pump throughout her skull. "Come near me, you son of a bitch, and I will tear your eyes out," she spat.

Nothing stirred.

Georgina was reaching the threshold of her tolerance, fuelled by a growing anger of resistance and not knowing her son's situation. She was waning, sensing the slightest tremble to her weakening muscles, trying to continue a battle so desperate not to lose. The grip on the chains turned her hands ashen white, as sweat raced her face. Her tolerance exploding as she cried out in pain and defiance. A wash of nausea clouded her senses as she noted the pooling blood around her elevated, shackled feet. A cold sensation of sweat slid down the arch of her neck and back, soaking her underwear as her grime-stained slip clung to her skin. She was noticing the effects of the blood loss as a numbness crept into her extremities, fuelling burning muscles. "Bobby, I'm coming home, baby," she whispered. Tears no longer stained her cheeks as she had none to give. A forced swallow against the dehydration she was suffering. She flinched at a solitary unfiltered light emanated from a recess off to the side. Georgina was becoming delirious, seeing shapes cross her vision as she battled to stay focused.

"Are you ready to confess your sins heretic?" Returned the sinister voice, taunting.

"What do you need from me?" Georgina pleaded.

"I want you to pray for forgiveness and renounce your sins as a heretic."

"What sins are you talking about, nothing is making sense?" She sank against the limits of the restraints.

"You are a heretic, straying from the path of the righteous by spreading lies through false prophecy."

The repetitive sound of metal on metal returned, and then a smell of damp, burning wood. A single flame of orange formed, growing with intensity, stoking increasing fear as the odour of an open fire filled the room.

Then strands of thin greying smoke stung Georgina's eyes, filling an already dry mouth and forcing her to cough, as attention remained transfixed on the growing light. A violent hiss made Georgina rear back to hit the wall with a violent blow. Another coughing fit tensed her body. Then, having little chance to react, a flash of heated metal struck her left thigh. The pain instant, intensifying throughout her side as she arched her back. A stench of charring flesh lingered. The brand removed to leave her twisting, eyes wide, mouth open, as she released a pitiful whimper instead of her intended scream.

She fell forward, drawing in a lengthy breath in desperation to stem the pain as she watched the orange glow return to the darkness. Her lower lip now lay open from her resistance, tasting the metallic texture of her own blood as she sensed her whole body tremble. A glance of her thigh showed the skin around the burn to be scorched black, smouldering in a shape of which she had no interpretation. Her ordeal continued with another brand thrust into her lower abdomen. The hot metal burnt through the flimsy slip to leave charred pieces of material in a wound glowing red. This time a scream reached Georgina's lips. "You bastard," she shouted. She had no time to react as another brand embedded under her left arm, supporting her suspended body. The impact and pain threw her back again, hitting her head with a deafening impact. Her last memory was the odour of burning flesh followed by darkness.

A gloved hand grabbed Georgina's chin, shaking her from her comatose state. "Our time is far from ended."

Through half-opened eyes, she endeavoured to focus on the figure returning to its implements of torture, stoking the flames of the heated burner. Georgina, dazed from her concussion, fought against her fog filled mind, then sensed floor beneath her feet which helped the strain of her wracked body. She tried to clear her vision, shaking her head. Flashes of light dissipated until the figure of a man dressed in hooded robes stood before her, only the lower part of his features visible under the hood. He resembled a cleric from her church, but his robes appeared thicker, of a heaver stained brown material. Not unlike the religious prints of clergy from the old books her grandmother had kept. The figure chanted in a language she did not recognise as he returned the irons in the burning embers that glowed white hot in the flame.

"What do you want with me?" she asked, her voice cracking, too hoarse to speak. The burner increased the stagnant heat of her prison, increasing the sweat rolling her cheeks, matting hair in tangled clumps around her smoke-blackened face.

"Explain your visions?" the figure asked.

"My visions, what visions?" She felt confused to the questioning, straining against her restraints that still held tight.

"For you spread heresy, proclaiming to have revelations of the past, present and what is to come. These interpretations spread falsehood, I'm I correct?"

A spark arched from the burner, its existence brief on the tiled floor at her feet.

"Your life resembles that ember, extinguishable if I so see fit. So tell me what we seek."

"I don't have any idea what you demand from me? I've never had visions." Georgina shook her head, trying for her life to remember anything that may save her from what came next. The increasing heat of the iron passed over her exposed skin. She twisted, bracing for the inevitable pain to come. Teeth clenched, permitting herself to open her eyes to find the hot iron a few inches from her left cheek.

The heated metal sizzled as it twisted in gloved grip.

Georgina's attention remained on the single white tip inching closer.

"What is the falling light and what does it bring."

Georgina sobbed, unable to answer the cryptic questions.

"Tell me of the coming darkness."

The iron moved closer, making Georgina flinch.

"We know you have the gift to speak for the false prophet. Explain their meanings and I will release the demon within you and rescue you from your pain and burden of the infliction."

Georgina tried to swallow. "I don't see what you mean. What visions? Who do you think I speak for, I don't understand?" In anger, she pulled on the restraints edging away from the heated iron. "I don't know what you want from me," she screamed. Her body convulsed as the iron burnt deep in to her cheek pinning her to the wall, her scream her only release.

Lukewarm water splashed Georgina's face, shocking her back to reality. With a gasp for air, she spat out the foul tasting remnants mixing with her pooled blood around her feet. Her senses screamed in pain, the rest felt numb. Her tormentor had been busy in her unconscious state. Further symbols had been burnt deep in her flesh. She struggled to stay conscious. The side of her face had swollen, reducing her vision to one eye. Searching, noting the far walls shared the same intricate symbols now adorning her flesh. Any further resistance failing, she felt broken and craved a release from her nightmare.

From inside the room, the chanting resumed in the unfamiliar language.

Georgina did not care, slumped against the restraints, her body numb as though her consciousness was being pulled from her chest.

The robed figure emerged, pacing, and reciting from a stained leather book.

The growing cold numbness in the dark recesses of Georgina's chest continued to warm, but she could not explain the sensation. Curling and twisting in desperation for freedom, causing an uncontrollable spasm spanning her entire flailing body.

Her tormentor continued in his chant, faster and faster, reading from the book.

Unable to control her own body, Georgina panicked as her mind grew cold from an approaching darkness. Then a calming silence, as though floating without the burden of her failed body. From the corner of her mind she heard a familiar voice, chanting the same language spoken by her tormentor. Her muffled scream was in the realisation that the voice was her own, and she was no longer in control as Georgina Appleby ceased to be.

The business card led Simon and Lisa into the heart of New Eden, fighting building traffic.

"Have I told you I hate driving into the city," Lisa confessed, knuckles white against the wheel of the little Ford as she tried to change lanes.

Outside, street after street of whitewashed stone and glass flashed passed.

The journey fascinated Simon sat in the passenger seat. Everything appeared clean and well maintained, and a far cry from the rundown streets of Sufferance. "What I remember you were most excited to volunteer," he smiled. "When you knew I needed to visit this place." With a twist of the embossed card, he reread the details for the umpteenth time. "And besides, if we are to get any answers this Reap Corp Inc. is the place to start, don't you think?"

Lisa half listened. In her nervousness, she played with the thin watch strap on her wrist, waiting for a break in the traffic. Soon enough one appeared, allowing her to manoeuvre and continue into the city.

"This Mr D was selective with his answers, so it's an excellent chance he knows more about what happened with my accident," Simon continued.

Lisa took her attention briefly from the road. "Please don't put all your hopes on him having all the answers. This complete adventure could lead to disappointment."

A pained expression crossed Simon's face, fuelling a growing doubt of his own. He had hoped she would share his enthusiasm in search for answers as attention returned to the card.

Lisa sensed the growing tension and was about to apologise when their destination loomed ahead.

Reap Corp Inc. was a vast entity, unique to the business district, unusual gothic architecture dominating its modern neighbours. The building took up the whole side of the street, as columns of black granite lined the facade and framed the dark filtered display windows. Those same windows housed an array of marketing screens flicking through the company's latest offerings. A grand and elaborate entrance lined with white stone steps leading to a choice of revolving doors. Already a crowed of bustling, well-suited employees and prospective customers hurried past in an endless stream as the car pulled to the side.

Lisa surveyed the surrounding street. "I will have to leave you here, need to find a damn parking space. Did I mention I hate driving in the city?" She turned to Simon, noticing his fixation to their destination, which until a few moments ago was just a name on a business card. "Are you sure you will be okay, Simon? I can..."

"No. It's okay. I need to do this. We can meet back here, I shouldn't be too long." Simon stepped out, closing the door with a wave and watched as the car manoeuvred back into traffic.

Passing overhead, an advertising drone drew attention to its virtual life like visuals depicting a woman with an elaborate welcoming expression. "Welcome to Mortis House, the hub of our international business, a place to connect you to the afterlife through our exclusive worldwide branches. We take the pain out of your last journey." The drone moved in perfect step as Simon approached, continuing her greeting as soulless eyes watched intensely, making Simon somewhat nervous to the attention. "We offer services to the soon to be parted. Whilst bringing comfort to those left behind in times of quiet reflection and contemplation." The virtual seller gave a well-programmed smile. "Why not visit our Suicide Booths? For a limited time we offer thirty percent off full booking if you recommend a friend."

Simon's pace quickened, caught in the crowd moving through a set of tall revolving doors.

Inside, the interior changed to neutral colours as crimson drapes framed large glass partitions, separating visitors from plush furnished seating and rows of grey uniformed staff.

A guide rope walkway controlled the flow of visitors to the public area, where Simon remained in awe until a virtual attendant ushered him forward. He joined a waiting line overlooking the entire length of the ground floor. On the far wall, embossed in gold and black lettering, was the corporation's mission statement 'Delivering Everyone's Angels to Heaven.'

Simon watched as staff went about their day-to-day business until another virtual attendant broke his concentration, requesting he moved forward in its unnerving monotone manner. His curiosity continued to notice assorted seating providing waiting visitors comfort until escorted to vacant Bereavement Booths at the far side of the welcome area. Throughout the reception area, piped calming music to help relax and add to the tranquil atmosphere as further uniformed staff attended to potential clientele.

Simon sensed to being observed and turned to find he had reached the front of the line where a physical human receptionist beckoned him forward.

Her customary practised smile and head tilt of sympathy was a customary greeting to make any visit as pleasant as possible. "How are you today and how may we be of service in your time of solemn reflection, sir?"

Simon glanced the full length of the reception desk, each window serviced by the same uniformed staff reciting well-rehearsed greetings before returning attention to the receptionist. "What... no... no-one's died," he responded. "I was hoping for information."

"Then perhaps sir is looking for our luxurious Suicide Booths on the eighth floor. We cater for all concerns with your own assigned Bereavement Councillor who will handle all your needs and those of your loved ones."

"That won't be necessary, thank you." Simon responded.

The receptionist's rehearsed smile slipped to a brief frown as Simon reached to inside his jacket pocket, retrieving the battered business card. "Is it possible to speak to the owner of this card, I have questions in need of answering."

The receptionist glanced from the card and back to Simon without breaking her expression. "I'm sorry, sir. I'm not allowed to put you through to that individual. May I direct you to our customer service department who will answer questions you may have." She offered another practised smile.

"You don't understand the importance I speak to the

gentleman who gave me this card."

"I'm sorry, sir. Company policy doesn't allow clients to contact senior management without an appointment. Has sir an appointment?"

"No, I don't..." Simon paused, scratching his cheek in building frustration. "Look! How do I get an appointment if I can't talk to the person in question to make a damn appointment?" Simon's agitation drew attention. So releasing a held breath, he tried to ignore the disapproving glares and get control. "The fact is, the owner of that card threw me off a roof. If you don't mind, I would like to know why," he continued offering his own forced smile through clenched teeth. "Please, it's important I speak to Mr HaMavet. Just five minutes."

For the first time since the start of the conversation, the receptionists' compassionate expression faltered. "I'm sorry, sir, but that is not possible."

The crack of Simon's clenched fist striking the desk partition brought the area to a quiet murmur, startling the receptionist who blinked back wide-eyed.

"Sorry." Simon tried to explain, continuing to rub the side of his face, exhausted by the past few days.

It was then two security officials came to flank him, and Simon understood his visit and hope for answers had come to an abrupt end.

After twenty minutes of waiting, Lisa wished she'd insisted on joining Simon on his quest. She was unbuckling her seatbelt when she jumped to the passenger door swinging open and Simon sat down next to her. His obviously forlorn expression told her all had not gone well, but she remained silent. So starting the engine, she flicked the indicator to pull out.

The car passed into moving traffic, and the next ten minutes of the return journey remained in silence.

With a hesitant breath, curiosity made Lisa ask a question. "Any luck?"

Simon's lip twisted, reluctant to come out of his self-imposed brooding. Instead, he shrugged and stared out of the passenger window at nothing in particular.

Lisa felt his disappointment. "That's not good." With a small sigh, she wished the visit had been more encouraging, maybe finding out why this D character was interested in Simon. She took another glance from the road, eyes narrowing, so wanting to help. What could she say to bring him out of his isolation these past few days? Her attention back to the road ahead, manoeuvring lanes leading out of the city to the harmonic gesturing of car horns from fellow drivers.

They had not been travelling long, Lisa gripping the wheel with nervous thumbs, tapping in annoyance to the slow-moving traffic around them. Her thoughts returned to earlier in the day, over hearing Simon's need to visit Reap Corp, Inc. She had jumped at the chance for the alone time, wanting to uncover the reason he had become so reclusive since the roof incident. Now perhaps her chance had come. As she chewed her lip and not taking her eye off the traffic ahead, she considered what she wanted to say.

"Complete waste of time," Simon interrupted, silencing Lisa's train of thought. "No help at all, just passed over these damn leaflets and requested I left." In annoyance, Simon screwed up the mentioned paperwork, depositing the crumpled ball on the dashboard. "Against company policy to give out contact details of senior management, and if I persisted they would ask security to remove me from the building, I got the message."

Lisa glanced over, understanding his frustration. "Kind of understand what they mean as this D person is the CEO of one of the country's biggest company's right? They wouldn't let just anybody off the street have his personal contact details, would they?"

Lisa's explanation gave minor consolation as Simon spun the business card between his fingers. "Suppose you're right, it was a long shot anyway," he concluded with a sigh. "But we had to try," he continued. The journey continued as familiar structures rushed past, making Simon sit up to notice. "Where are we anyway?" He asked. "I think I know this part of the town."

"You do?" Lisa got her own bearings. "Suppose you would, we are... coming to the tenements off thirty third and our turn home."

The car took a less busy side street, much to Lisa's relief as she nodded to the large tenements behind the seven eleven across the street. "Past those buildings are garage lockups were Jake found you after your accident."

Simon noticed a group of fern trees stood over an outcropping of smaller buildings at the top of an incline.

"I'm surprised you remember. You were out cold, according to the Father, as he brought you out."

"Pull over," Simon asked, almost half out the car before Lisa could slow to a full stop.

She parked and grabbed her bag to rush after him; soon finding him stood gazing at the trees, releasing shafts of sunlight through their thick wavering canopy.

With eyes closed, Simon listened to the birds nested high in the branches. "I remember the sounds, the wind through the trees."

"That's great, isn't it?" Lisa nodded to the base of the trees and the ramshackle buildings. "We found you in one of those garages." To Lisa's surprise, Simon grabbed her hand, pulling her towards the footpath.

"Come with me, show me," he asked.

As they reached the garages, they found the footpath blocked by crisscrossed police incident tape flapping in the breeze.

Lisa pointed to the bared path. "It was in that one with the double doors, but it looks like we can't go any further."

Simon gripped the tape.

"Guess the authorities marked it off as a crime scene," Lisa explained.

Simon, transfixed on plausible answers to his questions in

the garage, ducked under the tape.

Lisa hesitated, rubbing the back of her neck in search for witnesses to them crossing the tape. When she caught up, she clutched his arm for reassurance. "You shouldn't cross the tape line back there; we'd be in serious trouble if we get caught."

"So we'd better not get caught," Simon smiled. His apprehension vanished in trying the doors and found them unlocked. "Come on," he offered. "A few minutes to look around, jog my memory." He opened the doors wider so to enter.

Lisa peered in, surprised to find the room swept clean. Gone was the rubbish and debris littering the floor, nothing but bare space. "Still spooky dark but cleaner since we were here last," she remarked.

With the light from the opened doors providing the only illumination, Lisa went to the brown weathered door, which she found closed. "Past that door, the room beyond, that's where we found you."

Simon headed for the door, finding a brief resistance as it creaked, then dropped off its remaining hinge. He picked the door up, placing it to one side.

Lisa stood on her tiptoes, peering past his shoulder. "Wow, this place is clean."

The room beyond was bare, everything removed by the authorities.

Lisa knelt, wiping a hand across the floor. "Even the oil's gone. Not a trace." She pushed past, turning to see Simon glancing around the room. "There's nothing left, even the desk you slept under, everything gone." She did a full circle, taking in the space. "I don't like this, Simon. Why would they remove everything? I've never heard of the authorities doing such a thorough clean-up of a scene."

Simon slouched, recognising another dead lead.

Lisa took his hand, offering a gentle squeeze. "I'm sorry, Simon. It must be so frustrating for you. Nothing makes sense, but perhaps being here, do you remember anything?"

With a heavy sigh, he returned her gaze with a half-hearted smile.

She stared into his tired eyes, maybe seeking a glimmer of what he was thinking.

Still hands entwined, he squeezed back. "Why was I found here? I hoped, seeing, smelling the place would make it all fit into place, but I'm back to square one." Simon's face twisted, knowing the authorities were searching for something important or more likely someone important. It was easy to understand that someone was after him, for reasons still unknown. That meant time was running out. The realisation brought a knot to his stomach, of which he could not shift.

"If answers you are seeking, you're looking in the wrong place, bro." The voice was familiar, startled them both.

Simon shielded Lisa at recognition of the newcomer.

Lisa taking a cautious glimpse around his shoulder to see a tall man, dark complexion and dressed in a business suit walk out of the shadows.

Simon pushed against Lisa, keeping himself between her and the newcomer, eyes remaining fixed on the suited man. "It's okay, Lisa, we have met. This is Mr HaMavet and..."

D pushed past, offering his hand in greeting. The smile brought a slight chill to Lisa as he took her hand in his. She looked up into the ebony face, hidden behind darker glasses.

With a gentle bow, D kissed her hand with ice-like touch before stepping back. "Lisa Shelby, mother of Jake and a Pisces if I'm not mistaken."

With a nervous half smile, Lisa took back her hand and stood again behind Simon.

"How did he know?" she whispered.

Simon remained stony faced, glaring at D who stood back, ignorant to his contempt filled glare.

"Please call me D and its lists, my dear, everyone is on my list," D explained. "All accept you." He pointed a well-manicured finger at Simon.

Lisa watched both men share a glance before Simon broke

the deadlock.

"You mentioned lists before, if I remember, just before you pushed me off the roof."

D chuckled at the mere mention of their first meeting, holding up his hands. "Peace of mind and a need to know. Unfortunately for you, it involved needing to push you off the roof. But to be fair, it turned out okay as you're still here, aren't you?"

Lisa stepped back, shocked at the revelation. "You were telling the truth about the other evening?"

Simon turned with mouth open, understanding Lisa had doubted what had happened. "You didn't believe me?"

She offered a shrug, forcing a thin smile as an apology. "Sorry Simon, but it sounded so far-fetched, a well-dressed man appearing on our roof with an intension to shove you off."

"In his defence I had an excellent reason, but she has a point," D interrupted, still grinning.

Simon shook his head to being humoured the whole time.

"Okay, okay, you're mad at me, I understand, but had to make sure, see with my own eyes," D offered.

"Why did it call for me needing to free fall off a building?"

"Would you believe curiosity?" D flashed another grin.

"To see if I could fly?" Simon's patience waned with the riddle like answers.

"Oh no, I knew you couldn't fly, silly. No wings and all, well not anymore," He pushed his glasses down offering a wink. "No, needed to know you would survive the fall. Resilient little nugget aren't you."

Simon shared a look of surprise with Lisa, who asked a question. "Survive the fall?"

"Yes."

"Why?" She continued.

"Because he's not on my lists and no one is exempt, not even him. This makes him unique, and I enjoy collecting unique things." D threw his arms up in agitation before grasping Simon by the shoulders.

With a nervous flashback, Simon pushed him away.

A quick straightening of the suit jacket and tie, D composed himself, keeping his distance, and paced the room, trying to explain his earlier actions. "It's understandable you're hostile. But I'm on your side in all of this." His attention passed between both Simon and Lisa as he continued. "But you must have realised how special you are by now, bro." He finished pacing, turning to Lisa. "Tell me, aren't you a little curious how someone survived such injuries. Has it not crossed your mind how someone could heal in such a brief period?"

Lisa did not answer as Simon interrupted. "I was bedridden for weeks."

D ignored the protest, attention still on Lisa. "Ask yourself how that same someone could walk away from all those breakages, burns and ailments in record time?"

Lisa glanced at Simon, doubt crossing her face, still staying silent until with reluctance she looked away instead.

"It was Father Peters and Lisa caring for me that got me through it, nothing more."

D leaned in until Lisa could make out her own reflection in his dark lenses. She noted the solid black eyes behind, swallowing her whole and somewhat unsettling. With the dark direction of the conversation, she felt uncomfortable. With a begrudging sigh, she considered being blinded by her growing feelings for Simon. Too trusting that once they started digging into his past and not once had she considered what they might uncover and that troubled her? *Just how stupid had she been?* The thought made her angry with herself.

"What are you getting at D? Why don't you explain to us what you mean instead of the smoke and mirror bullshit?" Simon asked, spinning D. So they faced off inches from each other. "Why don't you tell me? I'm convinced you're not telling the full story. Have you got anything to do with me ending up in this garage, half dead?" In his anger, Simon had grabbed D by his suit jacket, roughing the fabric.

D motioned to the crushed jacket still in Simon's grip. "Do you mind?"

Frustrated, Simon released him, allowing D to step back, straightening out the creases in his suit. "Don't you a recognise twenty-five hundred made to measure suit from Harvard & Locks of London? Not including the extra shipping through the EU embargo lines." He continued, still pressing out the creases. "Ooh... sorry, forgot you remember nothing, do you?" D's laugh echoed the garage.

Simon slumped against the wall, sliding to the floor, placing his head in his hands.

Lisa, with a touch of guilt, unable to understand what was going through his mind as she knelt to stroke his face, showing he was not alone.

Just then, an electronic beep sounded, so D reached into his inside jacket pocket to retrieve his secpad. "Sorry, I'm always on the clock, got a VIP appointment across town in an hour, wouldn't want to miss this one." Once again, the perfect smile as he glanced from his device. "Almost like you, bro." Moments passed, and a few more hasty taps followed. "I would let the office handle it, but these VIPs are such a special case, needing the big boss." He knelt, placing a hand on Simon's shoulder. "Not only are there lists, bro, but they're rules we all must follow. Specific rules not broken under any circumstance, for the consequences are unpleasant for anyone crossing the powers that be. Understand when I tell you this, for it's the reason you're in this mess. You broke the rules and your free fall and memory wipe are the consequences. Here's the kicker, those same unbreakable rules stop me from telling you anything else that might help you remember. My pay grade doesn't cover giving you the full package, it's a free will, find their own path crap. They like those things upstairs. So, it's important that nut of yours gets sorted before too late. Remember who you were. It will protect you from the coming storm. It's started and you play an enormous part, so no pressure, okay?"

Simon raised his head, recognising sincerity for once behind the dark glasses.

D ruffled Simon's hair, and then stood to dust down his suit, checking his secpad and his watch.

Lisa put her arm around Simon, hugging him.

"It will come back to you, bro, and soon. When it does, an entire truck load of crap will hit the fan. You're about to face something not seen before and your arrival was the beginning and they know you're here. All the players are circling because you're the significant change. Take care of yourself, Simon." Leaving Simon to his own thoughts, D gestured Lisa over to where he stood.

She left Simon seated and followed D to the doorway.

"Can I give a piece of advice?" he asked in a hushed tone.

Puzzled, Lisa nodded.

"Grab that son of yours, get out. Go home to Cleveland and make amends with your family. Just be far away as possible. Make peace with your past before it's too late." With that last piece of advice, D left, whistling as he did.

"Simon," Lisa asked, offering her hand out to him. "Come on, let's get us home." She lifted his head, the stress of the day pictured across his face.

"Even after everything D has said, you're not nervous to be around me?"

"I will not lie to you Simon not knowing your past scares me. But it also reminds me about something Father Peters mentioned about bringing you to the refuge. He tried to explain the experience of renewed strength in himself after helping you. He had a gut feeling he needed to protect you, because you're important. Since knowing the Father, I have learnt to trust his judgement of people. Not once would he bring danger into the refuge unless there's a reason he would never put those he cared about in harm's way." She again offered her hand. "Let's get home before I change my mind."

Simon took the offered hand and followed Lisa back to the car.

Unnoticed, hidden in the roof space of the small garage, a device focused on them leaving. It had activated on their arrival, recording the entire conversation. The red light blinked, showing completion of the live feed through high-speed transmitter. The surveillance images processed for identification through an extensive database back at the remote surveillance console monitoring the area. Everything had changed, for those searching had found who they searched for, and for Simon and the refuge, trouble would soon follow.

CHAPTER SIX

Devil's Playground

Neither Simon nor Lisa wanted to discuss the mysterious D, achieving nothing but the meeting, culminating in a chain of events that had put an unforeseen strain on their relationship. As the journey home continued, both fell into the confines of their own thoughts.

For Lisa, D's words lingered as she forced herself to concentrate to the drive and the traffic ahead. On reflection, a conflicted guilt to having not told Simon the complete truth about her fears, trusting Father Peter's judgement whilst ignoring her own misgivings wrapped up in blossoming emotions. She became lost in enjoying the excitement, not considering there to be any consequences. D's warning resonated to get Jake and run as far as possible. With a cautious glance, she watched Simon slouched in the passenger seat, preoccupied with D's business card turning between his fingers. *What was so dangerous about Simon?* Her mind became a clutter of darkening possibilities. Just how prepared was she for the truth once he got his memories back. Regardless, if it came down to choosing between the safety of her son and her own personal needs, she would not hesitate. With wheel gripped tight, deciding that the first sign of trouble, she would heed the warning and leave the refuge.

Unaware of Lisa's concern, Simon had become consumed with the fleeting image of D's macabre smile ingrained in the door glass, the man behind a veil of secrets and half-truths. Whilst conveniently hiding behind the underlying rules, unable to explain those same elusive rules or who was behind them. The whole meeting fuelled more questions than answers. Suddenly an unevenness of the road forced him from his dark thoughts as the little red Ford pulled in to the backyard behind the Refuge of Lost Souls.

With them parked, Lisa set the handbrake, allowing the car to settle with the cooling ticking of the engine, neither occupant wanting to exit.

Lisa once again gripped the wheel, turning, but before uttering a single word, the kitchen door to the refuge burst open.

Both saw a figure manhandled backwards and flung to the ground in a dust filled cloud.

"What the…" Lisa cursed, alarmed by the sudden interruption, frowning at the silhouette at the door.

Father Peters, shirt and cardigan ruffled, glasses crooked on the bridge of his nose. His attention fixed on the figure struggling to get to his feet, in an obvious state of intoxication. "Go home and get sober," he pointed. "We don't want you back until you do. Always respect the rules of this refuge, no drinking or causing any trouble."

Lisa unbuckled her seatbelt, making her way to the front of the car to recognise who the Father had manhandled. Anger replaced her shock as she approached the scruffy individual in a crumpled floral shirt, unbuttoned to show a beer and sweat stained vest.

The figure's unkempt hair clung to his face as he twisted to meet her glare.

"Brian, I should have guessed it was you causing a scene here." Lisa offered, arms crossed in signal to her ex-husband all was far from happy.

Brian Shelby tried to focus, a wide unconvincing grin spreading across his face, resulting in a belch to Lisa's disgust. "He flung me out." Pointing to the priest silhouetted in the doorway. "Wouldn't let me see my kid, the Scottish bastard…"

Lisa with rolled eyes lowered her voice to calm the situation, helping her ex to stay still. "You're supposed to contact me first before visiting. Not turn up when you want." Moving closer, she smelled the stale alcohol oozing from his body. "And you're drunk." She cursed as the anger continued to build.

Brian struggled to stand to his full intimidating height, lasting a few moments until his body trembled with the effort. He staggered forward, resting upon the warm bonnet of the car.

Thinking fast, Lisa knew all too well how bad tempered and volatile Brian was when he'd been drinking. She still had the scars to prove it. "God, how dumb was I to think you would ever change Brian. All those failed promises of becoming a better husband, a better dad to Jake. The lies, apologetic stories once you sobered up and crept back home. We are so much better off without you."

"I've changed," he protested, wiping the spittle from the edge of his mouth continuing to focus.

Lisa rubbed at her temples in frustration. "Do you remember being in the same state and turning that anger on our son? You swore you'd never let that happen again, but look at you! You're a mess."

With a blink of concentration, Brian tried to answer but was sick instead.

"Over twelve months we escaped you, and then you track us down to that small apartment in Denver for it to start anew. You call around, saying you had changed. How many times did we have to move because of you? Barely scraping by after finding jobs, paying little to no wages. Only to hit rock bottom after losing another flea pit apartment because you won't stay out of our lives. We were hungry and cold before ending up here. If not for the kindness and fortune of the Father taking pity on us, offering us a place to stay until we got back on our feet. I'd dread to think what might have happened." She clutched Brian's shoulder, pulling him around so they stared at each other. "For years now the refuge has been our home, mine and Jakes. It gives us a decent life. We never asked for you to track us down and for this entire merry dance to start again."

Brian straightened, concentrating on what she was saying.

Lisa continued to glare.

"I might be a screw-up and a terrible husband, but that shouldn't stop me seeing my kid, should it?"

"Stop shouting and yes it does," Lisa replied, pulling his arms down to stop him waving about and losing his balance. "How dare you come here in this state, to where I work and live, showing yourself up in front of Jake?"

Both turned to the kitchen window, noting Jake had appeared with Sister Angela, his face a mask of concern, explaining how he felt in that moment.

Brian leaned back onto the bonnet and sobbed. "I'm so sorry, Lisa. I've so screwed up, and I needed to see you again. God, I've messed up so much this time."

Lisa mouthed she would handle the situation from here to Father Peters, who still waited in the kitchen doorway.

With a nod of acknowledgement, he returned to the kitchen, shutting the door behind him.

With a smile to help relieve Jake's distress, Lisa observed Sister Angela put a comforting hand on his shoulder, moving him away from the window. She hoped the scene would not upset him too much, but she would explain it all later.

Back in the car, Simon awaited a discrete moment to exit. With Lisa and her ex preoccupied, he opened the door cautiously to make no noise.

Brian raised his head from his drunken sobbing, taking a few seconds to focus on the shadow moving from the car. His expression flushed as he realised the stranger had exited the same car as his wife. In his alcohol-clouded mind, two and two equalled six, and he came to the wrong conclusion. "Who the hell is this?" He pointed.

Simon froze, looking to Lisa for guidance.

Brian squared up, using his height advantage to look down on Simon in a dominating stance.

Although reeling from the alcohol breath, Simon stood his ground.

Lisa pulled on Brian's arm to shove past, placing herself between the two to defuse the situation before it got out of hand. A push on Brian's chest gave them more space. "He works here at the refuge with us and besides, what has it got to do with you, anyway." Still pushing against Brian, not affecting the fact he had a good seventy pounds over her but being drunk he was unsteady on his feet.

The anger appeared to ebb and for a moment, Lisa recognised a brief flicker of the man she once loved, back in high school.

"I worry about you babe, strange guys come to this place, you know?"

Lisa sighed, stroking his cheek. "Get sober and get whatever else you're on out of your system before coming back again. You hear me, Brian?"

With a blank expression, he sniffed, wiping sweat soaked features on his opened shirt.

"Oh, dear god you are a mess," Lisa said shaking her head.

A crooked smile crossed Brian's face, "I have excellent news," he said.

"You're leaving the city?" she concluded, incapable to hide her sarcasm, and watched Brian's intoxicated confusion.

"No, but remember that job I got months back, plenty of prospects and stuff."

Lisa, ever sceptical, knew whatever came out of his mouth was a lie.

"Trouble is." He gave her a wry smile. "I've hit a snag, and I need working capital for the next part of the venture. The others in the deal, once I put in my share, will bankroll the rest. It's the biggest score yet, and the money we make on this one deal is twelve times what we put upfront. So I was hoping you could help me out?" He reached out, trying to touch her cheek as he appealed to her old feelings for him, but she was having none of it pushing his hands away.

"You turn up again. Even after telling you to stay away and you have the balls to worm money out of me." She put her hands on her hips. "I told you the last time you asked, I will not give money to a waster like you." She felt her anger building as she paced, scowling as Brian swayed with his arms out, still trying to appeal to her.

"Oh come on babe, this once. I've got most of the cash I need but I'm short, say sixteen hundred, two grand, max." He turned to point towards the refuge. "You could ask the priest, they have the money these days." The half-smile Brian gave was the last straw.

Lisa lashed out with her palm, striking Brian across the face with a crack, shocking even herself to her actions.

Brian reeling from the blow took a few unsteady steps back. His inebriation evaporating, replaced with darkening expressionless eyes that narrowed as his entire body tensed, reaching up to touch his cheek, still marked by Lisa's blow.

The entire scene for Lisa slowed, changing to an outcome seen too many times during their volatile relationship. She braced her legs, feet refusing to move and be as far away as possible.

With clenched fists, adrenaline took over and Brian lurched with a speed fast for a man his size.

The blow struck Lisa with white-hot pain as the force lifted her body off the ground. She slammed against the rear passenger door, hitting her head with a sickening thump. With the wind knocked out of her, she stumbled to make it to her feet. The acrid taste of blood filled her mouth, escaping the corner of her lip as her vision blurred from her possibly broken nose, unable to recognise Brian towering over her.

Brian was ready to put her down if she showed any sign of disobedience, but there would be none as Lisa slipped into unconsciousness. With breathing heavy, he stared upon the pitiful state of Lisa at his feet. "You bitch," he spat, rage behind his eyes. "I will teach you a lesson you will never forget." With his attention on Lisa, Brian was unaware of the shape moving fast from his right. The first he knew was the body slam, taking him under his abdomen as both men hit the ground hard.

Simon rolled and in one fluid motion was ready for any retaliation Brian might try, but he need not worry.

Brian was in no state for a quick counterattack and was still rolling on the floor, holding his stomach. "Son of a bitch," he shouted, pushing himself on to his knees, disbursing the remaining contents of his stomach over the floor. With a further purge, he wiped his mouth, studying Simon with coldness as he rose. "I will tear you up bad," he growled.

Not waiting for him to recover, Simon's boot swept in to catch Brian's ankle, tipping the man backwards and knocking the wind out of him.

Simon paused, concerned for Lisa slumped against the car.

Both men were seeing red.

Brian made the best of the delay by rolling to his side with another spit of bile. He stood to shake off the sudden attack.

Simon acted fast, knowing he had to bring Brian down before the man used his advantage of height and weight over him. The kick aimed for Brian's centre of mass, but Simon could not contain his surprise as Brian blocked it mid-air. Brian had grabbed the leg in both hands, giving no time to resist as he kicked out Simon's other, forcing him over in a cloud of dried dust. As pain sprang up his leg and across his lower back, Brian using all his strength and rage threw Simon hard against the dumpster.

During the commotion, Father Peters rushed out to see Simon launch his ill-fated kick and the painful consequences. He rushed to the car, finding Lisa's limp body as blood flowed from her nose and mouth. A quick stoop and he cradled her head, checking her over for any other injuries. "It's okay, child. It will be okay."

Lisa's eyes flickered open, and she gave a muffled response as she slipped in and out of consciousness. "Don't let Jake see… me. Not like this, please Father," she sobbed.

Father Peters picked her up, heading for the kitchen door

where it was safer. A glance over his shoulder had Brian on his feet, and Simon down, but still fighting.

Both studied each other for weaknesses to exploit, before Simon sprang forward, but Brian expected the move. He grabbed him in a headlock. A quick turn and knee to the stomach had Simon gasping for air. "I spent my entire life in situations like this. Scraps and fights throughout school and every dark, dank bar from here to Cleveland. Hell, I could have been professional if it was not for the wife and kid straight out of school."

"A professional wife beater, more like," Simon coughed.

Brian snarled a grin, waving a finger in warning. "What goes on between a husband and wife is nothing to do with anyone else." He gripped a clump of Simon's hair, pulling his head upwards. "Coach said I had an uncanny sixth sense in knowing what my opponents do next. Helped me side step any attack." His fist slammed into Simon's head, forcing him back down as Brian walked around him.

Simon gripped in pain, rolled onto his back as Brian continued to circle. Then a foot came hard between his legs, ending any fight left in him.

Brian cheered in triumph. "Have to fight dirty these days, pal," he spat, leaving Simon reeling in pain, hands between his legs. "You want her? Well, you can have the bitch." Brian looked up at the refuge, seeing no one at the windows but knowing they heard. "It goes for the bastard too." With a quick dust down, he swaggered out of the yard.

Simon rolled about the floor, coughing into the dust.

Back in the refuge, Father Peters helped Lisa to one of the kitchen chairs, and then went to retrieve ice from the small freezer. Wrapping cubes in a tea towel, he applied the cold compress to the swelling around her face. She winced as he did. "It hurts worse than it looks," he suggested with a reassuring smile.

Lisa offered the thinnest of smiles, pushing through the discomfort as she removed the compress. Then, with eyes closed, she tried to push past the grogginess she still felt. "Where's Jake?"

"The Sister took him upstairs, thought it was no place for a child to see his parents arguing."

With a reluctant nod, she reapplied the ice, calming the throbbing racing through her skull. "He isn't a parent, just the bloody sperm donor and waste of four years of my life."

The Father gave an agreeing grunt, wiping the drying blood with a clean cloth. "There, all beautiful again," he smiled, sitting back. "You're lucky your nose's not broken, but it's a beauty of a cut," he offered. "Vision will be fuzzy, so try to stay off your feet, okay?"

"I'm fine, Father, and trust me when I say he has given me worse. Besides, I have to see Jake, make sure he's okay." Lisa stood. Her balance was still off, and she sat back down with a jolt.

The Father moved closer, watching as she dabbed the ice pack back to her head. "He demanded to see Jake. Take him out."

"Huh!"

"Brian, he wanted to take Jake out, but I wouldn't let him, not without you saying so beforehand. Besides, he was drunk and so I guessed that wasn't the reason he came."

Lisa rolled her head back, trying to rest it on the chair back. "Money, same old story for the latest get rich venture." She moved the pack to another part of her head. "I lost my rag with a bitch slap. Felt good when I did it, but a big mistake afterwards."

She put down the ice pack, drawing her chair closer to the table before placing her head on her arms to rest.

At that moment Simon, the colour drained from his features, entered the kitchen, and headed to a spare chair. "How is she?" he asked through clenched teeth.

"A nasty cut and banging headache," the Father answered, concerned for his friend, watching him wince with the slightest movement.

"I'm okay," he answered, more concerned for Lisa.

"You got a pasting yourself looking at you?"

"The guy fights dirty, but I'll remember next time." Simon shuffled in the chair to ease the pain.

"I saw the dumpster take another hit. Has he gone?" the Father asked.

"He has, but I'm more worried for Lisa," Simon answered.

Father Peters watched her over the rim of his glasses. "She will be fine, let her rest."

Simon rose to examine his face in the mirror on the wall as Father Peters came over to meet him.

"You look like shit lad, but you did a grand thing tonight. Thank you," Father Peters offered.

Simon gave a half-smile, removing the grime and blood from his face with the torn shirt hanging from his shoulders.

Both left Lisa resting, Simon went to get changed and Father Peters crossed to the back door, ever mindful to close behind before standing on the doorstep. A quick fumble at his inside shirt breast pocket retrieved the opened packet of cigarettes. With the lighter, he lit the cigarette to receive a much needed calming of nerves from the day's stresses. Whilst enjoying the moment, he studied the thin white stick smouldering between his fingers. *After today's adventures, it could not get any worse?* He thought.

The electronic build-up stated a solid round being loaded before a distinct metallic click of a weapon safety being removed. "Don't move," a voice commanded, full of threat.

Father Peters, his cigarette forgotten, turned to face the visor covered face of a Guard Cleric of the Monastery of Light.

The entire side of the refuge then became bathed in light as a six wheeled armoured vehicle powered through the narrow entrance in to the yard. Clerics followed it, their sleek white-red battle armour made for an impressive sight, if not for the guns pointing in the priest's direction.

Father Peters placed his hands on his head as instructed, watching the surreal moment unfold. With a silent curse, he saw his day just got a lot more serious.

The Order of Light clerics secured all exits and herded the refuge residents into the main hall. No explanation to the intrusion or reason for the ongoing search. The disruptive movement upstairs a clear sign every inch was being searched whilst everyone could but look on, tempers fraying.

"Would someone please explain what is going on?" Father Peters protested as he watched clerics strew further content of the store cupboards across the floor.

"What reason is there to be so brutal with your search," Sister Angela added.

None of it helped as their pleas went unanswered, clerics continuing to violate every corner of the refuge.

"Father, do something, stop them, what reason do they have for this upheaval?" Sister Angela pleaded, physically shaken.

Father Peters shook his head at the disrespect, removing his glasses to smooth the top of his nose. "I don't know Sister, I don't know."

With a quick turn, her anger aimed at the priest. "Perhaps they search for someone, not something, Father." She had malice in her voice as she glared across at Simon, who sat oblivious to the suspicion. "Have you considered that?"

The Father clutched her arm, pulling her closer. "Now's not the time to point fingers, Sister." His tone was so not to raise attention. "I urge you to think first? Whatever your grievances are, I recommend you keep them to yourself until this issue becomes resolved."

The Sister grunted, pulling away to mumble in her native Gaelic.

"Do I make myself clear, Sister?" The final words made as a statement rather than a question. The Father peered over the rim of his glasses, his expression serious enough that she should keep any more opinions to herself on the matter.

Sister Angela was about to protest but thought better for it, so closing her mouth, the bitter crease of her face showed she would not press the issue further. "Fine Father, I might understand you have your reasons, but I need not like them." With a final mutter, her attention returned to the brutal continuation of the surrounding search.

Off to the side, Lisa sat cradling Jake, who had joined her from upstairs with Sister Angela. The youngster clung to his mother, not wanting to leave her side. His concern clear on seeing her injuries suffered in the earlier altercation with his father, not for the first time seeing her in such a state. Lisa content to hug her son and sensed his breathing against her chest as they tried to ignore the surrounding chaos. A medical cleric had tended to her injuries, suturing stitches above her eye and stopping any further bleeding. They administered pain medication, taking the edge off the dizziness and becoming a fight to keep her eyes open, for all she wanted to do was sleep.

Across the hall, Simon tense and nursing his own injuries sustained earlier with Lisa's ex. The mere thought of the altercation angered him as he stewed in his own misery. He tried not adding to his problems by avoiding attention from the imposing faceless clerics positioned around the hall, ever watchful of the small group.

The doors to the kitchen swung open for a single cleric to appear. He made a hesitant search of the hall to find the reason for his visit, striding to the stacked tables and chairs when not in use. Unnoticed by the others since entering the hall, sat a uniformed figure.

Everyone's attention was now on the hidden guest.

Father Peters recognised the black piping of a priest. "Perhaps we might get the answers," he offered, nodding to the newcomer continuing in silent observation of the group.

Their guest remained seated, acknowledging the cleric's salute with a dismissive nod. He then referred to the contents of the secpad passed to him, ignoring the curious glares of suspicion from those in the room.

Sister Angela nodded to the seated priest.

Father Peters offered a shrug, knowing as much as her.

The Sister continued to mutter under her breath, a light kiss of her crucifix a sign to her nervousness to how things were developing.

"Can I have your attention please, ladies and gentlemen?" It was the priest addressing the room, rising from his concealment to cross and stand before a foldout table. He placed the secpad down, all anxious eyes still on him, apart from Simon continuing his reserved posture at the back. A removal of helmet uncovered thin stern features, with a dark shaved head thinning at the temple. The priest's eyes narrowed, studying the room and confirming to having their full attention before continuing. There was no mistaking his authority, conveying confidence and leadership as he stood waiting.

In the brief pause, Father Peters inspected the priest's well maintained battle armour. It was spotless and intricate in design, with overlapping plating providing protection over an intricate internal hydraulic frame compensating mobility. The Father observed clerics countless times on patrol, but this was a first seeing them up close. Easy to understand why they're so feared. They were a formidable sight.

"I'm sorry about the disturbance and my hope is we shouldn't keep you inconvenienced for too long," the priest announced, placing his helmet on the table. "I'm Father Sebastian Clarke, 22nd Cohort of the Cardinal Guards." He tapped the secpad, activating its inbuilt functions to project the device's contents on the makeshift screen of the serving hatch shutters. The details refreshed, highlighting personal information and images on each person present.

Father Peters remained indifferent as his personal details appeared for all to see. He had no secrets as details of his upbringing in Granton near Edinburgh flashed on screen. Next was his time before the priesthood as an apprentice welder, but nothing shown was not already common knowledge.

Next up was Lisa, her well-respected parents, her father's

position in the new civil government and details on her disastrous marriage shown for all to read. She hugged Jake tighter as the details continued.

Father Clarke gave a few moments for the information to sink in before starting his speech. "As you will have noticed, we have full background details of each of you and this quaint little flophouse," he added. His mouth curling in satisfaction to the varying degrees of discomfort his captive audience were having to their life stories being open to everybody to read. It was all with relished knowledge. Worse was to come as he caught Father Peter's glare, easy to recognise the priest's growing anger. "Father George Peters, forty-eight and ex apprentice shipbuilder from the UK, promising earlier career as a boxer before joining the priesthood. Tell me Father, are you still packing in that thirty a day habit or perhaps the last bottle you have tucked away gets you through the day?"

The Father held his breath, anger replaced by embarrassment as he dropped his glare. A flurried cleanliness of his glass lens with the pocket lining of his trousers followed, as Father Clarke enjoyed the moment. His attention moved to the next unwitting victim to his scrutiny. "Sister Angela Kirkpatrick. Born Donegal Ireland to parents Marie and Father Morris Kirkpatrick, your father sentenced to twenty-four years for his involvement and conviction in the trials of 2022. Understand your mother never got over the shame before she died, but perhaps you could tell us Sister, does he still write for forgiveness from his little angel?" The Sister faltered, collapsing to a waiting chair, head in her hands as she wept.

Father Peters lent over to place a reassuring arm around her, comforting her and trying to explain everything will be okay.

With further satisfaction, Father Clarke moved on, eyes falling on the huddled mass of mother and son sat cross-legged on the floor. "Ah… yes, now the young Lisa Shelby and her little offspring Jake"

"Okay, don't bother," Lisa responded, raising her hand. "Yes,

yes, it's all impressive that you have every dirty little secret from us all here. We know how the Order works, so stop with the theatrics, okay." She flinched as she spoke, still nursing the blinding headache the tablets refused to shift.

Undaunted and not denied his moment, Father Clarke ignored her interruption and continued his detailed monologue. "Lisa Shelby, you fell pregnant at sixteen before marrying petty criminal Brian Shelby. Numinous minor theft convictions and one bank card fraud to date and now working as a kitchen assistant." His expression joyless as Lisa returned a forced smile, resulting in further discomfort.

"Ladies and gentlemen, the Order has detailed information on all those present." Father Clarke continued. "In fact, we pride ourselves that the Ministerial Bureau of Intelligence has excellent up-to-date information on all citizens of this great nation." He walked across the floor. "I hope you all appreciate that in doing so, it makes you safe in the knowledge we can weed out undesirables that threaten that security. It may then surprise that during our investigation we found no record of you, my elusive friend." Father Clarke turned his attention to Simon, refusing to raise his head.

The room fell silent but for the distant rumblings of the clerics still searching throughout the refuge.

Father Clarke was persistent. "Please inform us who you might be?" he asked, coming to stand in front of Simon, who continued to keep his head low.

Father Peters still comforting the upset Sister Angela tried to dispel the tension. "His name is Simon Alksey, and he works..."

Father Clarke cut him off with a raised gloved hand, leaning in to rest his opened palms upon the table, now close enough so no one else heard. "Who are you?" he asked. "You know we will find out, so the question you have to ask yourself is what the repercussions are for your friends to you staying silent."

Simon lifted his head, expressionless as he met the priest's challenging gaze. His motionless eyes narrowed as he sat back in his chair, arms folded in defiance.

Father Clarke recognised the challenge to his authority, the contempt in the body language. He could not suppress delight as he paced the room again. "Would you be so kind to inform us why the MBI cannot find anything on a Simon Alksey, living or dead? Nothing registered at immigration, birth and deaths fitting your description or age. Not even a parking ticket or bank account opened in that name, nothing. It's almost like you don't exist, and yet here you sit, living at this refuge, how fortunate."

Simon tried not to react under the scrutiny of the entire room, taking a moment to glance towards Lisa.

She remained seated, even suffering a half swollen face obvious to not notice her mistrust towards him.

A mistrust also shared by the others, apart from Father Peter remaining silent in his observation of Father Clarke.

"There is no reason to be missing from the central system unless someone had something to hide." Father Clarke explained. "So tell me, Simon Alksey, what are you hiding?"

"I have nothing to hide," Simon stated, trying to appear confident.

The priest took a small portable controller from his belt and gestured to the screen. "Maybe this will help?" he said. The secpad flickered to split the image into four separate mini screens. Various documents from old police reports flashed in sequence, including disturbing graphic crime photos.

There was a noticeable change to the hall, as everyone appeared horrified by what they were witnessing before attention went to Simon.

Simon could but share the same doubts. Without his memories, how could he claim to be innocent either? Every muscle tightened in reaction to the evidence building against him.

"Care to explain how your fingerprints appeared at the apartment of a Washington DC cold case from 2001. The victim kidnapped, bound and tortured before killing her with ritualistic intent." The priest tapped the remote again, the screens changing to a personal bio and photo. "Carla Simmons, twenty-four and an administration assistant from Newport."

With the revelation took all of Simon's resolve to hide the fact he recognised the name, the same name that had been on the edge of his memory for days. The accompanying photo confirmed a connection to his past, for it was the same mysterious dark-haired woman from his dreams. Details flooded back, her laughter as she danced and how happy she appeared until collapsing in his arms. The horror and loss he felt as he brushed away her long matted hair to show her mutilated features, those same tortured features now shown on screen.

Father Clarke approached. "How old are you, twenty-four, perhaps twenty-six?" Not waiting for a response, he continued his synopsis. "So what do we have so far? First, we have a 2001 crime scene of a brutal murder of a woman. The fingerprints of the prime suspect to that case matching an individual sitting here today. A suspect I may add appears to have aged not one day since the crime occurred. So please explain your reluctance to explain your connection to the death of Carla Simmons?"

"I know of no Carla Simmons," Simon answered.

Father Clarke pressed the remote, and this time the image was of a security feed. The video was of Lisa and Simon at the garage being joined by a suited individual.

Lisa, with a sudden intake of breath, felt an icy chill as the video played.

Simon's attention drifted from screen to Lisa, sat shocked, and they shared the same apprehension to knowing they were in trouble.

"Since you appear to be uncooperative with the cold case, would either of you care to elaborate on the reason you crossed a police crime line today? Where you met a CEO of one of this country's largest multinationals?"

The situation was becoming desperate as Lisa now found herself involved in the Order's ongoing investigation. "Site seeing," she offered.

"That so," Father Clarke asked with surprise.

"Simon wanted to see the sites and this other guy stopped to ask for directions."

At first Father Clarke ignored the flippant answer, coming to kneel close to Lisa.

She pulled Jake closer, bracing for the consequence to her insubordination, but all he did was to ruffle Jake's hair. Lisa understood the silent threat as the priest's eyes betrayed malice.

"Would you like to read the transcript to the video Mrs Shelby before answering the question again?" he asked, returning to stand at the front of the hall.

Lisa shook her head, any fight evaporating.

Father Clarke's returned to Simon. "The suited gentleman seemed to be interested in you, my mysterious friend. Please elaborate why you are not on our system or his lists?" With the thinnest of smiles, Father Clarke knew he had Simon rattled. "My, we are an intriguing individual, aren't we?"

Father Peters remained confused by the entire line of questioning, struggling to find anything in the evidence that might cast doubt to the Order having Simon as a suspect. Everything so far showing Simon's alleged connection, but back in 2001 he was but an infant. He struggled to shake the thought somehow they were being tested, forced to second guess his trust in Simon. Including allowing Simon to live at the refuge, but why? Was he wrong and could he live with the consequences his decision now involved Lisa? His attention returned to the images playing on the screen of Simon and Lisa's mysterious meeting with the suited stranger. A thought occurred to him to what he needed to do, so offering the slightest cough of interruption. "Can I ask why you have monitoring equipment in a disused garage in a rundown tenement block?"

Father Clarke, obvious tension in his jaw as he turned to glare across the hall.

Noticing the reaction and with a flash of confidence, Father Peters continued. "I'm trying to understand why continue watching an obvious compromised location? Surly, no suspect would return knowing the authorities had searched the building."

Father Clarke's arrogance up to this point appeared to slip as he switched off the secpad, returning the remote to his belt. "We were responding to a tipoff."

Father Peters nodded, knowing he was on to something, and kept probing. "All sounds plausible but still doesn't explain why continue the surveillance. I mean, you cleaned the entire garage out."

"We had our reasons." Father Clarke answered, brow lowered to the priest's questioning.

"Are they the same reasons the MOI are also investigating a cold case which would normally be an NEPD matter?"

Father Clarke continued to collect his belongings from the table, including the secpad. "That would be a classified security matter," he answered, facing down Father Peters before addressing the hall. "Can I recommend never trespassing on a crime scene or face the consequences?" Retrieving his helmet, he headed through the double doors.

Father Peters blew out a whistle of relief as he turned to those left in the hall. "That was too easy, and something tells me we haven't seen the last of that priest."

No one else spoke.

Outside the refuge waited a convoy of impressive six wheeled armoured multirole MAUVs.

Father Clarke strode up to the opened rear of the nearest and took the empty command chair. "Are we ready with the next stage?"

"Yes sir," replied the communication cleric. The man's uniform showed rank of deacon. His role as part of the MAUV crew was monitoring the multiple screens of real-time data, including videos of various rooms around the refuge, including the hall. "We have surveillance in all locations, including sound. Surveillance drones on adjacent rooftops for added visuals and covert observations with a standard two minute deploy time if needed. We have a tracker on their vehicle."

"Excellent." Father Clarke turned to his own consoles, satisfied. "Keep running the photos through all relevant agencies, including international past and present."

"Yes, Father."

"What did the labs say?"

The deacon transferred his consoles data to Father Clarke's own, so he could read the full details himself.

"Basic rubbish includes fused metals, whilst DNA results have three adults including the child present but nothing conclusive."

Father Clarke finished scrolling. "What of the blood at the scene?"

"Labs confirmed a match to suspect Simon Alksey. His file has been closed and made highest classification, as Bishop Nikolaos requested. He awaits an update on your questioning of the suspects as soon as you're finished."

Father Clarke pondered over the report and the information gathered, agreeing the case was a standard NEPD investigation, nothing to call for Order involvement. The whole situation was strange, for Bishop Nikolaos had taken a personal interest and requesting the classifying of any findings so far as high importance. A frown crossed the priest's face for during his long service within the Order, never questioning orders regardless how unusual the situation. Another scroll through the data included fingerprint supporting the suspect's involvement in the cold case. Protocol under normal circumstances would have the case passed to NEPD to make an arrest. Nothing about his orders explained a need for show and tell unless spreading mistrust amongst the group against this Simon individual. Father Clarke ground his jaw, closing his console. "Send all findings and reports, including data burst of the video of the questioning to the bishop's office. Then close and wipe. Also ask for an update with the bishop at his convenience to discuss any further developments."

With a nod of acknowledgement, the deacon completed

his orders.

Father Clarke sat in silence, watching the live feeds. *There's more to this refuge and its occupants, that's for certain. That meant the Order was just starting in its true investigation.*

The last of the Guard Clerics left after Father Clarke, leaving the refuge as though a small tornado had passed. The contents of cupboards, draws, and shelving lay scattered around the floors, every inch searched.

Sister Angela, tears welling, started her clean-up, picking up bibles and returning them with loving care to the shelves in the hall.

Upstairs and still nursing the throbbing headache from her altercation with her ex, Lisa took a moment to survey Jake's bedroom. "Well, I can't see the difference between what happened and the normal state of your room." The light-hearted joke appeared to fall flat, leaving her to chuckle alone as she continued folding clothes.

Jake offered a puzzled stare, then with a frown shrugged off his mother's try to make light of the situation.

Back downstairs, Father Peters and Simon had made a start on the kitchen. Both remained sullen, neither mentioning the search or later interrogation at the hands of the Order of Light. In silence they continued to pick up and salvaging what they could.

With a groan, Father Peters strained to lift a box of broken plates, before cautiously manoeuvring around scattered debris.

Simon, sweeping another part of the floor, sidestepped to allow the priest to pass and place the box onto the sideboard.

The movement was fast, like the boxer he once was, Father Peters grabbing Simon by the throat, pinning him against the wall in a powerful grip. What the priest lost in height, he gained in strength, holding Simon with relative ease.

Simon resisted, recognising the red rage behind black-rimmed glasses as air rushed from his lungs, desperate to not pass out.

"What have you brought to my home?" the Father demanded. "Who the hell are you?"

Simon fought to speak, clawing at the tight grip, not wanting to hurt his friend by lashing out in retaliation as his vision blurred.

Then, almost as soon as the attack had begun, the grip loosened.

Father Peters backed away, coming to his senses. With a shake of head, he stood shocked at losing his temper, hands still trembling.

Simon rubbed at the imprint of the grip. "I suppose I deserved that for what's happened."

"No lad, no you don't," offered the priest with a reluctant sigh. "I'm sorry, not sure what came over me," he confessed. Father Peters fell into the nearest chair, still shaking his head at his actions. "Yes, I'm angry at you, but not all the blame is on you, I should share responsibility."

Simon slipped into the chair opposite, struggling to understand. "Why blame yourself, when the Order was after me."

"Because I brought you here, and that involves all of us now," the Father confessed.

"But I've caused so much trouble, so will understand if you want me to leave."

Father Peters glanced over his glasses. "I had my reasons for helping you lad and don't regret doing so until that damn priest showed those pictures. He made me doubt myself, made me doubt you without allowing you to defend yourself and get your side of the story."

"You think I could inflict that on another person, to cause her death."

"I still believe I'm an excellent judge of character, but what I believe or not is irrelevant at the moment," he offered, scrubbing a hand over his face. "Once I used to believe God would show me a sign, to answer my questions." He sat back, pushing fingers through unkempt hair, gripping a clump at the back whilst deep in thought.

Simon sensed the old priest's frustrations. "My past is such a blur of fleeting flashes of people and places whose names I don't remember."

The Father's gaze narrowed. "Wasn't hard to notice your reaction to the pictures, so tell me the truth lad, did you recognise her?"

Simon swallowed, struggling to find the words. "No, not at first." He paused, frowning. "Her face is familiar, but I can't get my head around how I'm connected," he continued.

The Father eased from his chair, pacing the kitchen before attention returned to his friend. "For Gods' sake, lad, why didn't you tell me before all of this happened?"

"She's just another face out of a growing list I have no recollection to and didn't know existed. Believe me, I've never heard her name until today, and that's the truth."

Father Peters took his seat again, leaning forward. "Tell me everything you know about her. You said you remember her from a dream or nightmare?"

"Nothing to tell. Dream starts in an apartment, possible hers."

"Okay, then what?"

"Then there's a figure dancing, but I'm unable to see her face."

"So how do you recognise her?"

"I don't at first, she continues to dance until collapsing into my arms," Simon explained.

Father Peters lent back. "Then what happens?"

"I'm looking down, and move her matted hair, and she's like the photos."

"She resembles the woman from the photographs?" Father Peters asked.

"Yes, including the cuts to her face and that's when I find blood on my hands and as I pull away and she vanishes."

"That's it, nothing else? She said nothing to you, nobody

else was with you?"

"No. That is all," Simon confessed, seeking to recapture the details.

Father Peters rubbed his forehead, piecing together the evidence they had so far, and noticing Simon's frustration as he stared at the floor. He felt his own struggle, doubting his original trust in Simon and the possibility he was not so innocent? The images were of a person capable of causing horrific injuries on another without remorse. He sat in silent study, trying to recognise any sign to hide anything, but all he saw was a man troubled by his own memories. Over the years, the Father had prided himself on an ability to read people, knowing when someone was lying. The more he considered the evidence, the more he thought his first instincts had been correct. Simon had to be telling the truth but still doubt lingered, so it was important they found proof he had no involvement, which would not be easy.

The kitchen had fallen silent, both reluctant to share.

Father Peters knew he had to prepare for either possibility because if wrong, he would not hesitate to hand Simon to the authorities, answering for any crimes. The safety of the refuge and those living here was his priority. Still, deep mistrust lingered over everything happening these past few days as a test of his judgement regarding others. He contemplated their next move, remembering the strange experience back in the garages on first meeting Simon. The sensation had started in his hands until enveloping his entire body. Instantly ridding him of his anger and pain and forming a moment of clarity with a need to keep him safe. In remembrance, he sat with flexing fingers, glancing occasionally towards Simon sat with head in hands. "We work this out together, lad," he offered. "From now on, no secrets, okay?"

Simon returned his gaze, agreeing with a solemn nod.

Father Peters leaned closer, seeing straight into his soft blue eyes. "Understand the consequences for all of us if you don't?"

Simon understood the seriousness in his voice, knowing the priest would not tolerate secrets, for it bought nothing but trouble with the Order now being involved.

"Trust me, as I do you, it's our best chance of finding out the truth," the Father continued.

"Okay, so where do we start?" Simon asked.

"Start at the beginning, but first" He rose from the chair to switch on the small radio sat on the countertop. He tuned to a classic channel that echoed the kitchen. "Might be my paranoia, but can't be too careful." Back to his seat, Father Peters listened as Simon strained to recall anything important from the first night waking up in the garages.

Not until they had discussed everything did Father Peters stand, pushing out the strain from suffering the uncomfortable chair. "So to recap, the murder happened 2001, so explain how you're DNA and adult fingerprints got left at the scene?"

Simon shrugged, part answering the question and part suppressing the tiredness from the day's events. "Wish I remembered, but everything is still foggy, jumbled in my head, I'm uncertain of what I remember any more."

"Okay, this woman might be a family member, a memory from your childhood?" the Father offered.

Simon gave a deep, weighted sigh. "We can't be sure only the feeling I get when I remember her is the same feelings when I see," Simon's face flushed.

The Father peered over his glasses, offering no comment. "Well, that would show you're connected to this Carla Simmons, and that puts you on the Order's radar." The Father stopped pacing. "The question we should ask is why the Order's concerned in a 2001 cold case?" Taking a break from the conversation, Father Peters stopped at the coffee percolator, still thinking as he turned to Simon. "Something crossed my mind to how easy that priest let us off. They are usually more thorough in their investigations, more ruthless." He poured the black liquid into a waiting cup, sipping the contents before continuing his analysis. "We will have to watch our backs in future as they won't let this matter go." He offered a cup to Simon, who refused with a courteous nod. "Not surprised if we're not being monitored right now. Excellent excuse is a search of the building to leave behind surveillance."

Both men glanced the kitchen with suspicion.

In its present state, everything seemed out-of-place, so Father Peters gave a grunt to his paranoia and moved to the kitchen window.

"What's with the radio?" Simon asked.

The Father grinned. "Works in the movies and besides, not seeing anything lurking in the shadows does not mean they aren't there." With a sip of coffee, he continued his pacing. "Now that's true paranoia, but with many years of experience has taught me the Order's capable of anything. They will be back with more questions." His voice lowered, the music continuing in the background. "Look at this from a fresh angle."

Simon was fighting growing fatigue, raising his head as Father Peters continued. "I'm not following Father?"

"They mentioned having surveillance for the chance someone might return. I don't buy it. They removed everything, so why not leave the garage like it was?"

Simon shrugged, still confused with the priest's logic.

"They not interested in an old cold case. No, something does not smell right. It's all smoke and mirrors and it starts at that garage where we found you."

Simon tried to explain. "There was nothing there but trash, junk."

"You were there, lad," the Father smiled.

Simon sat back, stunned. "Me!" He frowned. "It's a coincidence, Father." Simon still tried to understand his importance. "They somehow have my fingerprints from the cold case. That's why they're interested in me, not where you found me."

"The MBI does not ransack a refuge for a cold case suspect. They are interested in something recent. It's you and what happened to you they're interested in, and they're willing to stick you as a suspect in a forgotten crime to do it."

"Okay, if that's true. What reason is it being me?"

"That is the question. Without your memory, we have no clues. You saw for yourself today, they have nothing too. Would put money on you having information they don't want going public. The Order does not get this powerful without having dirty secrets they will wish to stay buried. Perhaps you have the memories of this cold case because it links back to the Order somehow. If you and Lisa had not gone back, getting caught on camera, they would have known nothing."

Both men came to the same conclusion.

Father Peters continuing to keep his voice quiet. "Be careful, lad, even the refuge is not safe. We can't tell the others, the less they know the better."

Simon agreed with wanting no one else getting hurt.

"Now think, lad. What reasons are there to you being important to them, it could help us understand where to go next?"

"I have nothing..." Simon paused. "Unless," With a pinch of lips he sought to force another detail. "Remember when I pointed out the Hand of God monument and I said it felt familiar."

"You mentioned seeing it before the rooftop."

Simon rubbed at his temple. "There was the one nightmare where I imagined myself flying."

The Father gripped Simon's shoulder. "It will come to you lad, don't force the memory, just take your time."

Simon closed his eyes, clearing his mind and focusing. "No, it's okay. Whilst flying high above the clouds they turn black, as giant hands open out towards me and try to grab me." Simon thumped a fist onto the table in frustration as the details faded.

Father Peters clasped Simon's hands, seeking to keep him calm.

"I'm okay, Father; the shape the hands make resembles the open hand emblem of the Order." Simon opened his eyes.

Father Peters grabbed a glass from the sink to get water.

The strain to remember etched Simon's face, grateful for the drink.

"A potential connection to the Order, that's a start, but we have to build on it and find more details."

"I'm more worried about what it all means." Simon asked.

"May prove you're a person of interest, after today, I'm sure. That Father Clarke was interested in you, probing for answers, and he needed you to fill in the blanks." Father Peters went to refill the glass and passed it back to Simon.

"They wouldn't have left me here, surveillance or not. I mean, wouldn't they take me somewhere and questioned further?"

"Agreed," offered the priest with a hesitant nod. "It didn't seem right letting us go. My guess today's events were to scare us into doing something stupid or making us suspicious of each other. Not surprised, they are waiting for it to play out. Is there anything else you can remember, how about how it ended?"

"The dream you mean?" Simon frowned. "Well, the hand came out of the clouds, making a grab for me until I raised my hands to protect myself. A brilliant bright light pulsed from my hands, shattering the surrounding darkness, and then I woke up screaming."

"Bright light, you say, was there anything in your hand?"

"It's so hazy; you think I'm crazy, don't you?" Simon asked, noticing the priest's frown.

"Not at all," he smiled, giving Simon a reassuring pat on the knee. "You forget how we had to drag you back into bed because of your dreams getting out of control. We went through it with you, but fate has its reasons for you being here." With that, the Father rose from his chair, passing a sweeping brush back to Simon. "Come on, lad. Kitchen needs cleaning before the nights out, and besides, who knows who might listen," he winked.

Upstairs, Lisa had finished boxing and bagging all the items not salvageable from hers and Jake's bedrooms. The list included memorable and irreplaceable pieces, Jake's kinder garden pottery, painted with bright-coloured stripes and used to store her jewellery on her beside cabinet. Not that she had much jewellery, still had sentimental value and upset her to not have survived the search. Another item was a small wooden frame that had held the only picture she had of her parents. She had found it broken under the bed and sat sobbing, pressing the broken frame to her chest.

On hearing his mother's distress, Jake crept into the room and pulled himself onto the bed next to her. She held him with the photo frame before he gave her one of his enormous grins. "Don't worry mom, we will be okay," he offered.

Lisa gave the thinnest of smiles and hugged him again, wiping her hand against her cheek. She composed herself, drawing on the endless supply of tissues from her cardigan sleeve. "Thank you," she sniffed, rubbing her nose and grabbing Jake again for a further squeeze. "I wish I had your outlook on life, Jake."

Jake wriggled free again. "He says I must be strong, to never lie, for lying is a sin."

Lisa raised an eyebrow, chuckling at the peculiar answer from her still grinning boy as she played with his fringe. "What are you saying, baby? Did you mean Father Peters?"

"No mom, don't be silly. God says it's a sin to lie, so when he tells me all will be okay then it has to be the truth, doesn't it? Have the faith for the coming day's mom." With that, Jake shuffled himself off the bed, looking through a box open on the floor.

Lisa sat perplexed until wiping her face of the remaining tears, making herself a little more presentable considering the still swollen part of her face. "Shit, I've got to stop letting Sister Angela baby sit you," she responded. "Her holier than thou attitude is rubbing off on you." She rubbed the top of his head, making him giggle. "Come on, get this stuff downstairs." She picked up the two bags of rubbish, leaving Jake to grab the box he had been looking through and deciding nothing was worth salvaging.

"You know swearing is a sin too, mom?"

Lisa rolled her eyes, watching Jake struggling with the box. "Yes, and you might find it also a sin to correct your mother, now get yourself downstairs with that box before you drop it."

A quick frown of puzzlement, Jake considered his mother's comment, and then headed for the door. "Not sure mom, but will ask him tonight when I sleep to make sure."

"Okay, baby, you do that and whilst you're at it ask for next week's winning lottery numbers."

They soon navigated the stairs and headed for the kitchen. On entering, Lisa was pleasantly surprised it was almost back to its original state.

Jake placed his burdening box on the kitchen table.

Lisa left her bin bags at the back door.

"Can I make anybody a drink? Kettle still works," Father Peters asked, cleaning cups with a tea towel at the sink.

"Please," Lisa asked, somewhat out of breath from carrying the heavy bags.

Jake rounded the table and sat next to Simon, mimicking his tired composer down to his glum expression.

Simon noticing from the corner of his eye gave Jake a smile, resulting in a grin back, a temporary lift to Simon's gloom.

Father Peters arranged the cups, making the required drinks as Jake leaned for the biscuit tin left on the table. The resulting soft tap across the back of his head made him jump as Sister Angela entered the kitchen.

"Ask permission, young Jake," she said, as she took a spare seat around the table.

Still rubbing his head, Jake offered a mumbled apology and sat back down, legs underneath him as to see over the table.

"Make mine herbal, would you?" Lisa asked. "Don't think my head could take much more caffeine tonight." She grabbed the bags again and headed into the yard. "Back in five," she shouted.

The night sky was cloudless, a chill breeze to an otherwise warm night. The icy shiver passed down her back as she struggled with the weight over uneven ground. She lifted the bags with a grunt into the bin, letting the lid close with a thud. On heading back to the kitchen, a large black shape passed in front, pressing a cloth over her mouth. As Lisa's eyes widened, her body slipped into unconsciousness without a struggle.

When she came to, Lisa found herself draped across a plush purple lounger in a sizeable dressing room. Against one wall were half a dozen dressing stations stacked with coloured perfume bottles and makeup boxes. Large gold-framed mirrors hung from the wall, illuminated by bright strip lights.

The lights that now made her wince, the blinding headache returning with a vengeance. With eyes closed, she propped her back against the lounger.

"Christ, you're awake," said an agitated voice, a voice all too familiar.

Lisa's foggy vision cleared enough to make out the agitated figure pacing the other end of the room. "Brian, you complete bag of" The pain in her head stabbed her again as she tried to stand, stopping her in her tracks. *Better to stay seated,* she thought. Even in her diminished state she recognised Brian was nervous, biting his thumbnail as he paced. "Somehow I feel the nervousness you have is not for the fear of my reaction to this kidnapping. So tell me, Brian. What trouble are we in this time?"

Brian stepped over to kneel in front of her, taking her hands, but Lisa wanted none of it and pulled away.

"It's true, I've got myself into a little trouble babe and I need your help to solve it."

Lisa tried to suppress the slight laugh, watching Brian's pathetic expression of despair. Ten years ago, that might have worked, but now, she knew him to be a pathetic loser and desperate. This time it was different, recognising a fear behind his eyes that worried her the most. She had never seen Brian scared of anything in all their time together.

Brian resumed his pacing, watching the door in anticipation. He occasionally offered Lisa worried glances, knowing he would get no sympathy or cooperation from her. That invoked a change of mood, and a flicker of anger as he pointed towards her. "We could have avoided this; it's your fault, you, and that priest." He bit his thumbnail again. "If he did what I asked, we wouldn't be so desperate. No one else needed to get involved."

Lisa glared, not believing his explanation. "What do you mean, my fault? What did you do, Brian, and have you so rattled?"

Just then the door opened and two menacing men entered, both dressed in tailored suits, with a tone of seriousness that they would not tolerate any trouble. The first of the newcomers was a balding, heavyset man offering a fixed expression of contempt as he faced off against Brian, who shrank away.

Brian became more agitated as these men put fear in him as he backed off.

The knot in the pit of Lisa's stomach turned another notch, her attention on the second man taking position next to her.

He was of Asian descent with tight cropped hair, and he scowled in silent hint for her to stay quiet.

Lisa did not need any instructions as his open jacket showed two black handled knives on his belt. The whole situation brought on a cold chill as she swallowed hard, sinking back into her seat.

"Make this quick Shelby, I have a club to run," the voice female, full of authority with a hint of menace. From the doorway stood a tall woman of confident demeanour, her waist length hair tied back so as not to diminish her exotic Hispanic features. She carried her authority and beauty dressed in a two piece suit, which clung to her and emphasised her slim figure. "You have five minutes before I let my dogs here rip you apart with their bare hands."

The slight smiles of her colleagues made Lisa's stomach lurch.

"Lilith, always good to see you and can I mention how beautiful you look." Brian squirmed as he tried to move forward in greeting.

The bald bodyguard, placing a firm hand across his chest and blocked his way.

Lisa sighed, shaking her head.

"Cut the bullshit, you have the sixty grand you owe us?" Lilith asked, losing patience from being brought to this impromptu meeting.

A nervous sweat rolled Brian's face as he rubbed damp hands down his stained flowered shirt. "Tell Lewie I've got his cash, but I hit a snag, so I was hoping for more time. Two days and you get the monies in two days, promise."

Lilith's eyes narrowed at Brian's answer until her gaze moved to Lisa, sat cradling her head in her hands.

Somehow, Lisa sensed the attention and looked up to meet the dark-skinned woman's gaze from across the room.

"And who might you be?" she asked.

Lisa swallowed, clearing her dry throat. "Lisa Shelby," she stuttered. "This loser's thankful ex. So regardless of what Brian's plans are, I have nothing to do with them and hope to go home, back to my son," she explained.

"Then why are you here?" Lilith asked, tilting her head, awaiting an explanation.

"Ask him," Lisa explained, nodding to the sheepish Brian who gave a pathetic chuckle as both women glared at him.

"The agreement still stands, yes? So let me go now, leaving her here like collateral. You give me a few more days to get the cash together, pay off the debt or you get the boy as well."

"What did you say?" Lisa spat, finding energy to launch at the cringing Brian.

The Asian bodyguard's reflexes were faster, pulling her back down to the lounger.

"Enough," Lilith ordered, walking to the restrained Lisa.

She cupped her chin in a well-manicured hand, studying her face with a look of pity. "This you're work, Brian?" She turned Lisa's head to show the bruising cut around her swollen eye.

Brian shrugged again. "A disagreement earlier got physical."

"You like to hit women, do you?"

"Well, sometimes you have to put them in their place," he explained, smiling between the bodyguards for vindication of his actions.

The bald bodyguard shuffled position next to Brian, making him flinch.

Lilith gave the slightest of nods to his explanation. "I see."

What happened next, nobody could have expected.

Her movement was swift, Lilith's kick curled through the air, the back of her stiletto heel contacting the side of Brian's skull.

His entire body shuddered, spinning from the blow to crash against the far wall with a sickening crack.

Lisa sat upright, shocked at the suddenness of the attack as attention went back to Lilith.

She returned her suit to its pristine state, before heading out of the room, followed by her two bodyguards as if nothing happened.

Lisa glanced from the closed door to the unconscious Brian. Watching the blood trickle from his mouth and nose as she sat forward, putting her head into her hands again.

"What the hell happens now?" she sobbed.

They had searched until two in the morning, scouring every part of Sufferance for clues to Lisa's whereabouts, returning exhausted and no closer to finding out what had happened. Suspicions had arisen once Father Peters had noticed Lisa had not come back from the yard. A quick investigation found a chloroformed cloth near the bin area, raising concerns for her safety. The Father feared the worst, setting out with Simon to search the surrounding area, returning with disappointment in their efforts.

The little Ford returned to the yard, Father Peters switching off the engine before straining to get out. "So the hospital and the free clinics were a bust. Nothing fitting her description admitted in the past twenty-four hours." He pulled out a notepad, resting on the car roof to cross another name off his dwindling list of locations. "What puzzles me is why take her? What reason would they have?" he continued.

Simon closed the passenger door, watching the Father read through his list. Half listening, choosing to investigate the bins again in hope to find a clue missed earlier. He still brooded with guilt, blaming himself that it somehow connected her disappearance to his presence at the refuge.

Father Peters, not receiving an answer, frowned, then placed the notepad back into his pocket and headed for the back door, leaving Simon in his search.

The refuge remained shrouded in darkness, a sign Sister Angela had got Jake off to bed. The youngster had become agitated on noticing his mother had not returned. Father Peters made the subconscious decision not to worry him, whilst hoping for more positive news once they had made a full search. He approached the door, pulling at the bundle of keys from his belt, retrieving the back door key. It was then an uneasy sense ebbed in the pit of his stomach at not having any news. In silent thought he pushed past his disappointment, the key turning in the lock before stepping into the kitchen.

"Gentlemen," offered a voice from the darkness.

"What the hell?" Father Peters stepped back in alarm, reacting to the figure rising from a chair at the kitchen table.

Simon on hearing the alarm raced from the yard, pushing passed to confront what had startled the priest.

"My hero," Father Peters laughed, slapping Simon on the back as their attention turned to the figure moving into the light provided by a cloudless moonlight night.

"Father Peters, meet D, who has the uncanny way of appearing at the worst of times." Simon offered.

The stylish dressed D grinned.

Simon took off his coat, returning it to a spare hook next to the door as he switched on the lights, still ignoring D's pleasantries.

Undisturbed by the snub, D offered his hand to the sceptical Father Peters stood in the doorway, arms folded. An unimpressed expression as he gave a quick glance over the well-dressed D, then back to Simon. "This is the guy you and Lisa met? The same guy responsible for pushing you off the roof?" he asked, frowning to the still smiling D. "Looks like an infomercial seller," he scoffed.

D ignored the insults with a vibrant clap as he moved to grip the Father gentle by the shoulders. "The names D. It's a pleasure you being a man of the cloth and all. You're Father George Peters, correct, a big fan. Simon has told me... well nothing about you but it might surprise you we almost met years back but you would not have remembered. Hit and miss at one point, was it not? Guess you're a hard man to put down, but damn it you pulled through didn't you." D patted the Father on the chest. "But keep lighting up those little sticks of yours and we will see each other sooner rather than later, in a more professional capacity." He left Father Peter with mouth open, perplexed confusion as how to answer.

D's attention returned to Simon. "We need to talk, bro."

"Bro, what decade are you from the nineties?" Father Peters chuckled, heading for the table.

Ignoring the priest's sarcasm, D followed Simon to the far side of the kitchen.

"I'm done talking to you, now's not the time for your riddles and theatrics. We need sleep, so can this wait to the morning." Simon pushed past, starting for the doors leading upstairs.

"But I offer help."

"Not interested D, find somebody else for your mind games will you, I'm tired."

"I understand you're missing something special to you?"

Simon turned, grabbing D's jacket, lifting him off his feet.

"The clothes dude, the clothes," D protested. "We've talked about you messing up my suit."

Anger and tiredness made for a volatile combination at the best of times, but Simon brought his emotions under control, calming himself and released his grip. "Tell me what you know D and no riddles this time, straight facts. Why is Lisa missing?"

"Okay, going to tell you anyway," he said, pushing out the creases of his jacket. "The ex has her."

Both Father Peters and Simon shared a glance.

"Brian Shelby has her?" the Father asked, spinning D to face him. "Why would Brian want to take Lisa?"

"Payback," Simon answered as he leaned against the table. "The thought had crossed my mind after finding the cloth." He ran a hand through his hair, rubbing his face, forcing past the fatigue threatening to overtake him. "Lisa embarrassed him earlier in the day."

"Not quite, but close," D responded. "Something bigger is happening, the pieces are moving behind the scenes." D took a chair, placing his feet on the table to get comfortable, a smug smile crossing his face.

Simon fought an urge to throw him out of the kitchen. Instead, he sighed and waited for him to continue.

Basking in satisfaction, having information others did not, D pointed a long bony finger at Simon. "I warned you about what trouble you would bring on those around you. Even told Lisa, she should have taken her boy as far away as possible. But no one listens."

"Hold off with the 'I told you so' moment, you told us nothing," Simon responded.

"Congratulations to making the Order of Lights hit list. The search was proof of that. That means they're searching for signs why your arrival brings so many grim omens."

"What signs?" Father Peters asked, trying to understand the conversation.

"The cardinal, he knows of Simon's significance and his fall…" D closed his mouth, demeanour turning to nervousness as though he had said too much. So taking another glance around, he awaited any impending repercussions to his actions.

Both Simon and Father Peters shared the same confusion at D's apprehension until Simon lent over to D sat in the chair. "Stop playing with us and tell me what I need to know. You know more than you are telling. Once we find Lisa safe, you and me are having a personal chat, understand?"

D swallowed, trying a smile to defuse the tension. "Okay, I tell you what I can tell you," he offered, pulling out a small cylinder device from his inside pocket, activating it. "A little privacy, can't be too careful these days, keeps us safe from unwanted guests and prying eyes and ears." He pointed upwards. "Where were we, oh… yes, the cardinal? Well, he knows about you, and what you represent from reading the signs. It all starts with the first of three obscure prophecies, which he considers describing the end of his Order and the cardinal himself."

Simon frowned. "I've never met this cardinal, let alone had anything to do with him or these prophecies. What's Lisa and Brian's involvement?"

"Nothing, they are collateral damage to the coming storm. It's what I've been trying to explain. All of you are getting into something you can't comprehend. Step up your game for the alternative is getting burnt… again." D gave a slight laugh at the private joke, noticing nobody else in the room shared his humour, so continued. "Tell me ever heard of a place called the Fire Pitt club?"

"It's the hottest skin bar in the city before the Paradise Valley turnoff," Father Peters answered, trying to salvage the last of the peculated coffee from the machine.

Both D and Simon turned in surprise.

The priest stirred the lukewarm contents of his cup before noticing the room had gone quiet. "What, because I wear a collar, you think I'm ignorant to the seedy parts of life?" he offered.

"So you heard of the Fire Pitt Father?" D asked, grinning.

"The name came up when I supported a skin trade task force with the church and local police. We were to counsel the victims of the human traffickers operating throughout the state. It's horrible how they suffered, beaten and boosted, a grim life for all concerned." The Father, embarrassed by his admission, concentrated on his cup.

"I like you more priest, there's an air of danger about you I like." D said attention going back to Simon. "Well, the clubs owned by a not so nice character called Lewie. Don't let the name fool you. The guy is the worse character to cross, and nothing happens in the city without him allowing it. That's were Brian's connected. He offered a business opportunity to Lewie, who stumped up a caseload of cash for the venture before it went south."

"Lewie wants his money back," the Father added.

"Ten points to the priest." D pointed with a clap of hands. "But Brian is short of the full amount and interest is increasing daily."

"That's why he came to see Lisa earlier, for money," Simon added. "Still doesn't explain why he took her?"

"Damn Si, you came back a blank slate, didn't you? This Lewie's biggest operation is the skin trade. Anything you need, he has. Women, men and kids of all ages, whatever your taste. All brought to your door within the hour for the right price. Tall, thin or fat, whatever you prefer."

Simon looked across at the Father, nodding agreement.

"The ex is using her as collateral until getting the money," D continued.

"What about the police or the Order, can't they stop it?" asked Simon.

"You're kidding, right?" asked D, surprised at Simon's naivety. "There is rumour the cardinal has unsavoury connections with Lewie, no one dare get proof and go public. It's all power and greed, bro, corrupts all."

Father Peters scoffed at the mention of the cardinal. "The cardinal is the biggest religious icon since the last Pope. I might have grievances with the Order, but to insinuate there was a link between him and this crime lord, it's utter nonsense."

D's tone changed. "You think what you want there, priest. I have my sources and don't forget what happened the last time those within the church denied what was going on behind closed doors."

Father Peters took a step forward, face flushed, fists flexing at his side as he found his path blocked.

Simon intercepted him, stopping something he might regret. "This will not help Lisa if we fight amongst ourselves," he whispered.

The Father checked his anger, stepping back to glare at D, remaining unaffected by the reaction.

"What is the plan?" Simon asked, turning back to D.

"Well, the first thing," D offered, rising from the chair, clapping his hands. "You could embrace your true self, find what you have lost, delve deep in that fuzzy head of yours and get her out of there before lunch." He clasped his hands around Simon's face. "You've had the dreams right and pieced the details together. No?" D raised an eyebrow.

Simon pushed him away. "I've had dreams, vivid dreams, but I'm far from piecing them together to understand what they mean."

"Damn bro, you are so screwed up if you're thinking of going up against the forces gathering against you, whilst not having your real mojo. Lewie and his people will sniff you out straight away. There's no messing and they won't have an issue wiping the floor with you, to be on the safe side."

"Why would that matter, what aren't you telling us?" Simon asked.

"Because you're damn special, that's why and the sooner you realise it the better, for all of us."

"Then tell me," Simon frowned.

"I'm not allowed, it's that damn free will nonsense crap," D shouted, losing his composer for a moment. "Because you have human free will, there's no interference," he continued, the smile back as he adjusted his tie. "They bind me to specific rules, not broken under any circumstances. You must follow the path fate has set out for you, work it out for yourselves. My job is keeping the balance. None of us can act outside these rules without his say so."

Father Peters still listening to the conversation stopped D. "Whose say so would that be? You can tell us that at least?"

D straightened the priest's dog collar, then lent in to whisper. "Why God's who else?" He started for the door before turning back. "It's the whole good and evil grudge match. Time to repent boys as judgement day is upon us. So pick a side priest."

The colour had drained from Father Peters' face, as he tried to find the words, but nothing escaped his month. He just stared at D, who pointed between both. "You guys need to sleep, for tomorrow I'm taking you to see the big bad of all evil, so you will need your wits about you. The club is open twenty-four seven, so we will go in the morning bright and early. Oh, and we're taking my car, so be ready." With a last wave, D left both of them confused.

"What did he say?" asked Simon with suspicion.

The priest swallowed. "What... sorry, who?"

"D, you asked him about who was pulling our strings in all of this."

"Oh, yes," The Father answered with a chuckle of disbelief. "He said God, and we had to choose a side."

Simon stared at the Father. "He's having a joke at our expense."

The priest's expression turned to concern.

"You okay, Father?" Simon asked, sharing his concern.

"I tell you, lad, I've had unexplainable feelings of guidance of late."

"So what are you saying, that you believe him, and that God

is guiding us?"

Father Peters traced the outline of the cross hung on the kitchen wall, struggling with his thoughts. "As many before me who've devoted their lives to the same beliefs, all waiting for signs, it's not all for nothing. I can't help considering after these past weeks, many strange things have accrued to strengthen that belief. From first finding and bringing you here, to your miraculous recovery from horrific injuries and hearing an inner voice. Is it wrong of me to not dismiss feeling Gods guidance?"

Simon was uncomfortable. "You said it was because I was young and healthy, not divine intervention, Father."

"Okay, say you're correct lad, but I would be amiss in my role as a priest to disbelieve that somehow he had helped in your recovery."

"And if D is telling the truth and God sent you to find me, bring me back to the refuge to heal from my injuries. What reason has he got for denying me to remember who I was or the reason for me being here?"

"They say the truth shall set you free, for an honest man will find his own path to the light. Perhaps he wants you to come to those answers on your own because a better man finds out for himself."

Simon shook his head at the explanation. His memories so far were of scenes of blood, fire and pain, nothing resembling a normal life. Even the pleasant images of the park and the dancing woman turned sinister and disturbing. Then finding his connection to a victim of a murder twenty years ago, which the authorities were adamant to pin on him. Also there's the strange old man Samuel, what's his story? "If my current dreams are any sign to my life before the accident, Father, I'm not sure I want to regain more."

Father Peters placed a reassuring hand to his shoulder. "We are walking a dark path lad and tomorrow it's taking us to rescue a friend, I fear not everyone will come back the same."

CHAPTER SEVEN

The Coming Light

Even after the day's traumatic events, both Simon and Father Peters tried to get a few hours of much-needed sleep before dawn broke and, as promised, D arrived.

"Good morning, people, and a most beautiful morning for a drive, wouldn't you agree?"

The enthusiastic greeting to the sleep-deprived duo irritated them and goaded Father Peters' stretched patience straight away. "With no sleep, breakfast or morning cigarette, I might have to kill him before the days out." The Father closed the kitchen door, having left instructions for Sister Angela to handle the morning's duties, with the help of the volunteers. He considered it prudent to omit where they were heading, mentioning only to be following a lead on Lisa's whereabouts. Not wishing to worry the Sister any more than necessary, or endure her obvious objection if she knew they were going to the notorious Fire Pitt Club.

She had already made plain her objections to trusting D, grabbing the priest's arm and taking him to the side before they left. She had taken an instant dislike to the smartly suited stranger waiting in the yard.

The Father had agreed with her, deep down, sharing her concerns. D was untrustworthy, but he was their best hope of finding Lisa.

Sister Angela continued her objections with a disapproving glare from the kitchen window.

Father Peters could but offer a hesitant wave, unable to

shake an uneasy possibility to be seeing the refuge for the last time. Taking a deep breath, he turned to follow Simon and D to the awaiting car.

"Let's go people," D shouted, waving to hurry the pace. "My car is out front, I thought it prudent we arrived in something a little less rustic." To emphasise the point, he brushed a finger across the grime-streaked Ford, his unimpressed gaze falling on Father Peters.

The priest was muttering under his breath as he caught up with Simon. "As God is my witness, before the days over I will wipe that smug grin clean off."

Simon could not help raise a smile to D's uncanny ability to antagonise the priest within minutes of being in each other's company. "What about turning the other cheek, Father?" Simon replied.

"Don't you start, lad," he bit back, pushing past to then suddenly stop on turning the corner.

What greeted them was a gleaming, stretched limousine parked by the roadside. The car's luxurious black finish was spotless and out of place for such a rundown part of the neighbourhood.

Father Peters let out a slow whistle, before ducking through the opened door to choose a seat in the plush soft interior. He took no time searching the luxurious offerings until spying crystal decanters of various spirits.

"Yes Father, please enjoy the free bar, never too early for a drink."

The priest ignored D's sarcasm, relying on a silent hand jester as his response.

"So charming, I'm sure. As ever, Father, you're a credit to your profession."

Simon approached, appearing apprehensive towards the expensive transport.

"After you, bro. Age before beauty," D smiled.

It was easy to note Simon's suspicion. "Why can't I shake the notion that when in this car, I'm a lamb to the slaughter?"

"That's because you are," D replied, slapping him on the back with encouragement to take a seat. The smile evaporated into a grimace on entering to witness Father Peters pouring a generous amount of neat aged malt into a glass.

Now, with everyone present, D closed the door and confirmed to the waiting driver. "Fire Pitt if you would be so kind."

The engine started, and they were soon pulling out in to morning traffic.

"The club is across town so it will give us a chance to have a chat," D offered. A quick glance of surprise and disgust as Father Peters continued to sample the plentiful hospitality.

The priest, unaffected by the attention, continued to sip his drink. "We might as well enjoy the journey whilst it lasts, so cheers." He took another sip, cherishing the smooth, expensive taste.

"There's a fine choice of cigars and cigarettes, Father. I'm sure you..." Without letting D finish the sentence, and with gleeful enthusiasm, Father Peters pushed a generous hand full of items into the inside pocket of his cardigan.

"No, please continue to enjoy," D responded to the blatant raid on his generosity before his attention focused to the contents of his secpad.

The Father raised his half-filled glass, answering with a smug and content grin. "God bless, for it's never too early as it sets you up for the hard day ahead."

"Quiet, but you're confusing alcoholism with a healthy breakfast, but each to their own, I suppose Father," D answered, giving a judgemental glare over his glasses.

Simon smiled at the obvious baiting between the two clashing personalities before attention went to the world flashing past the darkened window as they continued their journey.

Time passed in silence until D glanced from his secpad, waiting for the right moment to lean forward without being overheard. He need not worry, for Father Peters had found the controls for the flat screen suspended from the ceiling. A pair of supplied earphones allowed him to hear as he navigated the channels in search for something of interest.

"Tell me, what do you remember about those dreams of yours?" D asked. "Have you worked out what they mean for you?"

Simon answered with a shrug, continuing to watch the world outside the limousine.

"What of the scars on your back, are you not intrigued how you received them?"

Simon's attention returned to D. "What do you know of my scars?" Almost as a subconscious reminder, he felt the hard bone like protrusions even against the cushioned backrest of leather upholstery. The unique questions increased an already heightened level of suspicion towards the mysterious D. "I remember nothing before the accident. The following weeks are a jumbled mass of images, and memories of nothing concrete. I'm guessing you know more about me at this moment, so how about you fill in the blanks? Including how you knew Lisa was missing and how convenient to knowing where to find her."

Both men shared a frosty stare until D, unwilling to push the matter, found interest back to his secpad.

Simon needed to press the secretive D, pushing down on the device. "Who are you? You come from your fancy office and rich going by the suit and this car? So tell me, D, what's your interest in the refuge?"

"I'm not interested in that flea pit, the girl or the damn priest here. What is important is the numbers and balancing my lists? Anything else is stats on a page. I can tell you I was so content with my purpose until the powers that be order me to find you and prepare you for what is coming. The shit doesn't stop there. Those same powers have sent you back Swiss cheesed brained, with no knowledge of why you're here or your importance. To top that off, I'm instructed to stay impartial to both sides, meaning I cannot influence events for either by telling you anything meaningful."

Both remained silent until a belch broke the increasing tension.

"Excuse me, it's the peanuts," Father Peters apologised, still searching through channels on the in car entertainment centre.

D rolled his eyes at the interruption.

Simon rubbed at his eyebrow, somewhat confused. "Okay, so say we believe God has a plan for us?"

"Not them, you," D corrected.

"Okay, but he sent you as a guide to help me find my true self, but isn't that breaking the rules of non-interference?"

"Kind of, sometimes I bend those same rules. This helps me find your friend, but it only goes so far. It's not like they're written on tablets." Unable to contain his chuckle towards his unshared humour, D returned to his secpad.

Simon shook his head, frustrated in the glib answers to his questions.

"We are putting a lot of trust and faith in you D in helping to find Lisa. Are you saying everything that has happened so far is God's plan? How can we trust a God willing to let those we care about suffer?"

"Well he does," D answered, nodding towards Father Peters sat occupied by the television and free bar.

"Father Peters trusts in God's word because it's his job to help others believe in the same message, spreading it to the masses," Simon answered.

D gave a thin smile. "Let me get this straight, even with all that's happened to you, including a rapid recovery. You still believe it was down to your stubbornness and will to survive, and not divine intervention and what you are?"

Simon glanced out the window, not wanting to return D's stare. "I don't know, it's almost like you're saying I'm not human."

"You had injuries that would have killed a mortal man, but you survived and healed from those injuries in a remarkable amount of time. You, bro, are special in ways you could not imagine. Unfortunate for you, you have a human side including a subconscious stopping you from reaching your full potential. That will continue until you face facts to your past and regain those memories. Our Father has reasons for you being here, and you need to be ready to do what's needed."

"But what reasons? You have explained nothing and make it sound like I'm on a grand mission from God. Do you hear how insane that sounds? You keep mentioning this impending battle I need to prepare for, but I can't even distinguish between friend and foe."

D peered over his glasses. "In the next few days you, and those close to you, will be in immense danger. You're stuck between a power play that has been going on for millennia, well before this cesspit of a rock cooled." With a glance at the priest, he continued. "Don't get confused by what the religious lot spout on about their interpretations of God's message. Most are nothing but stories and repackaged in booklet form and sold to frighten whilst hiding the genuine message. They needed something for them to follow, a Dark Age marketing ploy to keep the masses submissive. A crowd control to a God-fearing world, but the truth is God never considered humans would amount to anything, remaining the early primate they are. Hell, they surprised us all, being nothing more than a plaything in his giant experiment. A spark of life, a seeded plant and waiting to what grew, half expecting a flower but getting an invasive weed that spread out to take over, destroying everything else. Most blame that unique and pesky free will of yours." D laughed, soon regaining his composure, noticing Simon still did not share his humour.

"So it was never Gods intension to create man in His image or go fourth, just another experiment like bugs and plants?"

"Not quite," D answered. "Man is as relevant to the plan as the animals they slaughter daily. If it wasn't for the ability of religious leaders over time to spin the creation story to help a growing fear of the unknown. Think about what they could achieve, growing without that interference. Just allowed to be individuals without limitations, instead they follow those in power, to pay taxes and becoming drones following vain, equally dysfunctional celebrities on social media."

With a shake of head, Simon tried to understand. "Okay, so if he doesn't care about humanity, why does he need us to help in this coming battle?"

"It's because deep down God doesn't like to lose." D gave a heavy sigh, watching Simon take in what he was trying to say. "Look Si, there's an old force rising, and it has both sides running scared. This shit predates time itself when the universe was young."

"If God is powerless to stop this rising, what could I achieve? He's all powerful, able to move mountains with a wave of a hand."

"It's down to that free will again, man's own destiny. That's why it's important you remember all you have forgotten, the answers are there." D pointed to Simon's head. "You play a pivotal part in what will happen. When the greatest need is upon you, look to heaven, and salvation shall fall from the sky."

"Oh great, riddles again, D." Simon sat back in his seat, frustrated.

"Sorry, but they like the old ways for passing on messages. I keep mentioning it's the digital age. Send a damn text. They're still stuck with the whole burning bush thing and don't get me started on the cell coverage." D offered a slight smile, understanding Simon's frustration.

The rest of the journey was in silence until the car slowed to a complete stop. The occupants of the limousine peered out of the window, noticing they had reached their destination.

D's secpad chimed and with a swift brush of a finger, he checked the latest message.

Father Peters, glass still in hand, noticed the colour drain from D's dark features. "Problem?" he asked, intrigued on what might wipe the smirk off his otherwise smug face.

"It's nothing to worry about, an update from the office," D

answered submissively through a strained smile.

Simon shared the same concern filled expression as Father Peters. A sense of discomfort from the pit of his stomach in that it was too late to reconsider. Not sure if they were making a colossal mistake in trusting D.

To describe the Fire Pitt Club as lavish was an under-statement. White stone steps extended outwards from the coppery red frontage of glass, mirroring the raging flame pits burning the entire length of the club. Those lucky to enter were to enjoy their own private pleasure pits where discretion and anonymity guaranteed to whatever you desired.

Even from the enclosed luxury interior of the limousine it could not diminish the reactions of the excited party-goers surging the red roped railings surrounding the doors.

Simon felt hesitant, noting the security manning the doors brandishing the Fire Pitts distinct name in flame-embossed gold lettering.

"It's the hottest nightspot in the state," D offered, noticing Simon's darting gaze towards the crowds. "Everyone who's anyone parties at this club."

As they waited, two towering suited security staff des-cended the steps in greeting, opening the limousine door to a wave of excitement. The entire atmosphere outside elec-trified as the crowds surged in whooping celebration for a glimpse of the expectant rich socialite or VIP to step out.

D could not hide his amusement, glancing over at the both of them and smiling. "Boy, wait for their disappointment when they see you two." He was still laughing as he pushed past, waving at the screaming crowds on his exit. Those left in the limousine shared a glance in silent agreement to each other's drab and unshaven appearance, far from the norm for such an establishment.

"If I knew it would be so formal, I'd have changed my shirt," Father Peters grinned, getting out.

A flurry of synchronised flashes from the mass of photographers became overwhelming as Simon shielded his eyes on leaving the limousine.

All around the crowds continued to surge, screaming in need of attention from the newcomers, hoping it led to getting inside the club.

Security made an empty path through the throng to the entrance, staffed by further well-dressed intimidating security. Each shared the same expressions of menace, making the bravest think twice about causing trouble.

Simon noticed their professionalism as they studied the crowds, maintaining contact by concealed communications and more intimidating, revealing the occasional concealed weaponry under well-tailored jackets. The recent development added to his already growing apprehension.

"D, and who are your guests?" The question asked from a short stocky man, glancing from his small secpad to the latest arrivals with a distrustful glare. A distinct pencil thin scar crossed his left cheek, highlighting his sneer. "We have a dress code policy, you know."

D gave him one of his best smiles. "Anton, I know, but we aren't stopping long. Conducting a little business with a pickup as Lewie is expecting us."

"Lewie expects us?" Simon asked in a hushed tone, nervous from the growing stares and increasing vocal crowds.

Anton tapped his device, awaiting confirmation of their invite. "Please wait here," he asked, offering a subtle nod to his security, who took position by the recent arrivals in silent wait.

It was D's turn to appear nervous, turning to his two companions. "Relax guys, all is okay. We will be in soon."

Unable to share his enthusiasm, Simon became tense with balled fists, expecting trouble.

It was then the glass doors opened, ushering the group through to a grand reception leading to the club. Within moments the doors closed in silent wake, reducing the extreme noise from outside to a muffled roar.

Simon could sense beneath his feet the distinct base beat thump resonating from the club's music. He noted the luxurious reception spread out in elaborate decor, sharing the external dark theme with red curved furnishings scattered for customer's comfort. Off to one side was an elaborate reception desk staffed by two provocatively dressed female attendants.

One attendant, a petite blond, her lace bodice struggling to conceal her ample assets, offered a smile as she took coats from a young, well-dressed couple. The same couple turned to face the group, their expressions falling in shock and disgust. They reeled from Simon and Father Peter shared destitute and threadbare appearance for such an exclusive establishment.

The Father offered a mischievous grin. "Evening," he said. "Can I interest you in a sermon on the sins and evils of drink and impropriety?"

The young couple continued to recoil before scurrying to the side, uncomfortable to the scruffy priest's attention.

"I would appreciate you didn't talk to our clientele," requested a voice.

D rushed to greet the newcomer as she entered, flanked by more security. The bright lights exemplified her tall, slim figure as her untied hair rested across her shoulders, extenuating her startling beauty. As she stood, her single cut buttoned suit jacket trailed open to sliming trousers, amplifying her long legs with a pair of black small heeled knee-length boots.

Both Simon and Father Peters stood speechless as she held up a hand to the advancing D, stopping him in his tracks.

"Gentlemen meet the lovely and beautiful Lilith, Lewie's second and the manager of the club," D introduced.

Father Peters tried to remove the remaining crumbs of food from his cardigan, a failed try at appearing more presentable.

It did not matter as Lilith's attention remained fixed on Simon. She had not taken her narrowed scrutinising glare from him since greeting the group.

Simon, captivated at first, became uncomfortable from the intense interest.

A shared moment noted by D as he proceeded with his introductions.

Lilith ignored him, sweeping past to pause in front of Simon. Her perfume washed over him, an intoxicating scent that could not distract from her dark green eyes as she leant in close.

Simon thought she was about to whisper into his ear.

Instead she pulled away, a mild frown amplifying her dark, flawless features.

Unable to hide his embarrassment to the peculiar moment, Simon glanced to the Father who nudged him.

"Was it me or did she sniff you, lad?" he asked.

"Follow me please," Lilith requested, pointing to a side door, held open by one of her security entourage.

"We were hoping to see Lewie?" D asked, falling into step behind her.

"We came to ask about Lisa Shelby?" Father Peters offered.

Their queries ignored, as they ushered the group towards another opened door marked for staff only. They moved into a long corridor running parallel to the club. As they continued, passing rows of compact dressing rooms and storage spaces that housed groups of staff, including dancers and further security personnel taking no notice on their passing.

"I don't understand?" D asked, as they reached the end of the corridor leading to a double door marked fire exit. "What is going on, Lilith? This is about a friend of theirs, brought here by Brian Shelby."

Lilith remained silent, ignoring his questions.

A bleep from D's pocket made him retrieve his secpad, reading the latest message.

Lilith plucked the device from his grip. "You don't need that where your friends are going," she offered, crushing the device under her boot heal.

"What's going on, D?" Simon asked.

D retrieved his damaged device and joined the others pushed through the fire door.

Back outside, taking a small flight of steps adjoining a loading bay, tension rising for all concerned.

Agitated, D fell in next to the others. "I'm sorry guys, I tried, but it's getting out of hand."

The small group passed into an adjacent building to the club, a large multi-storey car park, lit with unfiltered strip lights illuminating the entire ground floor.

Their escort pushed them against the outer wall as further club security waited, guarding the shuttered entrance.

"What the hell is going on here?" Father Peters demanded, now agitated by the sight of so much security.

Once the parking garage was secure enough, it allowed the security to produce hidden weapons, chambering the first rounds with menacing intent.

Simon noticed Lilith tap her concealed ear piece. "You can bring them down now."

An echo of a scuffle came from the level above, where dark suited security dragged two hooded figures, positioning them where Lilith pointed, before removing their hoods.

"Lisa lass, what have they done to you?" Father Peters asked, clutching the terrified girl. Her frightened expression resulted from her ordeal, bound and hooded. On seeing a familiar face, tears flowed as she buried her head into the priest's chest as he held her tight.

Simon moved to share in Lisa's relief, but the nearest of the security team raised his weapon in warning. Taking a moment to glance from machine pistol to expressionless owner brought on a wash of anger and frustration as Simon felt helpless to do anything about it.

"Steady boys," Lilith said, pacing the line of hostages, making a curious inspection of each one, taking obvious enjoyment in their uncertainty to what happens next.

Brian Shelby was the other captive brought down the slope with Lisa, and he pushed himself forward to plead with Lilith.

"I will get the money, I swear. This time tomorrow, tell Lewie, please."

Lilith smiled, stroking his bruised face, almost concerned by his agitation until gripping a clump of his hair, pulling his head back. "You tried to offload your ex and your kid as payment for your debt. You then only brought the woman damaged, and that doesn't bode well with us."

"The priest wouldn't let me take the kid, not without his mother's say so." He winced in her grasp. "Two hours there and back, collect the kid and my debt's paid, right," he pleaded, stooping against her grip.

"If we ever get out of this you shit, I will rip you apart," Father Peters spat as he continued to cradle Lisa in his arms.

With attention on Brian, Simon considered his options. He needed a plan that would disarm the nearest security whilst enabling him to get his friends out of danger. All outcomes appeared bleak, and in Lilith's favour. He calculated even his fast reflexes were no match to overcome all security and save his friends. Someone would get hurt in the crossfire.

Lilith released her grip, tapping Brian's face, and noted the fear behind his eyes. She revelled in the power, savouring every moment. "We might have had a deal if you hadn't got the others involved, but now you bring them to our doorstep in search for your beaten ex-wife. In fact, you could have had your full debt paid off and made a tidy profit if you had told us about the half-breed being at the refuge." With a slight turn, she watched Simon's reaction.

"What him?" Brian asked, pointing. "The vagrant they picked up off the streets. What's so special about him?"

Everyone had the same surprise, apart from D trying to keep a low profile at the back of the group, putting his cracked secpad back together.

Simon tried not to react to the sudden attention.

A single shot broke the silence, amplified by the buildings cramped confines, making everyone flinch.

The bullet entered Brian Shelby's brain under his right eye, killing him instantly and not knowing what was happening as the bullet exited the back of his skull. A fine visual spray covered the shocked priest still cradling Lisa and D.

Instinct made Father Peters shield Lisa from the danger, leaving the shocked D stood open-mouthed.

Brian's body in a last spasm of life twitched and then slumped backwards to pool blood across the dirt-covered ground.

Lisa screamed, burying her head deeper into the Father's chest.

Lilith with satisfaction re-holstered her weapon.

Simon was the only one unaffected in the group by the sudden execution of Brian. His earlier apprehension and confusion replaced by clear adrenaline fuelled defiance and sudden need to survive. He braced, for now was the time to act, knowing he and his friends were to share the same fate unless he did something.

An electronic bleep broke the tension, D's secpad blinked back into life. "Huh… Oh yes, working again," he shouted, tapping rapidly on the blood-smeared screen. It was a surreal moment as everyone waited for an explanation as he turned the device to show the cracked screen displayed a timer ticking down to zero. "Guys, I would get to cover if I was you, it's about to get a hell of a lot messy in here," he grinned.

The entire parking garage shook as the far end, including the closed shuttered doors, exploded in a deafening flash. Thousands of razor sharp pieces of debris surged the lower level, engulfing the closest of Lilith's security and reducing them to a red mist.

Simon reacted, elbowing the man to his right, who reeled backwards. A swift kick to the knee incapacitated another, hitting the ground in a scream of pain. There was confusion all around, allowing Simon to lift Father Peters and Lisa up from the floor. With haste, he pushed them towards the ramp that led to the upper levels, with D keen to follow.

Lilith dragged the nearest of her men across her as a shield, as red tracer rounds emanated from what had been the entrance. Her improvised shield took the violent effects of the rounds, shredding the man's upper body. Then serving his purpose, Lilith pushed the body forward, allowing her to leap for the far stairwell doorway.

All around, increasing automatic fire continued to fill the lower level.

The stairwell gave protection, where Lilith caught her breath. She tried to understand how the situation was now out of control, as she watched lethal weapon fire tear apart the remnants of her security personnel. Then through the drifting smoke she spied Simon and his small group making for the safety of the upper floor.

Then everything fell silent.

With a curse Lilith checked her weapon, then peering around the shattered door frame, noticing the grey cloud of dust expanding the entire lower level.

Just then, from the side door leading back to the Fire Pitt, rushed two more of her security team, returning automatic fire towards the space that had been the entranceway. All proving futile, as returning fire saturated them as they ran, flinging their bodies to the ground.

In a blink it was all over, the only sounds came from damaged lighting and the cascading flow of water from an overhead pipe, ruptured in the explosion.

Lilith took another chance to peer around the splintered door frame, noting a bright high powered light swept the area. The light silhouetted ominous figures darting further into the lower level. Then a sound of heavy diesel engines revved, filling the air with an acrid taste of dust and burning flesh. Then, stepping in to the cascading light, came a figure to stand and offer a foreboding shadow over the full length of the ground floor. The light then extinguished, leaving the emergency lighting of the stairwell to contain the immediate area in a soft red hue. Lilith cursed as she recognised the figures fanning out to take up positions all around the ground floor, as they went, cautious to check for survivors and dead alike.

"Guard Clerics," D whispered, peering over Simon's shoulder from their vantage point on the next level.

Simon ignored the newcomers as his attention was on Lilith and what she would do next.

She remained crouched in the stairwell, calculating her escape. With her exits blocked, her only chance was to go higher, but she knew it would conclude with the same outcome caught once the clerics searched the upper levels. Her pained expression clear, for her only other choice being the far door and returning to the club. That proving suicidal under the gauntlet of weapon fire, she would face from the approaching clerics. Somehow she knew she was being observed, returning Simon's gaze and seeing him shake his head in warning, expecting her next move. Another quick glance around the door, Lilith turned back to mouth something before giving a defiant smile. Then with reluctance she tossed her weapon out, letting it slide across the debris-strewn floor.

Shouts rang out, ordering clerics to move forward.

Lilith stood with hands upon her head. "I'm unarmed and coming out," she shouted.

The armoured clerics swarmed around her, forcing Lilith to her knees and restraining her. At the same time she continued to watch Simon, a malicious smile the whole time as the clerics pulled her to her feet, weapons still drawn. The clerics parted, allowing a figure through that had cast such an imposing shadow earlier. The smile of arrogance vanished as Lilith recognised the tall, battle armoured man, the purple piping of his armour indicting rank of bishop.

Bishop Alexander Nikolaos cupped Lilith's chin in a gloved hand, so he could see her face. "Defiant as ever, Lilith, I see. Understandable that you surrendered, be a shame to damage such a beautiful host," he said.

Lilith pulled away from his grasp, staring at the floor.

"We made a mess, so sorry, but the door appeared locked." He walked away with a last laugh at Lilith's reluctance to trade words, leaving her in the custody of two waiting clerics. Now flanked on both sides by other clerics, weapons drawn, Nikolaos moved up the ramp. "Okay, you can come out now. We were monitoring the whole situation since you entered the club. I can assure you, you were in no danger." He paused, waiting, the usual background chatter of personnel communication the only response.

"Targets second level, moving." a voice confirmed, followed by clerics locating the sheltering group. "All secured."

Nikolaos approached the survivors, covered in dust and dirt.

Father Peters continued to comfort the traumatised Lisa at his side.

"Get these people medical aid," Nikolaos ordered, recognising shock and fear on all their faces, except for one.

Simon sat crossed legged, hands placed on his head, refusing eye contact with those around him.

"All clear, no weapons, bishop," a cleric confirmed, offering a salute.

Nikolaos returned it, as two medical clerics set about searching the survivors for any other injuries.

Soon enough, one of the medical clerics made his report. "Superficial injuries, sir, slight bruising, cuts, but nothing serious apart from shock. The blood is not theirs."

"Thank you," Nikolaos answered, returning the salute as the medical cleric left. "You three are free to go with my blessing."

Both D and Father Peters shared a glance before rising from the floor. The Father continued to support Lisa, clinging to his side. As they passed Nikolaos, Father Peters stopped. "Thank you, bishop, for our release, but can I ask? What about the lad, he's as innocent as the rest of us?"

"Oh, I'm sure he is, Father," the Nikolaos smiled. "He will help us with further enquiries. So please follow the waiting clerics instructed to take you back to your refuge." With a nod, the nearest cleric herded the group down the ramp.

With a last glance, Father Peters gave Simon a look of concern.

Simon acknowledged with a half-smile. "Take Lisa home Father, there's nothing to worry about, I will be okay." Deep down he wished it were true, but his situation was looking grim.

The last to pass Nikolaos was D, who flinched as the bishop placed a hand upon his shoulder. "Don't think this hasn't gone unnoticed, what you have been doing these past few weeks, you know the agreement. You're supposed to not take sides." Nikolaos lent in closer. "The cardinal is most displeased."

D blinked, somewhat reluctant to plead his innocence, considering it was neither the time nor place for his usual showmanship response. With a shrug, he freed himself from Nikolaos's grip, hurrying after the others, sharing the worries of the possibility that they might not see Simon again.

The assault on the parking garage created toxic clouds of dust that hung the ground floor. Not helped by the advancing Guard Clerics heading for the upper floors to complete the dramatic assault. An assault that had freed Simon and the others from a local crime boss, starting with Simon and Father Peters arriving in search of Lisa, abducted by her ex-husband Brian. The day's shocking events cumulated in Brian's sudden execution by a local crime boss's lieutenant, Lilith. Simon was the only remaining member of the group held by the Order of Light forces, the others freed to return to the refuge.

Now bound and seated cross-legged on the floor, Simon watched cleric clean up teams continue around him. *Could things get any worse?* His fleeting thought answered when the bishop in charge of the operation returned.

"Please stand him up," Bishop Nikolaos instructed to two clerics. "Remove his restraints too."

A female cleric did as instructed, cutting the plastic bonds around Simon's wrists, and lifting him to his feet.

With his restraints removed, Simon eased out the knots in his shoulders. An immediate relief from the pressure of his constricted muscles, with a subconscious rub of wrists still bearing the red indentations of the restraints. He acknowledged his gratitude with a begrudging nod whilst trying to clean the dust and dirt from his clothes. A futile gesture with the realisation he was rubbing at the dried blood of Brian Shelby. "Am I under arrest?" Simon asked.

"Have you done anything to call for an arrest?" Nikolaos removed his helmet to answer almost quizzically.

Simon remained silent, confused to not being released with the others.

That allowed Nikolaos for the first time to see the object of their supposed demise. He tried to comprehend what threat this dust covered, bruised and beaten poor excuse of an individual represented to bringing the end of his beloved Order. "As I understand, a situation arose where a security monitoring team observed four individuals and one known felon being dragged into an underground parking garage by armed assailants." He pushed a gloved hand through his short grey flecked hair, a welcome release from the confines of the helmet before his attention returned to Simon. "That said team, concerned for their safety, investigated the situation further and resulted in a slight altercation."

Simon watched Brian Shelby's body being zipped it into a body bag. "Suppose you could put it that way."

Nikolaos scoffed. "The question you should ask yourself is what reason had they for you and your associates to be dead?"

"To silence us, our friend was being held against her will and we came to find her," Simon offered, rubbing his tender wrists.

The bishop could not suppress the laugh. "And your plan was to walk through the front door of the biggest crime lord on the coast and ask him to give her back?"

"With hindsight, it wasn't the best plan, but getting Lisa back was our priority," Simon offered.

"That priority would have got you and the priest killed. Never trust D without understanding the consequences."

Simon turned to meet the bishop's gaze. "Guess we thought no harm would come to us with a priest in our group."

Another deep throaty laugh as Nikolaos slapped Simon on the back, pitching him forward. "You would risk your lives on Lewie's compassion. You are the bravest sons of bitches or the dumbest putting your hopes in Lewie not killing you because you brought a priest." Nikolaos shook his head, continuing to laugh.

Simon stewed in his embarrassment.

Soon enough, Nikolaos stood against the guardrail, attention on the clean-up on the lower level.

Clerics cleared the bodies to a waiting MAUV where local emergency services had responded in a wail of sirens and lights. They were trying to gain access to the scene, their efforts hampered by a deacon guarding the entranceway.

"Let them handle the PR." Nikolaos pointed to the heated altercation by the entrance.

Simon watched as the deacon took the police captain's arm, leading him back towards the taped off security line, where the rest of the emergency personnel waited. As he watched the heated exchange, he was unaware of Nikolaos's observation.

"Did you know our Order is one of the world's largest religious organisations, followers in the billions," the bishop explained. "What singles us out from the others are our successful business interests, putting the Order number one in the top five global entities."

Simon was unsure of the sudden change in conversation and let the bishop continue.

"This means the Order controls vast amounts of resources, including the expensive lawyers and the best public relations money can buy for incidents like today." He nodded to the altercation, continuing with the local authorities. "Any problems are well under control. In fact, the masses have got used to news of the Order's cohorts pacifying pockets of insurgent radicals and other undesirables. The same groups bringing their religious holy war to our streets, so we take it upon ourselves to pacify that hatred and violence. In doing so, we keep the public safe in their homes and we're loved for doing so."

"Why are you telling me this, bishop?" Simon asked.

"Because it's the world around you, and your little band of misfits needs to understand what you're involved with, being so out of your depth. Tonight you almost became a statistic in a crime file." He left Simon to consider that revelation for a moment.

"Should I be thanking you for telling me, or are you worried for our future?" Simon asked.

"That's up to you, but offering a courteous warning to the fact you interest the Order. That makes it my responsibility to investigate you and your friends and decide if you're irrelevant or a threat."

"I'm not a threat to anyone. I'm not even sure why I'm still here?" Simon confessed. "The others aren't a threat either, we have no secret agenda. We wanted to get our friend back."

"Everybody has secrets, most of all those trying hard to stay off our radar."

Simon remained focused ahead, trying not to show his emotions.

"Wonder how eager you would be to throw your life away in helping your friends, knowing the truth about them? Perhaps, ask yourself if they would do the same for you. What sacrifices are you willing to make to uncover the truth?"

Without realising, Simon was gripping the railings, his knuckles turning white.

Nikolaos, satisfied his questions were having the desired effect, continued pushing a little more. "There is one thing that puzzles me, we have your friend's histories, but there's the curious question of a twenty-year-old cold case. The incident the only confirmation you ever existed until now."

Simon avoided his gaze, unsure how much the Order knew.

His mind was a whirl of doubts and questions of his own as he lent against the railings. An image returned of a robed figure, hands out stretched grasping for him. With a furrowed brow, Simon let out a slow breath, considering the possibility of the Order's involvement in his past before the accident. If so, was the bishop playing mind games, trying to slip him up, have him make a mistake and give himself away. It was obvious he had become a piece in an elaborate power play. How had D explained it, Gods big plan? The revelation brought on a wave of nausea.

It was then a cleric approached, with a well-practised salute offering over a secpad to the bishop.

Nikolaos confirmed the details and passed the device back, his expression unbroken by the interruption as he noticed Simon resting his forehead upon his arms. "I've confirmed the release of your friends, including the charismatic Mr D. We may need further questioning when we see fit, but for now they are free to go. Our medics have checked over Mrs Shelby and apart from the bruising and shock of today's events, she's in a remarkable fit state."

"Am I free to go?" Simon raised his head, regaining his balance.

"Not yet, we wish your company for a little longer, and explain the gaps in your history."

The knot in Simon's stomach tightened.

"Have you studied the works of Reformation?" Nikolaos asked.

"I'm having a hard time separating fact from fiction from my life these days, without adding religion to the mix."

"The cardinal's teachings tell us his word is enlightenment."

Simon stirred, feeling further tension as the conversation changed again.

Nikolaos raised a hand, relaxing his stance. "We brought order where there was none. Peace to the country after the collapse of government as the people needed leadership to stem the breakup of the union as times were dire for all."

"Father Peters talked about what happened, how people suffered," Simon offered.

"But it's not the same as experiencing it yourself, the hardship, the desperation. You are lucky not remembering those bleak times of mass unemployment, food riots, and embezzlement at the highest levels of the establishment. Then there were the escalating wars in Europe and the Middle East. They brought the country to its knees. Our enemies seeing our weakness took advantage, but the Order brought a light of hope and salvation. His Eminence sent out clerics to spread the word as shared with him. It brought hope to the masses, giving something to build with from the chaos. As New Eden grew, we offered infrastructures in helping others recover from the troubles. From that small beginning, the Order empowered people to flock to us, worship in a place symbolising the true God. Those that showed worth, realising the message, joined the Order's growing ranks, to pass the message to those wishing to listen."

"What of those who don't share the true message. What of them?"

Nikolaos turned back with a courteous smile. "His will is pure, as it always shall be, striking down those who speak ill of that word with all of His anger. Then cleanse the world, for we shall have Eden. The Book of Reformation, Chapter 12, verse 4." The bishop's answer took a darker tone.

It made Simon shake his head.

"We force no one to become a believer in His word." Nikolaos continued. "Those not sharing our teachings, and who fight us every day in their need to destroy what we build here…"

Both men shared a glance before reacting to the sudden interruption of a deliberate cough.

They turned to face a nervous priest, stood to attention.

"What is it?" Nikolaos asked with irritation.

"You requested confirmation when the convoy was ready

to escort your guest back to the monastery, bishop. We need your authority of transit." The colour had drained from the priest's face as he offered the secpad.

Nikolaos snatched the device, allowing the orders before passing it back. "You're dismissed, Father." The statement acknowledged with a hesitant salute before the priest retreated down the slope.

Nikolaos gestured to two waiting clerics, who slung their weapons and came to flank either side of Simon.

"I'm sure we will continue our conversation soon, Mr Alksey. I so look forward to reading your debrief report." Nikolaos paused and lent forward. "May I offer advice?" His tone hushed. "You might try to be more, should we say, talkative? Silence isn't a choice you have under the circumstances."

Simon felt the dread of uncertainty returning before being escorted to the lower floor.

Bishop Nikolaos's stony stare of scrutiny remained on them as they left, considering the gains from the brief meeting. *How was this pathetic child the bringer of darkness the cardinal was adamant was coming?* With a grunt, he retrieved his helmet. *What reason did the cardinal fear this man's arrival, and how does a group of refuge misfits fit in the prophecy? Are those fears justified? If so, is it still necessary to resolve the issue by whatever means were necessary?* A quick change of helmet strap, he strode down the ramp. *Whatever the reason, his cohorts were ready.* As he continued, another passage of text came to him. *Under the light of the true God, whose light shall never falter. For no man will ever turn his back on that light, for fearing his soul forever consumed in the darkness.*

MAUV is the acronym for the ominous waiting armoured vehicle, whose sleek combination of sloped design and brute strength sat upon a reinforced six-wheeled frame. Encased in twenty-two tons of Talamite reactive armour and designed by the Order of Light's military division. To offer multiple role capabilities to carry eight armoured Guard Clerics and crew complement of three. Capable of a top road speed of fifty-five kilometres per hour, powered from its dual diesel engines. Since its induction, becoming the workhorse of the cohort's arsenal, seeing deployment in various pacification projects.

As Simon and his escorts approached, his chest tightened to understanding there had a well-earned reputation, they were an intimidating vehicle. His anxiety increased observing a cleric overseeing one of two duel fifty automated heavy weapon systems mounted on the roof. The situation returned his thoughts to his recuperation, having spent long hours reading about the Order and its cohorts. Father Peters had left books, hoping something might jog his memory, including archived histories and recent news articles. Simon soaked up the information, recognising the MAUV had become a symbol of the Order's authority. Their first deployment was supporting the stretched emergency services around the country, becoming instrumental in quelling citywide food riots in Boston and Seattle. To start a grim time of civil unrest, as a result Congress passed the Reformation Act, a bill allowing integration of Order forces into all states, civil and military organisations. The cohorts deployed on mass and the MAUVs with them, outfitted with non-lethal armaments and other pacification control systems, quashing riots that had broken out throughout the country. Its unique dual role as escort and security for food transports proved how resilient it was in even none volatile situations. Throughout his study Simon had never questioned why a major religious organisation had need for such a militarised security measure. Father Peters tried to sum it up once, during one of their lengthy discussions. The way he described it, the masses need to feel safe, especially after all the troubles. That allowed the Order to patrol the streets, giving the public a false sense of security, little knowing they gave up their freedom and liberty for progress and vigilance. He also had described the Order as thugs in combat boots, zealots using religion as a tool of oppression to make all see their way of God. The speeches and uniforms might change, but it was the masses who always suffered. Simon's attention went back to the waiting MAUV. The same vehicle that had assaulted the parking garage as evidence of the assault still covered its exterior.

His escorts brought him to the rear where they found the external ramp open. The interior comprised two rows of canvas seating, the forward section filled with an array of screens with readouts and system diagnostics all provided by external and internal sensors. Sat at one console was a deacon engrossed in getting the vehicle prepared to be underway.

The Guard Cleric escorts manhandled Simon to a seat, taking positions either side of him, deterring any ideas of escape. They need not worry, as Simon glimpsed the waiting convoy from the confines of his seat. He counted three more MAUV, their crews a hive of activity for departure. The entire scene offered an intimidating show of strength.

Simon's attention returned to the vehicle's interior, noticing the driver sat with his head encased in the vehicle's operator headset. The back of the headset connected various cables and optics feeding the wearer direct access to a multitude of sensors and sub systems duplicated on the surrounding consoles. All giving detailed real-time information on an eight-block radius. The sloped profile design of an MAUV offered no windscreen. External cameras immersed the crew with a virtual three hundred and sixty degree display, including drone and satellite surveillance.

As he settled into his seat, Simon somewhat relieved not restrained for the trip, thankful Bishop Nikolaos had been true to his word but still felt he was a prisoner. That realisation did not dispel the lingering apprehension, nor did one of his escorts miss interpreting his agitation as a precursor to seizing an opportunity to escape.

The cleric's sinister grin appeared under his visor faceplate, tapping the rifle resting across his lap with intent. To show escape was futile.

Simon returned a half smile and with a quick push of a hand through his hair, he closed tired eyes, hoping his ordeal over soon. "If ever I needed a miracle," he muttered before a sound of footsteps forced him from his thoughts, recognising the priest from earlier with Bishop Nikolaos.

The priest took the command chair behind the driver. "Ramp up please and prepare for departure," the priest requested, confirming the instructions through his own console.

A steady vibration of the diesel engines increased, revving. A motorised hydraulics sounded as the ramp door closed, followed by an airtight hiss of the seal. With the light from outside extinguished, the interior fell in to darkness but for the consoles until the interior lights bathed everything in an ominous red hue.

The commanding priest adjusted his posture, choosing a sequence of commands for open communications as his fingers crossed his console's screen. "Alpha 2-2 to Alpha group confirm please."

One by one, the other MAUV of the convoy confirmed their readiness.

"All units confirmed ready. Alpha 2-1 takes point," the priest ordered.

"Understood," was the response.

With the convoy underway, the priest leaned back in his chair. "Green lights on the civilian system please, there's no need being stuck in traffic."

The deacon completed the task as the priest returned to open communications again. "Alpha 2-2 to command ETA is forty-seven minutes."

"Understood," replied the speaker.

Simon leant forward, curious to view the screens of live images from outside the vehicle. Another showed all the MAUV in the convoy within a mapped city grid display, coloured icons representing their own convoy in blue, and civilians in yellow. He felt the entire experience reminiscent of playing

Jakes handheld video games. With his interest waning, Simon sank back, closing his eyes again, still wishing to be back at the refuge. Not long into the journey, he was struggling to ignore every bump and jolt regardless of the canvas seat.

The two cleric escorts were faring better, being used to the cramped space of these vehicles, remaining motionless and unaffected.

A growing sensation of pins and needles crept into Simon's finger, and no amount of flexing made it go away. As time passed, the sensation spread to bring on a need to rub his arm to help circulation.

The MAUV made a hard left turn, engines gunning to increase speed.

Simon slid sideways, nudging into the cleric, whose response was a grumble of annoyance and the order to stay still. By now, nausea and numbness had made Simon uncomfortable as he made a quick glance around at the crew showing to be unaffected. Only a faint static interference appeared to be affecting the display screens. The sensation made the hairs on the back of his neck rise. Also, increasing the dread of apprehension that something was about to happen.

The deacon, his attention now to the interference, tried to isolate the problem. "Commander, we have a localised EMP build up reported effecting systems. I'm unable to isolate or track the source, but confirm its close."

Just when Simon could not imagine his day getting any worse, the entire MAUV rocked on its wheels.

The driver fought with the controls, bringing the vehicle to an abrupt stop, his muffled scream resonating as he tore at his helmet. His entire visual senses became overloaded as he saw the MAUV ahead vanish in a bright multi-coloured array of flames. One moment he had the vehicle in view, the next something reduced it to a smouldering charred wreck, unrecognisable as it lay in the street ahead, burning.

Everyone sat in silent shock until the priest reacted, opening full system communications. "Command, command, we have a situation..."

Anything electrical suddenly within the vehicle went dead, all screens, systems including communications but for the emergency lighting flickering to stay lit.

The clerics escorting either side of Simon shared a glance as the situation developed with another enormous explosion, close, rocking the vehicle.

A metallic rain hit the roof, as muffled automatic fire rung out nearby, followed by cries of alarm.

The priest shifted to the deacon, trying in vain to get life from his dead consoles. The priest grabbed his shoulder to get his attention. "We're shielded against such attacks, how the hell have we lost all systems and power?"

"We registered a static pulse before the attack. Father, we're dead because secondary redundancies have not kicked in after losing power. With all systems down, I'm trying a manual reboot and have switched to solar cells, regaining partial systems in ninety seconds, including power. That will trigger secondary systems, including drone release."

The priest swivelled in his seat, pointing at the seated clerics. "You two, topside, without power we have to go manual with the fifties and give me a visual on the convoy. We are blind without systems and need information ASAP."

Both clerics stood, levering the locking bars to the outside hatches. Bracing shoulders and with a grunt, heaved the hatches open.

The sound of gunfire more intense now echoed, and an acidic taste of burnt rubber and diesel flooded the interior.

"We've lost Alpha 2-3 and 2-5, both in flames, multiple casualties. Alpha 2-1 is tracking unknown targets with heavies and has deployed small arms," answered a cleric, pulling the duel weapon system around to face the street.

The priest reached for the hatch above his own chair to see for himself. What he found was whatever had knocked out the system's electronics had taken out the power for the entire block as high as the sixth floor. He knew of no EMP device capable of specific targeting. That showed high-grade technology, not including the ordinance to take out two armoured MAUV with single shots. Whoever was attacking was well-armed, mobile and intent of achieving what they wanted with this convoy.

From a nearby shop, a group of civilians broke cover, the shop's frontage gutted by the explosions. Two civilian vehicles were also burning by Alpha 2-5's destruction. Wreckage let off a firework of colour from its remaining ammunition. The first explosion had also blown out the ground-floor interiors of the businesses across the street, raging in flame. Devastation of the attack had caused thickening black smoke to cover the full length of the street, causing chaos for anybody caught in the ambush.

The priest recognised shapes scattered between the burning vehicles, as the unfortunate charred remains of the dead Alpha 2-5 crew. He offered a silent prayer for the fallen. He tried to get control of the situation and understand what they faced. Their attackers had planned well, choosing the narrowest part of the journey where the convoy turned on to a single one-way on the outskirts of an extended business district. That meant most properties were still vacant or under construction, reducing the chance of citizens being caught in the attack. He turned to the rear of the convoy, which appeared just as bleak as Alpha 2-3 rested on its side, burning. This meant their immediate exit blocked by the two burning vehicles and separated from the other remaining MAUV.

Dense smoke continued to hang low in the cramped street, turning day into the gloom of night for visibility.

The priest knew they equipped all Order cleric personnel with the latest in battlefield optics. So with the slightest movement of the user's eye allowed navigation of various visual options within the helmet. He scrolled the list, navigating from normal to infrared, and picking out heat sources as glowing tracer fire lashed an office block on the corner of the street.

Alpha 2-1 fired its heavy fifty calibre weapons, adding to the sporadic automatic fire of its ground forces. That showed power loss had not affected them unlike their own transport. There came a tremendous sound of shattering glass as portions of masonry rained down onto the opposite sidewalk as further rounds of heavy weapon fire tore into the neighbouring buildings.

The priest tried to track any targets, but it was proving impossible. It was then to his relief his communications stuttered to life, only static at first. He then heard shouts of alarm, including voices of the other clerics. The priest tried to make sense of the confusing chatter, recognising the voice of his opposite number commanding Alpha 2-1. The voice of the female priest sounded stressed but in control as she issued orders to her crew.

"Watch for targets, stop firing wild. Pick your targets and engage."

With contact restored, he cut into the chatter. "Alpha 2-1 a situation report."

"Alpha 2-1, the situation is multiple targets on an elevated position. Contacts are using surrounding buildings for cover, and we are taking light ordnance. Have deployed ground forces and instructed them to make their approach to your position, but hindered by wreckage."

The priest reacted as communication became overwhelmed as the front of a coffee shop buckled and then exploded. He watched as heavy tracer fire hit the corrugated security shutters, scattering debris, covering the top of the MAUV. Both the priest and exposed clerics ducked back inside as super-heated debris showered them.

The few remaining civilians in the area fled, screaming from the intense violence.

"Check your fire, Alpha 2-1. Friendlies in area," the priest shouted as he recovered.

Inside, Simon was desperate to comprehend what was going on from hearing the restored chatter. Obviously it was a war zone outside the MAUV. Much like the nightly news bulletins of the conflicts in Northern Europe and the Middle East, never once thinking he would experience the same on the streets of New America. Just then, he lost his balance, clinging to the seat strappings as the MAUV manoeuvred. Deducing they wanted a better firing position so to add their own heavy weapons against whatever was attacking. All attention was on the battle outside, so Simon slid back an observation plate to get a view of the battle.

A sudden wash of flames lapped the side, as the driver fought to get any functionality from his screens, which remained blank. With a need to know what was happening, he slid open his own view plate, so to see the street ahead. Without power steering it was a fight to reposition, but he did the best. Then the order came to use heavy weapons, needing to increase the suppressive fire down the road.

From Simon's position, he thought to have seen a figure lurching across an adjacent building as tracer fire arched towards it.

The priest tapped his console. "Alpha 2-1, break out and meet up on our six, we will give suppressing fire."

The reply was nothing but static.

"Alpha 2-1 what's your situation, report." Still no reply as he noted the heavy weapons from their last position had stopped, but for occasional automatic fire from concealed positions. A quick sweep of the area, greatest magnification, resulted in no obvious movement. "Everyone stay alert, pick targets when you see them, understand?" he ordered.

"Friendlies incoming," shouted a cleric, pointing into the smoke.

Three clerics weaved their way around a burning minibus, awaiting the all clear to approach.

The priest waved them over, watching as they made a brief sprint to the side of the MAUV. He leant over to acknowledge the salute from the senior cleric.

The man's appearance blackened and speckled by blood,

appearing not to be his own. The cleric caught his breath before making his report. "We lost Alpha 2-1, Father, and have to report Sister Haywood and the rest of the crew didn't make it. Don't know what hit us, but it was like a shooting gallery, Father."

The priest held up his hand. "Give me something I can use, who hit us, insurgents?"

"Not insurgents, too fast and organised. We weren't able to get weapon locks on them either and their weapons appear high-end tech, energy based."

The priest with scepticism digested the report. "Energy weapons, you're certain?"

"Yes Father, cut through body armour like it was nothing," the senior cleric confirmed.

The priest thought for a moment; the description reminded of an earlier briefing from research and development. They were developing energy weapons for frontline service, but experimental and years off. He also remembered the prototypes took an entire MAUV mount for firing.

A shout of warning brought their attention to the cleric manning the rear weapon system, pointing further down the street. "Target closing, it's using the building ledges for cover." The heavy weapon he operated lifted and thumped into action. Tracer fire raced towards the target, dispensing spent shell cases that clattered through the hatchway to settle around vehicle's interior, smouldering.

Simon strained to see, but thick smoke hindered most of the scene. What he saw was a glint of light keeping tight to the building, almost oblivious to the fire power raining down, for nothing was stopping what was coming for them.

Duel weapon systems of the MAUV erupted with glowing red tracers tracking multiple targets, tearing out both sides of the street. The survivors of Alpha 2-1 took up positions further up the street, whilst the commanding priest adjusted his optics to track movement. The diamond-targeting icon flickered, unable to gain a lock. It was unclear whom or even what was fast approaching their position.

Two blurred shapes raced the building facings, using the ledges as cover.

With the slightest shift of eye, the priest's optics returned to normal view as he needed to trust his own eyes.

The heavy weapons of the MAUV ripped into the buildings, shattering glass in desperation to take down what was stalking them.

"Automatic targeting is none functional and we are at highest elevation for the fifties, permission to go to small arms?" The question shouted from the nearest cleric.

"Permission granted," the priest replied, reaching to retrieve his own MP-92 mounted behind his command chair. On returning, a glimmer of light highlighted the nearest target, leaping the ten feet gaps between ledges. *Impossible, no human could move like that,* he thought. Instinct made for a corrective shift of the weapon's weight, then releasing a silent breath, he squeezed the trigger. The resulting force of the weapon releasing the nine millimetres full-jacketed rounds at a rate of three shots a second was harsh against his shoulder. Every fourth round was a tracer, helping the shooter to adjust their aim, and so the weapon flared again at the still moving target. Even with the inbuilt compressors a mark, four MP-92 dual assault rifle still bruised his shoulder through the heavy padding of his battle armour. In a silent whisper, he recited a small prayer. "By grace of the true God, let my aim be true."

The rounds hit the building through cascading masonry in all directions, but the target leaped with a dancer's grace, to stoop to a crouch on a corner of a ledge. There came a sudden streak of blue accompanied by a cold scream, as a cleric took the hit square to the chest, almost the size of a fist. He turned in shocked reality, inspecting the burnt wound, offering a gurgling groan as blood bubbled the corner of his mouth. Then, with eyes sliding back, his body slumped into the interior of the MAUV.

The surviving crew reacted in shock as the lifeless body fell at their feet, blood pooling the floor as the smell of smouldering flesh filled the compartment.

Simon, with an immediate need to escape, sensed no reason to believe whoever was attacking the convoy would be any friendlier once the shooting stopped. He had no chance to react as an accompanying shot incinerated the helmet and skull of the remaining cleric manning the last weapon system. The man's body convulsed, collapsing inside to the crews' increased horror.

The priest, numbed by the sudden loss, recovered to reclaim his target through his weapon's sights, as his assailant continued a macabre observation high on its vantage point. A quick change of the optics magnification had sight of his assailant, making him pause on noting she was female. Her slim build wore what appeared to be armour like Guard Cleric armour, less restrictive and almost... primitive in design. A throwback to a darker time, in the style of old riveted armour over chain mail, down to the reinforced boots. The whole effect finished by a helmet, and face plate embossed with a gold trim nose guard. Nothing about her explained how she moved with such grace and speed. Just then, as though expecting his intensions, she raised her own weapon. Another peculiar aspect that made no sense, for it appeared as primitive as her armour, a hunting bow.

The priest drew a breath to gather his wits, steadying his aim until pulling the trigger. In a blink of an eye, the target disappeared within a cloud of dust and glass. His helmet optics unable to compensate as critical seconds passed with the need to be certain of a confirmed kill. *No one could have survived that, surly?* In his haste, he had fired a full clip, and now his weapon was empty. With a silent curse he fumbled, the replacement becoming entangled in his webbing, forcing a need to duck back into the MAUV. He reached out. "Extra clip... give me a damn clip, hurry!" he shouted.

Inside, the remaining crew were still cleaning the remnants of the dead clerics from their darkened consoles. The deacon, the first to react, retrieved a clip racked above his console and passed it across to the waiting priest.

With well-trained determination, the priest ejected the empty clip, locking the replacement in one fluid motion before hurrying to regain his target.

Before he could, a tremendous weight dropped onto the roof of the MAUV, which rocked back on its wheels.

The priest with weapon reloaded cautiously pushed through the hatch, greeted by a scene that will haunt him for the rest of his brief life.

Stood before him was an armoured man from head to toe, so close to make out intricate layering of the elaborate plate armour he wore. The edges appeared etched with symbols or writing of an unfamiliar language, and the man stood larger and broader than any Guard Cleric.

Still crouched, the priest in stunned silence watched as the giant appeared to ignore him, as attention went to the weapon at the giant's side. A broadsword of elaborate design and crafted with silver and gold, almost the full length of a man, decorated in the same strange symbols as the wearer's armour. The priest remained hesitate, unable to move, costing him as the armoured giant's attention finally fell on him.

Both men studied each other.

What the priest looked upon was an intricate faceplate, adorned with the morbid expression of a weeping man. The design sent an icy shiver down his spine, his gaze fixed on the solid cold dead eyes behind the crafted faceplate. They offered nothing but insignificance and contempt, almost as though staring upon death itself.

Both men continued in their study, one in fear and the other in disdain.

It was then the priest's arms refused to move, paralysed in fear, but it did not matter.

Scooped from the hatch, the priest clenched in a single

powered grip with minor effort, his insignificant weapon swatted to the side as he floundered. In his struggle, panic set in as lungs burned from squeezed breath as resistance became futile. His last clouding thought was to the grey wings unfurling outwards, followed by a deep beast of a roar as his windpipe crushed and his lifeless body discarded.

Inside the MAUV, the terrified crew, witnessing the death of their priest through the open hatch, now opened fire. It had little impact, as the hollow tipped rounds cascaded from the armoured hide, more an irritation than wounded.

There came another terrifying roar as the armoured giant unsheathed the broadsword, clasped in both hands and thrust through the thick armoured hide of the MAUV as though cutting paper. The blade sliced through electronic circuits and conduits, showering the interior in a violent cascade of sparks. Then in a decisive last thrust it sliced from groin to shoulder the cowering driver, reloading his empty weapon.

The cleric's curdling scream echoed as bullets from his reloaded weapon deflected around the compartment.

Simon and the deacon dived for cover at the far end of the MAUV, rounds continuing to ricochet until everything fell into an eerie silence.

Simon lay still, listening for further danger, but none came. "It's stopped," he remarked.

In the distance came sounds of approaching sirens, signs that reinforcement were on route.

With hesitation Simon peered through the view port but could see nothing but smoke hanging thick from the uncontrolled fires.

The deacon sat back in his seat, obvious shock as he looked about the destroyed interior and the bodies of his dead colleagues. He removed his helmet, sweat matting his cropped hair, as he put his head in his hands. The crew slaughtered in the matter of minutes; the convoy broken and burning.

With a quick search, Simon found a locker retrieving a weapon. Without a second thought loaded a fresh clip, slinging it over a shoulder, his earlier hesitation gone. Then with caution pushed his way out of the nearest hatch, searching for the priest's assailant, only to find he had vanished. Now outside, he took in the devastation, as flames from burning buildings on both sides, mixed with the smouldering remnants of an overturned MAUV. Their situation was dire, so ducking back he offered a hand to the still stunned deacon. "Whoever pulled out the priest could come back, I for one am not staying around to suffer the same fate, are you with me?"

The man blinked before coming to the same conclusion, and so retrieved his helmet and weapon. Whilst remembering to push spare clips into his webbing before accepting the offered hand.

Outside there was a strong odour of burning fuel, plus the danger of a ruptured gas main adding to the surrounding threats.

Simon reeled, covering his face to the sudden stench of burning flesh.

"It's the crew." The deacon nodded to the overturned vehicle. "They had a full crew and cleric complement when hit, they had no chance." He checked his weapon's safety again, expecting further trouble before the day ended.

Simon could but nod, following him off the roof, soon making in the direction the convoy had entered the street.

"Our best chance is getting to the monastery for reinforcements," the deacon offered.

Simon agreed, better to put trust in someone trained under the circumstances.

"Let me check that." The deacon took Simon's weapon, examining it. "You used an MP-92 before today?"

"No, never," Simon answered, taking the weapon back.

"Well, you loaded this weapon like a pro. Had any military experience?"

He shook his head. "I remember very little these days."

The deacon made a grunt of suspicion before taking the lead.

Soon, both men had found their way through the mass of debris, including burnt-out cars littering the entire area. They came across the priest's lifeless body, his helmet-less head turned at a grotesque angle from his shattered body.

Simon felt as if the dead man's open eyes stared out in judgement.

The deacon offered a quiet prayer before continuing, watching the surrounding buildings for any sign of danger until raising a clenched fist to stop and nodded to movement ahead.

Simon crouched, trying to discern why they had stopped.

"Three shadows hunched in an alley about twenty metres away to our left." With a tap of his personal communications linked through his helmet, he tried to confirm their identity. "Alpha 2-2 to any clerics in my location, please respond." Receiving nothing but static, he tried again. "Alpha 2-2…"

A voice shattered the silence. "Alpha 2-2, Alpha 2-1, we are in your location. Do you have a visual on us?" One of the three shadows gave a flash of helmet light.

"We see you, Alpha 2-1." The deacon felt a sudden weight from his shoulders lift in knowing to be joining other Order personnel. But turning to Simon, he noticed he did not share his relief. With a confused frown, he followed Simon's gaze towards the building nearest to the alleyway.

Simon had sensed a presence almost at once and noticed the stalking figure.

The deacon's optics shielded his eyes from the flash of reflecting metal as he countered to the threat, raising his weapon, but Simon gripped his arm.

"Fire that weapon and you give away our own position," he advised.

It was too late. The figure leaped from concealment, silhouetted in twisting free fall, unfurling enormous wings in controlled descent. Shouts of alarm rang out as the winged giant landed in front of the senior cleric who had earlier sent the visual response giving away their position. The giant rose before them, contracting its wings as the terrified clerics had no time to react. The giant was fast, bringing a huge battle mace sweeping upwards with pulsating blue energy emanating from its entire length.

A blow struck the senior cleric in the chest, lifted him off his feet as his dead body disappeared into the smoke-filled street. The remaining clerics reeled backwards.

Simon turned to watch the deacon level his weapon, unleashing a flurry of rounds only ten feet away from his target. The rounds, designed for the greatest impact against any modern body armour at three times the distance, struck the giant's upper body between retracted wings.

The giant reeled in response from the assault, automatic rounds continuing to walk its spine. As it spun, it once again extended its huge wings to their full length in a powerful display of rage.

It proved ineffective as the deacon shouted for help. "By the true God, open fire." The other clerics recovered, adding their own salvos, a last hope to take out the giant.

The combination turned out to irritate it more, stepping forward under the onslaught but somehow still standing.

Simon became a reluctant witness to the extraordinary battle unfolding. Unable to help, consumed by the same strange sensation experienced back at the MAUV. He felt a rush of familiarity to the giant, recognising the fur trimmed armour and helmet, its elaborate design resembling crossed blades.

The brute reeled again as more rounds hit him at point blank range.

Moving into the open, Simon shouted. "Raguel stop!"

The giant spun on Simon, a glare of recognition of its own, before a last roar of defiance as it turned back.

In desperation, the clerics continued to pour round after round into the armoured hide as coloured sparks cascaded in all directions.

As did the deacon pushing forward, keeping his own rate of

fire until empty ammunition clips littered the ground.

Still, the winged giant did not give ground; the effort only appeared to enrage it more.

The cleric's visibility reduced to zero as greying fog swept around them. Without a target, they stopped firing. That same fog becoming electrically charged, swirling around the clerics with a haunting sound as though something parted the air.

Cleric First Class Richards, his life ended as his neck broke on impact from his broken body hitting the road side after being struck by the mace. His colleague, First Class Valcess, her wife and daughter, her last thought, as a sword severed her spine.

The remaining deacon crouched with Simon, cursed as his weapon clicked empty. His last act was to turn in confused response as a bolt of pure energy struck his body, severing his out-stretched arm. With eyes wide, Second Class Deacon Davenport died, his body slumping to the floor.

Simon looked at the slain body of the deacon before attention passed to the armoured man stood before him.

The newcomer carried an air of authority as he strode forward. At his side, griped in a gloved hand, was a blade of brilliant white gold steel.

Simon noted the etched intricate lettering down its full length, as it emitted the same blue energy seen earlier. His focus moved from blade to the unfurled wings, retracted with a flurry. A noise of scrapping metal on metal brought his attention to the other armoured assailant, the one he had referred to as Raguel. The giant surviving the onslaught with no obvious injury, its helmeted features could not hide a grin that did not dispel Simon's dread. The macabre grin remained as Raguel rested the bloodstained battle mace over its shoulder.

Simon resembled a mouse trapped between two hungry cats. He knew he could not resist, as he glanced at the weapon still in his hand. It was easy to discard, being virtually useless for the clerics.

No one spoke, the group waiting, watching in equal curiosity.

Simon licked dried lips, breaking the silence. "Raguel, that's your name?"

The giant nodded.

A sudden crash made all those present turn to the latest arrival, crouched on the bonnet of a parked car. Her bow gripped in one hand, a sideways glance of interest at the dead man at Simon's feet.

Simon surmised she must have killed the clerics earlier and took a step back, hoping to keep an equal distance between all three.

The group made no further movement towards him or appeared hostile. The female of the three greeted Raguel, both exchanging curt nods before their attention returned to Simon.

"Raphael," Simon asked.

She gave a slight bow.

A sudden, violent and vivid flood of images forced Simon to stumble forwards as though a dam had broken; names, faces, and places to the front of his mind. "I remember others too," he said through gritted teeth, forced to his knees, clutching the side of his head, struggling with the sudden intense pain. His senses overloading with the rush of a fraught mind, trying to control his body as he stumbled and darkness overtook him.

CHAPTER EIGHT

God's Fury

Helen Zimmerman was a successful lawyer, ambitious, motivated and had earned the associate position with the Commercial Acquisitions Division, a subdivision of the Order of Light. Her days long, relishing the pressure, excelling in the challenge it gave. She was at the top of her field, and the money was fantastic. In fact, the pay gave her a lifestyle she had only dreamt of back home in Georgia, where she had shared a small trailer home with her teacher parents. They had become products of the civil authority collapse, losing their jobs after the state streamlined, and then closed the state education system. With no money, the bank foreclosed on their comfortable suburban lifestyle, forcing a transfer to the dilapidated single bed trailer, but they had continued to make the best of it. It also meant Helen was home schooled until congress signed the Reformation Act into law. The act allowed the Order to become the primary investor in the country's reopening education system. To invest in fresh minds of the future as the clerics recited at each assembly. They also influenced building a streamlined system, unburdened by bureaucracy and federal red tape. It emphasised a change in education in New America, focusing on learning for a better tomorrow.

Helen was one of the first graduates from the Order funded high school. She left achieving grades in the top three percent in her last year and then awarded with a prominent opportunity to join the Order's scholarship program. Leading to a move to New Eden to continue her studies and take up a graduate position in the Young Business of Excellence program. The first year set her up with a chance to meet with Mike Zimmerman, a graduate on the same program, the chemistry instantaneous, and a relationship blossomed. The following years after graduating included a move from the small apartment they shared. To take residency in a luxury three bedroom townhouse in Paradise Valley Estates, welcoming the first of two beautiful children. Life could not get any better. But that had been five years ago. Helen caressed the family photograph enclosed behind the window pocket of her purse. She gave a strained smile to the brief reflection of a happier time, a temporary reprieve from the growing issues turning her life for the worse of late. Those same issues formed a strain within her family and the perfect world she thought her life had become. It had started a few months ago, resulting in visits to various doctors about her sleep apnoea issues. There shared diagnosis was stress related to her demanding job. Advised a change to her working life style, not taking on too many cases and maybe cutting back her hours. She followed the recommendations, but sleepless nights still plagued her. Too frightening real and increasing her stress level each day. Any medication prescribed did not help and now she was having physical symptoms, awaking screaming and drenched in sweat, restrained by Mike as she lashed out. Her expression darkened with the memories, fearing the dark dreams and disturbing visions whenever she closed her eyes. If she did not regain control, these dreams would tear her apart. A slew of therapists had her discussing her issues and thoughts with her husband so he could understand what she was dealing with, but it proved futile. He tried to understand, but could never comprehend her suffering. He soon became frustrated in not able to help and worried she was harming herself. Whilst at the same time how it affected the children growing warier of their mother with her actions. Helen was awash with guilt, remembering their strained expressions, like a stab to the heart. She knew she had to fight to get better, to beat her demons. It all came to dreams, one worse than the others, and the thought bringing a bitter chill in remembrance. The dream started with her walking barefoot upon a deserted street. With each step tall grey washed structures thrust upwards on either side of the cobbled road, to cast foreboding shadows as they rose above her. There was nothing familiar about the scene, until recognising the white walled complex of the Monastery of Light, shrouded in a darkening sky of violent reds. More horrifying were the flames engulfing the tall towers of glass and metal, and plumes of thick smoke billowed skyward. The entire landscape erupting in violent flames as Helen ran forward in panic on hearing the shouts of those still trapped.

Others lucky enough to escape stumbled past, struggling over the fallen as they pushed on in panic as the firestorm intensified.

A sudden lash of heat made Helen reel back, her skin blistered red as she raised her arms in protection. As the air filled with smoke, chocking her as she fought for breath.

All around her crowds of survivors continued to flood past, clothes and skin burned alike to peel away in their haste to escape. Then from the walled structure came a sound of crashing stone and screams of tortured metal.

Helen hesitated, uncertain to what to do next, becoming caught in the crowds pushing back. The cries of the suffering, still trapped, tore at her, so desperate she was to help. She fought the need to scream, frustrated tears flowing as she watched the destruction unfold around her.

Another crash from inside as a glass-domed roof buckled, falling inwards, followed by an external wall cracking from the heat. From the depths of the flames appeared an ominous shadow, unfurling within the chaos and devastation. The shadow appeared unhindered by the arching flames, forcing through gaps in the splintered structure to gasps of internal pressure.

Helen could but stay mesmerised, as the shadow emerged

from within the crumbling structure. Growing in mass to take the shape of a man, shrouded in white robes as the inferno continued to lash around him. In horror, Helen recognised the frail features of Cardinal Ambrozij.

His eyes as red as the flames, frail hands stretching claw like as survivors struggled from his grip.

This time Helen screamed, dropping to her knees, witnessing a river of blood cascade down the street over taking her, choking her breath. She held on, nails biting into the cobbles until drenched. Her rest short lived as the screams of thousands of lost souls overwhelmed her, fighting to block them out. She pushed through blurred sight to see the cardinal's face distort, racked with anger and ending her nightmare with the sound of her own internal screams.

Helen pushed out a hand to steady her balance, detecting cold sweat race down her back as she gasped. The vivid and disturbing images faded as she rubbed at her temple to ease the pain overcoming the tiredness. *No wonder I can't sleep,* she considered.

Mike had recommended further professional counselling and had booked her in with the Order's in-house counsellor, a sympathetic female cleric offering spiritual and conventional medical guidance. During the first appointments, she sat in the comforting, inviting office to share the details in hope she would find answers.

The cleric sat scribbling her notes, ready to explain perhaps the violent nature represented by the pressures of her job, underlining a fear of failure plaguing her from childhood. The Order was her career so, unable to cope with the demands of the job; she was destroying what she had built.

Helen listened to the plausible explanations, considering the same conclusion. The next few weeks she continued her appointments with the cleric who brought a remarkable change in her. She no longer feared her limitations, understanding her issue was her own pressure to achieve. The cleric introduced calming techniques to help whenever she thought she was relapsing. Those same techniques included mild medication, resulting in the past few nights passing without incident. She was feeling like her old self and looked forward to reconnecting with the family to enjoy quality time together again. It was then her smile wavered to an anguish of guilt, guilt to keeping secrets, unable to admit everything during her treatment. There were details too revealing, maybe fracturing her relationships further, a risk she was not confident in taking. She kept the secret of a particular dream that stood out from the rest, not sharing the nightmare-filled themes. Helen flushed with embarrassment at the thought. An expectant arousal, a primal urge within making her chew her lip in anticipation as her mind returned to a scene of a small apartment. The evening light filtered through the curtained windows as she observed her surroundings. She found herself sat cross-legged on the floor opposite a chest of draws. On it stood a faded cream narrow lamp, its dim light shadowing the room's dated furnishings. Then rising to her feet, she moved to a double bed to lounge in lazy anticipation. A quickened pulse making her breathing increase, the hairs of her neck bristled from the tingle of electricity coursing through her body. She smoothed out the textured black lace trimmed slip, clinging to extenuate her slim tanned figure. Wishing to appear presentable for whoever emerged from the shower still running. The bathroom door closed to muffle the sounds of running water, which now stopped. There came a precursor to movement appearing under the door, making Helen's fluttering sensation intensify. Opposite, stood a full-length mirror and slipping from the bed, she straightened the soft fabric of her slip again to stand at the mirror. In the softened light she stood in half shadow, aghast to see a stranger staring back. Her mimicking posture included the same shocked expression. With hesitation Helen traced the features of the unfamiliar face, beautiful exotic features framed by long straight hair sweeping her shoulders. The stranger in the mirror appeared petite and slim, no visual sign of two children and many failed diets.

A pang of jealousy surfaced as she pushed her hands down the curvature of the body that was not her own.

Then a noise brought attention to the bathroom, the room's light extinguished.

She rushed barefoot to the bed, her breathing stressed but not from panic as her pulse quickened.

The door opened to show a man whose sculpted midriff gave way to a towel covering his modesty.

Helen traced every part of the man's glistening body. Meanwhile, an urge of familiarity stirred as her lustful glance rested on the man's smouldering smile. That same smile filled her with electricity, making her body tingle as he drew closer. Their eyes met, Helen became lost in the blue pools of his eyes, sharing lustful intent as she moved back on the bed. The blue-eyed stranger pushed forward until their lips were inches apart. Helen, awaiting the impending kiss, opened her eyes to witness the stranger arch his back to unfurl large speckled white grey wings. Birdlike in appearance, they extended to their full-length with a shudder. She remained captivated and unperturbed. Uncurling, she slipped a hand around the stranger's waist, feeling the soft feathers between her fingers. Both fell into an embracing kiss as the giant wings entwined them both.

"Simon," Helen gasped as the lift doors chimed, pulling her back to reality. The doors had opened on to the parking level as she struggled to regain her composure, face flushed from the experience. A final push through her fringe, as she hurried to the waiting car whose electronic flash showed it had unlocked. On opening the drivers' side she threw her handbag, briefcase and spare jacket onto the passenger seat. Then manoeuvring in to the driver's seat, she took a deep breath to grip the steering wheel and start the engine.

The radio made her jump as it played the local monastery channel she listened to during the morning drive in to work. A talk show was breaking to the half hour news bulletin announcing grid locked traffic.

"Emergency services have the entire area blocked off with fear of further explosions of a potential gas explosion earlier today. They have taken civilians injuries to local emergency centres, and we await further updates." The news report continued, but Helen had heard enough. "Radio off, please."

The radio complied.

"Navigation, quickest route home, please."

"One moment," came the soulless response from the car's internal system. A street map appeared on the bottom corner of the windscreen, loading an alternative route as she placed the car in reverse.

It was not long before Helen pulled up at the security gate of the private parking garage. She fumbled for her security pass from the discarded handbag on the passenger side, swiping the ID to lift the barrier.

"Thank you, Mrs Zimmerman, have an enjoyable weekend." The Guard Cleric operating the security position smiled as she passed.

"And you too, Paul. Good night." With a last wave, she turned into passing traffic and was on her way via the alternate route chosen.

Thirty minutes into the journey and it was clear the route was well out of the business district, heading into the less savoury area of the old town. As a result, unfamiliar boarded-up shops and dilapidated high-rise businesses streamed past, but Helen stuck to the route, having faith in the latest state of art navigation system. The traffic ahead thinned, relieved to be missing the holdups caused by the emergency in the city. She was soon crossing the over pass, glancing at the grid locked lanes of traffic below, frantic to get in and out of the city.

There was a small chime as her mobile re-docked to the car's hands free programme in the dash. "Play messages."

A brief search for unread messages resulted in none pending, due no doubt to the lack of cell coverage she was experiencing, so she switched off the message display. Her navigator instructed her to take another left. Complying as instructed, still not recognising the area or finding any familiar landmarks showing where she was since leaving the freeway. It was another few miles and a further instruction to turn. Her patience had grown thin, so pulling over, she stopped. The navigation system expressed a need to continue forward to what appeared to be a dead end.

With a heavy sigh, Helen sat facing the loading bay compound of a closed down factory. A silent curse for her reliance on obviously useless technology still requesting, she continued two hundred yards ahead. A quick slap at the controls on the wheel forced the device into silence. In the meantime, Helen retrieved her phone from the cradle, hoping for a signal, but the display flashed no service. A desperate search of the immediate area showed there were no public text booths and needed to tell Mike she would be late.

The closest rows of shops remained boarded or rundown, so she checked her phone again, with the same result. With a shake of head, she chastised herself for taking an unfamiliar route. "Well done, Helen, you're lost." With a subconscious bite of lip, she put the car into reverse, wanting to retrace her journey. The motor whined as she turned to make certain the way was clear before reversing. A sudden thump under the back wheel resulted in colourful expletive as she braked and checked all mirrors. "Please, not a dog," she repeated. With an exasperated breath, she unhooked the seat belt before making her way to behind the car. She peered around the bumper for evidence of what she may have hit, but found nothing.

The street appeared deserted but for an occasional vehicle speeding past the road junction, past the intermittent neon sign of the closed cyber cafe. An eerie silence fell on the street, nothing but the gentle chime of the door alarm echoing.

An unusual sense of an icy chill urged her to head to the safety of the car and to lock her doors. Once again taking solace behind the wheel, she tried to shake the rising fear, and felt her nerves become calmer. She started the engine, leaving it running. Her glance went to the rear-view mirror, a last check, and that was when she screamed.

The sun had set behind the horizon as Simon's eyes opened, flinching at the violent red tint expanding skyward. All in stark contrast to the chilling air sending a shiver down his body. Everything an instant struggle, including breathing as he pushed to his feet to find his bearings from the city stretching out below him. At first, hard to recognise any landmarks, the effort forcing the need to shield eyes in fighting waves of nausea in a battle to stay upright. His senses opened to overwhelming white light as jumbled memories flooded back. Fingers pressed against his temples, massaging the thumping strain persisting to shut down his body, forcing concentration from pain management to once again finding his location.

Off in the distance loomed the prominent floodlit towers and glass domed rooftops of the Monastery of Light.

The recognition brought a wash of relief to still being in the city, a relief not to last as a brutal wave of nausea threatened to make him pass out. Suddenly losing his balance, he tumbled forward, bracing his fall against a high mesh fence that appeared to circle an unfinished rooftop. Every muscle protested as he clawed his way back onto his feet, yearning for the safety of the one place that had become his home. The refuge and its distinct flat white roof came into view, bringing on a rush of emotion. Simon's eyes welled on reaching his breaking point, sliding to the floor to stay crouched as time passed in silent fatigued thought. Then, with reluctant eyes opening, he forced a racked body to stand, making hesitant steps to see an obvious construction site, confirming his earlier suspicions to his location.

On both sides of the rooftop rose the gleaming sister constructions of the Reformation Towers, their skeletal frames etched against a darkening sky.

Still unhelpful in explaining how he had ended up here.

"You're safe, as no harm will befall you. You have my word."

A shape separated from the shadows. The tall stranger carried a demeanour commanding authority and fear whilst clad in intricate armour.

"Forgive me if I don't take your word, especially after watching you lay waste to an entire armoured convoy." Simon commentated, recognising the decorated armour and crafted broadsword, hung against the stranger's hip.

The stranger removed his ornate helmet, uncovering short black hair matted with sweat to frame the expressionless features, cold and unwelcoming and including dark filled eyes scrutinising Simon's dishevelled appearance.

Neither spoke as though in silent truce as they watched each other with suspicion.

Simon noticed a flick of irritation as the stranger gripped the hilt of the sword. "Perhaps you think me the threat here." Simon nodded towards the broadsword.

The stranger released his grip, attempting a less threatening posture.

Simon frowned, fighting through an increasing nausea. "It's making sense, all of what's happened, as though a veil has lifted to fill my mind with a knowledge of times and places... names." His mind raced, searching for the details. "Your name is... Michael, and you are a... archangel."

The slightest of bows confirmed the revelation, including a look implying a smile would hurt his face. "Hello brother, welcome from your forced slumber."

Simon kept his distance, stressed with the implausible situation as he struggled with his sanity to what was true.

"Don't fight the process," Michael offered. "Let the memories realign until regaining your true self. Remember, your human side has limitations as the transitioning can be painful for minds so... primitive."

Simon gave a forced smile. "Thanks for the reminder." His expression pained as further details flashed to the front of his mind. "It's coming back," he offered. "But what I'm remembering cannot be true and yet..." He rested his head against the fence, eyes closed, navigating memories of a lost life. For the first time since his accident, Simon felt clarity, able to concentrate on long-forgotten memories, offering answers to questions absent since his first wakening. He felt back in control, tentatively pushing at the fringes of his returned mind, frowning at certain parts remained clouded, fragmented, refusing to return regardless how hard he tried. The ordeal fuelled a growing suspicion as he returned Michael's glance. "Strange you've neglected to return the reasons for my punishment."

"We give you back only that deemed necessary and critical, nothing more. The rest complicates the task ahead."

"Tell the truth, Michael?" Simon found strength to stand and face the archangel. "You're hiding something, why else neglect the reason for my banishment or for the fact you're here after centuries of isolation."

Michael's attention went to view the city. "Our need is urgent, and under the circumstances we found it necessary to speed your recovery."

"You say we but you mean you Michael..." A thin smile broke out across Simon's face now understanding. "That's brave of you, not obeying His every word, since only Father can grant absolution for a fall from grace."

Michael turned, eyes narrowing towards Simon's glare. "You're far from absolution, Simon especially for what you did, but in war things change. We do what we have to do as Father has become... preoccupied of late, so responsibility falls on the garrison to continue the fight."

"Things must be desperate if you don't see the consequences to being seen, let alone laying waste to the convoy in broad daylight. Don't you know what knowledge of your existence would do, especially getting out to the masses?"

"As mentioned, needs must for waiting any longer risks us losing our advantage and to lose means consequences changing the balance for both sides. That is why it's necessary you fulfil your quest. Besides, we break no rules as long as the conditions for your banishment stay denied until atoned. Let me worry about repercussions." Michael approached, placing a gloved hand upon Simon's shoulder, making him tense. "You are still a battle brother, an angel of the Legion, and so we return the knowledge needed."

Simon shrugged away, stepping back. "You're making little sense, Father sent me back Grigori, an abomination in angelic and demon eyes, neither human nor angel. Your very hand Michael clipped my wings if I remember, so what reason could you have to come to seek a banished half-breed left stranded here?"

"Because of your uniqueness, Father found it important you kept the strengths of the celestial being you once were. He also endowed you with the compassion of humanity, something lacking as archangels, especially free will."

"And the two scars on my back. What reason are they but a reminder to what I have lost?"

With a flicker of apprehension, Michael responded. "The truth is the powers stripped your wings as a reminder of your fall, including penance to live amongst His children of which you grew so fond. Fate has many challenges ahead until deeming you worthy to transcend back to our ranks."

Simon flinched, unable to hide the betrayal in his voice. "That's bollocks," he cursed. "That's what Father Peters would say, bollocks."

Michael drew in a slow, steady breath to the insubordinate tone, checking his own building anger.

"The truth is I'm your last resort Michael. No cosmic enlightenment or your destiny crap. I'm expendable in your war and being a half-breed I'm not seen as influencing either side as freewill chooses what I do. Isn't that the truth?"

Michael's jaw tightened, seeing no reason to continue the delicate pleasantries as his expression darkened. "Correct, in the eyes of the Celestial Temple, you are an abomination. Unworthy to be in our presence but you have freewill, unique to Father's favourite creations. And yes, that makes you a weapon I can use as I see fit. But remember Simon to choose your next words and actions carefully. For they will not save you or the lives of your friends if you decide against the greater good in this ongoing war."

"What greater good would that be? You told me nothing, and why is what I choose so damn important?" Simon shouted, throwing hands in the air. "You're as frustrating as D, all riddles and no answers."

Michael's wings quivered in impatience, resulting in the archangel striding away.

That left Simon to return to the floor, placing his back against the chain fence, shaking his head as he struggled to understand the chaos his mind had become. Eventually he took a deep breath. "Why are you here, Michael, why today?"

"We deemed it necessary to extract you from your predicament with those calling themselves the Order as they hinder our plans."

"That makes little sense, isn't the Order here for Father's bidding, in His name?"

"It's complicated, for humanity for generations misinterpreted Father's message. A message twisted and manipulated for those in power, exaggerating to something that no longer envisages the true meaning." Michael pointed towards the monastery where floodlit beams lit the darkening sky. "Father never required his creations worship him as a deity. This world is an experiment to allow free will to develop like any other organism scattered upon the surface. As long as they lived by the values he set. He never intended to have built monstrous buildings in his honour or appoint religious representatives over the common masses. His wish was for them to be free, think for themselves. Instead, those who say to speak in His name live off the masse's faith in Him. To amass wealth and influence leading to corruption and greed, where evil festers and manipulates."

"You're talking about human civilisation over the past two thousand years."

"Time is irrelevant, as Father made everyone and everything equal. He wanted them to tend the land, live their lives in peace. But many grew jealous and desired what their neighbour had built, fuelling a growing hunger to amass lands and wealth, a vicious cycle going on to this day." Michael gestured to the open city, emphasising with open arms. "They build affluent and extravagant constructions so to show how much they love Him. Not unlike a spoilt child craving attention from an absent parent." Michael returned Simon's stare, noting a mask of sorrow as he continued to explain. "There is a darkness stirring, waiting since before this world was still a boiling mass of gas and rock. An evil as old as Father, and this causes great apprehension for our future and consequences for both sides."

Simon made his way over to Michael, both watching the city.

"So you're here to stop this rising darkness," Simon asked.

"It's the greatest threat ever faced. Your quest is one of a much larger conflict, and failing has the potential to destroy everything you hold dear. That is why we return, for together we must purge this evil from the earth by any means necessary. The threat is that great."

"So what are you saying? We either purge this evil or you are to judge humanity corrupt, and then what, wipe out and start again?"

The archangel considered the question before answering. "Yes."

Simon struggled to believe what he was hearing, shocked to the emotionless response from the archangel. "You're talking Armageddon, the day of reckoning." Simon walked away. "I was happier not knowing, and now I find Father has allowed the Legion loose on the world?"

"It's the ultimate solution, win the coming battles and turn the tide is the only way to allow humanity continue unaware," Michael continued.

Simon felt a rush of nausea, fighting a sudden urge to retch before composing himself. "What is this darkness you speak of, and why has it got you so sacred?"

"The returning evil has no name, scripture calls them pure bloods. This one returns from old times, waiting for over a millennium in the shadows, to plan and manipulate the weak willing to embrace it."

"So it's a demon, you're talking demons," Simon said.

"Demons are creations from the original pure bloods, tainted energy needing a vessel to walk the earth just like ourselves. But unlike angels who seek permission to coexist with our vessels, guarding the soul until our mission is complete. Demons devour the host's soul, interning it to an eternity of torment before eventually burning out the vessel."

Simon rubbed his chest, imagining the soul within his own body.

Michael noticed his apprehension. "Your host's soul ascended many years past, I can assure you."

"Don't make it right or comforting to take someone else's body for a joyride to do Gods bidding."

"That's your human side's emotional response and unique quality we find to be a hindrance. Recommend you learn to suppress those feelings." Michael's turned to stride to the centre of the rooftop, looking skyward. "Raphael, Raguel come join us," he commanded.

A sudden rush of huge beating wings signalled the approaching archangels, descending to greet them.

"You should thank Raphael for she helped return your memories and stopped your weak brain leaking around your feet."

Simon, hesitant of the newcomers, acknowledged his gratitude with a nod. The larger of the two, he recognised from earlier, who had attacked the sheltering clerics. The smaller of the archangels removed her helmet, offering a curious smile and none of the brutish posturing of the others. Her delicate features framed by shoulder length hair and shared Michael's black eyes, but none of the arrogance. Just curious scrutiny as she continued to watch him.

270

Then Michael stirred, bringing attention back to him. "Time is brief with much to discuss. Do you understand what we need from you?"

"No," Simon answered. "I understand nothing at the moment, but I'm a quick learner."

"What was the reason they gave for being held by the Order?" Michael asked.

"Nothing, they were as clear as you about answering questions."

Michael gave a reluctant grunt. "They know not of your true existence or your quest here?"

"They didn't get a chance, your assault saw to that, and the fewer finding out the better, no point innocents getting hurt in the crossfire, okay?"

"Agreed," Michael nodded.

Simon offered a pained look, rubbing at his forehead as he remembered an earlier altercation. "But we might have a problem though." Attention returned to the archangels before continuing. "The one called Lilith knows something, the way she acted and the fact she called me a half-breed back at the Fire Pitt Club."

Michael glanced at the others, nodding in silent agreement. "We know of Lilith and her kind. They are the demons we spoke of, a stout adversary in the ongoing war. She has taken many in battle, but my concern is who she serves."

"D mentioned this character called Lewie," Simon confirmed.

"A more common name would be his celestial one, Lucifer."

Simon hesitated. "Wait, Lewie is Lucifer. The biggest gang boss in the city is the devil?"

"There is not a human vessel strong enough to host the full essence of Lucifer, so he spends time between realms, here and his own dominion. That is where Lilith as his minion completes his day-to-day bidding."

"So, let me get this straight, having her knowing who or what I am is bad, yes?" Simon asked.

Raphael answered his question. "There is a significant bounty for an angel fallen. Most hunted and slain on sight or taken to Lucifer himself were the outcome is unpleasant."

Simon swallowed, finding his throat dry. "So where does that leave us?"

The others remained silent to the question as Simon glanced between them. "Oh great, he's me thinking this day couldn't get any worse."

"Malach," Michael shouted.

Not far away a black shimmer appeared, taking the form of a man whose attention went around the waiting group. D offered a silent curse of recognition to the looming Raguel, flinching as he saw Michael. He continued to back off, palms out as he tried to keep his distance. "Michael, how good to see you," he half smiled, not his usual confident self.

Michael stood, arms folded.

"Raguel, I see you're still working out, bro." A deep growl emanated from the glaring archangel as D continued to scuttle backwards. "Dear old Raph, looking beautiful as ever."

"Enough of your pathetic pleasantries," Michael ordered, closing the scant distance to grip D by the collar and pulling him over to the group.

Stood at the back, Simon stemmed sudden laughter. "This all makes total sense now, the name on the business card, Malach D HaMavet, the Angel of Death."

D offered a thin smile, shrugging from Michael's grip.

"No wonder you are the boss of undertakers." Simon fought to get his laughter under control until a stab of pain from his unhealed injuries made him regret getting carried away.

With a flash of defiance at the demeaning comment, D adjusted his designer tie. "I'm CEO of one of the biggest multinational corporations, over one hundred and twenty thousand employees worldwide, and if you don't mind a little respect, thank you."

"You're supposed to be helping Simon to achieve redemption," Michael snapped, needing to keep order to the conversation and stopping further interruptions.

"Hard to do when the damn rules refuse to allow me even mention his earlier life. Add the fact the powers send the kid back messed up, memory all over the place and…"

"Wait, is that why you pushed me off the roof?" interrupted Simon, facing off to D.

D half laughed. "Not quite, had to be sure you're not another unlucky reject off the street, suffering the fall to earth in a flaming fireball of light issues. The big guy enjoys going old school, so no email or twitter bio with a picture attached on the poor sap he had chosen. No, I had to find out myself." His trademark smile again as D tried to defuse the tension, but received a look of disapproval from all those present.

Simon's eyes narrowed, stemming a growing anger, aimed at the complacent D. "How about I throw you off this building, see if you are who you say you are." As Simon approached, D cowered away.

"Enough of this bickering," Michael interrupted. "We are here for the Blade of Light and we must retrieve it before they realise its power."

D and Simon shared a glance, then back to Michael.

"Never heard of it," Simon confessed.

D shrugged, too.

"Simon has his orders to seek this blade, taken from safe-keeping as the ambition of man once gain uncovers its hiding place. We cannot stress how important it's returned to the Celestial Temple. We fear it's in the hands of someone who knows its true potential with ambition to shift the balance on this pitiful planet."

"The Vatican bombing," D answered with a click of fingers, turning to a confused Simon. "After the bombing, there was total chaos in the city. Law and order gone, people got rich by plundering the massive vaults the bombing had uncovered."

"Why did the church have it?" Simon asked.

"The story starts with having to understand faith in religion has declined for decades. With mass defections of followers turning to the Order, scandals and lawsuits had hit the church hard over the last few decades. Then the economic crash wiped billions of their investments overnight, and so they faced bankruptcy. Then in twenty-two the bombing killed over four thousand people." D paced, continuing his explanation. "One of our busiest days as I remember, I can tell you, we were crossing names off left…"

"Malach," interrupted Michael as his tolerance became tested at D's long-winded explanation.

"Huh, okay. Sorry, where was I? So following the destruction and civil breakdown of authority meant looters uncovered vast vaults. They pillaged a wealth of items and I'm betting your Sword of Light was one of those items being stored there."

"Blade, not a sword but a blade," Michael corrected.

"Okay, whatever," D waving off the comment with a roll of eyes, before cleaning the top of a cooling vent with his handkerchief and getting comfortable. "Those treasures heralded from before the crusades and even the dawn of Christianity itself. Most wouldn't understand its value, just ending up on the international markets. Museums and private buyers of less respective scruples bought up many items in their droves."

"You're one of them, aren't you?" Simon asked with a suspicious glare.

"I might have a few delicate pieces that sit in my private collection." He answered, finding something of interest in his fingernail. "What's the point of having money if you don't spend it?"

Simon could not help laugh at D's candidness to any situation. "Here I am on top a high-rise, finding out I'm a fallen angel, suffering penance back on earth by God himself. Who has sent an archangel to order me to find a mystical blade, lost no one knows where? Whilst this goes on, I'm given history lessons by Death himself. Who unlike scripture wears two thousand new dollar handmade suits and drives around in a limousine carrying lists of the soon departed on a damn secpad." Everyone watched Simon, trying to control himself again at the surreal moment. Finally getting control, he offered an opened hand in apology. "I'm sorry, so what is this Blade of Light? Same as a Knife, big, small, and why are you guys so willing to wipe out an entire city to get it?"

Michael answered. "It's a weapon, proving fatal to angel or demon alike by those who wheel it."

"I just saw you take the full power of modern weaponry. How does a blade hurt you, never mind kill you?" Simon asked.

"They forged the blade in the Celestial Temple, blessed with the power of our Father to smite his enemies and carried by one of our highest brothers in battle. Becoming lost until found four hundred years ago, at the time its significance was unknown. Revered as an artefact of importance by the church and placed in their safekeeping. That was until recent developments unearthed it again." Michael paused, emphasising the importance. "As you know, both sides have need of a human vessel, when a vessel becomes damaged or is dying. The entity can leave to return to their original sanctuaries and realms. With the blade forged with the essence of our Father, it means it can bring death to that entity and its host, even threatening an archangel. The threat of just owning the blade could change the balance of power on earth if wielded by the wrong side."

"You think a demon has the blade?" Simon asked.

"Demon or human, it matters not, each potential threat to our brothers," Michael continued.

"Make more blades, wouldn't have more keep the balance, surly," D offered.

An air of nervousness circulated between Michael and the other archangels before Michael answered. "To forge more of these blades would need Father's power to grant his blessing," he frowned. "That is impossible now."

Confused, Simon looked at D for clarity, but he shared the same confusion.

"Can't you ask him, I mean Michael, you are his right hand?" Simon queried.

The archangel appeared hesitant to answer. "God has been absent at the Celestial Temple, for he has grown disillusioned with humanity."

Silence descended over the group.

"How do you do his bidding without speaking to him?" Simon continued.

"Communication is through the Ophanim when he so wishes."

"That's great. When needed most, he goes off in a sulk because the kids are misbehaving." Simon ignored Michael's obviously scornful glare. With a sigh, he tried to stay on topic. "Any ideas as to finding this blade, lost and found, or advert in the papers, perhaps?"

With another click of fingers, D interrupted. "That's what we can do."

"No serious D, it was a joke."

"Listen, I put out feelers with my contacts in the rare artefact circles and say I'm in the market for a blade or weapon of sorts."

Michael stirred, stretching giant wings, thinking over the proposal.

"It might work better than just tearing the city apart," D offered.

"Make it so," agreed Michael.

Raguel grinned at the mention of levelling the city, resulting in a nudge from Raphael.

D headed for a quieter part of the roof, tapping away at his device for information about the blade.

At a loss, Simon's thoughts returned to more questions. "Tell me why the powers brought back after stripping my wings."

Michael scowled, remaining silent.

"I've had visions, dreams of another life. Including a woman called Carla Simmons."

Michael took a lengthy breath. "Your penance is atoning for your wrongdoings, completing this quest will go towards that atonement. Allowing knowledge of the other details takes you from that path."

"So what, you give me part of my memories, but not those I might consider important."

Just then, Raphael came to Michael's side, watching Simon walk off to be alone.

"Allow him to remember her in part, leave out the details and her connection to his fall."

"Doing so will cloud his judgement to the task ahead," Michael said.

"That may be, but knowing what he had lost may strengthen him. Give him something to fight for," she continued.

"Revenge, you mean."

"Perhaps, but he needs to understand his past, not have his judgement clouded," Raphael continued.

Michael nodded agreement, allowing Raphael to walk over to Simon, kneeling where he sat watching the last of the evening light fading in the night.

"Carla was your charge," the archangel smiled, taking his hand in her own, her touch warming and an instant lift to Simon's sombre mood. "She hid an extraordinary gift, a gift that made her one of the Chosen." Raphael moved closer, placing her forehead against his, both closing their eyes as they shared the same thoughts.

Simon's clouded mind cleared to an image of the face of a dark-haired woman, her smile and laugh intoxicating, as she beckoned him to follow. The entire time, the archangel's narrated words continued to provoke further lingering images. Opening to a familiar scene, cleansing Simons senses to ones of peace.

The street resembled any other, crowded and nameless

as the people continued their hustle and bustle of everyday lives.

The memory still narrated by Raphael, her calming voice encouraging Simon to concentrate. "Our Father had need of messengers to teach His word to the masses, to give light to the darkness when needed. This power lay dormant within those chosen until called upon to spread that message. The Chosen can foretell the future, making them cherished and in need of protection. That responsibility fell to the Legion, and that Simon was your task, becoming her Watcher, ever vigilant as her charge." Raphael's voice became a guiding tether to Simon's mind. "She loved life," she continued.

The crowded street parted for an adolescent girl, walking between proud parents, lost in the happiness of their attention. She was no older than ten years old, and Simon recognised the warming smile of Carla Simmons as she held both parents' hands. The image invoking sudden emotion until fading to present day as Archangel Michael stood over them. "Your purpose was to safeguard her Simon. A guiding voice throughout her life when needed and shield her from whatever evil would do her harm. You were the voice of wisdom to her purpose, remaining vigilant, as a shadow or insignificant glimmer hidden in the corner of an eye. But you broke the rules of her guardianship, Simon, to keep your distance and never let your charge see your Celestial form." Michael's tone turned hostile. "You showed yourself and made her aware of your presence. From that moment she became vulnerable."

Simon pulled away from Raphael, tears welling as he remembered finding her blood soaked body back in her apartment. He shared in the moment of her death, sensing her soul leave her body. In that moment, the rooftop became chilled, requiring him to pull his coat closer around his shoulders. "Can you show me more," he asked Raphael, a tremble to his voice.

She glanced to Michael, who stood, arms crossed, with an unreadable expression. With silent authority she leant forward, cupping the back of Simon's head with a gloved hand to press foreheads together again.

Once again everything appeared blurred and unfocused, until opening to a sense of falling as Simon opened his mind, transported within a familiar memory of a rain-lashed street. The nearest structures had neon facades straining to penetrate the limited visibility, adding to his concealment. From his hidden position Simon watched the approaching woman battling the downpour in haste.

Carla Simmons, the woman who brought such powerful emotions for Simon as he concentrated, Raphael continuing to narrate the scene, minds entwined.

As the blending of the recovered memory intensified, Simon watched Carla unsuccessfully flag down a cab. All around the rain fell, increasing in strength as she struggled at the kerbside.

Simon remained in the darkness afforded by an adjacent alleyway, unprotected from the elements but unconcerned to his own discomfort. All attention remained on Carla as her presence brought a swell of uncontrolled emotions.

She reached out to flag another passing cab, her short suited jacket and pencil skirt inappropriate for the weather. She appeared drenched, but doing her best to stay concealed under the inadequate umbrella.

Another blacked out cab sped past, ignoring her desperate wave.

Simon continued in vain to suppress the strange growing feelings for his charge. As time passed those same emotions grew stronger, so unfamiliar, he was becoming lost and overwhelmed with every waking moment. For the first time in his existence he sensed insecurity gripping him, almost dare he say... emotional feelings for another person?

The downpour was relentless, blurring approaching lights.

Carla strained to grab attention of another speeding cab. Just then, from the opposite side of the road, another one approached, its sign showing availability. She had had enough and stepped out, navigating the steady stream racing the curb edge, so desperate to gain the drivers' attention. A cruel combination of poor viability, haste, and the wish to be out from the dire weather made her unaware of another approaching cab.

There followed a mixture of treacherous conditions and brief loss of concentration, culminating in the driver not noticing the woman until the last moment.

Carla's reaction was an intake of breath, frozen as she closed her eyes for inevitable impending impact to her desperate error. That was when her world around her slowed, becoming lost to flight, forced within a twisted spin but to her surprise landing on her feet. No pain, only a tightness gripping her upper body in an unexpected embrace. Somewhat dazed, daring to open her rain lashed eyes to a face of concern.

Simon had swept her up and out of danger of the speeding cab, the driver relaying minor concern with a blast of horn as he sped by into the night.

Carla's breathing remained heavy, adrenaline coursing, but regaining her composure. With a last swallow of relief, she raised her head to once again look upon her saviour. She tried to pull away, finding reluctance to relinquish at first before being let go. "Thank you," she offered with a slight frown, curious in the strangers clear blue eyes, forming a sudden chill of familiarity, like they had met in another life.

"Yep, we lost him again," D remarked, rocking Simon out of his dream state. "Come on bro, snap out." He turned back to Michael. "It's no good, we broke him."

Simon pushed D away. "I'm okay," he said, with a rub of face, forcing himself to return from his dazed state. "Things are coming back," he frowned.

D glanced to the others for guidance, remaining statuesque in their posture, offering little aid. So attention returned to Simon with a roll of eyes to his colleague's inability for concern, knowing all too well what awaited Simon now. The memories were returning.

"This girl Carla is the same girl from the murder scene photos and my dreams. I knew her and was there when she died," Simon asked.

Subdued from his usual enthusiastic manner, D answered. "Before I give you any details you have to understand, the Celestial Temple forbids angel and human interaction unless instructed by a higher power. The consequences are too dangerous to imagine, and it's why the powers didn't tolerate your disobedience, and why they recalled you. That left her vulnerable to various parties seeking her gift and leading to her murder. You then disobeyed the powers again to return, but by then it was too late. Sorry, bro."

Simon, unable to suppress his emotions at the revelation, gripped the chain fence, fighting to keep the fleeting remnants of memory before they faded.

Michael interrupted. "There are paths travelled alone, Simon. You have your answers and so live with the consequences." The archangel continued to watch Simon struggle. "We digress from the more pressing mission, the Blade of Light."

Simon bit back his sudden anger, knowing it futile to argue with an archangel who could not comprehend the slightest human emotions. So with reluctance, he pushed past that anger, for now was not the time before offering a nod of agreement. "I will not deviate from the need to search for the blade, but I will get my answers Michael and will find out the truth about Carla's death."

Both faced off through a silent glare.

Then Simon offered out a hand, noting the glimmer of hesitation from the archangel before he nodded, and both clasped each other's wrists in agreement.

Simon understood when he was being lied to, or at least told half-truths. How far could he trust the archangels and D, nothing was certain, for deep down he knew he was being played? What other choice did he have? So he made a silent promise to find answers and focus on his true quest, which was only the beginning, the outcome impossible to foresee.

The last few hours had Lisa content to watch Jake sleep, snuggled on his bed. Affectingly brushing a few strands of hair away from his face as he stirred, absorbed in the rise and fall of the boy's chest as he slept. Ever thankful he could sleep after all that had passed, just relieved to know he was okay. She struggled with her own need to sleep, hard to achieve, trying to ignore the relentless headache, an unpleasant reminder to the injuries she had suffered. With a final watchful gaze, she finally succumbed to the tiredness until a single gunshot pierced the darkness of her mind, startling her from slumber. Her final image lingering of her ex-husband Brian's lifeless body, his blood pooling at her feet, forcing her to question how to tell Jake his father died. The prospect filled her with dread. True, there had been no love lost between them, but still he was Jake's father. Father Peters had advised her to take a few days, come to terms with everything that had happened, but it just gave her more time to remember. As she lay next to Jake's still sleeping, she struggled with unresolved questions, including how had Brian's death affected her? Easy to recognise the usual signs of shock and numbness to such a violent death, but there was a growing guilt. Guilt to being relieved as though a colossal weight lifted with Brian's death, suspecting this relief was the true reason for not sleeping. With a slow rub of tired eyes, she turned on to her back, cautiously removing her numb arm from under her sleeping son.

Jake stirred but remained fast asleep and turned onto his side

Lisa pulled away with need of a warm drink and maybe finding tablets as the painkillers she had taken earlier were wearing off. On exiting Jake's room, the chill of the floor crept into her bare feet as she headed for the kitchen. Fearful in making any sound on the warn flooring at such a late hour, soon descending the stairs and passing through double doors. She crossed to the kettle, flicking a switch to illuminate a small light underneath the extractor. The kettle's contents enough for her need, as she basked in the low light, deep in thought as she waited for the water to boil. A low whistle allowed Lisa to switch off the hob, crossing to the dinner table. She filled the waiting cup. Gentle stirring brought out the aroma of the herbal tea before returning the kettle to the hob.

"Got enough for two?"

The voice startled Lisa, whose nerves already fraught from the past twenty-four hours.

"Sorry lass," Father Peters apologised, pulling over a chair. "I didn't mean to scare you."

"It's fine. You can't sleep either, Father?" she asked, reaching for another cup and spooning out a measure of coffee from a jar.

"Something like that, I've been finishing up on leads of Simon's whereabouts." He rubbed a finger under his glasses against tired eyes before continuing. "The authorities are stone walling, so I have passed the case on to a lawyer friend who owes me a favour, helpful if we need to bail him out too."

"Would it come down to that, Father?" Lisa asked, pushing the coffee cup across the table and sitting opposite the priest.

With a quick smile of thanks, he blew over the contents until taking a tentative sip. "I'm hoping not, but I still don't understand why he's being held, as we are all innocent of any crimes that should account for something."

Lisa shrugged, unable to think straight and becoming lost in the contents of the cup. She suppressed a yawn before cradling her head in one hand, stirring her tea with the other.

"If it was just the club incident, then they would have kept us all for questioning." The priest continued, taking a moment to stretch out the knots in his back. "No, they singled Simon out and the whole situation sounds suspect from the start. My guess is his past has come back to haunt him or worse, he hasn't been honest with us."

"You think he's involved in actual murder like the Order

priest mentioned?" Lisa asked, somewhat taken aback by his explanation.

"Asked me that question yesterday, would have said no. Today I'm not sure." The Father had questioned his own reasoning. "I'm unsure what to believe. Time will tell, so I guess it comes down to trust." He took another sip of coffee and yawned before proceeding to explain his concerns. "We have to trust in finding out the truth." Noticing to getting no response to his explanation, attention went from drink to Lisa, sat slumped and asleep.

Her head cradled against her arm, her own drink untouched.

"Bless you, child," he said with concern for her comfort, retrieving a jacket from the stand by the door. He draped the garment over her shoulders and retrieved his own drink to finish upstairs.

A shattering scream woke Lisa with a jolt, adrenaline racing. Startled eyes scanned the darkened kitchen, searching for the source, but she was alone. *Did I imagine it or was it a dream?* A touch of her cup found the contents cold. Standing, she stretched her knotted back, sensing sweat roll down the curve of her spine as she rubbed sleep from her eyes. She sensed a slight tremor remained in her hand as her heart continued to race. With a frown, she sought to recall the dream that had woken her. The scene fading fast as she fought to hold on to the details. She took a mouthful of lukewarm tea in clearing her dry throat, trying to focus.

The dream had started with finding herself in a darkened room from which limited light uncovered a scene of frightening horror. In the centre stood a long, crude steel table bolted to the floor.

Lisa approached with hesitation to touch the surface, holding the chilling coldness of the room, before focusing her mind on the smallest detail. As she moved about the room, she felt her body to be floating, a disembodied witness to the distinct shape of a woman bound.

The woman's unconscious body lay bare but for her under-wear, sweat and blood drenching her skin from obvious strug-gle to be free. The scene raw and vivid, as parts of the woman's skin lay open and brutalised with strange symbols, making little sense to their meaning. Those same cuts appeared deep and bled into swelling pools around the woman's restrained body.

From the shadows, Lisa noted movement.

A robed figure of a man approached to check his victim's breathing, remaining shallow and weak before continuing to circle the table.

Lisa's subconscious faltered to being a reluctant onlooker to the building apprehension to what was to come. She fought for control, and desperate to push passed a growing fogginess to regulate her own breathing. Lisa took a deep breath, focus-ing with disturbed reluctance to be a voyeur to the cruelty and torture of an unknown woman, unable to intervene.

The robed figure resumed their work, producing from dirt stained robes a faded leather-bound book, opening the stiff-ened pages to chant words of a language unrecognisable.

Lisa's perspective still unable to uncover the identity of the figure and instead focused on the victim. Her brunette hair fell in unkempt clumps around her face, masking any chance of recognition.

The robed figure's own breathing now became heavy to the point to be enjoying their victim's predicament and discom-fort, relishing the power over her. Then gentle traced a gloved finger up the victim's stomach and between her breasts, be-fore parting strands of sweat-soaked hair from her delicate features. Cupping her throat, applying the correct amount of discomfort to force her eyes open in alarm as she struggled for breath.

"Helen," Lisa gasped, forcing her from her dream state and back to the safety of the kitchen. A sudden rush of nausea re-turned as she tried to shift the unnerving fear from what she saw had been real. Her body trembled from experiencing the pain and fear the woman endured. Nervous sweat trickled her back, making her uncomfortable as she ran hands through her hair, wincing from brushing her bruised features. She wished her own injuries had been a dream too. She moved to the washbasin to splash cold, refreshing water across her face. In her mind the remnants of the dream lingered, so brutal, blood soaked and all too vivid and disturbing. The dream increased her vengeful headache as she reached for the tablets from her bag, placing two into her palm before swallowing with the tepid tea.

"Momma!" The tired, filled voice made Lisa turn to the hall doors, finding Jake stood in his pyjamas rubbing sleep-filled eyes as he stumbled to the table.

"What is it, baby? You okay?" Lisa asked, noticing his agitation as she pushed past her own concerns. She crouched to scoop the youngster up in her arms, allowing him to wrap legs around her waist, carrying him to a chair. His head settled on her shoulder. "You're getting too big and heavy for me to carry, you know?"

"I know," he offered, content to cling to her for a moment before pushing away so he could see her face.

Lisa recognised his weariness and let him clamber onto the chair next to her, placing a kiss on his forehead before running a hand through his spiked messy hair.

"I'm okay momma, just couldn't sleep cos the bad dreams," he explained, reaching for the coffee mug. With a curious sniff of the contents, his face twisted at the smell of mint, berries and cinnamon.

His reaction made Lisa chuckle as he pushed away the cup.

"Can I have breakfast, please?" he asked with a weary smile, swinging legs in anticipation.

Lisa returned the smile, not wanting to disappoint by mentioning it was far too early for breakfast until realising the time. "It's after seven thirty," she cursed, late in starting the preparations for breakfast.

Jake giggled as his mother's sudden haste to pull out the

needed cooking pots. All thoughts of her disturbing dream of the mysterious Helen, and her brutal demise temporary forgotten, lost to the start of another normal day.

CHAPTER NINE

Haunting Past

Morning broke to slip between the protruding spirals, making up the Reformation Towers, concluding a macabre evening as Simon stirred from his brief slumber. He rose to witness the warming glow as he pushed from between two heating vents that had offered welcoming warmth during the cold hours. Memories from the earlier nights' revelations returned as he regained his thoughts until sensing to not being alone. Turning, he found the curiously watchful D stood navigating his secpad. "The others returned to the Celestial Temple," he offered.

"What, no goodbye?" Simon rubbed his face, shrugging towards the healthy hint of sarcasm he felt whilst trying to push through the remaining tiredness. "What's with them leaving us here on this damn roof, couldn't they drop us at the refuge?"

"Michael said it was important they returned and left me to answer any further questions."

"Oh, great, that's what I need more riddles," Simon mumbled walking the rooftop.

"Huh! What you say?" D asked, looking up from his device.

Simon waved off the question to continue his search. "Never mind... Guess we walk from here." His search uncovered the stairs and wearily started his descent. "How many floors is this building, anyway?" He asked.

D following, as ever preoccupied with his secpad, frowned. "Well, including the roof one hundred and thirty, give or take." He paused, agreeing with his assessment before continuing after Simon. "With the money spent, you'd have thought it possible to have working lifts."

"Look around D. This place is a shell, we're lucky the lights are working," Simon scowled as D continued to complain for the next four floors, increasing his darkening mood. With a released breath he reflected on one remaining nerve D continuously tormented until the stress and tiredness built to a sudden release of loss of patience. He turned to face D. "You're Death right, the Grim Reaper and taker of souls and all that?"

Taken aback by the sudden confrontation, D gave a forced smile. "No one croaks without my..."

Simon interrupted, raising a hand. "Busy collecting souls requiring guidance to the afterlife and such, save me the sales pitch, I've seen the infomercials. The question I have to ask is, how do you complete this task?"

"Someone as important as me, bro, and CEO of a multinational company, I delegate. We are a twenty-four-hour service, full of care and..."

Simon nodded, interrupting again. "Okay, but what do you do to complete this role?"

"Reapers, like me, go where we're needed. Its poof and we are there. Saves on travel expenses but without the air miles and..."

Simon raised an eyebrow as D considered his answer, soon realising the point Simon was making.

D smiled a brimming smile. "Ooh... I see where you're going with this."

"You're an idiot, D," Simon answered, turning to continue down the next flight of stairs. "You've got so used to being driven around in a limousine, you forget who you are."

"It's a modern time, my friend, luxury is in, you know?" D answered.

Simon ignored him, continuing to the next level.

D put away his secpad and with a final shrug hurried after him.

Nothing could prepare Simon for what happened next as D

placed his hand upon his shoulder. The staircase shimmered and contorted, dissolving into a bright light before Simon could react. Then, in a moment's breath, his vision cleared as they materialised in the dawn light of the refuge rooftop. The disorientation of the intense journey hit him like a freight train to the guts and forcing him to grab the nearest vent for balance as he struggled to stand.

D unaffected retrieved his secpad from his jacket pocket as though nothing had happened.

Simon coughed the contents of his stomach as though frozen from the inside out. "Warn me next time before doing that again."

With a quick reassuring slap on his back, D walked past him. "Sorry bro, what would be the fun in that, forget you're half human. Usually transporting recently departed means no complaints, and wasn't sure how it would affect you, so guess we do now." With a perplexed expression, he pointed to Simon's face. "You appear to have... something icky dripping from the edge of your mouth... there." D walked away, unable to hide the smug smile of satisfaction.

Simon, getting to his feet, wiped the remnants from his mouth with the back of his hand. Then, offering a silent curse, headed for the roof exit leading into the refuge.

"So tell me, out of interest. What are you going to say to your friends?" D asked, taking a leisurely position against the nearest vent. "Last time your friends saw you, the Order were marching you to the rear of a waiting MAUV, on your merry way to being questioned by Inquisitors. There number one suspect in a twenty-year-old murder enquiry."

Simon turned. "Not sure." A look of doubt crossed his face. "I haven't thought about it."

With a sympathetic frown, D watched Simon wrestle with what to do next. "Thought so, but you expect to walk in there all smiles with no genuine explanation. Especially after the last few days raising a few questions to your life before your accident, including your involvement with the Order back at the Fire Pitt. Who no doubt have enough unanswered questions about how you escaped their armoured convoy. You might know yourself, but my guess is telling your friends and hoping they understand isn't the best plan?"

"What do you suggest?" Simon asked.

"How about having an answer for walking into that kitchen without a scratch, for one? The convoy incident will be news by now and plastered over the early morning vids, and it will raise even more suspicion on you."

Simon considered the repercussions, coming to the same conclusions. "So how do I explain the truth without the result being they never trust me again? Hi, guys, by way archangels and demons exist. With Deaths help, we are to complete God's mission. Oh, and I'm a half-breed angel human sent back in service of my penance."

"We all undertake Gods mission by living our lives by His guidance and teachings lad. If you want to earn our trust, my experience is to begin at the start and let us decide." Father Peters had appeared at the door to the roof.

Simon stepped back, embarrassed to answer.

With a stoic stare, the priest peered over the rim of his glasses. "There I was going to my office, when on hearing voices I came to find you two discussing what, may I ask?" His expression remained stern.

Simon had learnt to never underestimate his friend, often keeping an open mind when understanding complex problems regardless of how fanciful they may seem. So taking his advice, he started at the beginning.

For the next hour Father Peters experienced a flurry of emotions, testing the priest's resolve and faith to its limit as he sat listening, eyes wide.

Simon went into detail, explaining how the man they had found near death and in need of help was an angel cast to earth in search of penance. To undertake the fight in a long secret war between good and evil that had raged since the dawn of time. Then there was Carla, a woman chosen to spread the word of God, and how she had been his charge and what his connection was to her violent death.

Taking a moment during a break in the conversation, Father Peters removed his glasses. He blinked tired shocked eyes, a sign to what he was thinking, regardless of how incredible everything sounded. "Let see if I have this right."

Simon looked up to meet the priest's emotion filled gaze.

"You're under instructions from angels of whom you are one, correct?" He pointed to Simon, who gave a weary shrug as a response.

"The others are archangels, the big guns of the Celestial Temple. Simon here is, was, a soldier. Stripped of his wings to face a whole redemption, repent your sins scenario thing," D answered.

Simon placed a hand over the Father's, stopping him frantically to rub the lenses out of the frame of his glasses. He sensed a tremor, understanding the priest was having a hard time with being told the truth.

Father Peter's mouth opened, but no words followed. His emotions continued to swell as his eyes reddened, giving the slightest of nods. "I've given my whole adult life and soul to the church." His voice sounded strained. "I've followed its virtues and teachings, tested many times, even doubting my faith after watching scandal after scandal. Then came the rise of the Order and..." His voice trembled as he took a deep breath.

"Are you okay, Father?" Simon asked, concerned. "I'm asking a lot from you, but you have to believe everything I have told you is the truth."

"It's a lot to process lad, give me time." He stood, returning the spotless glasses to the bridge of his nose, offering an apprehensive smile. "I will take on faith you are who you say you are, and this Blade of Light is as dangerous as your warning." He shook his head. "God had a purpose to send you to us, so how can we not offer help in your time of need."

"Everything I said, doesn't it sound far-fetched and unbelievable?"

"I'd admit lad, yes, but many consider the book I put faith in everyday sounds just as impossible. Now I haven't seen God, but that does not mean I don't sense His presence watching over us. That is my faith, and wavering of late I'd admit." He paused. "But after witnessing the miracle, that was your recovery. Not forgetting an overwhelming need to help you back at the garages to keep you safe. Just hearing your story to what has happened makes sense in part."

Simon's glance flitted between Father Peters and D, sensing relief. "Thank you, Father."

"I have committed myself in God, and so I now put that same faith in your quest if you're willing to let me." He held out his hand, offering it to Simon, who clasped it in his own.

"Think I might cry," D remarked.

"I still owe you a throw off this building, D," Simon remarked.

The smile slipped from D's face as he stood straight, unsure if the threat was real.

The Father raised a thumb towards the nervous D. "You say this guy is Death, the Reaper himself?"

"What were you expecting, a black robe and rattling chains?" D offered somewhat offended before heading towards the exit. "It's the 21st century priest, social media, smart phones, designer suits and Cyber space rules. Sooner you get your arses out of the Dark Ages and that dusty book you hold so dear and embrace the future, the sooner you could rebuild your dwindling flocks." The rest of his passing comment lost as he continued out of earshot and down the stairs.

"Have to say I'm disappointed, lad," Father Peters said.

Simon laughed. "Father, meeting Death is nothing, wait until you meet the archangels."

Father Peters stopped to turn back to Simon, concern etched his face. "Tell no one else, Lisa or Jake, no one. Understand?"

Simon agreed.

"It causes problems for everyone, the fewer people who know the better. Follow me to my office as we have a lot to plan." Both men headed down the stairs, unsure what would happen next.

Later in the morning, the television in the hall continued with rolling coverage of the major gas explosion rocking New Eden and dominated the news circle on all channels. "Fourteen confirmed dead, including ten clerics caught in the first blast," continued the report. "Civil engineers have stated property damage will run into tens of millions..." The screen blurred to a video of burning and damaged vehicles overturned in a devastated street. "Eyewitness reports describe valiant survivors pulled from the damaged buildings, whilst earlier reports of terrorist involvement dismissed by the authorities. They stated secondary explosions were of ammunition carried by Order personnel caught in the first explosion. Because of spreading fires, this has hampered any rescue efforts to reach further injured until the early hours." The screen cut to a live feed of a straight-faced reporter wearing a protective vest and helmet. His attire befitting a front line reporter covering conflicts in Europe rather than a domestic gas explosion in an urban city. The reporter tried to convey the dramatic course of events with the help of an enthusiastic eyewitness stood next to him. The camera panned towards the distant devastation in the street.

"Then whoosh," explained the eye witness, exaggerating his description to events with open arms. "There came this giant fireball in the street's centre, so awesome man."

"Thank you," the reporter answered, nodding with intense interest before pushing the man away and turning back to the camera to finish the live feed. "There you have it, a city in mourning. Our thoughts to those caught in this terrible accident. This is Jason Talbot for MGN News, downtown, New Eden. And back to the studio..."

"Turn it off will you please," the Father asked entering the hall.

Sister Angela operated the remote, blowing into her tissue as the screen switched off. "Oh, those poor, poor people, shocking."

Simon glanced towards the Father, offering the slightest shake of head as they headed for the kitchen.

"What is he doing back?" Sister Angela's tone and remorse evaporated on seeing Simon stood behind the priest. "I thought he was helping the Order in further investigations?"

"He was Sister, they released him early this morning and now it's why I have to talk to you all, please sit."

Her disapproving glare remained as she took a seat at the table.

Father Peters stood, cupping hands behind his back as attention went to the small group, noticing one missing. "Where is Jake?"

"Upstairs Father, do you want me to fetch him?" Lisa answered, untying her piny and draping it over the back of her chair.

"No, that's fine." Father Peters appeared tense, glancing at each present. "I've asked for this meeting because of what has happened these past few days. The stresses and disruptions of being held by the authorities and questioned at length, and we are still unsure why." He paused, judging the mood of the room. Each face shared the same despondency, but no one wanted to interrupt, so he continued. "During the next few weeks, it's important that we stay vigilant. This includes noticing any strangers around the refuge." From the corner of his eye, he caught Sister Angela stir in her chair. With anticipation, he interrupted before she gave her own thoughts. "Hundreds of strangers come through the door every day, Sister, I understand. With that, it's with regret I've been in contact with Father Thompson and Father Conner. They agreed to take in our regulars and cover meal times for the foreseeable future. They will pick up our donation supplies later and anything else you can think they would need. Lisa, if you could arrange that please, I hope we all make this transition as quick as possible."

The Sisters' mouth opened then closed, glaring hostility as her chance to air her own opinion vanished as Father Peters continued.

"It's with deep regret we need to shut the refuge for how long, I'm not sure. I've taken it upon myself to let the volunteers know of my decision. It's for the best until resolving these problems."

"And if they are not?" Sister Angela interrupted.

"That will be my call, Sister, questions?"

Simon uncomfortable during the announcement, as an air of disapproval at his presence descended since entering the kitchen.

Sister Angela sat glaring whilst Lisa refused to return his gaze.

That disapproval increased, as no one said a word until the Father broke the silence, continuing to explain Simon's reappearance. Embellishing the facts to explain what happened after the parking garage, taken for further questioning but released without charge because of the case of mistaken identity.

The mistrust remained, but Simon hoped to get their trust back, eventually.

For now, Father Peters had recommended he did not mention any involvement in the attack on the Order's convoy, using the media cover story of a gas explosion.

Observing those around the table, Father Peters felt satisfied everybody agreed, if a little reluctantly for the need to close the refuge, but understood why.

Even Sister Angela, agitated by the upheaval, agreed and so did Lisa, who felt relieved for a few days off to spend with Jake.

The small group dispersed, allowing Simon to speak to the Father with nobody over hearing. "What is our next step?"

"Not sure lad, giving everyone time off might help so we can plan our next move. I want them out of harm's way if we can."

"How long until the Order comes searching for me again?"

Father Peters shrugged. "Not sure. They still have to shift through the remains to ID bodies, once realising you are not a casualty, the refuge will be the first place they search. That reminds me, whilst you were absent we swept the place and found most of the monitoring devices, but we cannot be certain we got them all."

"I need to leave," Simon offered.

"And go where? You have nowhere else to go, lad. No, not yet. We wait for D. Where is he anyway?"

"He left to check his artefact dealers for leads on blades coming from the Vatican collection."

"Okay, we wait and decide then." With a gentle reassurance, he put a hand upon Simon's shoulder. "Question is, how long do we have?"

A knock at the main door interrupted the conversation as both men shared the same worried expression.

The idea had started as a co-operation between agencies, combining the assets of the Monastery Bureau of Intelligence, known as MBI, and local law enforcement across all states. This digital suppository of new and past crimes, cross-referenced in real time, known as the HubNet, accessible by all levels during domestic investigations. In theory, the result would be better coordination of resources and streamlining police investigations with a wealth of criminal database access. No more waiting for crime lab results, if it's in the system it's instant, including decades of recent digitised paper archives. This integration was the reason for the red flag registering at a detective's mailbox.

Detective Jacob Colby of New Eden Police, a veteran officer of twenty-eight years, from Washington beat cop to New Eden detective. The constant chime emanating from his department assigned secpad was an annoying reminder that in an age of technology, advancements. His superiors monitored him day and night via the same HubNet. He sat in silent irritation, pushing out the increasing stiffness of his back. A sign of the time spent confined to his unmarked cruiser and released a yawn from another lost night's sleep. Not surprising when adding the constant boredom with long stakeouts. This was what he considered proper policing, looking back with fondness to a time before drone surveillance, instant data uplinks, and facial recognition monitoring. Today's policing was towards hi-tech changes made in the departments' fresh way of thinking, looking good on reports, and making the job appear more efficient. The recent intakes of recent recruits from the academy were volunteering for the new cortical implant connections, mandatory for MBI field agents. Even the classic stakeout was being completed by surveillance drones these days. Gone were the uncomfortably long hours, terrible food, and even worse coffee. Colby felt a need to cling to the old ways of policing being phased out, considering it better to rely on human eyes and intuition over the latest AI algorithm. It was day three of staking out a little dive called Bella's diner, the last known location of the suspects of several liquor store holdups across the city. He released another triggered yawn as the electronic notification continued to flash on his secpad. With attention between the diner and the device, he scrolled the unread messages. There were various updates flagged for his attention. The daily most wanted of various undesirables, internal memos, departmental overdue report requests from his Lieutenant and personal case file updates. A daily routine was deleting all messages, but today one caught his interest. The heading showed a cold case ID; he tapped the icon and opened a security page. Offering his password, it then highlighted details to fingerprints of a recent suspect crossmatched to an unsolved cold case. The primary suspect details and current whereabouts omitted for MBI clearance only.

Colby frowned at trying to remember the original case. Why the sudden development? He had forgotten he had left an update tag on the case. Still racking his memory, he recovered details to the case, surprised at being assigned way back when still in uniform for Washington PD. The case was a gruesome murder of a woman, left unsolved as the lead suspect, the victim's mysterious boyfriend, vanished without a trace. With no further evidence or leads, they shelved the case with no further investigation. Since his earlier career, experience had taught him to distance himself from the victims of no win cases. Many an unpleasant case broke excellent cops if they let the victims get to them. His outlook on the job had changed, for no longer that eager rookie out to prove something, but he had continued to visit the details when the chance arose. Needing to find something missed to bring closure. As he read the details, a pang of guilt rose to allowing years to pass since last reviewing the case. With his attention on the secpad all interest in his current case lost, he reread the report, considering this fresh development.

An hour later and with a little creative data diving in the department HubNet, Colby pulled up outside the doors of the Refuge of Lost Souls. The MIB had classified the recent case file, but the personnel assignments associated with that file were not. Colby had completed a data trace of other Order surveillance authorisations for the past seventy-two hours. The result was the hunch paying off as he sat watching the primary entrance to the refuge. Another quick check of the details showed the same priest classifying the original case had requested surveillance on this building in the old town and on two particular occupants. A weak link, but perhaps the occupants of this refuge had information about his cold case. *Thank you inter department co-operation.*

On exiting the cruiser, instinct made him check the clasp of the concealed service weapon and a quick glance of the surroundings before walking over to the doors. With a distinct hammer on the door panel, Colby hoped to attract attention. As the moments passed, he stepped back to check for another entrance, pausing on hearing the grinding sound of heavy locking bolts drawn back. Then a slight gap appeared.

A pair of tired eyes hidden behind thick-rimmed glasses peeked out, using the door as a shield from the bright glare as he struggled to focus.

"Hello, names Detective Colby, and was wondering if you might answer a few questions about Simon Alksey and Lisa Shelby." As a sign to his authority, he showed the badge hanging from his belt. "Are you Father George Peters by any chance?"

"That is correct, but can I inquire the reason you have to talk to them? Have they done something wrong?"

"Just routine questions Father, their names came up linked to an old cold case. It's a courtesy call in wanting to rule out any further investigation, as you might guess." A small smile hid the bending of truth a little for his visit.

The Father opened the door, inviting Colby in with a wave towards the main hall. "Please take a seat, detective," he asked. Watching as Colby placed his secpad on the table, scrolling the contents until reaching the point he wanted. "You are Father George Peters, is that correct?"

"I confirmed my identity at the door," he replied.

Colby picked up on the evasive tone towards the questions. "Sorry Father it's a formality and for the record we record all conversations." Colby patted the secpad.

There came a pliable decrease in the room's tension, Father Peter's posture relaxing as he took a seat. "I'm sorry lad, just tired, for it's been a long few days. So please continue with the questions."

"You are the priest of this establishment with a... Sister Angela Kirkpatrick, is that correct?"

"Correct."

"What's your relationship with Mr Alksey?" Colby waited for the answer, adding observations on the secpad screen as the Father sat, curious to the attention. This was not the priest's first time being questioned by the authorities, so he tried to stay calm and courteous regardless of the interruption. Nothing to hide, he told himself. "Simon is the handyman here, responsible for odd jobs around the place, in return for lodgings."

Nodding to the answers, Colby watched the Father clean the lens of his glasses awaiting the next question. "Has he worked for you long?"

"About three months." The priest frowned as Colby continued with his notes. A sense of doubt rising to that he was giving something away. "If you're recording, then why still write notes?"

"Sorry, Father, recordings for the internal file. It's an old habit, but I like my own notes about personal observations during the interview, don't worry. So, Mr Alksey, may I get to speak to him?"

"He is a good Christian detective," the Father offered, hoping a priest's judgement might sway the detective's own.

"That may be, but according to records he doesn't exist on the network. No job records, security number or even driving licence, nothing before becoming your handy-man. So you can understand how that raises a few flags."

"Can I ask the actual reason for your visit, detective?"

There was no need to continue the facade, so Colby confirmed what Father Peters had thought since the beginning. "I'm hoping he could help in the investigation in to the death of Miss Carla Simmons of Washington DC. His prints match those taken at the original scene and a recent MBI investigation at this shelter."

"Carla Simmons." Father Peters tried to hide the fact to knowing the name.

Colby leaned back in the chair, noticing the slightest flash of recognition. "You know the name, Father?"

"She came up in questioning by the priest in charge of the rather intrusive search on the refuge. They mentioned a connection between the case and Simon, but were more interested in completing their search. We supposed with the obvious age of the case, Simon wasn't under further investigation and it was a case of mistaken identity, a clerical mistake. I suspect you might have had a wasted journey, detective."

"That may be. Still, I hope to clear up any need for further questions," Colby said.

"Why investigate such an old case, anyway? One thing that's plenty of in this city is more recent crimes to solve."

With a slight sigh, Colby continued his notes before scrolling the screen. "It was one of my first cases, Father and I always hated leaving things unfinished. You understand my need to give Miss Simmons's remaining family peace and closure if possible. With yourself being a man of the cloth, I'd hoped you might understand the need for closure."

Father Peters recognised the sincerity in Colby's words, sympathising whilst trying not to stall an official investigation. "To find peace for a lost soul is a virtue always encouraged. As long as it's not at the expense of an honest man's liberties," he replied, leaning forward, trying to read what Colby was writing.

Colby raised an eyebrow at his curiosity. "Just wanting to close the case, that is all, and hoping Simon Alksey might help."

"What information do you have about her death?" The question made both turn as Simon appeared from the storage room, hidden since the start of the conversation.

Father Peters released a distinct groan of disappointment to Simon, not taken his advice to stay hidden.

"Mr Alksey?" Colby asked, rising from the chair in surprise to the sudden appearance.

"Simon is fine."

"My Polish is a little rusty, but your name means defender if I remember, right?"

"It was a surname the good Father recommended I used."

Colby turned to Father Peter's rolling eyes as the whole cover story agreed unravelled before them.

"There is no reason to hide Father," Simon said.

"I see," Colby said, somewhat confused. "Well, if it's okay, please verify for the record and clear any miss understandings." Colby handed over the secpad to Simon that requested his identification.

With a press of hand, Simon watched as the screen flickered to confirm identification was complete.

"Thank you." Another chime from the device verified earlier findings that he was the same individual from the cold case. It was not a surprise to Colby. "Ninety-eight point two percent match to a suspect in the homicide of Carla Simmons." The detective offered over the secpad to show the results. "I have to caution you Mr Alksey or whatever you may call yourself, for we are still recording this interview. Now if you would prefer to explain your connection to Carla Simmons for the record?"

Simon faced with a chance to explain, to tell the truth regardless of how incredible, now appeared unsure. Father Peters had explained if ever facing questions to his past he should be cautious and not give too much detail and stick to the plausible basics. To stay quiet, for they have no actual evidence to who he was and for everyone's sake don't mention angels, he had advised. So remaining calm, Simon prompted for everybody to retake their seats. "I have no real recollection to the woman's apartment came the lie, but have dreamt about her and the details of her death."

"You dreamt about her." The surprise to the admission etched Colby's face, pausing his writing for a minute.

"Yes."

"What are you doing in these dreams?" Colby asked.

"She danced as I watched."

An incoherent grumble from the Father made Colby glance between both, his confusion increasing with each answer. "She danced?"

"Yes, until falling into my arms where she died," Simon continued showing no readable emotions.

Colby scratched at his temple, reading back his notes.

"Up to a few days ago detective, I had no memory of who I was. The good Father found me suffering amnesia, but during my recovery I've recalled my name during a dream state, and further flashes of memories have returned."

"It was through a dream state you realised your name?"

"The old man on a bench told me, whilst he fed the birds and we talked."

"An old man told you," Colby asked. "So this old man on the bench said your name was Simon Alksey and did he know Miss Simmons?"

"Just Simon, the Father recommended using the surname, and I don't recall that the old man knew Carla."

It was Colby's turn to roll his eyes in frustration to his questions. "Thank you for making that so clear for me."

"It wasn't until an Order priest arrived with further details of the case I put a name to the face."

Over the years, Colby had developed a sixth sense when questioning suspects. What he was getting from Simon was calmness to borderline arrogant, topped off with part crazy. *This guy believes what he's telling me regardless of how implausible it sounded.* The thought passed, and with a scratch of stubble chin, he scrutinised Simon for a moment. *You're comfortable, confident. We need to get you in unfamiliar surroundings and away from outside interference.* He took a slow intake of breath before continuing. "You have no recollection how they found your fingerprints in her apartment?"

"Perhaps in my past I was there, I dreamt I was, but I can't be certain."

"No idea at all as never meeting her before her murder?" The detective opened a paper file he had brought and inside were crime scene photos of Carla's lifeless body, which he fanned out to show Simon.

"I don't know. I'm not sure," he replied, watching the pictures pushed across the table.

"Is that so?" Colby asked, surprised.

"He said he wasn't a detective and I'm sure if he remembered her he would say so," the Father offered.

Colby's attention remained fixed on Simon, whose emotionless expressions slipped on seeing the prints. Colby pointed to one print in particular. "You're sure? Look again and imaging what she went through in the hands of her killer, the suspect ripped her apart like an animal."

The pain and remorse Simon felt was clear as he reached for the print, tracing Carla's pained and blood-matted features.

"Can I ask your age?" Colby queried, trying to get Simon off balance with a change of direction.

Simon continued to stare at the print, half listening to the question. "I think twenty-six."

"You think… you don't remember how old you are," Colby pushing for an answer.

Simon felt frustrated and flustered, losing his train of thought.

"The crucial question in this case which I can't quite get my head around is how your prints match our original suspects. There is also a significant likeness to the witness description of the boyfriend. For now, that and his prints are the only leads we have to her murderer." He continued to study Simon. "There is an obvious age difference, unless you're looking good for a man in his fifties."

No one answered.

"I believe the prints could be a clerical error, sometimes things get miss filed during digitising cases onto the Hub-Net." Colby paused with a tilt of head, curious. "What still intrigues me is you're telling me you have been having dreams about the victim, but no memory of ever meeting her." A few moments passed until Colby sat back again, blowing out his cheeks, somewhat frustrated. "Nothing makes sense with this case, but by your own admissions it would be prudent we continue this interview back at the precinct."

Father Peters stood to protest. "I don't understand detective, you already mentioned his age during the case but still want to take him back for further questioning."

"I have to Father, your friends' details don't add up to being innocent, no doubt about that. It's convenient to have amnesia resulting in his recent loss of important details. Consider he was there, perhaps as a child, the traumatic experience suppressed memories until later in life." His attention returned to Simon. "You said you had an accident, head trauma might have brought back those suppressed memories of your childhood."

"The fingerprints, how do you explain the close match?" the Father asked confronting Colby as he stood to collect his secpad from the desk.

"It wasn't a full match, and convenient he has no remembrance of his past before his accident. My job is to find out he isn't covering for an older relative. Maybe as a child he saw a robbery gone wrong, the victim returning home, disturbed them, and killed to silence her?"

"They took a child on a robbery with them. Do you realise how absurd that sounds, detective?" Father Peters protested.

"Father, it happens, who knows what goes through the perpetrator's mind when their plan goes wrong," Colby responded. He made his way to Simon, clutching his arms behind his back.

Simon did not resist.

Now handcuffed, Simon let Colby lead him to the main doors. "I want to show him more prints of the scene in the hope it might help jog his memory. Maybe answer the questions we all have."

"I'm uncertain about this detective," the Father still protesting until Simon interrupted.

"It will be fine, Father. Don't worry. We might find the reasons for the dreams and either way we both need answers."

Father Peters was not so confident about Colby's motives for needing to take Simon back to the precinct. For now he needed to put his trust in Simon, but since his return that morning, he had felt a change in him. Gone was the shy, aloof lad nursed back to health a few weeks ago. "Could we have a moment please detective," he asked, resting a hand upon Simon's shoulder.

Colby considered the question before nodding.

The Father pulled Simon to the side, needing to talk in private and concerned in the intense observation of the detective. "I know it's important you find out, lad. I hate to say it, but you can't keep telling the truth about how your prints got to be in her apartment."

"Why not, when it's the truth, Father?"

"Those archangels did a number on you, lad, somehow stopping you from thinking straight." The priest thought for a moment. "Simon, telling the truth now would complicate things for all concerned, opening a Pandora's Box of problems if the police get involved. You need to understand that." He waited for a response, somewhat conflicted to what to do next, not having any answers. "They could still charge you on the thin evidence, throwing away the key or worse section you with a life in a padded cell."

Unknown to Father Peters, Simon had considered the consequences, but he had to take the risk. "Helping with the investigation might give me answers to my own questions. Please, I need to do this, Father."

"What of your quest, the blade. Remember what happened last time the authorities took you for further questions."

"I have this, Father. Trust me, I have a plan."

Colby watched the huddle, closing his secpad and returning it to his inside jacket pocket. "You're more than welcome to follow us to my car, Father?"

"Which precinct are you taking him to, anyway? Would like to confirm he isn't being arrested, for something he didn't do."

"Twenty-third Father, no worry and we will not be too long, depends on his co-operation in the matter."

Outside, Father Peters watched Colby push Simon into the back seat of his unmarked police cruiser.

Colby offered a slight wave before walking to the driver's seat, and soon the cruiser was pulling away.

The Father headed back inside, closing and locking the

doors behind him. He sensed an uneasy dread that Simon was walking into more trouble than he could handle. With haste, he headed for the kitchen to find details of his lawyer friend. The man's services needed soon enough to get Simon out of police custody. It was then the room grew icy cold, sensing no longer being alone.

The last bolt slid across to secure the doors. Father Peters could not shake the fear the whole situation was getting out of hand. Then a sudden coldness came over the hall, a dark chill making the priest turn and stumble in alarm. "For all that's holy... I wish you didn't do that."

The tall figure of D sat against a table, unconcerned to the effect his sudden appearance had on the priest as he continued to scroll his secpad.

"Scared me to death, you idiot," he said, clutching his chest.

With a chuckle at the irony in the priest's choice of words, D tapped his device. "There's still plenty of time yet, Father, but remember Fate has a funny way of changing your stats at the last minute." Still keeping his trademark macabre smile, he searched the hall. "So where is our boy wonder? We have news on the blade, thingy?"

The Father had started for the kitchen. "He's helping the police with their enquiries."

With a concerned frown, D followed. "Enquires and you let him go?"

"No choice. Detective Colby picked him up and took him back to the precinct for further questions about the Carla Simmons girl. There's a mess up with fingerprints and Simon the prime suspect in the investigation."

"Carla Simmons," D replied, hesitating at the name.

The Father turned, recognising D's apprehension. "What aren't you telling me, Mr HaMavet?"

D paused before answering. "You're mindful of the Simmons murder, right?"

"Well yes, they say his prints were at her apartment." The Father felt a sudden pang in the pit of his stomach. "Simon said he dreamt of her but had no direct connection to her murder?"

"That was true... but not... if you understand my meaning." The answer was cryptic and made Father Peters turn on D. "Are you suggesting he's involved in her death or not?" He pulled out a spare chair at the kitchen table, gesturing for D to do the same. "Tell me the truth, was he involved in the girl's death?"

D sought to get comfortable, placing his secpad on the table, unsure how to interpret in a manner the priest would understand. Their earlier conversation on the refuge roof had rocked the priest's whole belief system and faith, and even himself as a person. What he was about to tell could destroy what little faith the poor priest had left to trust anybody, especially Simon, but deep down knew he deserved the facts. So with a heavy sigh D tried to explain. "Be aware how it works, death, I mean."

"The lists of the dead, I remember my scripture."

"Please don't get me started on that," D responded with a roll of eyes. "What you follow is that taught by your superiors because it's their interpretation of the truth? Why, because it's chronicled wrong by scholars ever since the Dark Ages. They knew it only benefits the few for their own gain, being such a barbaric representation of God's word, a way of keeping law and order. The masses working from the same hymn sheet, no pun intended," D continued.

The Father scowled at D's ramblings.

"Recognise our Father intended his creation to live in harmony with everything else. Never contemplated you would create factions, putting yourselves higher than his other creations in his name. That's the flaw in free will and it might be a shock, but he never intended to treat the apes any different from any other creature spread across the planet. Even now you interfere with the balance, it so infuriates how you take this world for granted."

Father Peters remained silent, emotions rising, including

irritation. "So you're saying it's all a lie and we pray to him for nothing?"

"Not quite," D answered. "In the beginning, the Chosen guided to spread teachings of His word. But over time the word became distorted and changed by those with power to manipulate for their own gains. Commanded to not kill, but undertake wars in the name of religion or greed for centuries, saying it was His will to do so. Did you ever stop to consider the message was not for the rich to prosper while the masses became poorer and hungrier? You can understand our Father became disappointed in the poor shadow of what He intended."

Father Peters twisted his rosemary, sadness welling.

"You think its Gods will when something happens?" D continued. "When it's Fate who dictates when someone lives or dies, regardless how that individual prays or repents but where it gets tricky is from that moment of birth. An individual's life is in a continual state of flux, sprinkled with pivotal moments from that pesky free will affect life decisions that also affect your last date. Do you follow me?"

"What you are saying is your times not over until you decide to either step off the curb or continue down the road," the Father answered.

"More or less, yes, but when the ultimate time arrives, it's because of freewill and fate, not any divine power's influence. It's the get-out clause in the contract of sorts. When your time is up, Fate herself summons Reapers to guide the soul on its journey to the afterlife. There's no proper control, and here's the deal breaker. There are deaths that are special cases, fixed points in the Plan regardless of that individual's freewill because their death affects the status-quo."

The knot of Father's stomach twisted again, realising D's meaning. "Are you saying Carla Simmons died because Fate foresaw and God willed it because it had to happen?"

"Sometimes something has to happen for a certain event to continue to its conclusion. When I heard one of the Chosen would die, such important souls needed personal handling and understand no one knew of Simon and Carla's indiscretion before her death. The powers forbid such things from happening as it's a great sacrilege."

"You're insinuating they had a romantic relationship?" The Father in shock cleaned a lens on his pocket lining.

"It wasn't the first time they had banished an angel for unfitting conduct unbecoming of their position. This rock provides many temptations to the most worthy." Unable to stem his laugh, D stopped once noticing the Father's disapproving gaze.

"So you were there when she died?" he asked.

"I'm called upon once the soul is ready to leave the body, not the exact moment of death. Sometimes hours pass after death until it's time, sometimes minutes." The Father pushed his glasses back up his nose, placing a hand on D's shoulder. "Did you see Simon on the day she died?"

With slouched shoulders, D sighed, his expression sombre as he shook his head. "As I understand, they recalled Simon before her time of death, leaving Carla vulnerable."

The room fell into silence.

D broke the silence after a sort few minutes of thought. "The girl tortured and killed for the knowledge she knew."

"Which was what?" the Father demanded.

"She had foresight in predicting future events. As a Chosen, she had extensive amounts of celestial knowledge, and so they carved her up so she would give direct access to that information."

The colour drained from Father Peter's face, and he could not find words.

"I'm still surprised what humans can do to each other," D confessed. "They forced her predictions by carving Enochian incantations into her body. That gave them control over the power of her gift."

"Wait a minute," Father Peters interrupted, griping D's arm. "Whoever killed Carla recognised her gift for what it was?"

"They would otherwise have no reason to kill her that way. Where are you going with this, Father?"

"They hoped to gain from those predictions." The priest paced the floor, trying to piece together the entire story in his mind. "Who could force her predictions?"

"The ability is there, for those willing to seek it Father, most of the required documentation held by your religious academics and authorities for centuries."

"Still a small list, though? That should give us a place to start for answers." The Father watched D consider what he was saying. "Today, where would someone, unaware of their gift, go for treatment as though seeking help for an illness?"

A flash of clarity crossed D's face with a click of fingers. "Professional help, like a doctor or therapist?"

"Well, yes, perhaps." The Father did not want to stem D's enthusiasm. "We need access to her medical files, find out who she confided in about her nightmares." Father Peters went to find the digital telephone directory.

"Sorry Father, I'd almost forgotten the reason for my visit. I've got a lead on who purchased the Blade of Light."

The priest paused from what he was doing, staring at D. "Well, who has it?"

D retrieved his secpad, a quick scroll across the screen to stop at a communication received earlier in the day. "This is from an Asian connection in rare antiquities that had traded in various items liberated from the Vatican attack. About two years ago, a big buyer bought every available item, regardless of price. A lot of money changed hands with no questions asked. My contact sold the buyer rare items and for a price gave me a full inventory list."

"Who was the private buyer?"

"It's not who, but what. The buyer was an Indonesian-based hydraulic company."

"I don't understand," the Father asked. "Why would they want to spend a fortune on buying up religious relics?"

"Listen to this, doing a corporate cross reference, we find

it's a subsidiary of a Hong Kong building division of Jinjing Guang Corporation. Which in its self is a holding based in New York called Achievement of Spiritual Enlightenment?"

"I'm not sure I follow, I've never heard of them."

"You wouldn't have." D continued. "They're all shell companies for the Order. The person in question spending money on relics is the cardinal, believe me when I hope he isn't aware of the power he has in his collection. This weapon has the potential to bring the war of Heaven and Hell to the streets of New Eden and start the end of days for all of us."

Simon remained handcuffed and restricted to the rear seat of Detective Colby's cruiser, almost grateful that the journey had been short, for neither man spoke. Their only connection shared was scrutinising glances from the rear-view mirror as their destination came into view.

Simon eased across the seat to get a better view of the twenty-third precinct.

One of the oldest buildings of Sufferance, its red brick structure had ornate archway emphasising the steel main doors with the precinct's weathered designation engraved in the stonework. The precinct stood out from the newer post-war buildings of the last century surrounding it. Sharing the same neglected facade of daubed graffiti as barred windows made for an uninviting sight. The entire perimeter was ringed in reinforced chain fencing and formed a prime fortified example of front line inner city policing in Sufferance.

Colby escorted Simon through the precinct entrance to the front reception, where a crowd of civilians jostled the protective screen around the main desk. They clamoured for attention from the desk officer shouting over the noise, ordering them to wait their turns. None reacted to Colby pushing on through, heading for the security gate for police personnel beyond that led to the inner workings of the precinct. A grilled door barred the way, entry granted by electronic security card reader imbedded in the wall.

Simon noted a uniformed officer in full body armour waiting behind the gate and protected by a further screen. The slightest nod of acknowledgement confirmed their entry after Colby swiped his badge and moved them into the booking window passed the gate.

Simon tried to hang back as Colby went to sign him in for the record, observing the throng of civilians and police filing through the precinct.

There were a dozen desks, three rows deep, manned by uniformed officers continuing with their everyday workloads. As he waited he became desperate to appear inconspicuous, as two Guard Clerics manoeuvred towards them. A sudden sense of dread, of the possibility of being recognised, but his apprehension evaporated to relief as the clerics pushed past and out into the reception.

"Come with me this way," Colby instructed, gripping Simon's arm, and led him towards a row of interview rooms. They occupied one side of an open space to what appeared to be a waiting area. A quick search found the nearest empty and with a flick of florescent lights they entered. Colby unlocking the handcuffs as Simon sat at a table. "Not long now and we can get started, can I call you Simon?"

Now relieved of the restrictive handcuffs, Simon nodded, taking in the bleak grey room as he massaged his wrists.

A uniformed officer entered, offering a bundle of paper files to Colby. The detective sorted through and spread out one particular file, before retrieving a data card to place into a spare port of his secpad. With a tap of the screen, a projected image flickered on the far wall.

Simon tensed, recognising the image of Carla Simmons's smiling face. A lost feeling of a carefree time flooded back, remembering her positive outlook, which nothing could dispel.

Colby sat back, studying Simon's reaction to the image, confirming a flicker of emotion seen earlier at the refuge. "August fourteen, twenty-seven, interview with Simon Alksey,

Detective Jacob Colby presiding badge number NE1438. I'm proceeding to question with a link to reopen cold case file Carla Simmons CC237890-3." Colby retrieved two more files. "Also connection with ongoing investigations of the murders of Georgina Appleby case A456789-45 and Helen Zimmerman case A456846-23."

There was no way in hiding Simon's surprise to Colby's opening description for the record. Father Peters had warned him to be cautious about being taken for further questioning and now, away from the sanctuary of the refuge, Colby's true motives emerged.

The detective's whole demeanour changed. For gone was the kind, supportive and sympathetic officer replaced by stern and determined investigator, wanting nothing but answers to his questions.

Simon braced in his chair as Colby fanned the contents of three folders out in front of him. One picture was of Carla, the others were of women he did not recognise.

"Can you explain where you were on tenth and thirtieth of August this year?" Colby asked, proceeding to push further pictures towards him.

The photos were of other crime scenes, of women in various degrees of mutilation and obvious torture. Their hair and features matted in blood and there similarities to Carla's crime scene photo uncanny.

Simon reached out for the picture of Carla appearing to be in peaceful slumber, forcing back emotion as he tried to stop eyes from reddening.

Colby pressed his questions. "Night of the tenth, can you explain where you were?"

"I don't remember," Simon replied, his attention fixed on Carla's picture.

Colby's frustration flared, gathering the file's contents and slapping down a photo of an unknown woman. "Georgina Appleby, do you recognise this woman?"

Through a forced frown, Simon's concentration slipped.

"Don't think so. I don't understand the question. Who are these other people?"

"I'm asking the questions, now, Helen Zimmerman, do you know her? They found her body this morning. Close to that refuge you live at," Colby continued. Not allowing Simon to regain his concentration, perhaps slip up and incriminate himself about the other murders.

"No... I don't," he replied.

"You don't." Colby searched through the case file. "It states her son goes to the same school as Lisa Shelby's son Jake. So tell me. Was it a chance meeting at the refuge or the school? Maybe followed her home? Things got a little out of hand? Is that how it happened?"

"No, no... I don't know her. I've never seen these women before," Simon protested, tension in his voice as he got agitated under the barrage of questions.

"But you admitted knowing Carla Simmons, don't you? That is obvious from the reaction to her photo."

"Yes... but no. I mean, I did... but you are confusing me, detective."

Colby sat back with a grunt, frustrated at the lack of co-operation. "You stated you have dreamt about her? Did you dream about the others too?"

Simon put his head into his hands.

"Explain how your fingerprints get into the apartment of a twenty-six-year-old cold case? I mean, you are what... twenty-five, six? No... perhaps you've invented time travel or are immortal. Whatever, it's an excellent party trick you have." The detective rubbed his unshaven chin before leaning forward, his voice low. "You're covering for an older family member? Is that the case? Would explain why you're not on the grid. Did daddy take you on a little family field trip? Now you're picking up where he left off with your own little murder spree. Is that it?" Colby pressed the secpad screen, projecting a flurry of scrolling images of each crime scene. "Look at that screen, Simon. Tell the truth, what's your connection to their murders or do you know who did it?"

Simon lifted his head, blinking through red eyes as the screen continued to scroll the graphic images.

"They mutilated their bodies in such a way that we couldn't let their loved one's ID the bodies. So explain the weird shapes. Is it a sick religious cult thing?"

Simon remained silent with head down and reluctant to answer.

"Here's what we have... the prime suspect's fingerprints found at the original crime scene of a religious motivated murder. Years later, a connection to our original suspect uncovered living in a church-run refuge. At the same time two victims with the same religious themed deaths to our earlier murder turn up, see the coincidence." Colby, getting little to no response, pressed on with his questions. "Look, we have all night and you better give me answers. I'm this close in letting the District Attorney recommend throwing you inside a compact room, never seeing the light of day again. How does that sound?"

"Detective Colby, do you have a moment?" The voice came from the doorway.

"What?" Colby rounded on the interruption, unable to stem his frustration and annoyance to being disturbed. Stood at the door was the officer who had brought his files earlier. Her face appeared flushed and agitated. "Sorry to disturb you detective but we have two gentlemen from MBI here for Mr Alksey."

Colby looked at Simon, sharing his confusion to the recent development.

"Get comfy, I'm not letting your friends from MBI to undermine my case and take you yet. I have a lot more questions for you, my friend." Colby turned off the secpad before collecting the files in to one pile.

Simon leaned forward, placing his hands on the desk, not wanting to provoke the detective.

"Think introductions are in order, detective. I'm Father Sebastian Clarke of the Twenty-Second Cohort of the Cardinal Guard." The tall, imposing priest moved to the side, allowing a Guard Cleric to pass.

"I don't care if you're the cardinal; you're not taking my suspect."

Father Clarke appeared unruffled by Colby's lack of courtesy and professionalism, instead directed the cleric towards the files on the table. Who gathered up the files and attached a small device to Colby's secpad.

"What's going on here?" Colby moved to take back his secpad, but Clarke intercepted him. "You've got no jurisdiction in taking my files," Colby protested.

The secpad lit red, then green, showing the program had completed, and the cleric removed the small device and left with the paper files.

Colby was about to intervene again when Father Clarke stepped forward, blocking the exit once again. "You will find your captain has the relevant paperwork for Mr Alksey's transfer, and we have retrieved all interview notes and background data from your secpad. Your suspect interests us in a delicate matter, so would appreciate you desist in further investigations."

"This isn't right. These are ongoing murder cases, and he is my prime suspect."

"About your ongoing investigations, we've sealed all relevant files for review by MBI. NEPD will investigate no longer about Mr Alksey on this matter until further notice."

Colby cursed, rubbing fingers through his short hair at having the Order over rule him on his case. He lashed out in anger by kicking the table.

Father Clarke ignored any other objections, nodding to another waiting cleric who assisted Simon from the chair, helping him to the door.

"I'm putting in an official complaint to my captain about this, Father."

"As you may detective and thank you for your cooperation," Father Clarke responded, watching Colby's frustration before leaving after the others.

Falling into his chair, Colby scanned his secpad and cursed again. They had wiped all references to the three cases from his main network file directory, even taking the data card from cloud backup. Still cursing, he navigated the device for a hidden secondary partition holding access to an offline backup system off the main department HubNet. A folder icon appeared, a quick scroll of sub folders finding the options required. He pressed upload, and then waited for a progress bar to appear, increasing to one hundred percent. Another scroll of the main directory satisfied to have retrieved the deleted data. *Always take remote backups of your folders,* he thought, closing the secpad. This case is far from over, promising he will have his suspect and they will meet again soon.

CHAPTER TEN

Wolf in Sheep's Clothing

Simon hoped to never find himself back inside the illuminated hulk of an MAUV, but fate transpired against him. Once again sat between two intimidating Guard Clerics, the recurring circumstance not lost as he noted the crew in the cabin's red hue.

Father Clarke sat at the command console, monitoring the journey's progress through his own screens, unaware of his passenger's lingering observation.

Simon suppressed a silent laugh in contemplation of the irony of his predicament and the lingering sense of déjà vu as he regained his composure. A quick sideway glance at the clerics reassured him his silent hysteria remained unnoticed as they remained ridged and stony faced under half plated visors.

"We are about ten minutes from the monastery," Father Clarke shouted over an intense roar of the twin engines as he twisted to face Simon. "You will have the honour of meeting his holy Eminence, who is most eager to meet you."

"Why?" Simon responded, drowned out by the sounds of the engines.

Clarke tapped his helmet and pointed to behind Simon's seat.

Simon reached back, retrieving a spare headset, placing them over his head, and an immediate silence cancelled out the noise of the vehicle, to his relief.

"That's better, is it not?" Clarke's voice came through from his own personal communications.

"I presumed you'd take me to the monastery, but what reason has the cardinal for wanting to see me?" The question asked as Simon adjusted the headset for comfort.

Clarke's eyes narrowed, a discerning grin appearing from the corner of his mouth. "Oh, don't sell yourself short, for you are privileged to meet the most important person on the planet, the speaker for billions and voice of the true God."

Simon returned an unconvincing grin, nodding at the priest's answer, and sat back in his seat, removing the headset that ended the brief conversation.

Father Clarke somewhat disappointed and with reluctance returned to his consoles.

The motor park at the Monastery of Light was a vast underground complex. Several large hydraulic lifts manoeuvred two MAUVs at a time, hissing out pressure, as they descended inside the complex. The journey all too brief as it stopped at a level marked nine, Detention Level in bold black lettering. Manhandled from the vehicle, they escorted Simon through a security gate, where he noted monitoring surveillance and more white uniformed Guard Clerics.

Father Clarke continued ahead to speed up the process through each further checkpoint, and soon they came to a lift as the doors opened, allowing the small group to enter. A brief sensation of ascending followed until the opening again to a pristine white corridor. The group continued through a labyrinth of inter-connecting corridors and walkways, sometimes passing observation platforms offering breath-taking views of the vast monastery. Then they reached their destination, two enormous oak doors. A security scan of the approaching group resulted in the doors opening to an elaborately decorated room with two ornamental tables occupied by two modern dressed female clerics. They busied themselves with their work, without acknowledging the recent arrivals as they entered.

"Father Clarke, thank you for your prompt retrieval of our guest. I hope you had no problems with the NEPD." The authoritarian voice of Bishop Nikolaos greeted them, his tall frame dressed in full white and red battle armour. He stood with hands behind his back, staring out through the nearest observatory window. His view overlooked a lavish garden of trees and shrubs, appearing out of place for a modern business like environment the monastery appeared to portray.

"None bishop, all data purged as instructed, including our journey's log files," answered the dutiful priest remaining at attention while giving his report.

"You will relinquish the guest to my escort if you please," Nikolaos ordered.

Two intimidating clerics approached, both wearing to Simon what resembled standard cleric armour, but with changes. These appeared more intricate with extra layering, making the wearer bulkier without impairing movement. A more obvious change was the full plated helmet protection, including neck and shoulder plating. Their appearance did not diminish Simon's increasing apprehension.

Now noting that apprehension, Nikolaos allowed a slight smile as he approached. "They are the cardinal's personal security, the Legion of the Hand. They are the best of the best and have sworn to protect his Eminence to the death."

Simon peered between his new escorts, their purple shoulder pads embossed with the emblem of The Hand of the True God in gold in its centre. The bishop's explanation did little to calm his unease.

Nikolaos greeted Simon in a welcoming grasp of shoulders, like old friends meeting after many years. "I'm so glad to see you and without incident this time." There appeared not an ounce of malice in his voice. The bishop's friendly greeting made Simon tense, half expecting the start of a terrifying interrogation to how he survived the convoy attack that resulted in such a loss of life.

Nikolaos's face expressed almost concern for his wellbeing. "As I understand, you had a run in with the NEPD today?" He asked with a curious frown. "An awful, awful business these murders, I'm sure our city's finest will get their culprit soon."

"Detective Colby has me as his prime suspect."

"But we both know truth has many faces, don't we?" The smile remained as he turned to retrieve a secpad from the nearest desk. He quickly navigated the contents whilst cautiously keeping a watchful eye on Simon as he did.

Simon considered his predicament, sensing perhaps he had walked in to a trap. Were the kind words and soothing tone a front to drop his guard, to expose his intentions or worse, the identities of Michael and the others? His response was a nervous swallow against a dry throat, trying to shake the suspicious thoughts. Certain the cardinal would not let him live after today if he knew the truth. His apprehension increased as he observed Father Clarke salute the bishop and leave with his own clerics.

"Follow me please," Nikolaos requested, ushering Simon towards the far doors at the end of the office.

The new escorts fell in step behind as they passed adjoining rooms and entered a long corridor. The further they went on, the more extravagant the interior became. Unlike the earlier rooms, pictures depicting various religious settings and historical scenes spaced out the full length of each corridor they passed. They soon arrived at an observation window opening to a beautifully tended garden that appeared to be a central hub to an expanse of office spaces spiralling upwards. As they proceeded, the gardens connected to an atrium where two large branched trees dominated the central space. Offering a green canopy separating outwards to form a delicate covering for the entire garden, as sunlight broke through heating the gardens that flourished in splendour of colours.

Simon could but stop to admire the beauty of nature.

"Gorgeous isn't it," Nikolaos remarked, watching Simon admire the scene. "The atriums are self-contained, to regulate the garden's ambiance with the power provided from the dome's solar collection system. Any spare power then gets fed to the monastery's other power needs. They gather over thirty-three percent of our entire power in this way, and the gardens give clean air and a place of reflection and relaxation."

The blending colours of plants and shrubbery were stunning, awash with exotic sweet scents. Occasionally robed clerics emerged from the undergrowth to tend to a particular plant or shrub before scurrying back into the greenery. It made for a surreal moment to otherwise desperate circumstances.

"Very impressive," Simon agreed, remaining transfixed as two small birds swooped between a small cropping of conifers.

The group moved on, using a flagged pathway crossing the well-tended lawns, arriving at an entranceway leading into another white corridor. At the far end stood three priests dressed in ceremonial white robes. Two stood with heads covered whilst listening to the third, the shortest of the group whose head remained uncovered with his back to them as they approached.

Nikolaos quickened his pace in greeting as the third priest turned and gave a slight bow.

Simon recognised veiled disdain behind the thick glasses towards the bishop as he did.

Nikolaos gestured Simon to go through another set of impressive doors as he spoke to the older priest.

Unable to hear the conversation, Simon noted the suspicious frosty glare from the glass-wearing priest as he passed. The man's frail features were unmoved, as his narrowed eyes remained fixed on him.

The room Simon entered furnished in soft draped silks drifting in the gentle breeze that warmed the room. Further works of art decorated the walls befitting the ornate furnishings, including handcrafted table and chair offset to one side. There was one piece of furniture not fitting with the room, a large curtained four-poster bed. Thick plush drapes of red and purple hung open against a backdrop of a large pictured wall depicting a scene Simon did not recognise. Also out of place and centred in the far wall, offsetting the gothic architecture of the room was a stained glassed window, offering an array of colours.

Simon could not help marvel at the extravagance until unnerving realisation all eyes were upon him, making him unsure what to expect next.

Nikolaos stood by the ornate table, arms crossed, and an expression giving nothing away.

Their escorts took up position around the door the group had entered.

The aged priest and his two hooded companions stayed in the shadows.

Simon summoned all remaining courage, fists clenched at his sides in apprehension, knuckles white from the tension.

A gentle click sounded and part of the pictured wall exposed a hidden doorway where the three robed priests bowed to the arrival entering the room. The newcomer's face remained hidden by the purple hood of their dress robes. A strained shuffle to their walk and slight arch in posture showed a man in later years.

Nikolaos moved forward to stand next to Simon, placing a hand on his shoulder and offered the modest of bows. "Your Eminence, may I introduce Simon Alksey. Simon, can I introduce his Eminence Cardinal Vladislav Ambrozij, the first of the Order of Light and founder of this monastery."

Everyone in the room remained bowed as Simon watched, somewhat troubled and hesitant, before offering his own clumsy bow to the approaching cardinal.

The stooped robed man introduced as Cardinal Ambrozij paused, turning with caution to keep features hidden. "You are the same Simon Alksey who survived the attack on my convoy?" The voice sounded strained and dry.

Simon hesitated, looking to Nikolaos for guidance, who nodded in silent confirmation to answer the question. "I was there, your Eminence."

The cardinal continued to shuffle over to the large crafted

writing table, reaching out with a frail hand for a glass of chilled water. Pausing again before in one fluid motion pulled back the hood to expose fragile and gaunt features of a man ravaged by age. The cardinal's white milky sunken eyes shadowed by black rings but still hid a spark of intelligence. Clumps of white hair hung in patches around a balding head darkened with blotchy covered skin. The books and online news feeds Simon had watched while recuperating had depicted a stronger-looking man, less ravaged by time. This cardinal sipped the contents of the glass before returning it to the table and turned to Simon. "So you survived where an entire company of Guard Clerics perished?" he asked. "You must be a unique man with particular talents Mr Alksey or do I need to have better trained clerics."

The insult not aimed at Simon observing Nikolaos shuffle with discomfort next to him, hiding his agitation to the comment. "I could not say you're Eminence," Simon offered.

"Is that so?" the cardinal queried, the slightest of icy smiles showing a calculating mind as he continued. "I'm sure you're aware of the uniqueness of the perpetrators of the horrendous attack, but those questions are for another time. Please join me on a stroll." He reached out, taking Simon's elbow for balance as both men fell into a gentle pace. They headed for the opened door in the picture wall. "The doctors say I must exercise twice a day. So please, walk with me as we have a lot to discuss, the two of us."

Nikolaos and the three priests that had been waiting fell into position behind them, followed by the Legion Guard bringing up the rear. The door closing behind as they headed through another office.

Simon adjusted his pace, matching the slow pace of the cardinal, concentrating on not walking too fast.

"You are a remarkable man, Mr Alksey, if that is your correct name?"

"I'm not sure you're Eminence. Father Peters recommended I use the surname."

"Ah yes, because of your accident and convenient amnesia."

Simon frowned to the questioning, considering that the Order admitted having surveillance in the garages and even had shown recordings during the refuge search. So it was no surprise they have briefed the cardinal before this meeting. "Yes, my accident," he answered.

"Brought on by your spectacular fall from grace, I presume."

Simon tried to cover his hesitation. "I do not know what you mean…, your Eminence?"

"Come now, I've travelled far and wide during my long lifetime to enlightenment. During my travels I've been fortunate to meet many intriguing individuals willing to share their own experiences and knowledge." He stopped, taking a moment to stare at Simon with dark, tired, scrutinising eyes. Then clutching his arm again, steadying his balance before continuing their slow pace. "Can I tell you a story, Mr Simon Alksey?"

Simon remained confused in the change of direction of the conversation, but agreed with a nod. The deep sense of apprehension remained in the pit of his stomach as they continued, passing through a corridor that continued to circle the domed gardens.

"Please sit," the cardinal asked, pointing to a marbled bench placed in a small recess under a patch of overhanging trees. As they did, a short bald cleric appeared from an adjoining cloister, producing a red cushion for the cardinal's comfort.

In his frail form the cardinal strained, releasing a slight groan in relaxing with the aid of the cleric. The rest of the party mulled around in their own groups, observing with curiosity as the two sat to continue their discussion.

Cardinal Ambrozij discerned Simon's apprehension as he lent in, so not overheard.

"Please ignore my Secretary Jozafat's glare. He felt a slight irritation towards not being involved in this meeting. My subordinate's opinion is he must know what does not concern him. The same goes for the loyal bishop, for the two of them hover around me, waiting for me to show the reason for bringing you here."

"I must admit to wondering that myself," Simon asked.

"Ah yes. But back to my story, for you must have many unanswered questions, wanting to know the truth, but what would the truth be, I wonder?" The ageing cardinal's gaze fell upon a small bird, hopping a small patch of grass in search of food. "Would you recognise the truth if you heard it, or would you take it as the truth because of who spoke the words?" The cardinal's attention returned to Simon, who felt irritated as he struggled to understand.

"I would like to think I would know the truth, regardless who spoke it," he offered.

The cardinal considered the answer with a simple nod. "I have a vast amount of people who follow my every move, following my teachings in the true God's name. You might call it blind faith Mr Alksey but faith none the less including those who understand the teachings of the truth."

"I've considered it's better to tell the truth rather than live a lie?" Simon offered, sure the cardinal knew more than he was admitting. His questions part of an elaborate cat-and-mouse game.

"One day soon you will have to face the truth. For your past will have far-reaching consequences for everything and everyone you hold dear." He rose from the seat. "Please let's continue our walk, Mr Alksey, this way." He took Simon's arm for support, manoeuvring towards a door leading from the gardens. The small entourage fell in behind as they made their slow pace.

Simon felt a creeping dread swelling inside, struggling with doubt to the questions of how and what this man knew about his past and the outcome for all concerned.

An imposing steel security shuttered door filled the end of the corridor ahead, entry granted by a palm security scanner plate built into the wall.

Cardinal Ambrozij pulled back a robed sleeve, placing his hand to the scanner to wait for a light to pass under his palm. The panel turned green, offering greetings before the hydraulics stuttered to life to open the door.

The room beyond came to life, as automatic lights flickered in sequence as sensors monitored movement from the group entering and rows of display cabinets lit from floor to ceiling. From above came a sound of air conditioning, emitting a cold mist to flow around the static displays, keeping the space to a constant temperature.

Simon supported the aged cardinal who casually waved a hand towards the illuminated room. "Over time and through great expense, I have gathered an extensive collection of artefacts, many items dating before the written word. Most unseen for thousands of generations, understood to be pivotal to spiritual and religious doctrines throughout the ages. To what our historians, academia, and scholars perceive as the world's greatest knowledge of our time."

Unsure what he was witnessing, Simon watched further displays of light one after another to fill the full length of the vast room. Then encouraged to continue browsing the displays as the others hung back to give privacy.

In front stood two large cabinets displaying feudal shields, their flaking canvasses depicting emblems of heraldry from the first and second crusades and damaged from wars in the holy land.

Simon felt the urge to study each item, fascinated at such a collection brought together outside a museum.

"We have the first written bible, the only copy to survive undamaged for over two thousand years," the cardinal explained.

Simon read the description plate of another artefact, well aware of the cardinal's intense fascination in his reaction than the priceless contents.

"This collection houses not just Christian relics either. We have an entire section of early Persian and Moorish antiquities including delicate crafted tapestries documenting the early rise of man's beliefs in Middle Eastern culture. This includes a hand-printed Quran taking pride of the collection in its own secured display over there." He pointed to a large display where a beautifully crafted gold and black book took pride of place in between Middle Eastern tapestries and banners. "There are sections for Buddhism, Hinduism, Shinto and Judaism." The cardinal seemed to know what Simon was thinking, expecting his questions as they continued the tour. "We have sections for all known religions, including those long forgotten." They stopped, the cardinal in need of rest as he supported himself against a railing.

Simon continued his curious fascination at the nearest display.

"You will recognise many items but others you may not, forgotten Gods whose names not uttered in tens of thousands of years, but still represented in this collection."

"Why?" Simon asked, crouching to read the plate of a worn tablet from an early Mayan dynasty around 8000BC. "I don't know why you hide the collection? Share it with the world?"

With a begrudging nod to the query, the cardinal straightened, gesturing for Simon's support, and once again they continued their journey through a labyrinth of cabinets. "To share the collection is not the question to ask. The question is the world ready to accept what this collection holds? It's true that items are important to history, others for religious significance, but others are too dangerous to have knowledge of their existence."

Simon frowned. "That's still no reason to hide such historical and religious importance?"

The cardinal considered the question, offering the slightest of smiles. "It's keeping the statues-quo, as not everything is for the masses to know, and that certain secrets have to stay just that, secret. For their knowledge could cause widespread panic or conflicts between nations to gain such items."

Simon paused, turning back.

"Please understand, for centuries the few controlled the many, either for religious or political reasons or just sheer greed for power," The cardinal watched intensely at Simon's reaction. "All in the name of civilised progress, keeping those in power through the need for law and order, and the masses remaining happy in their sheltered lives. The best example is the expanse of the early Roman Empire conquering the known world and inflicting Roman way of life on those deemed un-civilised societies now conquered. Suppressing or destroying those societies' religious beliefs, converting the populations to their own. When that didn't work, they assimilated those willing to follow and sacrificed the rest who continued to practise the old ways. The same continues to this day." The cardinal prompted Simon further in to the corridors of the collection. "Please come this way and follow me."

"It's fascinating your Eminence, but I don't understand why you would show me this priceless collection?"

"It's all about the truth and the bigger picture to our exist-ence." He gripped Simon's arm tight, continuing to walk. "As I asked earlier, would you recognise the truth if told? Would you believe the truth when faced with it, even though it contradicts everything told to you by those you trust?" The cardinal released his grip, shuffling to brace against a cabinet.

Simon's stomach churned violently with an increasing knot of discomfort as he sensed the cardinal's narrowed gaze fall upon him. A macabre expression of glee and fascination stretched his face as he noted Simon's hesitation.

The sensation Simon felt was instant, a sudden weakness and a chill ran down his spine as he flexed out his fingers from their numbness. His gaze went around those watching, shar-ing the same expressions of anticipation. "Is there something you want to ask me you're Eminence?" He asked, trying to control his composure and stand upright.

The cardinal, head tilted with a curious smile, features cold and uninviting. "It's not me needing answers, Mr Alksey, for I know the answers you seek, and have done so for quite a while. Which allowed me to prepare for today. But out of courtesy wanted to give you a chance to explain the reason for your presence here and what your fall means for us all." His once frail expression turned to a mask of stern defiance, unmoving as Bishop Nikolaos reappeared flanked by the Legion Guards.

Simon edged back to press against a small pedestal display. His body flooded with adrenaline, heart racing but strength failing. The prickle of electricity continued to numb his fingers, spreading through his hands and upper body. The sensation resembled the same sensed before the convoy attack, but more intense. It caused him to stumble, legs strength ebbing as he felt his body heat leave his limbs. As panic set in, he glanced at his hands as though holding answers to the numbness increasing with every passing moment.

The cardinal's interest intensified in Simon's floundering and inability to stay standing. "I thank you, Mr Alksey, for without your help we could not confirm what we had in our procession was the genuine item." His eyes flashed with satisfaction, raising a frail finger, pointing.

With a wash of nausea and dizziness, Simon staggered to turn to where he pointed, and for the first time noting the contents encased in the glass pedestal.

Sat on a red cushioned base, was a unique item radiating a hypnotic blue glow rippling its entire length and intensified to Simon's presence.

"The Blade of Light," Simon whispered, closing eyes in realisation to understanding why they had brought him to the monastery.

"Old texts chronicled the item reacts to a unique presence, your angelic side. That slight Celestial spark is enough to start a chain reaction to allow the blade to tap your essence and with time reaching its full capacity."

Simon cursed for his stupidity and arrogance, anger replacing the increasing pain. For once again the archangels neglected to mention a prime piece of information about the blade. He tried to push away, returning attention back to the cardinal and Nikolaos, watching with satisfaction at his discomfort.

"See bishop, kind words rather than brute strength get quicker results."

Simon struggled to stay on his feet. "You knew of what I was from the beginning," His body tensed at a wave of pain to his life essence draining from his body.

"With the knowledge I have gained, easy deciphering prophesies to understand what was coming. The hardest part was pin pointing when but with the vast resources of the Order in place monitoring for your arrival. It was a matter of time, although it was a surprise to hear of your rescue by a child and priest. A complication rectified in time before becoming a more serious problem."

Simon lurched forward, but his legs gave out, crashing to his knees.

"The boy has spirit bishop, if you would be so kind. A few more minutes will relieve him of that spirit."

Nikolaos supported Simon's unresponsive body back against the display case housing the blade.

The cardinal moved to clutch Simon with a bony hand under his chin, forcing eyes to flicker open.

"So you needed me here, it all makes sense now," Simon strained to speak, breathing becoming heavy.

"We don't have the capabilities yet to control a full angel, let alone one of your formidable archangel friends. Our sacrifices earlier were a necessity in gaining a chance of capturing a half-breed, being more susceptible to our needs."

Simon remained pinned against the glass as the blade's glimmer intensified to wrap around and envelope his upper body.

Nikolaos adjusted his grip, pushing against Simon's chest, fascinated in the light emanating from the blade as it responded to Simon. "Your Eminence, what is it doing?"

The cardinal chuckled, releasing his grip to let Simon's head slump against his chest. "See how it responds to him, even though the security glass. Remarkable, I was sure we needed physical contact for the transfer to begin, but I was wrong."

"But what is it doing to him?"

"Think of the blade as a battery, charging on celestial energy from our young visitor. Once returned to a self-sustaining level, it will then draw slight amounts from the surrounding life force of the planet itself until discharged." The cardinal appeared exhilarated and clapped with excitement. "The blade dormant for so long, its own spark depleted when found in the Vatican archives. Instantly, I knew its value regardless of its miss labelling as another relic of little importance. Few would recognise the scripture etched its edge and little did they understand the power they had."

"The celestial energy you speak of, what is it?" Nikolaos asked, curious attention remaining on the resonating blade.

"Every living thing has a God particle and the blade can collect and store such energy. The energy forms the building blocks of everything around us. In humans it's called a spark of life, but angelic beings are pure celestial energy within a human host which makes them so powerful. Think of them as one giant reactor walking around, but their one weakness is a weapon forged in the celestial temple, and now I have it."

Nikolaos remained speechless, unable to find words.

His subordinate's silence amused the cardinal. "Yes, bishop, in your grip is an angel, a bastard half-breed. Mr Simon Alksey here is a fallen angel, stripped of his wings to suffer penance on earth for his sins."

"Which was why we watched the sky for a falling star," Nikolaos responded. "The one foretold by the Chosen?"

"Yes, and much more, my dear bishop."

A sudden flash of concern crossed Nikolaos's face. "That would make him the threat you warned us..." He paused, unwilling to continue his sentence, as both continued to study Simon's interaction to the blade.

Simon was unresponsive, eyes filling milky white as the colour flowed from his skin, turning ashen grey.

Cardinal Ambrozij stood back. "If he is the threat mentioned and foretold, let him be the blade's first victim."

Stumbling for balance, Simon's body quivered. Almost unable to take much more, he pushed against the bishop's grip, breaking free to stagger a few paces before crashing against another display case.

Nikolaos sighed, pity filled expression to the semi-conscious Simon at his feet. "Perhaps he has limited time left, your Eminence."

The cardinal signalled to the guards to pick up the comatose body as attention went to the blade. The slightest touch of the cabinets' glass sent a static charge throughout his fingers as he pulled away, the sensation lingering. "Take him to level nine," he instructed.

Nikolaos pointed toward the door, confirming the Legion Guard takes Simon away.

From a side room, a robed cleric appeared to transfer the blade case to a waiting trolley.

Cardinal Ambrozij waved for aid and took the offered arm of his private secretary. "No, wait a moment." The instruction aimed at the Legion Guard. "Sit him down there."

They placed Simon on a small bench, appearing more lucid to his surroundings, away from the influence of the blade. He sat cradling his head, trying to shake off the nausea. A sudden tight grip of hair forced him to look upon the cardinal's sneering face.

"As a half-breed I would say the blade has a negative influence on your body, Mr Alksey."

All Simon could answer was with a pained response, suffering from the brightness of his surroundings as colour returned to his features.

"It doesn't matter as your usefulness will end," the cardinal snarled as he continued to grip the back of his hair. "Take him away," he glared, letting Simon's head fall forward.

The Legion Guard gathered Simon and carried him to a waiting detention cell.

The rest of the group gathered around the cardinal on entering the green-canopied garden atrium.

"We should kill him now, your Eminence, and remove the threat," Jozafat suggested.

"He still has his usefulness before that deed is complete. Besides, it would look better if he were... maybe... injured escaping the authorities after incriminating evidence resurfaced linking him to recent brutal murders."

Jozafat nodded. "I will see to the arrangements myself, your Eminence."

Both men rejoiced in their achievements before the cardinal leant towards Jozafat. "Is everything in place as instructed?"

"They are ready, you're Eminence," the secretary confirmed, bowing.

"Good and bishop, have you followed my instructions to the letter?"

Nikolaos shifted his stance. "In place your Eminence and awaiting your command."

"With the blade reactivated, my aim is to prove the prophecy false with this half-breed's death. Before then the last pieces of my plan have to be in place, for I await a bigger prize. Before then we deal with all other possibilities before the element of surprise becomes lost."

The three men observed robed clerics place the display case on a waiting pedestal between the bases of the trees of the ornamental atrium.

"From here the blade can feed on the essence of earth itself, to reach its full potential before we complete the last stage." The cardinal resisting the thinnest of smiles as everything hoped and dreamed was coming to pass. "Long live the true God," he said.

The Legion Guards hauled Simon to his incarceration, somewhat unresponsive, but as time passed and gaining distance from the Blade of Light's influence, he felt the return of his strength. Muscles ached and his vision improved to the point he could make out the hulking shapes of the two guards dragging him to a pair of lifts. Once inside, the doors closed, and they sped on their journey.

Simon sought to stand, and though unsteady, shrugged off his escort's support. He pushed past the persisting numbness and protest from every part of his body. The glare emanating from the fast moving lift needed for him to shield his eyes and apply pressure to his temples in temporary release from the nausea building. Simon tried to replace his pain with anger, anger towards becoming an unwitting pawn in Michael's celestial grudge match against the cardinal's plans. What was obvious, he was expendable to both sides? It begs the questions to his usefulness to the Order and why was he not already dead? None of it made sense as Simon's darkening thoughts interrupted with the lift doors opening to a sign posted corridor showing they had reached the detention level.

On existing, their heavy footsteps echoed the passage leading to a security checkpoint. Guard Cleric observed from his position behind a protected screen as a Legion Guard stepped forward to scan a pass over a reader plate. With access granted; the cleric nodded towards the waiting doors, now parting. "Pass the prisoner to security through the gate, and we will take him to a detention cell for processing."

What greeted them were two waiting clerics, pacifying batons holstered at the hip within easy reach for the slightest provocation. Not that they needed to worry.

Simon had no intension of attempting escape under such

tight security.

Both groups exchanged silent nods, completing the exchange, and the new escorts took Simon towards rows of waiting cells lining both sides of the detention block. Most cells appeared empty but for the occasional unfortunate appearing at the viewing port with curiosity to the latest arrival.

Simon kept his eyes low, struggling to avoid the glares as he passed, until sensing a peculiar interest. An icy stare of hatred met his glance as he noted the dark-featured woman brandishing the distinct bruising of her own unpleasant incarceration. Her injuries did not diminish her strange, alluring beauty as Lilith watched them pass.

Simon could not break her gaze until passing out of sight to his own waiting cell. *Guess I can add another name to the fast-growing list of enemies out for my blood,* he thought.

They stopped a few cells down as the escorting cleric offered a secpad, instructing Simon to place his right hand upon the screen. A red to green flash confirmed his identification into the system as the cleric typed a few commands into the secpad. A metallic clunk accompanied the distinct unlocking of steel bolts as the cell door opened.

Simon entered to the sound of the solid cell door closing behind, leaving him to familiarise himself with his new sparse surroundings as the electronic locks engaged. "Cosy," he remarked, pulling down a fold out shelf doubling as a bed. The thought of having to use it disgusted him, the stained plastic of worn cushioned mattress offered minor comfort as he clicked it into place.

On the wall were two printed signs, toilet and basin. The press of the first resulted in a hydraulic hiss releasing the metallic amenities from the wall, followed by the uniquely unpleasant smell of a blocked system. He swallowed an urge to wretch, returning the unit with automated flush and hoped his stay would be short. As he sat, a wash of tiredness overcame him, needing to rest. With reluctance, he pushed his tired body across the foldout bed seat, groaning under his weight. He rested his head against his arm, eyes closed with a need to clear his head with hope to relax enough to sleep. With time his body won over his mind and he slipped into sleep.

Not to last. Memories of the past few days stirred him from slumber, awaking to his unfamiliar accommodations before remembering where he was. Simon lay listening to the distant muffled noises of the cell block. He endeavoured to ignore the lingering odour seeping into the cell until the distinct sweet scent of ozone suddenly filled the air. The familiarity made him sit up to rub sleep-filled eyes, trying to focus around the cell. He noted a small pocket of shimmering air distorting with an array of colours before morphing into a solid mass. The mass continued to increase until Simon had to pull up his legs to allow for the materialisation of two huddled figures. Both clutched in an embrace until parting to allow Simon to recognise the arrivals.

"Bro, get up, hurry. We are here to free you." D's familiar voice and beaming smile greeted him as Simon remained huddled in the corner, baffled by the unforeseen appearance of his friends.

The other figure hunched over to retch, bracing against the far wall. Turning with a stressed expression, he struggled to speak before returning his head between his knees to retch again. "For all the saints in heaven, don't you ever do that again, you crazy son of" Father Peters let loose a torrid rant of profanities.

The bewildered D consoled him with a reassuring pat on the back, hiding the obvious enjoyment from the priest's discomfort. "Steady there, Father, I said we could take a quicker mode of transportation."

"I thought you meant your limo, you jumped up, pasty faced..."

Simon interrupted. "Father, what are you doing here?"

"Were here to rescue you, lad. Mr Malach found who possesses the blade."

"I already know who has the blade," Simon interrupted. "Because of me, the cardinal has a reactivated blade. I'm sorry I didn't listen to your warnings, Father." He sought to mask his guilt, but Father Peters with a shake of head tried to reassure him.

"It's not your fault, lad," he remarked. "How could you conceive what would go on, but luck has it if you hadn't, we wouldn't have been able to pinpoint your location?"

"But why wasn't I warned what would happen when I came into contact with the blade?"

The question aimed at D, wiping the splashes of vomit from the tip of his shoe with a pocket tissue. "In my defence, I was not aware of the consequences either," he explained with a sympathetic shrug. "I'm as much in the dark as you were."

Father Peters took a deep breath, still suffering from his unusual journey. "We can discuss that later. The fact is, the blade tagged you with an energy signature we could track."

D took in the newly confined surroundings with disgust. "You're in a cell, oh, that's great," he responded, unable to disguise his disgust.

"I'm sorry Father for getting you into this mess." Simon swung his legs down and greeted the priest with a clasp of hands. "Thank you."

"Group hug time," D called stepping towards them, arms outstretched, resulting in an unwanted push away in disappointment by Father Peters.

The trio shared a glance, happily reunited once more.

"We tracked him?" D protested as he caught up with what Father Peters had said. "What's this, we business priest... as I remember it was me who tracked Simon's location."

The Father with a roll of eyes let D protest his involvement so far in the escape plan.

Simon unable to stifle a smile let them descend for a moment into their petty argument of who was helping who before separating them. "Guys were still in the cell," he commented. "It won't be long until they notice the extra occupants."

Both men stopped close to blows as they stared at Simon.

"Oh, yes, hold on to your lunch." D grasped each of them.

"No, wait," Father Peters protested, but too late.

All senses became overwhelmed in pure white light, muffled as though submerged, followed by a sudden rush of air forcing breath from lungs and then silence.

Simon's next realisation to his surroundings was his scream of alarm as he fell towards the ground. The hard landing was painful, a sledgehammer blow to the chest. The only consolation being the cushioned grassed area breaking his fall. With a stifled groan, he rolled onto his back to view a canopy of green foliage stretching above him.

A faint mummer and Father Peters stirred from his own forced landing a few feet away. "Where are we?" he asked, retrieving his glasses as he stumbled to his feet, blinking to the light breaking through the trees.

"Not far, one of the private atriums inside the monastery," Simon replied, getting his bearings. "What happened, D, why aren't we miles from here?"

With no answer, Simon crawled over to turn over D's comatose body. Blood trickled from his ears and the corner of his mouth.

The Father checked his airways, putting his head to his chest before checking for a pulse. "Faint, shallow rhythm, no idea if that's normal for him, surprises me he has a pulse at all."

With concern, Simon surveyed the atrium. "We need to move him to one of those side rooms before someone sees us." Supporting their unconscious friend, they headed for a vacant office.

"Please stay where you are." The command came from a familiar figure blocking their path. Bishop Nikolaos pointed his sidearm, advising surrender.

From a side door rushed half a dozen Guard Clerics, fanning out around the room to surround the small group, weapons drawn.

"We have the boy and his accomplices, all units on alert for further incursion."

"This was a trap from the beginning, they knew we planned an escape," the Father whispered, placing hands on head, and knelt as instructed.

Simon checked D's condition again, finding his breathing remained shallow, before placing him to the floor.

Tension within the room increased with weapons drawn, all pointing in their direction.

"But it does not explain how they knew D would help?" Simon said, the Father offering the slightest of shrugs in response, as both met Nikolaos's self-righteous glare.

The bishop towered over them, revelling in their misfortune, satisfied the cardinal had expected everything so far. "Did you think it would be that easy escaping?"

Simon's lips thinned as he remained silent, determined not to give him any more satisfaction.

"We watch all cells and know of your unconscious friend's abilities. It was a matter of waiting until attempting an escape and capturing your accomplices."

"You're aware of D, who he is?" Father Peters asked with hesitation and surprise in his voice.

"They do," Simon offered, glaring at the laughing bishop. "They planned it all with the knowledge I'm part angel. Easy to consider they knew of D and his abilities. Besides, they have Lilith in one of the other holding cells. Guess interrogation is not beyond them, extracting the information they needed."

The priest's mouth opened, but he said nothing.

"It was fortunate we could persuade her to divulge information, but she told us nothing we didn't already know," Nikolaos confirmed. "Besides, not that I still didn't take great pleasure in the responsibility of verifying the details with her." He crouched down, looking between them with a thoughtful frown. "We also knew keeping you alive would bring a response from your celestial friends. Unlike the attack on the convoy, you will find we have planned for their arrival. The cardinal is a master of the waiting game." Nikolaos glanced at D's unconscious body. "On learning the plan, I had reservations of it working until D teleported in to your cell. All we had to do was deploy psychic countermeasures, raising a temporal barrier to disrupt teleportation abilities. The results you experienced when you encountered that barrier. Our plans rested on this happening and with you captured it brings the most logical response."

Increased communication chatter resonated from Nikolaos's helmet, confirming the next phase had begun. "Now it gets interesting," Nikolaos smiled.

The floor shook, lights around the garden flickered before the surrounding lighting switched to emergency mode. Deeper inside the monastery, alarms sounded, followed by shouting of orders and hurried footsteps outside the atrium.

"Situation report," Nikolaos ordered, recoiling from a sudden flash of static interrupting the security link. Once cleared, replaced by voices relaying situation reports.

Simon saw the bishop's eyes narrow, face betraying his frustration as he listened to the first reports.

A door opened and in strode Father Clarke, escorted by three Guard Clerics.

Nikolaos moved to talk in private with the priest.

"Wish we could listen in to what they were saying," Simon said, straining to overhear the conversation between the two men.

Father Peters shuffled for a better view of the conversation, concentrating on their faces. "The main power generators are down, but they have backups for security and communications, including uplink to the main city grid. All cohorts holding at designated positions, awaiting orders."

Simon, surprised at the detail of the Father's interpretation, raised an eyebrow.

The Father smirked with a wink, concentrating on the conversation again. "Learnt to lip read from a nun working with disabled children in Africa in the nineties and taught me in our spare time. The priest mentions unknown assailants attacked the generators before containment in a sub level. The bishop is asking how many targets, two says the priest."

"Is it Michael and the others, did they say anything of what they planned for recovering the blade?" Simon asked.

"They were not forthcoming, just suddenly arrived and instructed Mr Malach to track the energy readings to its source and get you out. They never mentioned an attack on the monastery."

Simon contemplated the situation, noticing the Father's rather calm composure at the events unfolding around them. "How are you coping, Father? It's not every day you meet an archangel."

The priest shrugged. "Guess I'm doing okay under the circumstances, operating on adrenaline and blind faith at the moment." He lent forward. "Lad after the past weeks, nothing surprises me anymore. We have death catatonic on the floor, and my handyman's a half angel atoning for his sins commanded by Archangel Michael. Who instead of the spiritual imagery of my Christian beliefs turns out to be an arrogant dick with daddy issues? Under different circumstances I would be a basket case and drinking myself catatonic right now if I had a choice."

Simon stemmed a laugh. "Michael has questions to answer..."

"The guy's a tool lad."

Simon shook his head. "Not how I imagined. That's for sure."

The Father understood. "You're not like them, lad, you're better. Your human side makes all the difference."

"Hope you're right." Simon half smiled.

"Look lad, God made man with what archangels consider a flaw in the design, that being emotions. Instead, it makes us unique. The archangels are a blunt instrument of God's will, no reasoning with them as they follow orders. You don't, never forget that."

Simon hoped his friend was right, but since meeting the archangels and retrieving parts of his forgotten memory. Those returned memories, deeds done in service of their Father, had been unpleasant. He feared losing his humanity to his angelic side, which he felt growing stronger as time passed. His priority was reclaiming the blade, but what was the cost to those around him, those he now called friends. What were the archangels willing to sacrifice? He had experienced first-hand during the convoy attack how the archangels wiped out everyone without remorse. Could he allow that to happen again, or was he destined to become as emotionless and nar-row minded as Michael? Simon's attention returned to Bishop Nikolaos, returning the salute as Father Clarke left, followed by his escorts. He caught Simon's stare.

"Bit off more than you can chew bishop?" Simon asked, un-able to hide his amusement.

The bishop ignored the comment, waving over the senior Guard Cleric guarding the captives. "Pick them up and follow me," he ordered, striding for the exits across the grassed area.

The half dozen clerics gathered up their captives, ordering them to take the weight of their still unconscious friend be-tween them.

With backup power diverted to key systems, the lifts were not operational, so the group headed down the nearest stair-well, lit by emergency lighting. Under the red glow illumin-ating the stairs, alarms sounded, evacuating all civil and non-essential clerics. As the group descended, others evacuated and streamed topside via the fire safety points. Another two levels down, and they brought Simon and Father Peters into an already evacuated level.

Far above and outside the monastery, unknown to those inside, more Guard Clerics reinforced the cohorts preparing a defensive perimeter. A mass of MAUV and support vehicles stationed themselves around the primary entrance point's traversing weapon systems, waiting for orders.

Unnoticed from the prime vantage point of the uncompleted Reformation Towers watched Michael. The archangel studied the increasing activity, his black eyes emotionless and quizzical with the speed the Order had mobilised such a sizeable force. "This is taking too long. Our brothers should have returned with the secured blade and the half-breed freed with Malach's aid."

Thick spirals of smoke rose from the ventilation vents on the far side of the monastery. The plan was to disrupt the internal power grid to allow the escape of Simon and the others.

"Something has gone wrong Michael, the humans reacted with speed, it's as if someone prepared them for our assault," Raphael replied also surveying the scene.

Michael's eyes narrowed. "And something blocks my communication with the others, and I sense a mastery of the old ways against us. This is alarming."

Raphael concentrated, opening her mind in a search, sensing confusion and terror from the crowd's evacuating but nothing else. She felt hindered in her abilities, blocked by an increasing darkness enveloping the monastery. "I'm blocked from any connection with inside. You are right. Could be the reason Malach doesn't return?"

"I concur," Michael replied, considering their next move, placing a gloved hand upon her shoulder. "It's time we find our battle brothers. We trust in God, our Father, to complete his bidding in showing his light to those who embrace the darkness."

In unison they dipped their foreheads in silent salute, then parted and leapt from the edge of the building. Both plunging until unfurling wings, allowing them to soar between the buildings, circling unnoticed by the masses swarming below, hidden by the billowing smoke now enveloping the entire monastery. Once in position, Michael drew back his wings and plummeted feet first, crashing through the domed roof of an atrium garden. Glass cascaded in all directions, scattering birds from hidden roosts, startled by the sudden entry of armoured figures. Even under controlled descent, the archangel created impact damage to the mosaic flooring around a small rock pool. Unconcerned he raised to his feet, assessing the surroundings as alarms continued to echo.

There were two distant thumps of further explosions, followed by muffled automatic gunfire reverberating deep in the bowls of the monastery.

Michael closed his mind to the distractions, concentrating. "Raguel, Seraph, report brothers?"

The connection was instant. "They were ready for us, Michael," Raguel responded. His usually gruff voice sounded pressured and distracted by his situation. "We infiltrated and disrupted the power systems but have encountered heavy resistance and cannot retrieve the blade as instructed."

"Is Seraph still with you?"

"I'm here, brother, making slow progress as their weapons are proving most formidable in hindering our advance."

"We will come to you, then assault on two fronts, crushing all opposition. Retrieving the blade is paramount." Michael turned to Raphael, joining him from her observation from a stone outcropping in the ornamental fountain. "We appear to have pierced the black veil interfering with our communication," she confirmed.

Michael concentrated. "I sense the evil power behind it... warlocks. They cast a physic barrier to hinder our connection."

"Also makes celestial communication impossible with the rest of the Legion."

Michael agreed, heading for the nearest corridor leading to the levels where the battle raged.

Raphael fell in behind, ever watchful for signs of resistance.

Back at the detention level, Simon, Father Peters and the unconscious D returned to the cells, with instructions of being confined until the current emergency passed.

The nervous Guard Cleric in charge saluted and watched Bishop Nikolaos leave. Then, with his superior gone, relaxed as another cleric appeared at his side.

Both felt a sudden tremor through the floor, making them share the same apprehension to wondering what was happening.

"Heard from an admin cleric on six, says the main generators went critical during a controlled shutdown test. Now we have secondary explosions as they try to get the fires under control."

The first cleric ignored the obvious gossip, staying silent, but his colleague continued. "Another on eighth heard gunfire, something big has all the top brass hopping about, so it has."

On hearing the repeated rumours with no facts, he stopped what he was doing. "This isn't getting these prisoners processed, is it?"

With a shrug, the second cleric returned to his duties, listening to further distant rumbles.

As for Father Peters and Simon, their incarceration now appeared to be considerably longer than planned.

They had separated the prisoners into two separate cells, where Father Peters relied on his limited medical knowledge to care for his unconscious companion.

D lay bruised and beaten at his feet, dirt stained designer suit torn open and covered with blood. He showed no signs of recovery from the trauma of their failed escape. An unsuspecting result of contact with a physic electromagnetic barrier that had been violent, and the priest was not sure if he would recover. The only choice was resting his unconscious body on the pull-out bed, making him as comfortable as possible.

Simon, in the adjacent cell, spent his incarceration noting what little activity there was through the observation window. In frustration he pushed against the frame in hope to force it open, sensing intermittent vibrations followed by a distinct rumble throughout the cell block. The lights flickered as he stood back; the vibrations increasing under foot as though something was burrowing upwards. Shouts of alarm came from outside as the whole block shook, releasing dust and plaster across the entire level. The following explosion threw Simon to the ground, taking what little cover offered.

The cell filled with resistant cries of support struts buckling under extreme pressure as the cramped space filled with choking dust and debris.

When returned to his feet, eyes stinging from the toxic air and fighting the urge to cough, Simon groped forward towards the door. What he found was a cascade of sparks falling from ripped out electronic conduits in the roof, fizzing and spitting. The once solid door, unmovable moments ago, now lay twisted and open.

Simon clambered across the debris and peered outside, noticing distinct shapes of others stumbling as they too ventured out. He focused on the need to find the others clawing around to the adjourning cell. To find Father Peters and D spread out across the floor and unmoving.

Just then Father Peters rolled onto his side, appearing to be unharmed from the explosion.

Any effort to draw the priest's attention at the window got no response. Simon touched the side of his face, retracing blood from his ears. In his haste, he had not noticed the constant ringing muffle that was his hearing. An obvious result of the blast, hoping to be temporary as he considered the others, suffered the same disorientation. He quickly wiped away the congealing blood, flinching from the instant pain and disorientation, waiting for the sensation to pass before prioritising to getting the others out. But unlike his door, theirs remained locked and undamaged, and a search of the immediate area proved hopeless for something to lever the door open. It was then a sudden crackle of sparks drew attention to the cleric station, where part of the detention block had taken a major proportion of the blast.

Simon moved around the console, searching for a door release. Everything appeared dead, and including the senior

Guard Cleric who had manned it, for a support beam impaled his shredded body. Ignoring the horror, Simon searched the body before noticing in the scattered debris a rhythmic flash of green light. He stooped to retrieve a secpad, and with cautious dusting he found the device still active and unlocked. Navigating the main directories found what appeared to be the security command listing for the entire block. By now his hearing had returned, and distinct alarms sounded and accompanied by further tremors. He understood time limited, so searched for the commands needed.

All down the entire length of the wrecked detention block, the undamaged cells unlocked with a metallic clunk, their occupants freed but somewhat reluctant to step out.

Simon ignored them and headed back to his friends to find Father Peters sat up, nursing a bleeding head wound with a handkerchief.

"What in all things holy happened, lad?"

Simon completed a quick once over of his friend searching for further injuries and found none.

"It's nothing, lad, just a scratch," the priest grumbled, returning the blooded handkerchief back against the gash.

"The cell block took a hit. The clerics are dead or unconscious, but we have to hurry. Others will investigate what happened. You fit to travel, Father?"

"Get me to my feet and I will be okay lad, help me with him will you."

They're both grabbed D, sharing the burden between them as they clambered over the debris-strewn corridor towards the stairs.

"The explosion caused confusion and will give us an excellent chance to escape. No one will notice three more survivors once we are outside," Father Peters offered.

"Wait," shouted a voice.

The small group of fugitives froze. Simon and Father Peters sharing a glance before turning to find an MP-92 assault rifle levelled at them.

"Shit," expressed the priest, looking down the barrel.

A dust-covered Lilith glared down the rifle's sight. "Where do you think you are going?"

"No time to argue, Lilith. More clerics will investigate this explosion, and somehow, I don't think they will ask questions. No doubt shooting first and dispose of bodies later," Simon explained. He was desperate to defuse the situation so stepping in front of the pointed weapon, hands raised to show no threat.

Lilith's eyes narrowed, adjusting her grip. "That maybe, and I'm sure you're not bullet proof half-breed so I wouldn't come any closer."

Simon took the hint, stepping back. "Lilith, we want to leave, so come with us."

Father Peters pulled Simon to the side. "Lad, you sure about that, she tried to kill us not so long ago, remember."

"She wants out as much as we do, Father." Simon answered.

"It's your fault I'm in here in the first place," Lilith snapped, stepping forward, weapon still pointing. "You brought us a shitload of trouble."

"Your arrest was your own doing." Simon held up his palms, trying to still defuse the tension. "If you want to blame someone, blame Brian Shelby. He was the reason we were at the club after he took Lisa. If he hadn't, I'm sure the Order wouldn't have stormed the garage."

Lilith gripped the weapon tighter. "They broke an agreement to neither interfering in each other's business, and it had nothing to do with Brian. He was just a street thug out of his depth. The Order wanted you the moment you stepped in the club, they knew what you are, a danger to both sides. So tell me why I shouldn't put a bullet between your eyes and do everyone a favour?"

Simon flinched as Lilith pushed the weapon closer to his face.

"Then allow my friends to go." Simon requested.

Lilith shook her head. "The cardinal craves power that no

mortal should ever wield. You and your friends are part of his plans." The rifle barrel was no further than an inch from Simon now, as he braced for the inevitable.

"He already has the active blade," Father Peters shouted.

That got a reaction as Lilith's eyes widened at the news, "The cardinal has the blade."

"You know about the Blade of Light?" Simon asked.

Lilith lowered the weapon. "We know about a blade that can kill angel and demon alike. Does the cardinal understand what he has?"

"He knew from the start, it's why the archangels are here seeking to retrieve it before he can get to use it," Father Peters continued.

"Archangels are here too?" Her anger was instant. "What have you done half-breed?" Lilith growled, repointing the weapon.

"Help us, please," Simon pleaded, trying to read her intentions.

"Is Michael here?" Lilith asked as her posture tensed.

"We aren't sure. We think he had others attacking the lower levels as a diversion to our freeing Simon. But they have a mystic shield stopping D from doing his teleport trick," Father Peters explained.

Simon, on seeing the weapon lowered, relaxed. "We could use your help, Lilith, taking the blade back and getting out of here."

She threw him a half look, thinking a moment before nodding and pushing past to head for the stairs.

The Father watched with suspicion as she left, turning back to Simon, "I guess she's joining the band." They both gripped D, following Lilith out of the Detention Level.

It was a strain, but the group reached level three, lucky to find the stairs deserted but for a few individuals trying to evacuate. They did not appear interested, no one questioning two dirty survivors helping an injured man up to the higher levels. Even the well-dressed woman with a savage stare, brandishing an assault weapon, got no second glance.

"What are we waiting for?" the Father asked, breathless.

Lilith had stopped further up ahead, watching for activity through the stairwell door before turning. "On this level is a service hatch, takes you up and out behind a small motor pool. If you follow that topside and mix with those evacuating, it shouldn't raise any suspicion."

Simon approached. "What then?" he asked.

"I go for the blade. It's too dangerous to leave in the cardinal's hands." She checked her ammunition, returning the magazine and chambering a round before removing the safety.

"I'm going with you, it's my fault he has the blade," Simon offered.

Lilith gave him a chilled stare.

But he was adamant to make things right to what he believed was his fault, so stared her down until her face mellowed.

She gave the slightest grin. "Okay, half-breed, stay close." The door pushed open, Lilith covering both directions of the corridor with a sweep of the rifle, and then waved the others to follow. They did not get far, rounding a corner when Lilith dropped to one knee, pointing to Simon to crouch behind her. "Movement up ahead," she said, rising back up, keeping tight to the side as they moved forward again.

"Don't kill me please," pleaded a business-suited man crouched before a cross section of corridor, the opposite wall riddled with bullets. It was also where a body of administration cleric lay with robes drenched in blood.

Simon eased past Lilith, kneeling down beside the suited man. "What happened here?"

The man, his tear-filled eyes wide, sobbed. "Damn trigger happy clerics, they're shooting anything that tries to go past them. They have orders to not let anyone leave."

"How many clerics are there?" Lilith asked as she adjusted the strap on her weapon.

"Two, yes, two," sobbed the man.

"We will find another way around, don't worry," Simon offered.

Lilith with a roll of eyes pulled Simon behind her and went to peer around the corner.

In a heartbeat, gunfire erupted from further down the passageway as tracer rounds tore in to the wall, ripping away more plaster.

Both Lilith and Simon jumped back, the man wailing until the automatic fire stopped.

Father Peters rubbed the dust from his glasses, nodding further up the corridor. "So much for the vent," he said.

Simon agreed, looking around for another way, catching the frown on Lilith's face, reading her intentions to other ideas.

She stood up, grabbing the cowering man with her. He blinked at the intent stare she gave him before being kicked into the adjoining corridor.

The man floundered, a sudden expression of horror crossing his face at the realisation of his predicament. Weapon fire racked the ground around his feet. For a moment he appeared to live a charmed life until further tracer fire rounds found their target. His business suit erupted in ripples of red. The force knocking him further back, each round hitting his body until, unable to support himself, he collapsed to the ground, next to the dead cleric.

Simon stood shocked as Lilith then levelled the rifle and rounded the corner to aim. The rifle bruised her shoulder, firing individual rounds in quick succession, and then all fell quiet. "Done, follow me," she confirmed.

Father Peters crossed himself, seeing the motionless suited man. He gave a small prayer before Simon put a hand on his shoulder and nodded to help lift D. "Did you see what she did, lad?"

"I did," Simon offered with reluctance.

"She murdered him in cold blood, as if she pulled the trigger herself so she could draw their fire," he protested, loud enough for Lilith to hear.

"I know Father," Simon said, straining with the still uncon-sciousness D.

The group stopped at a small barricade made from furniture dragged from the surrounding offices, then placed across the corridor. Two Guard Clerics lay amongst the makeshift barri-cade. The first lay on his side, a bullet hole to the chest, second through his helmet faceplate and under his left eye. A second cleric, still alive, tried to crawl to an adjacent office.

Lilith strode over to him, using her boot tip to flip the cleric on to his back.

His faceplate was open and blood covered his face and chest as he tried to speak bubbles formed at the corners of his mouth.

"Simon please take D we have to get him help," Father Peters said, moving to the cleric, rolling up his sleeves of his cardigan.

A sudden shot ran out, and the cleric was silent, eyes open, still looking upwards. "He doesn't need your prayers now, priest," Lilith remarked, lifting the still smouldering rifle to rest on her shoulder.

"You lousy bitch," he cursed, anger getting the better of him as he came to block Lilith from walking away. "You're one soulless bitch, you know, Lilith." He pushed a finger into her shoulder.

Lilith remained expressionless to the protest, clutching his throat in a tight grip.

Father Peters floundered, struggling to break the grip.

"Stop it, let him go, Lilith," Simon shouted, grabbing Lil-ith's arm to help the still floundering priest.

It was Lilith's turn to express anger as she turned on Simon, a look of sheer contempt for them both. "About time you bur-ied your human half, embrace who you are half-breed for the coming war will cost you if you try to save everyone. Do you expect your archangels would show any remorse and mercy to these meat bags? I hate your kind with every breath but still respect them to carry out the job, whatever the cost. When will you realise both side treat the meat bags as slaves, fodder to do with as we please?" She released her grip.

The Father coughed for air, collapsing from the ordeal.

"I'm well aware of what I am, Lilith. It frightens me as I remember my past, what I have done in His name. Don't think I'm not prepared to do what's needed, but I will not sacrifice innocents just because you can."

Lilith studied him, eyes narrowing as they faced each other. Her expression softened and her ebony beauty showed through the dirt and grime as she chewed her lip in thought before pushing him to the side and striding away. She headed to the far end, tapping the service vent on the wall with the butt of the assault rifle. "This is where we part company. That vent leads to behind the motor pool. Keep to the tree line and you're out."

Simon walked to the vent, pulling free the metal grill. A quick peer inside the narrow space, finding a single ladder secured to the inside of the shaft to the top.

Father Peters recovered from his confrontation, pushed D into the vent.

"What are you going to do?" Simon asked as Lilith checked around the dead clerics for spare ammunition.

With a forced smile, she stood, tapping Simon's face. "I will find this blade. It's not in my boss's interest to let the cardinal control it. It's a threat to both sides." She put two retrieved clips under her belt, picking up her rifle again, and headed back the way they had come.

"Simon lad, give me a hand, will you?" Father Peters shouted, struggling to take D's weight up the ladder.

Simon watched Lilith stride away before returning to help his friends.

On the lower levels, Michael and Raphael had met brief resistance. The Order cohorts had not expected assault from the rear, nor medieval armoured monsters brandishing Dark Age weaponry. With a battle roar, Michael fell upon the small group operating a defensive line. The first sweep caught a cleric under his right arm, slicing through his collarbone, almost decapitating him. His lifeless body fell against another cleric, struggling to raise her weapon. The downward cut sliced into the cleric's struggling body, silencing her alarm. No one stood a chance, and their last taste was their own blood. The remaining cleric made her stand against the towering armoured man. After witnessing the savage slaying of her comrades, she froze. Her finger hovered over the trigger, ready to release vengeful fury on the approaching target, but her brain refused to send the signal. The cleric's final thought was the realisation to a knife blade reaching under her chin, severing her throat in a spray of red. Her eyes rolled back in to her head as her body convulsed to the floor.

Raphael returned the weapon to her belt, remaining bird-like on top of a barrier as Michael approached.

Gunfire echoed, warning the two archangels that further bloodshed was far from over until the job done.

Smoke and burning fuel filled the air as Bishop Nikolas gave orders to the waiting priests stood around a digital display of level sixteen, Engineering Level. The virtual map designated the area as the Testing and Development Division split into three vast complexes. At the far end housed smaller test labs and offices for the army of technicians and engineers normally assigned to this level. The position a perfect choke point to the upper levels of the monastery and with all non-combat personnel evacuated, it became a massive military staging ground. The Order had pushed the unsuspecting saboteurs in to a murderous crossfire from two levels. Allowing ranged automatic fire to rain down from the elevated gangways, and armoured blast barriers being manoeuvred forward across the open space.

A young priest flinched as an explosion rocked a steel gangway. A quick regaining of composure, he continued his report. "We have them contained in the lower right corner. Two targets, armoured by the amount of firepower we are pouring down on top. They're resisting. Casualties are light and manageable, but we have extensive structural damage reports throughout. These include major ruptured power conduits on levels six, nine and twelve. Engineering clerics have control and are rerouting power as needed."

Nikolaos flicked through the large schematic of each level, acknowledging the report with a quick nod before enlarging parts of the screen. "There, bring the MAUV's up to here, suppressive fire with heavy weapons, pacify the intruders whilst Father Clarke brings up the new weaponry for containment. How long do you need?"

Clarke studied the map. "Ten minutes, twelve tops. The transport lifts are still operational but have fluctuating power issues on all levels."

"The tech guys say you have two, three shots max until the coils need to cool, they still haven't resolved the heat issue, so make each shot count."

"We will do our duty bishop or die trying," Clarke responded.

Nikolaos gave a wry smile to the priest's determination to his duties, slapping his back. "I like your spirit Father, let us hope my other priests have the same determination once facing the enemy today." The others around the table straightened as Nikolaos glanced at each. "Well, you have your orders. Let the true God guide you in his name we trust."

With a salute, they left to take up positions with respected cohorts.

Nikolaos continued to study the plan again, making sure he had left nothing out. His thoughts drifted to an earlier meeting with the cardinal, warning of the coming battle and more to come. Also, how the true God sent warnings of a weapon from the old days, wielding an extraordinary power, a power to destroy all enemies. Then trying to hide his surprise, when told a flophouse handy man was a fallen angel. He had stood in wonder as the boy's presence sparked the legendary weapon, almost draining him of celestial life essence. Nikolaos pulled back from the earlier thoughts, attention needed for the battle raging around them. Thankful the cardinal remained safe, and the elite Legion Guard protected the blade and so awaited the next stage of the plan against the intruders. He tapped one section of the screen, viewing multiple video feeds supplied from drone surveillance monitoring the battle, picking one image to drag and expand. He studied the hunched shapes sheltering from the murderous onslaught of his encroaching cohorts. They were larger than an average person, even a battle armoured cleric. Their weapon's design primitive but generated a tremendous amount of power, the same blue energy that emanated from the blade. He concluded their weapons condensed the energy into a solid projectile capable of ripping through the thickest defences like paper. As he pondered the image playing out, one figure rose from concealment to release a bolt crashing into an armoured barrier being manoeuvred by a group of advancing clerics. The light engulfed them, exploding outward and ripping plating and bodies alike. Nothing remained, but a blood spattered blast barrier. *What in the true God's name, are we fighting here?* His jaw twisted in thought, closing the image and retrieving his weapon. He left to watch the battle unfolding, the constructed cavern vast and the length of nine plane hangars. The far corner was awash with flames and explosions. Smoke hung in the airless atmosphere, hindering visibility of the manoeuvring cohorts as they moved forward into the maelstrom as though stepping into a hell on earth.

Only a few levels above, Lilith continued through the labyrinth of corridors unnoticed, but found her way blocked as the stairwell had collapsed. She pushed at the twisted metal and uncovered electrical wiring that sparked in final death throes. Forced to retrace her steps, she slipped through a side door into another battle-damaged corridor and noted another emergency stairwell, which appeared unguarded and undamaged. The quietness of the stairwell was eerie, and she felt surprised in not finding resistance, unlike the level above, coming across a platoon-sized squad of dead clerics. They had suffered various blade injuries and now her senses had become heightened, expecting trouble. She panned her weapon for any threats lurking as the corridor split in three directions. Lilith stepped over the remains of a dead heavy weapons team, no longer protecting the junction. A kick against the nearest body made certain he was dead before searching for signs of where to go next. "Shit," she cursed, lowering her weapon to the realisation to being lost in the maze. Another expletive and rifle ready, she continued but got no further than twenty yards before stopping. The corridor turned right and battle damage had taken out the lighting up ahead, casting her route in flickering darkness. She wrapped the rifle strap around her forearm, pushing forward.

A shape loomed from the shadows, gripping the barrel of her rifle and pulling Lilith off balance as a huge gloved hand gripped her throat. Lifted off the floor, Lilith thrashed whilst pinned to the wall, grappling against the grip. Air squeezed from her lungs as she continued to struggle, her vision clouding in a fight to stay conscious. She floundered for her weapon, dangling from her arm by its strap, but she needed both hands against her assailants' grip, never feeling such strength.

"Michael, release her," came a shout. "She helped us escape, Michael. She is trying to retrieve the blade just like us." Simon gripped Michael's arm, trying to make the archangel loosen his grip.

Lilith's lips turned blue as she fought against losing consciousness until Michael slackened his grip.

His disgust was clear as he snarled, still pinning Lilith against the wall. "Her kind is demon and to break its neck will release the vessel's torment, a more human response, would it not?"

Simon sought to reason with the archangel who stood back from the semi-conscious Lilith collapsing to the floor to get her breath. "I know she is a demon, Michael, I felt it when we first met back at the club. In fact, the entire club was crawling with them. But that doesn't mean you should slaughter everyone that moves." Simon tried to help Lilith back to her feet, but she pushed him away, staggering back at the suspicious glare by Michael with loathing behind jet-black eyes.

"Touch me again winged freak and it will be the last time," Lilith offered with bitterness. She loaded a round, aiming her weapon at Michael, who continued to growl as he stepped away.

Simon came to stand between them, holding up his hands. "We need to help each other if we have any chance of getting the blade back, Michael."

"She wants it for herself, nothing more. Demons do nothing they don't want to unless it benefits them."

"For a blade that kills archangels and demons alike. Your damn right, I'm here to get the blade, nothing more and the first thing I will do is smite your arse flyboy." Lilith grinned, lowering her rifle.

Michael rounded on Simon. "What are you doing here? Malach was giving the task to have you miles away."

"D ran into trouble, but I helped the Father get him to the surface, and then doubled backed after Lilith. This is my fight too."

Lilith pushed past both.

"I don't trust demons, I smite them," Michael said, watching her go.

"There is a trust issue, I would agree, but she got us this far."

Michael remained silent, brooding about letting Lilith go.

"Have you found the reason for stopping D to escape the monastery, anyway?" Simon asked.

"They have a physic web over the entire building, nothing teleports through and it also hinders our communication. We had to descend into the monastery to reach our battle brothers, but we are now out of direct contact with the Celestial Temple."

Simon detected concern in the archangel's voice as he spoke.

"We have never come against such resistance. Whoever's responsible, they're using old practises against us, dark practises." Michael continued with a flash of uncertainty.

"What do we do?"

Michael retrieved a discarded weapon, turning it over in his hand, before thrusting it at Simon. "We fight, that's what we do."

"We shouldn't be fighting the clerics, they are only following orders. It's the cardinal who we have to stop."

The archangel was not listening as he strode off to join Raphael, waiting. "Learn fast if you are to survive this battle," he shouted.

"Here, give it here," Lilith ordered, watching Simon frowning.

"Safety, eject to check the clip, snap back, chamber and release," Simon responded. "Not my first time."

Lilith gave a begrudging nod and followed the archangels towards the fighting. "Then make sure you watch were your pointing and don't shoot me in the arse, I'm already having a shit day." With that last piece of advice, she left Simon alone to continue staring at the weapon, forcing himself to consider what to do next. Not that he feared a fight, but the fact was that bloodshed was all he could remember from his past so far. How much blood had soaked his hands from the countless battles. The dark thoughts evaporated with another explosion rocking the building, flickering the strained lighting. With a final deep breath, considering how it had all been leading to this moment, where he had to fight or flee.

Unknown to Simon, fast approaching from a dark recess of the blackened corridor, something moved silently, a shadow hidden from sight. He was unaware until too late, as the darkness enveloped him, a tight vacuum to snatch him without a sound.

Cardinal Ambrozij waited in the luxury of his quarters,

where usually the ornate window flooded the room with coloured light. Not today, for the monastery had become shrouded in thick black smoke. The latest reports filtering through from the lower levels were less than encouraging as he sat sensing distracting rumbles shaking the monastery's foundations. To the others of the room he presented confidence and patience, remaining deep in thought, calculating in silence the next phase of his intricate plan.

From the corner of the room paced Private Secretary Jozafat, having pleaded for the cardinal to evacuate until safe to return. The response to that plea was swift and unpleasant, resulting in his brooding with his clerics.

The sound of raised voices brought attention to the doors shuddering open.

Two robed clerics unsuccessfully attempted to halt Bishop Nikolaos sizeable frame from entering the room.

"Your Eminence, there's an urgent matter we must discuss," Nikolaos requested over the heads of the clerics, still trying to stop him entering.

Jozafat moved to aid the flustered clerics, adding his own voice to the commotion.

"Enough," the cardinal ordered, eyes remaining closed with the slightest flicker of irritation before attention fell upon the small group. A swift wave of hand had the clerics disperse. "Bishop enter, the rest leave us."

Jozafat was about to protest but found it prudent to stay silent, bowing before ushering the clerics from the room, ignoring Nikolaos's unnerving glare.

The bishop's stance appeared ridged, features expressing minor stress and fatigue to the fight still raging.

Cardinal Ambrozij showed no signs of compassion towards his subordinate's state, nor reaction to his usual pristine armour displaying battle damage. Noting parts of the intricate plating lay open and scorched black. "Bishop, please sit and give me your report." The offer was a chair by his desk, suitable to accommodate the bishop's armoured frame.

"Thank you, your Eminence." Nikolaos removed his helmet, hair matted with sweat tracing the lines of his face, appreciating a chance to sit. He moistened dry lips before continuing his report. "We have control of the situation but have reports of further infiltration within the monastery. Casualties are manageable and confident of holding as requested. We have implemented a complete news blackout and PR teams are working on a cover story."

The cardinal's expression never changed, the black ringed shallow eyes observed as Nikolaos lent back in his chair. "Is the new weaponry deployed?"

"Combat drones confirm we are ready for live fire deployment on your orders and once again confident of their success."

"On the capture and containment of the subjects, make sure they're transported to the holding facility with all relevant precautions taken."

"Understood, you're Eminence."

The slimmest of smiles crossed the cardinal's lips. "You have questions, bishop."

Nikolaos with a nervous pause cleared his throat. "You're Eminence; I struggle to understand the reasoning, to have them attack the monastery and contain them. Why provoke their wrath, as we have the blade, is that not power enough."

"You will understand in time, my loyal bishop, for a bigger game is being played out and not all pieces are in position. Once I'm certain, and only then will we strike, until then I ask your forces to contain and wait?" He rose from the chair.

Nikolaos stood also, watching as the cardinal offered his arm.

"Walk with me, bishop, I wish to share something that will make your sacrifices so far worthwhile." Nikolaos fell into slow step, aiding the cardinal. "We offer nothing but obedience to you and the Order, your Eminence," Nikolaos confirmed with a courteous bow. "The true God will reward in the next life, as written."

Both men paused, the cardinal raising a palm to touch the bishop's cheek. "This is all I ask my friend, but the next few hours will be crucial to our Order. The blades pivotal to me regaining what I have lost. We must have everything in place, including a major piece of the plan." The two men passed through an assortment of deserted offices, leading to a corridor flanked by Legion Guard at attention. At the far end, the room expanded into an enormous glass domed atrium, its trimmed shrubbery and well-kept flora in full bloom. A picturesque scene if not for the suspended body hung between two trees, blooded and beaten, the man stripped to his waist. Somehow sensing their presence as he slowly raised his head, features bruised to include his right eye swollen shut. A fine line of blood bubbled from his mouth as he tried to speak.

Nikolaos smiled in recognition to the dreadful specimen hanging in front of him.

The cardinal went to sit in a prepared chair as two clerics bowed in greeting as he became comfortable. "You know Mr Alksey, bishop, such an intricate part in our plans and he will decide the last stage."

Nikolaos recognised a creature that had all resistance beaten from him.

"With the bait in place, time to spring our trap," the cardinal smiled, signalling to two darkly robed clerics stood under an outcropping of shrubbery.

Elsewhere in the monastery, Michael greeted Raphael, returning from her scouting. "Report please, Raphael."

"The blade's safeguarded on the upper level, in one of the many gardens under heavy guard. I could not get any closer, but I sensed its power."

"It will not help them, for we are his might, we shall never fail."

"I confess to having reservations, Michael. Our ignorance of the humans has hindered us these past few days, and I must express caution as we did not sense the blade until now."

"Nothing but primitives Raphael, meat suits to the demons

and our vessels when needed. Why Father chose them over the celestials has angered many since they first walked on two legs."

"Perhaps striking them directly has...?" The archangel's wings ruffled as though she spoke out of turn. "Our assault has proven ineffective in recovering the blade."

Michael turned with a flash of anger behind his eyes.

Raphael gripped his arm. "Brother, we are not questioning your leadership, rather hoping for a more tactical approach for its retrieval."

The anger lessened as he considered her words. "You are right, we have underestimated the humans in their audacity to stall our progress so far, and it's disturbing." He grasped the hilt of the sword at his side. "Their reliance on technology gives them an advantage we have never faced. In addition, their knowledge and use of the ancient ways grows stronger the more we stay here."

"Something evil dwells here, something old," Raphael said, placing her helmet and bow on a table. "This old magic not only hinders our communication but shields something from us, something not faced before, and that makes me ask for caution."

"I agree." Michael had sensed the same. "But that's secondary to retrieving the blade. We must end this." The archangel handed over an item of curved white ivory. "You will know, Raphael, when to use it and when the calls needed the most."

"What you are proposing, Michael..." Her words went unfinished as Lilith entered the room. Both archangels turned to her, leant against the far wall, arms crossed. "Hate to break up your little team huddle but were missing one half-breed. Neither of you thinks it suspicious that he was right behind us, then gone."

Her companions remained silent until Michael headed down the corridor. "Not our concern, he proved his usefulness, and the blade is our priority and nothing more."

Lilith shook her head to the emotionless answer, picking

up her own weapon to follow the two archangels further into the monastery.

Back at the atrium, the cardinal lifted the matted and blood stained head, confirming that Simon still lived. "It's a pity you have to die as you amuse me. A little older than my usual tastes, but your essence could sustain my needs for a while, I suppose." His stained teeth appeared from behind pencil thin lips, twisting into a macabre smile.

Simon's response was to cough blood, trying to focus before reacting to the Blade of Light raised to his bruised face.

"It seems you have outlived your usefulness as the blade no longer draws upon your life essence. Perhaps it senses your demise is imminent." The cardinal released his grip, stepping away and letting Simon's head drop to his chest.

"You call yourself a man of God," Simon spat in last defiance, blood lodging in his throat.

The cardinal swung around, spittle spraying Simon's face. "You dare judge me, was it not your own God that sent you here as a penance for your sins?" With a jagged finger, he pointed at Simon. "Your another sacrifice in his name, in a war of who loves him the most, angel, demon and human alike."

Simon could smell the stench of wine on the cardinal's breath as he came to grip the back of his head, pulling him backwards.

"You are nobody to him. Tell me, where is your God now?" The cardinal snarled, his grip tightening.

"There is a purpose in everything. If I die today, then let that be the reason."

The cardinal hissed, easing his grip in frustration. "You have blind faith that your God will save you, do you? How touching to find such stupidity in one so worthless." Utter contempt crossed the old man's face.

Simon mustered what strength he had, straightening his back against the restraints. "You stand there talking about faith when you're the spiritual leader for a religion of billions. A hypocrite in robes, like so many before you, craving power over those you believe beneath you. You sit with entitled arrogance judging over them, but God shall be the only judgement over man."

"Well, that is the sixty-four thousand dollar question isn't it," the cardinal replied, circling. "You question my faith and that of my followers, but the question you should ask is which God they follow."

An icy chill came over Simon as he observed the cardinal laugh at his struggle.

"God didn't create the earth in seven days. This planet was cooling when your God was a fledgling in the stars, a flea amongst true Gods and masters of the cosmos," the cardinal continued pacing.

Bishop Nickolas stood, observing with fascination.

"You put faith in lies spread for over two thousand years to masses following teaching of stories, encouraged by those hungry for power and disguised as religion. You're God. Instead of eradicating the problem as the cancer they had become, he waited and watched as his reckless creation plundered and destroyed. To then turn on their creator, ignorant in allowing them to question that faith resulting in centuries of death and hate, all in his name. Today, far across the globe, people suffer, dying as the rich and powerful bring countries to their knees. What I bring is salvation from that darkness. A fresh hope to those lost as they embrace a true God rising to wash away suffering and bring a faith in a new truth."

"Enough!" The command filled the atrium with authority, shocking the room to silence.

All attention turned to the sudden crash of an armoured figure striking the stone tile floor, rising to stride towards the cardinal.

In the heartbeat, everything slowed in reaction to the newcomer.

Only the cardinal appeared to react with menacing speed and pointed. "Now," he shouted.

With the command given, a flurry of activity sounded and

from all around the atrium Legion Guard took up positions, weapons drawn.

Michael ignored the threat of hostility, attention on the cardinal stepping back with an apathetic hand clap. "Archangel Michael, I presume? Such an impressive entrance, but I thought you would be... taller."

Michael crossed the distance between them until hindered by Legion Guard.

The cardinal raised a hand to stop the archangel.

"I want the blade," Michael commanded.

"You do, do you?" The cardinal answered with surprise. "You think you're capable of taking the blade from me, archangel?"

"I command it."

The words brought a sudden transformation to the ailing cardinal. "You command it." He appeared to mull over the words until with a burst of anger his entire body changed. His posture straightened from his hunched form, frail and tired features morphing to express sheer hatred as his hands clenched into fists. "You dare... command me! You are nothing but a pet to a pathetic absent Father, you insolent pup. How dare you have the audacity to command me?"

Simon, his beaten body still suspended, could only flail at the confrontation unfolding.

Then from the cardinal's robes emerged the blade, its intricate design radiated a blue haze increasing to Michael's presence. Without hesitation, the cardinal once again displayed speed unseen in a man his age. He lunged, the blade piercing the thinnest part of the archangel's armour to the side of the chest plate and protective chain mail. A deep thrust embedded the blade into flesh and muscle, releasing blood that soaked the cardinal's fingers and robes. With a satisfying twist, he took pleasure to the seething pain expanding throughout the archangel's armoured side.

With a roar, Michael gripped the cardinal's hand, still clutching the blade. His expression turned from disbelief and confusion to panic as the old man resisted him with equal strength.

"Tell me, Michael, how it feels after a millennium of servitude in the Celestial Temple to face an adversary capable in matching even you archangel." The cardinal grinned through clenched teeth as he pushed the blade deeper, revelling in the pain he inflicted. "I've been preparing for this day, training clerics in the old ways to hinder you in practises lost to even your precious temple. In fact, I thank you for being so predictable, for you're an integral part of my plans today. Using your hate and ignorance towards the humans, your hubris was always your downfall."

From the tree line appeared hooded clerics, moving in unison, reciting memorised scripture.

Michael struggled over his own body, excruciating pain racking his side as the blade twisted.

Simon, with newfound strength, battled his bonds, proving futile as the cardinal glanced at his insignificant struggle, and then returned gleeful attention back to Michael. "Your arrogance astounds me Michael as much as your Father's claim on this world." He drew Michael closer. "You're ignorant to believe he's the only God to walk this earth. Let all rejoice for a new kingdom shall reign for His time is ending and we reclaim that stolen, so says a true God."

CHAPTER ELEVEN

Darkness and Light

They had set the trap, resulting in an intensity pinning the two archangels under the onslaught from the advancing legions.

Two MAUVs tore across the concrete on their six traction controlled wheels, navigating the battle field with ease to manoeuvre into position. The mounted weaponry resembled large satellite antenna, elevated to face the archangel's position. From the dish's core emitted beams of solid white energy, ripping swathes of masonry and debris from all around the concealed positions, stripping away what little cover it offered.

From Seraph's vantage point, the Order's forces were manoeuvring another blast barrier, frustrating him to not able to hinder the advance. The engagement had exhausted his strength to muster celestial energy to power his weapon. With a grim expression to his impending fate, he watched his battle brother do no better behind a blast barrier disintegrating with each passing shot. Further suppressive fire arched around them as Seraph concentrated in search for his brother's thoughts in the chaos. "Raguel, brother, you must hold for as long as you can, Michael shall not forsake us."

"We need to break out, stop this hiding and fight as warriors of God, smite them for defying his will." A salvo of heavy ordinance followed the growled reply to spray masonry across Raguel's winged back.

"That may be, but we wait for Michael's guidance, remember our orders. Have faith, our time is at hand," Seraph replied with another cautious glance from his position. Observing smoke trails rise into the air, arching down-wards towards his battle brother's concealed position. With a metallic clang, the smoking canisters bounced and rolled towards the crouching archangel. The resulting florescent flash engulfed Raguel and lifted him off his feet, depositing him far beyond his original position. The body of his brother lay still, smouldering as giant wings unfurled around him.

"Raguel," Seraph shouted in alarm, grasping his bladed staff to launch himself towards his fallen brother. The sight of Raguel being brought down brought a sudden lull in the fighting, but it did not last as Seraph broke cover.

Not far away, Father Clarke gave the order to push forward. "Target two, engage." The cleric to his right struggled with the unfamiliar weapon resting on his shoulder, crouching as his partner tracked the recent target with the weapon's control secpad.

A stream of smoke left the weapon as the missile took over the programmed trajectory mid-flight, compensating for the target stumbling across open ground.

Seraph scooped up the discarded hatch plate from a damaged MAUV, shielding his body as the warhead detonated against the steel. The accompanying white flash temporary blinded him, launching him backwards, and for the first time in his creation he felt the jarring sense of pain coursing throughout his body.

"Target is down, sir." Father Clarke used his helmet optics, expanding the image with satisfaction as his cheering clerics stood sharing in their victory.

The celebrations were short-lived as deep from inside the monastery. A reverberating horn rumbled in eerie call, the sound haunting in tone in an ancient call to arms.

"What by the true God's name was that?" Clarke shouted.

"Still calculating Father, we are still trying to pinpoint its location. It emitted a high frequency interference that's affected electronics and optics, and we are trying to compensate."

The sound continued to echo the confines of the underground complex, unnerving the clerics across their entire front line.

High above and hidden from view crouched Lilith, watching with surprise at the hesitation gripping the Order legions. *Have to hand it to the winged freaks they love their theatrics.* "That you making that screeching noise?" She nodded to the ivory horn hung from Raphael's belt as she fell in beside her.

"That was Michael's call to bring to battle the garrison. He instructed me to use it when I sensed it was time."

A flash of anger crossed Lilith's face. "You've gone nuclear."

The archangel did not flinch to Lilith's anger, as her attention remained on the clerics. "I did as commanded by Michael."

"What about using that little trinket an hour ago before we got our arses kicked and saved us a shitload of trouble?"

Raphael unfurled her wings, meeting her glare. "We had to make certain the cardinal possessed the blade, and we knew of its location. We also needed to have their forces engaged before signalling. My brothers Seraph and Raguel volunteered to draw their forces out as a distraction to our retrieval of the blade."

"What about the physic shielding, you said it was stopping celestial communication?"

"Nothing stops the summoning of the Legion. Not even old magic." She nodded towards the battle. "Before day's end, we will discover those responsible for projecting the shield and deal with them." As Raphael closed her eyes, she concentrated. "I summon the garrison, Michael, now's the time to lead them." She frowned, trying the connection again. "Michael, our garrison approaches."

"Is it the veil?" Lilith asked, sharing her concern.

Raphael tried again before a frail voice spoke. "So it starts Raphael, time to do God's will." Then, silence.

The archangel's eyes opened wide, sharing the pain through the link. She stepped back, unfurling giant dark wings. "He suffers immense pain, we have little time."

Lilith grabbed her arm, pulling her back into a crouch so not to give away their position. "Who does, Michael?" She pointed towards the far end where the first archangel attack had appeared. "The big guy gets to fend for himself, can I remind you, an entire world of hurt is about to drop on us."

As the eerie sound faded, a static crackle of interference had taken out his communications. The last message Father Clarke received from the surface was a confused description of the sky darkening above the monastery. He organised a senior cleric to instruct the waiting forces on the surface to prepare for a secondary attack. Then retrieving his weapon, he found the same interference affected by all other systems in the command bunker.

Various screens flickered with white static as clerics struggled to get any life out of their equipment.

"In the true Gods name, what's happening? Have we lost contact with the other cohorts?"

A young deacon, working at his equipment, turned to answer. "Father, all communication is down, including with the surface. We have line-of-sight only. The last reports before the blackout were weapon fire on the gantry levels. We might have enemy forces engaging on those levels."

The news incensed Clarke to their intricate plan unravelling. "I need to know what's happening above and confirm earlier reports." Another deacon stood by his blacked out screens, Clarke pointed towards him. "Take a half section to the upper levels and send runners for further reports from the surface. In addition, have two sections of the twenty-third take position on the levels above and give me a situation report as soon as possible. Father Jenkins..."

A thin-faced priest covered in grime stood to attention on the mention of his name. "Find Bishop Nikolaos and explain our situation. Ask if he will command surface forces to make their way level by level towards us. Also confirm if he has the same communication problems as us and tell him I've already sent runners for updates. I want a hard line connection to the surface forward positions ASAP, understand?"

"Yes sir," saluting the older priest turned to complete his orders.

Clarke took his weapon from the table, checking its readiness, before walking out to pass the overhang of the above level. A quick sweep of optics showed no hints of movement above, so attention came back to the battlefield. Smoke drifted from various fires across the entire forward positions. Injured personnel were being ferried for treatment while further equipment and replenishment well underway. There were no suggestions of any imminent counter attack, but still felt uncomfortable as a lull fell over the area as he turned to the command position.

Going unnoticed high above, a shape slipped from the railings into the overhanging cover of smoke that the industrial scrubbers in the ceiling struggled to disperse. The shape moved fast, disturbing the atmosphere as it crossed the full length of the complex, before holding in a circling pattern. There was no chance to react as it fell with speed towards one of the parked MAUVs mounting the new weaponry proving so effective against the archangels. A thunderclap of sound erupted, rolling from the vehicle's position. The MAUV rocked backwards as a blue arc of light emanated from inside and through exposed hatches and rear door. The resulting flames engulfed the unsuspecting clerics caught in the inferno. With no time to reel from the loss, the remaining MAUV a few yards away exploded in a fireball as its remnants showered the surrounding area.

"Give me reports," Clarke shouted, desperate to see what was happening.

Sporadic automatic fire flared their forward lines, increasing in intensity.

Clarke watched the valiant defenders silhouetted against

the flames, as screams of warnings echoed as black shapes rose amongst their positions. The priest loaded a fresh magazine, tracking the nearest target.

The enemy appeared human in appearance, armoured but slimmer in design to the cleric's armour. They also moved with surprising agility, one leaping a blast barrier. It carried what appeared to be a long spear cradled under its arm, thrusting to remove the top of an unsuspecting cleric's skull that had been operating a heavy weapon. The cleric's colleague stopped loading the weapon and fumbled for his sidearm as the spear pierced his breast plating. He gripped the shaft, pulling his pierced body along its length. In an ultimate act of defiance, spitting blood across his assailant's faceplate as it watched quizzically to his last throws. A violent wrench of the weapon left the lifeless body collapsing to the floor.

The MP-92 dug into Father Clarke's shoulder, releasing the rapid rounds, hitting the spear-wielding figure from hip to shoulder. His target recoiled to the red tracer ricocheting off its armour and pushed backwards before suddenly exploding in the brilliant white light. No trace left. Clarke, adrenaline flooding his system, lowered his weapon to realisation to holding his breath. With an exhale of relief, he could not believe what he had seen. An entire clip of armoured piecing rounds emptied into the target. "We need special weapons, ASAP," he shouted.

All around, more ominous figures hunted small pockets of clerics.

Once again resorting to helmet optics, Clarke magnified an area to pick out three clerics, putting up a futile defence against a sword-wielding assailant.

The figure swept from behind, with three savage thrusts reducing the team to a blood-soaked mass of flesh, before disappearing.

Clarke felt a small tremble start in his left hand, fighting to get his emotions under control as he took a deep breath. A quick tap of communications resulted in nothing but the continuing static. Switching to the laser communications, a small device emerged from his shoulder mount, rotating to track the nearest clerics, their positions then appeared in his helmet's display. "All cohorts fall to the second line, cohorts rally. Use LOS and pass on the order."

At first, all along the forward line, nothing appeared to happen.

Clarke considered his orders went unheard before noting clerics disengaged from their small skirmishes to retreat with trained discipline.

A deacon nursing an injured arm crashed into his commanding priest in desperate haste, the man's visor open

Clarke recognised fear on his ashen white face as he grabbed the man's armour. "We have to combine and form a field of fire. Do your job and get clerics moving to secondary positions around our command position," he pointed.

The deacon reluctant at first nodded and got his fear under control before heading to relay the instructions to the other clerics.

"Are we retreating, sir?" a cleric asked, reloading his weapon.

The urge to berate for an impertinent question flashed through his mind, but Clarke recognised apprehension in the man's voice. "We're never beaten, for our trust in the true God shall prevail. We are His might, His hammer, and we shall strike down those who oppose His teachings." A cheer resonated from over a dozen clerics, rallying as they repositioned, covering each other's retreat.

Soon the joint rate of fire from the second and repositioned gantry slowed any further assault, keeping their attackers at bay but at a cost.

Father Clarke kept his men in line, moving between them, offering encouragement. He glanced behind, noting the return of Bishop Nikolaos leading the defences of the second position. "Thank the true God, for we will make it," Clarke shouted and turned to track another target, firing with a rapid head shot that disorientated rather than an outright kill. Frustrated, he adjusted his aim, but the target had disappeared into the lingering dense smoke rolling across the whole area.

Deep within the complex came an animal like roar.

Many clerics unnerved took comfort in Clarke continuing to move amongst them, offering encouragement, but understanding time had become an issue. He commanded his clerics into forming a staggered double line. "Deploy shields."

Across the first row, clerics knelt and activated a device expanding into a protective shield, almost the height of its user. The line behind pushed weapons through provided firing holes in the shielding, the linked shields becoming an impressive, almost impregnable wall watching for the next attack.

An icy chill came over Clarke as his helmet optics reported no further movement from the enemy lines falling into a deathly silence. He continued to pace behind his clerics, receiving updates via the LOS system, confirming all enemy elements had retreated. The lingering smoke made a need to spit bile clogging his throat, wiping his mouth with the back of his hand. He took another pass of the weapon's optics, more sensitive than helmet optics, providing an image flaring over a raging heat source that had been an upgraded MAUV. The wrecked hulk was still discharging ammunition in all directions in a macabre eventual death. Clarke continued to pan his weapon, catching sight of a shape appearing on top of another destroyed MAUV, unaffected by the flames lashing its armoured hide.

"Here they come." The shout came from the gantry level.

Clarke's attention moved to a line of silhouetted figures emerging from the smoke. With a drilled motion, he ejected the almost empty clip and reloaded a fresh one in expectation for what was to come.

High above came a sound of reverberating wings, making clerics hesitant to know what made such a noise growing in intensity.

Clarke passed from cleric to cleric, reassuring to hold their ground, mindful of the unnerving sound high above in the circling smoke. *What is making that noise?* He asked himself, unclipping a side pouch on his belt, retrieving the cylindrical object marked flare. The round cambered into his weapons grenade mount bracketed underneath the barrel. He braced the stock against his hip and fired. The thud resonated as the round arched upwards, exploding in phosphorus bright light to revealing what made the strange unnerving sounds. The sight would claw at his remaining strength as Clarke hesitated.

High above, suspended from the cavern's roof, were hundreds of overlapping winged figures, jostling for position.

Clarke braced for the inevitable as the first of the enemy dropped amongst his clerics. He watched helplessly as a female cleric emitted a grotesque scream as she was flung floundering against the gantry railings with bone crushing force.

A sweep of a battle mace took three clerics in one pass, the returning pass scattering the bodies of two more. Countless more clerics lay dead or screaming all across their line as more winged figures descended. Then from the forward position another wave of enemy joined the melee like water over stone as they launched themselves over the cleric's broken shield line with inhuman force. All across the Order's line buckled before breaking as Clarke tried to rally, but attention went to an enormous shadow looming over him. He had time to turn, facing a giant of a man clad in dull grey armour.

The beast released a deafening battle cry.

The roar startled Clarke, forcing him back away as his aggressor's swing severed the head of a passing cleric. That gave Clarke enough time to leap to the side to witness the giant's swing arch back. Time slowed as though sensing his impending death, bracing for the unavoidable with eyes closed, hoping for it to be quick.

There came a sickening sound of impact and breaking bones followed by an ear shattering scream as his assailant's mace struck an unfortunate cleric crossing between them. The cleric's blood sprayed Clarke's visor as her body struck him with intense impact, forcing air from his lungs as both tumbled across the ground. Every part of Clarke's body burned with pain. His final thought was of the giant stood over him as his mind faded to black. Captain Sebastian Clarke's battle was over as he fell with his beloved twenty second.

"Congregate all forces here." Nikolaos pointed to the screen. "Is there news of the twenty second and twenty fourth?" he requested, noting the forward positions before returning to the detailed display showing the scene unfolding. Various icons showed clerics retreating in what at first appeared organised order before breaking and scattering towards the rear positions. Their winged enemy descending upon them, throwing all chance of organised retreat into a rout.

A young deacon appeared to deliver a hasty salute.

Nikolaos acknowledged with a regrettable sigh, reading the physical stress on his face as he tried to deliver his report. "Remnants of the twenty forth and twenty fifth have pulled back to second position, twenty third are holding gantry and upper levels as instructed by Father Clarke."

"Is there any word on the Father Clarke's whereabouts?"

"Not since calling the retreat to the second position, then overseeing the fall-back of the rest of the twenty second, sir, coinciding with the latest attack." The deacon flinched at another explosion erupted nearby.

"What about the special weapons?"

Father Jenkins, a tall thin priest who joined the Order with Nikolaos in the same year. He had an often-volatile relationship with authority, an issue stalling any chance of promotion. Four years on Nikolaos's staff had proven him to be a competent priest and stepped forward to answer the question. "Heavier weapons are out of action in the opening assault. The fire teams are holding well on secondary lines. The new MP-92 ammunition appears to be effective against these enemies, but their attack coincided with our redeployment."

Nikolaos watched erratic tracer fire wind towards unknown targets all across their positions. "You said the twenty third has the gantry level?"

"They regained the level with brief resistance and are linking up with surface forces as requested." Jenkins pointed to the digital map, rotating the image to another level of the monastery, showing positions.

"What resistance?" Nikolaos asked, studying the new images.

Jenkins nodded to another deacon, shifting at the sudden scrutiny. The man stepped forward. "A lone sniper, casualties are three killed and five injured."

"Have you retrieved a body for identification?" Nikolaos asked.

"Nothing as yet, but further sweeps are being carried out, confident they cannot get far."

Nikolaos continued to stare at the deacon before nodding in agreement. *Lost too many clerics today, but we can suffer the losses. At least Clarke expected the second attack, saved lives and maybe this whole engagement.* All attention returned to the digital display before acknowledging with a low grunt to losing almost a third of their strength. The remaining legions pushed into small pockets around the office complex that was the command position.

"Now we're not overstretched, we can concentrate firepower better around this complex. How are they receiving reinforcements from the surface? I thought we had all entrances covered with surface forces?"

"A vehicle service lift shaft in section D, they used the smoke from the power plant sabotage earlier to cover their decent in to the monastery." Father Jenkins expanded a section of the map, highlighting the entry point.

Nikolaos watched each of his senior priests, all waiting for further instructions. "We have to keep pushing them until the job's done and give the cardinal as much time as possible. Make our stand here, and at gantry level. Regain communications with the surface and our reinforcements and setup another command position two levels above this position. If we have to, we can contain them in the corridors of the upper floors, stopping any further incursion. The cardinal has their leader, so a leaderless assault will fail and we will then push out when surface reinforcements arrive." The priests acknowledged Nikolaos's quick dismissal with salutes as he called over a waiting cleric. "Pack up and move to level ten meeting hall. I will follow."

The clerics gathered their equipment and cleared out.

Nikolaos, the last to leave, watched clerics rush past, ushered in by priests unaware of the proud observation of their commander.

Far below, from the cover of a wrecked MAUV, Seraph wiped blood from his staff blade. Greeting Raguel crouched beside him, offering a slap of his back and a wide grin across his blackened face. With a slight nod and through a forced smile, Seraph tried to share his joyful mood.

"They flee to higher levels," Raphael offered, jumping from the wreckage of a burnt out MAUV. "Time is of the essence if we are to retrieve the blade and find Michael, for I fear the worse for our brother."

"We felt his pain too before the attack," Seraph offered. "We will retrieve both soon enough but first we must regroup."

"What of the special weapons used against you," she asked.

Raguel laughed a throaty laugh. "They are effective against our fledgling brothers, but not archangel..."

"But the garrison lost many today," Seraph confirmed scowling at Raguel, shrugging off his brother's disapproval.

Raphael was the first to break cover. "Leave the garrison to contain the clerics, we will find an alternative way to the blade."

Four levels above, Lilith fired a quick burst down the hallway before sinking to the floor, clutching her wound that soaked her jacket lining and not so white blouse. With a wince she tried to get back to her feet, but she had lost a lot of blood and fell back against the wall. She had received the wound when the clerics forced entry to the gantry level where she was hiding. Now well aware of the pain, her injury not life threatening for her. That was not true for the Hispanic body she inhabited. If not treated, this would prove fatal. *Need to stop and rest, let myself heal,* she thought. Another check of the wound, noticing the bullet had passed straight through, which was lucky, but she was still losing blood. Further spasms of pain shot up her side. *Do not die on me now, I like this body.* Through gritted teeth, she pushed away from the wall, taking another glance down the passageway. Bullets tore plaster from the walls, forcing her to flinch back, a tight grip on her weapon, waiting for the right moment. She cursed the archangels for leaving her to die. So in desperation she fired another rapid burst, making the advancing clerics reposition before she was back behind cover, catching her breath. *What the hell were you thinking, trusting them? Well done, Lil, now you will lose an A+ body and get roasted over a slow open fire by Lewie when he drags you back.* She gripped her side, the warm blood congealing against her hand as she chambered another round and fired again. The rounds struck an advancing cleric, the last shot tore out his throat as he convulsed to the floor, as other clerics clambered for cover. "Well, if all I have to look forward to is a slow death and agonising torture, then I'm taking souls with me. Fire in the Hole, arseholes." The last of her grenades fired from the front mounted launcher, the resulting explosion caused her ears to ring in such a confined space. She coughed through the dust covering the entire breadth of the corridor, admiring her handy work.

A four-metre length of ceiling and support wall collapsed, covering the remains of the clerics. Strip lights hung from exposed wiring, sparking in protest as a small fire started in another section of erupted wall.

"That should slow them down while I take a rest here," Lilith mumbled, collapsing into unconsciousness. Her next conscious thought was a warm sensation covering her wound, making her eyes flicker open as the soft-spoken voice re-assured her.

"Your vessel needs to heal."

Lilith's sight cleared to look upon the features of Raphael. A spasm of pain increased until making her convulse. "I'm not letting a stinking archangel touch me, no way." She pushed through the pain, gritting teeth as she attempted to push Raphael away.

"It will take but a moment to heal your vessel and promise to not interfere with the demonic entity."

"I am the demonic entity you bitch, now get off me."

"Done," Raphael said, pulling away.

The pain subsided, and the only sign of injury was her blood-soaked clothes. "Oh man, a four hundred new dollar shirt and never getting that stain out." Back on her feet, she glared at Raphael.

The archangel returned a thin smile. "You're welcome."

"There be no thanks from me sister, I was doing just fine until you put your grubby paws on me."

Raphael frowned. "Your vessel was dying."

"Screw you," She held up a hand, pushing past and out of sight.

"Tell us again why we did not smite the demon," Seraph asked, letting Lilith walk away. "It was not her time, or our Father would have willed it so." The archangels continued through the winding corridors as the battle was far from won and still no contact with Michael.

Simon's senses attuned to the gentle tone of birdsong, eyes opening to the surrounding expanse of the picturesque park. His only disturbance to an otherwise cloudless day came from the rustling response of low hanging willows in the gentle breeze. The scene filled with summer colour as Simon slumped against the bench, the warming sun a welcome relief. Everything until this moment forgotten as he slipped into rested contentment with eyes closed, slipping in to the peace and solitude.

"Your challenge is not over yet, Simon."

The voice all too familiar and forcing him from his lethargy. Turning, Simon recognised the Panama wearing Samuel.

"You must face the effects of your past, embracing that hidden underneath all your doubts, becoming that you were and awaken to your full potential." The old man's unique silver tipped cane twirled in his hand as he waited for a response.

Simon chewed his jaw, scowling at the figure that had become a menacing figment of his fractured mind. "Okay, I play your game, who do you think I am?"

"You know what you are." Samuel chuckled. "You've been fighting that realisation since regaining your memories." He turned to meet Simon's frustrated glare, offering a thin smile. "Use that strength to fight, find it within you."

Simon's attention went back to picturesque surroundings. "What if I'm not ready to embrace who I am, as doing so risks losing what makes me human?"

"It's a risk you have to take, for the alternative will be unpleasant for all concerned."

"So that's your play, pulling me to a safe space of my mind when life turns traumatic. Just to tell me I should sacrifice everything and wake up, is that it?"

"Well, aren't we getting philosophical?" Samuel smiled. "We both gain nothing from you failing. In fact, right now your physical body hangs like a birthday piñata and is bleeding out as we speak. So would you rather die a slow death or continue the fight?"

Simon sensed the anger build. "You know, I'm done being a chew toy for you all to control. Perhaps I might stay here and find peace?"

Samuel could not suppress the laughter. "Oh Simon, did you think you had a choice? We have so much unfinished business together, you and I, and besides, I'm fond of you and would hate seeing you go down before the big finale." Samuel rose from the bench, dipping his Panama in farewell. "Oh... there's one other question for you to consider."

Simon's attention returned to the old man.

"What gave you the impression this place is yours?" Samuel offered with a hint of malice.

In a flash, tired, hazy eyes struggled to open. Simon's vison reacted to the bespectacled Secretary Jozafat, peering up as he gave him a soft slap to the face. "He's awake, you're Eminence."

"Good, have him released and brought next to this pathetic celestial parasite." Cardinal Ambrozij waived a robed hand to the bleeding Michael lying across the lawn at his feet as the Legion Guards untied Simon.

Unhindered from the restraints, muscles failing from his ordeal, Simon fell to his knees before dragging and deposited next to Michael. Everything was a struggle, with a voice weak he could offer but a whisper. "Michael, hold on for all our sakes."

The archangel's eyes opened briefly, his expression strained. "Fear not for the garrison comes to our aid."

"Enough." The interruption erupted from the cardinal rising from his seat, the Blade of Light gripped tight in a bony hand as its hypnotic blue light continued to resonate. "Witness the full potential of this blade's power." He pointed the tip to the two stricken figures addressing all those watching. "This blade not only takes life but also prolongs it to those who wield its power." Gripping the blade in both hands, the blade's pulsating aura intensified as it enveloped the cardinal's forearms. "For too long I've sustained my weakness with the spark of youth, limited by an ageing body but from today no more." The light quickened, wrapping around the top half of his body. "The Celestial Temple holds power far greater than even the essence of life, and this blade harnesses that power."

Robed clerics circled the garden, reciting a language familiar to Simon, but unable to make out the words as he lay next to the stirring Michael.

"It's Enochian, spoken by the Celestial Temple. This evil

uses our sacred scripture to harness its power, twisting it to his dark bidding, sacrilege to the Legion." His last words spoken through grated teeth as he fought against the wave of pain.

Simon pushed himself across the floor towards the archangel. "What do we do to stop him?"

"Get the blade and stop the regeneration from completing." Michael clutched his arm. "Stop him, Simon, before it's too late." Another stab of pain racked his body before falling into unconsciousness.

Simon watched as the cardinal now engulfed in angelic blue light. The spectators stepping back in awe from the spectacle unfolding.

Everyone preoccupied, Simon recognised his chance, forcing himself to his knees. He ushered the last of his strength to lurch forward. Any chance of warning came too late as he grasped the blade. Pushing his full weight into a strike, surprise crossed his face as the cardinal withstood blow after blow with incredible resilience.

Both men became engulfed, every molecule of their bodies rippling with burning energy as they grappled, as the light intensified around them in a desperate battle neither could lose.

Secretary Jozafat hesitated, fighting an urge to aid the cardinal, but fearing interfering could harm him, so held back ordering the Legion Guard to do the same.

In a desperate battle, the cardinal sneered. "You're too late half-breed, it's already begun, the power coursing through my body, transforming me, I feel it." At that moment his eyes grew wider, the liver spot blemished skin and red veined neck faded as his features grew tighter. The once thin features filled as sunken eyes became sharper, further defined as did his age ravaged hands. "Yes, my strength returns as I become whole again." Wisps of black hairs grew across his hands and wrists. His once white balding scalp grew thick youthful hair. As the transformation continued, the cardinal stepped back to touch and marvel at his rejuvenated self.

Simon stood back, reacting from his own damaged body healing from the power of the blade. From the deepest recesses of his mind emanated a voice. *Stop before it finishes.* The words prompted him to act. *Do it now, before too late.*

The blade pierced the cardinal's neck, his reaction instant reeling in shock to clutch his blood soaked wound.

Simon fought to keep his control, twisting the blade, becoming super-heated in his grip. Ignoring the discomfort until a brilliant flash of white filled the atrium, throwing both men and all those around to the ground.

"What have you done," the cardinal repeated, screaming in desperation to stem the loss of blood. "Guards finish this."

Simon remained sat and stunned with what appeared a dormant blade still in hand.

Unnoticed and hidden amongst the foliage of the observation terrace overlooking the atrium, a shot rang out. Almost cutting the nearest chanting cleric in two before another shot removed the unprotected head of a second. The man's brain matter sprayed Jozafat before reacting to the attack.

What followed was chaos, as Legion Guards swarmed the atrium, rushing to protect the still protesting cardinal floundering on the floor.

Barrage of returning suppressive fire peppered Lilith's position, filling the air with glass, plaster and eviscerated flora cascading in all directions.

Simon flung himself over Michael's unconscious body, remembering the blade which he pressed against the archangel's wound. He hoped any residual energy would heal, but nothing happened.

An animal roar boomed pre-empting, two armoured figures crashing through an adjoining wall, sending Legion Guards sprawling.

A sudden lunge of spear sliced through the chin strap and skull of a guard reaching for Simon. The victory short-lived as a volley of automatic fire struck Seraph, pushing him back as more guards entered the fire fight.

Raguel fared little better, no sooner crushing the ribcage of one unfortunate assailant against the wall with his mace. He too fell to a heavy impact across the bridge of his nose, sending him spiralling backwards.

"Help his Eminence," Jozafat screamed to those forming a protective ring around the wounded cardinal unseemly pulled across the floor screaming for the deaths of all those who opposed him.

"Seraph, rescue Michael," Raphael instructed.

A rapid barrage of shots rang out from high above the atrium, as another guard slumped forward, his battle armour peppered with smouldering holes.

Through gritted teeth, Lilith regretted what she had just done. "I'm saving a frigging archangel." She pushed past the annoyance, ducking as a glancing shot ricocheted past before choosing another target and squeezing the trigger.

Seraph spun his weapon, opening the collarbone of a guard loading a fresh clip into her weapon. The returning downward stroke disembowelled another, before sprinting to recover the still unconscious Michael.

Simon flinched as tracer fire pulsed all around until a tight grip under his arm pulled him backwards. His last view of the atrium was the huge armoured figure of Raguel in its centre, surrounded by advancing Legion Guards. The archangel swinging his mace in a wide arc followed by a roar of defiance as the beast within relished physical combat. He gripped a helmeted skull with a gloved hand, crushing with satisfaction before pressing forward. Two more guards hurtled backwards, their floundering bodies striking the far wall with bone crushing strength.

"Raguel to us, protect Michael," Seraph shouted, heading through the doorway made by their unconventional entrance. Michael's passive body slung over his shoulder as he raced for safety as the atrium continued to fill with Legion Guards.

Even Raguel calculated the fight unwinnable.

"A tactical retreat would be more prudent, brother." The

caution filled voice was Raphael connecting to his own thoughts, calming his battle rage. With a reluctant grunt, he was soon following Seraph.

The Order forces outnumbering the others gave chase, but an enormous explosion rippled through the support struts holding up the entire observation level. The collapsing debris foiled any chance of pursuit as the entire area fell silent as both sides retreated to tend to their injured and regroup.

Lilith came to re-join the others gathered around Michael's unresponsive body. "C4 worked, but it won't stop them finding another way to us," she explained, pointing a thumb toward the collapsed corridor.

"Thank you for getting me out of there," Simon responded to Raphael, continuing to examine him, returning his smile. "The blade appears to have healed the worst of your injuries. You were lucky and you're welcome."

"Can you help Michael?" he urged with concern for the still comatose archangel.

She gently checked Michael's injuries. "The wound is deep, but I will try." She placed her hands upon him, concentrating as a glow emanated around the damage, making Michael stir and flounder under her grip. "Hold him still."

Simon gripped his shoulders, pushing down to stop any further movement.

Tracks of grime and sweat traced Raphael's face in concentration, but could not hide her anxiety as she backed away. She tried again, frantic moments passing until Michael's eyes opened.

Simon released his grip and held breath.

"We thought we lost you," Raphael explained as she rested from the intense exertion, the strain clear.

Michael caressed her cheek, making her return his gaze.

"Michael, my care is a temporary binding. The wound made by celestial blade requiring treatment at the temple."

"But you have the blade?" he asked.

"I do," Simon answered, producing the Blade of Light from

his belt.

Michael placed a hand upon the blade. "They depleted its power, no longer posing a threat. The cardinal, you stopped him from corrupting its power?"

"It's complicated," Raphael explained. "The regeneration had already started, but Simon interrupted the process before completion. We have no knowledge if we were successful."

Michael stirred, nursing the wound, experiencing extreme pain and discomfort. "Recall the garrison and tend to our wounded and prey for our fallen."

"But the cardinal is still a threat?" Simon asked.

"More than you know." Michael turned to him, considering the question. "Even with partial regeneration there's a fear he will become more dangerous, but we need time to recover before uncovering his true plans."

"I don't understand why that would make him more dangerous?" Simon said.

Michael's pained expression faltered to a more concerned look as he remembered the altercation. "As we battled over the blade, I sensed something within him, something not human, that is why."

The others shared concerned glances as they waited for an explanation.

"It was a glimpse as we connected, maybe his actual form."

Seraph stepped closure. "You sensed a demon within him?"

Michael shook his head. "Something not seen before, I felt a presence deadly than anything faced in our garrison's history."

"What's more dangerous than a demon.?" Simon inquired.

"To describe what I felt would be a pure blood, an entity of pure evil from before Father."

"Explains knowledge of old rituals and Enochian text," Raphael added as she helped Michael to his feet.

Simon returned the blade to his belt. "We need to warn the others at the refuge." He searched the group. "Where's Lilith?"

Michael frowned as Raphael reminded him. "The demon female, she was most helpful covering your retrieval from the enemy."

"She's not our concern; something bigger is at work here."

In all the chaos inflicted on the monastery, the group retreated, taking flight to return to the higher ground and safety offered by the Reformation Towers.

Simon remained sombre; watching smoke rise from the monastery, in desperate thought to everything, was getting out of hand. For the moment they had dealt the Order a blow, and he feared the repercussions as he closed his eyes to consider the uncertain future.

"Your time here has ended, we have neutralised the immediate threat, and so it's time to return." Michael awaited a response as he struggled still with his injury. The slightest movement brought a flash of pain as he tried to keep his staunch posture.

"What of the refuge and my friends? The Order will come searching for me and you want me to give up my friends to suffer the consequences."

"The Order and the cardinal shall fear the repercussions defying the Celestial Temple."

"How certain can you be they will not retaliate? You don't understand humans, Michael. Admitting yourself, you sensed pure evil within the cardinal, something you can't explain. We can't leave my friends to face that alone, without celestial help."

"True, we don't know, but will leave protections in place, warnings to any human or demon around the refuge."

"You can't guarantee anything if I return with you," Simon asked with concern.

Michael lowered his head. "Your judgement is clouded."

"I have to go back, I've brought my friends into this, how can I leave them unprotected from whatever happens next?"

The archangel's jet-black eyes reflected nothing in the evenings dying light. "To leave you will mean you're a liability for the garrison, they could use you against us."

Simon's eyes narrowed, jaw tight. "So now my usefulness

has ended, you need me back up top. That reduces the chance I'm used for my celestial knowledge and any dirty secrets I might know."

"It's not like that Simon." Raphael joined the conversation. "What Michael is referring to is the repercussions of someone with awareness of the temple, could expose us to our adversaries. It's important you return until the threat passes."

"When…? Days, months or years even? Years passed after my last recall. What about Father Peters and the others, they're innocent? So what happens when the Order breaks down the refuge doors looking for me? What then? You mention precautions, but it needs someone to watch over them, keeping them safe."

"It's in Fate's hands, it's none of our concern," Michael offered.

"None of your concern, its innocent lives we are talking about here." Simon rounded on the wounded Michael. "We got them involved in our dirty war, now we are to leave them to deal with the aftereffects."

Michael tensed and moved forward, but Simon stood his ground.

With a ruffle of wings, Raphael intervened. "Your humanity gives an insight we as archangels lack. You show compassion and benevolence towards others not of our kind." She shared a glance between both as her softening smile defused the tension.

Michael sighed. "What do you ask of us, Simon?"

Simon stepped back, pushing fingers through matted hair, trying to think what his options were.

The sky grew black and in the distance the monastery continued to be a hive of activity as emergency services attended all around the vast building.

Observing for a moment, Simon's attention changed to the waiting archangels. "I will not join you."

With a tilt of head Michael studied him. "You refuse a return and reinstatement of wings?"

Simon nodded.

"An opportunity offered once Simon," Raphael added, concerned.

"I'm not leaving them to face the consequences because of me."

Michael appeared agitated. "We cannot allow your knowledge to fall to our enemies."

"Then remove it." Raphael offered. "Just the secrets of the temple, leave his memories of being earthbound."

"Is that even possible?" Simon asked.

"With a deeper scan, we can remove memories altogether. I can't be too specific, so will need to remove up to your fall of grace," Raphael said. "You will have an awareness of our existence but nothing else and understand you will suffer significant pain until it's completed."

Michael gave a nod of agreement. "That's acceptable; you will keep your abilities, healing, heightened strength and speed, but no memory of your angelic life. Also, your human side will make you vulnerable, so if your body dies, your celestial entity will not gain entry to the temple."

"I could live with that," Simon said.

Michael moved forward with an intense glare. "Do you, Simon, you wouldn't be so willing to agree if you thought about those consequences. You are as petulant and ignorant as the apes you choose over your own kind. Still, we will honour our side by leaving memories of your brief time on this debouched planet."

"Also, if possible will keep knowledge of demon kind," Raphael continued.

"We offer nothing more," Michael added as he strode away.

"I'm sorry for you, Michael, as you can never understand why I'm doing this." As his words got no response, Simon gestured to Raphael. "I'm ready."

As the emergency around the Monastery of Light continued, the authorities congregated those evacuated to staging areas marked out. Here hundreds herded to these safe areas, all well away from the security cordon being setup around the entire area.

During the confusion it was easy to go unnoticed. No one gave a second look to a dust-covered priest and his semi-comatose companion navigating the crowds, steered towards another evacuation point a few blocks past the last checkpoint.

An Order priest stood on top of a parked MAUV, instructing for the crowd to keep moving further back. "If you need medical attention, please go ahead to the far corner of the plaza where you will find a medical centre offering aid."

Still unnoticed, Father Peters pushed on, keeping a watchful eye on the surveillance drones hovering and monitoring the crowds. An opening appeared, so pushing forward to make for a side street. It was here they rested, hidden from prying eyes. Father Peters retrieved a pocket tissue, wiping away the beads of sweat. Now able to catch his breath as he tried to swallow, flinching from a smoke-damaged throat.

D was semi-conscious and somewhat lucid.

Father Peters left him holding his head in his hands, propped against a wall and hidden behind a pair of dumpsters.

"You okay to walk a few blocks?" the Father inquired.

"Just trying would finish me," D responded, incapable to lift his head from his hands.

Father Peters observed the crowds. "What the hell happened, do you know?"

D winched. "A mystical barrier used to block energy passing through, very painful and ancient magic. Someone has a lot of mojo to wield enough mystical power to envelop the entire monastery like they did."

Father Peters made a last glance to check no one investigated their loitering in the shadows. On finding none, he went back to D to ask more questions. "That would mean they knew about your abilities and that you would try to rescue

Simon."

"Simon being taken to the monastery was a trap from the beginning. Just means to get all the players under one roof." D lifted his head, flinching from the light. "I miss my glasses."

"So the cardinal set a trap and played us from the start, but why? What would he gain?"

"Apart from a blade of unimaginable power, forged in the Celestial Temple? Then there's the human-angel hybrid, enabling such a weapon that's capable of killing an archangel or demon. So take your pick."

"Well, put that way, it sounds like we are in deep trouble... you okay?"

D rose to his feet, pulling at his jacket to see the back. "In all hell's fire pits, what have you let me sit in here, priest?"

"It was dark, we needed to hide." The Father turned away, incapable to hide amusement at D's revulsion to the stains covering his expensive suit. "You're welcome." Father Peters offered.

"For what, the mind blowing headache and every muscle in my body still buzzing or perhaps the expensive dry cleaning bill which you will pay."

The Father rolled his eyes and headed for the other end of the alley, leaving D to continue his rant alone.

Traffic had backed up bumper to bumper with a chorus of horns expressing frustration at the holdup of emergency vehicles blocking the interchange.

As Father Peters waited, sensing tightness down his right arm and a slight tremor forming in his palm. He stared at the uncontrolled limb, a sure sign his body was returning from the adrenaline fuelled rush experienced since escaping the cell block. He placed his hand inside his cardigan, retrieving the cigarettes from his shirt pocket with his shake free hand. A cautious flick of the lighter had the cigarette lit, returning control of his nerves as he drew in the calming effect.

"Got two of those, priest?" D asked as he sidled up next to him, startling the Father from his quiet contemplation.

"Huh…, yeah, sure." He offered over the crumpled packet. "You have a light?"

Sparking the lighter, Father Peters was thankful the tremor had gone.

"Such a calming experience smoking, don't you think?" D continued as he studied the lit cigarette in his hand. He took another long intake, releasing smoke that became trapped in the breeze. "It masks all troubles and fears, this one slender stick."

Father Peters took a quick intake, continuing to search for anybody recognising them escaping the monastery, and an unnerved uneasiness grew at how vulnerable he felt.

"It's one of the biggest contributors to my business, you know?"

Father Peters had paid little attention to D's ramblings as he turned with a quizzical frown at the unusual conversation. "What is?"

"I'm talking about cigarettes, as these insignificant things are in my top ten causes of death each year, just ahead of fast food and DIY in the home."

"DIY?" the Father asked, now curious.

"Oh yes, amazing how many people die each year from DIY. In my experience, beer and power tools don't mix," he explained with a half-smile.

The slight chuckle they shared went to releasing the tension the priest felt, as his expression loosened, nodding his response at D's try at humour.

"What is our next plan of action?" D asked.

"Guess returning to the refuge," the Father answered. "There's no chance of a taxi in this gridlock. We need to walk."

"Who needs a taxi?" D offered, extinguishing the half-spent cigarette under foot before stepping out between stationary traffic heading into the city.

Not wanting to separate, Father Peters hurried after him. "Where are we going," he shouted over the noise of traffic.

"Two blocks down, my driver's waiting," D offered.

"Your driver, you had your car waiting for us this whole time and you didn't tell me?"

"Slipped my mind, honest." D shrugged.

"I carried you for almost two blocks and you had a car nearby?" the Father protested.

D strode off, oblivious to the priest's rant.

The Father balled his fists to release the anger under his breath.

As promised, the long-stretched limousine waited, and both men hit the mini bar on entering the luxurious comfort.

Father Peters measured out a generous twelve-year-old scotch from the crystal decanter, drinking the contents in one before refilling his glass.

Unable to hide his disgust at once again the abuse of his hospitality, D selected a chilled mineral water and sat back into the leather interior, sipping from the bottle. "The driver informs me we will be back at your refuge in two hours once through the worst of the traffic. So Father, continue helping yourself to the expensive scotch, I insist."

Through a forced grin, Father Peters continued to pour another measure, sitting back into the comfort, the plush leather taking the strain out of his tired body. "Any news of the lad, did he make it out?"

D, reunited with a replacement secpad, sat scrolling its contents, shaking his head as he read page after page of names. "It's been a busy day today, but our friend doesn't appear to be amongst them."

"Can't you sense him to tell if he is in danger?"

"I'm not a bloody golden retriever. It might surprise you priest I have many talents, but mystical mind tricks are not one of them. Leave them to carnivals and late night cable channels."

An uneasy silence fell between them, neither wanting to speak until D rubbed the side of his face, leaning forward. "I'm sorry, guess it's the stress of the day. It doesn't work like that. We were lucky today and what we know since Simon's convergence with the blade enabled us to track the energy like a flare in the night sky. The archangels then undertook a clandestine assault upon the monastery, but Michael underestimated the Order. That resulted in a full scale assault from the garrison. There have been reports of multiple celestial signatures flooding the city, so it makes finding Simon like a needle in a haystack right now."

Father Peters sensed his stomach turn to the thought of no pleasant news. "There must be something we could do."

"We return to the refuge and wait their return." D returned to his secpad to uncover further news.

Father Peters gave a low grumble of doubt sipping his drink, deep down sensing helplessness, but common sense dictated going back to the monastery would be suicide. That did not stop him worrying for his friend.

The smart-suited reporter held his composure, determined to break the story as the crowds jostled him against the human barrier of shielded Guard Clerics. The same thin white line held back the baying masses of rival press and concerned onlookers clambering to view the emergency around the floodlit Monastery of Light. "Damage, as you can see, is immense throughout the whole building, fires continue to rage." The camera panned wide, viewing the massive structure enveloped under a bank of grey smoke. "As we report, secondary explosions resonate throughout the underground complex. One source described the first explosion occurring during a routine armament audit. As we speak, clerics are trying to evacuate personnel and clergy. There is still no news on the cardinal himself as worried and traumatised onlookers await any further developments."

The image of the reporter disappeared as Sister Angela turned off the screen and returned to setting out the places for dinner.

"It's dreadful seeing such destruction. I will add a prayer

tonight for those affected." She glanced at the table setting. "Should I set extra places for the Father and our guest?"

Lisa was checking a tray of browning bread rolls to go with soup bubbling on the hob. "His names Simon as you well know Sister and I wouldn't set any other place for the moment."

Father Peters had phoned from D's limousine, dismissing her fears, adding they would be late because of the emergency in the city. More worrying to Lisa, he omitted to mention Simon or his whereabouts. She tried not to think about it as she retrieved the hot tray from the oven, pushing the heated rolls into a waiting basket.

"You mean about his arrest for murdering those girls?"

Lisa's lips thinned at the comment before switching off the hob. "Not arrested, Sister," she corrected with a groan. "Simon is helping NEPD in their enquiry and confident it's a misunder-standing."

The Sister offered a raised eyebrow as her smile narrowed, continuing to polish the cutlery with a tea towel. "Oh yes, dear... enquiries."

Slamming down the used baking tray, Lisa glared out the window at nothing in particular, her emotions and the stress of the day getting the better of her.

"Did you hurt yourself, dear?" the Sister asked, startled, feigning concern.

Then, turning, Lisa offered a forced smile. "Since the Father left, you have expressed your opinions about Simon con-stantly. A snide comment here, a little dig there, and I'm tired of it."

The Sister's cutlery cleaning intensified with feverish in-tent. "Never my intentions to undermine the Father, but re-cent judgements about the stranger have been... somewhat lacking. I for one haven't become blinkered about seeing him for what he is."

"What would they be, I wonder?" Lisa asked, crossing her arms.

Sister Angela placed the tea towel on the table, smoothing

out the hem of her apron, and faced Lisa's glare. "Can I remind you he is the prime suspect in multiple murders and it would be a miracle of God if not connected somehow? What do we know about his past and may I also remind you, he's been trouble since setting foot in this refuge from day one?"

Lisa held a breath, searching for words on the Sister's opinions.

The Sister could not help herself. "Police have visited us, including a search by the Order. Now we can't help those in need because the Father has shut us down until further notice."

"That's not Simon's fault, you can't blame him for everything that has happened. The Father was right in closing the refuge, what with the trauma of the search and the fact someone murdered my husband in front of us."

"Yes, the fortunate death of your husband." A hint of a distinct smirk crossed Sister Angela's lips as she continued. "A situation culminated from the altercation with our guest earlier in the day."

"Simon, his name is Simon." With temper flaring, Lisa gripped the table edge. "Now you wait one minute… what are you insinuating? We saw what happened and Simon had nothing to do with Brian's death."

"I don't disagree, but it comes at a convenient moment for you both and also having the good Father witnessing too. What other reason had he to frequent such a club of sin? Perhaps those criminal elements wouldn't have murdered your husband if they hadn't gone searching for you."

"I can't believe what you're saying," Lisa said, reacting to a wash of sudden nausea, a sign her earlier headache was making a dramatic comeback. "You're blaming Simon for causing Brian's death, but you weren't there, so how do you know?" She felt flustered. "If they hadn't come to find me, I would be dead, or worse, sold to a sordid sex house, drugged up to the eyeballs."

The Sister folded her arms, glaring down her thin nose

behind thick-framed glasses, her demeanour dismissing Lisa's explanations. "What about the grizzly pictures of those unfortunate brutalised girls, and they found his fingerprints in one of those girls' apartments?"

"The prints are from over twenty years ago, and besides, that is why he is helping Detective Colby to sort out the confusion because it's a big misunderstanding. Once done we can reopen the refuge and you can get back to your dreary little bullying life just how you like it, Sister."

"Maybe your judgements clouded by having a youthful man under the same roof. It's obvious the way you act around each other, sharing lustful glances whenever you're in the same room together. You should be ashamed of yourselves."

Lisa stood open-mouthed. "How dare question my motives? There may have been something between us but we are not throwing ourselves at each other like lovesick teenagers, my priority is Jake and will not see him hurt. Also, there's Simon's earlier life before his accident to consider."

"Well, that's an ongoing problem, isn't it, with the continuing questions to what he's done before the accident?" The Sister pushed at her glasses with a bony finger. "A life about which we know nothing, yet he's brought under our roof only to find out he's a suspected murderer and nothing but trouble."

Lisa took a step back. The muscles of her face quivered with the tension that had been building for weeks. The Sister had been itching to speak her mind all that time, but for Lisa, tired and stressed, she felt her shoulders dip. She had enough of her venom filled opinions. The time to stop pulling punches was past as she leant forward across the table again.

Sister Angela sensed the sudden change, her own posture ridged as she held her ground, her defiant expression narrowing to a mousy glare.

"You are a hypocrite, Sister. You stand there preaching right and wrong. Deep down you're vindictive and manipulative old women unable to recognise goodness in others, or even see others happy. You're so full of bitterness, hidden behind that old cross of yours, unable to cope when faced with human feelings." Lisa's malice filled words shocked even her as she stood straight following her outburst. She felt regret at once as the Sister floundered a response. There was a sudden flash of fury as Sister Angela's cheeks reddened, flustered for words in her agitation. "How... dare you," she spluttered. "Why you jumped up little trollop... worming your way in to this refuge using Father Peter's kindness, fluttering your sad eyes at anything passing. But I saw straight through the act of innocence from the beginning, young lady."

Lisa's eyes narrowed. "It's better to think with my heart and consider other's feelings than turn into a bitter and a cantankerous old woman. The only love in your life is that long dead guy on a cross around your neck." The regret filled thought clamped her mouth shut. *Shit, you did it now, Lisa. Ways to go, now bitch, slap her and get it over with while you're at it, why don't you.* She recognised anger eclipsed by hurt and shock in the Sister Angela's welling eyes as she staggered for the nearest seat. Lisa's remaining action was to squeeze her eyes shut, regretting the words as soon as they had left her lips. *How do I come back from this?*

A tense silence befell the kitchen until Lisa drew a slow, lengthy breath. "I'm sorry, Sister, I didn't mean to sound so cruel." Her words followed with a sigh as she got no response. "The whole situation is so..."

The Sister raised a hand, stopping the apology. "You said the words... you can't take them back. Whatever you say will not change the fact you said them."

Lisa pulled out a seat and sat down, touching the stitches above her eye, continuing to irritate. She pushed past the urge to scratch as her thought went to the Sister sat twisting her rosary, lost in quiet contemplation of prayer. *Just great, on top of all the other shit today you've sent her to a rubber room of her own making.* She gave another heavy sigh, knowing she desired to make amends, so Lisa rose from her seat to kneel in front of Sister Angela. She took her hands in her own. They appeared cold and clammy to the touch as Lisa tried to see her face. "Are you okay, Sister?" She bent lower as the Sister continued to whisper her words. Over the years, everybody at the refuge had become accustomed to the Sister's little quirks and oddities, and today Lisa put this latest down to stress and anger towards her. So she edged forward to hear what she was saying. They were not her native Gaelic, so perhaps Latin, she was not sure. "What are you saying, Sister?" Lisa received no response, so cupping her chin she lifted her head.

No one could have prepared her for what happened next. For a purple misshapen tongue lashed out from between dry cracked lips, the bulbous protrusion just missing Lisa's face as she flinched backwards. One moment she was arguing with a colleague, the next struggling against a warped representation of her. The pair became entwined as elongated claw-like hands protruded from the woman's ripped cardigan to grip Lisa's wrists, pulling her off balance. The sudden assault had both crashing against the table with a painful jolt. Lisa reeled as it forced the air from her lungs. The ensuing struggle scattered crockery across the room with a volley of noise. A pitiful scream was all Lisa could muster as pain gripped her arms as she struggled to regain her footing.

The once clear mousy eyes of Sister Angela turned a veined red, straining in their sockets. Her dark-rimmed glasses lost in the confrontation as blood strained veins throbbed underneath her leathery skinned temples. One vein erupted under the transformation, releasing a fine spray of blood in all directions.

Lisa screamed out as the warped features lurched forward, snapping like a demented animal. She became desperate to push against the weight pressing down on her, transfixed in horror at the Sister's continuing transformation.

The Sister's dried lips slid back to show fanged teeth. They protruded from a spittle covered mouth, as she released a grotesque gurgle, her features continuing to distort before Lisa's eyes.

Lisa fought to break free of the grip as they both rolled, scattering plates and chairs until hitting the stone floor. The corresponding jolt knocked any further resistance from her as she tried to roll away. The creature that had been Sister Angela released a haunting screech before vaulting the table to straddle Lisa on the floor. Its grotesque features pushed forward, depositing spittle and drool across her face as she pulled her legs under its body. With all remaining strength, she pushed out with her feet. The creature leaped to the ceiling, clamping the tiles with elongated clawed appendages. Not wasting her chance, Lisa pulled herself to her feet to scurry for the back door, but the creature was fast and blocked her escape. It remained hanging from the roof, mimicking her moves, scuttling crablike to the slightest movement for the door. So Lisa hesitated, watching with horror as the creature rotated its bulbous head with a bone cracking snap to face her. With a last scream of revulsion, Lisa flung herself to the side, expecting the creature's lunge. She was a fraction quicker and ducking low she slid but struck her head against the double doors. In her haste she had become stunned and disoriented, and noted the creature fared no better as it had struck the sink and cooker hob.

The still cooking contents of heated soup cascaded the front of the hob, spreading across the stone floor. It was almost laughable. The clawed limbs of the creature struggled and floundered, slipping on the soup slicked stone floor.

Lisa finding her own feet broke into a run to rush and open the outside door, as her attention remained on the still floundering creature. Her mistake was being unaware of the hooded figure stood in the doorway, clamping a gloved hand over her mouth. Lisa felt the sharp sting to her neck, and in her final conscious struggle she looked upon the creature resembling Sister Angela.

The abomination skittered to the doorway, its macabre features etched with an expression best described as glee.

Later that evening, Father Peters and D re-entered the kitchen, finding the door open and no one in sight. The scene was of an obvious struggle, for pans lay scattered with broken plates and uneaten food mixed with overturned furniture. A disturbing find was the traces of blood covering the kitchen table. "What in all the saints happened here?" Father Peters asked, picking up an upturned chair, returning it under the table.

"I would say, bad housekeeping?" D responded cautiously in side stepping the remains of broken crockery and pooling soup.

Father Peters ignored the sarcasm, bending down to retrieve a shoe. "This is Sister Angela's."

"Perhaps, she needed to leave in a hurry."

"The doors are wide open and there's evidence of a struggle and Lisa is missing too. Something terrible happened here."

D shrugged, nudging debris with his foot. "Perhaps the good Sister and Lisa had a slight disagreement and are taking a deserved time out somewhere."

"The Sister caught a greyhound to visit the convent in New Haven this afternoon. She needed time away and with the refuge closed and all the troubles I couldn't blame her wanting to leave. Lisa sent Jake to stay with friends, so she was the only one here. Do you think the Order could have taken her?"

"Not sure, they're hurting and still licking their wounds back..." D's face changed as he checked his secpad.

"What's it," the Father queried, concerned.

"Huh," D acknowledged. "We're requested upstairs."

"Upstairs." The question asked in confusion, pointing upwards. "Oh, you mean the roof."

D nodded with a smile, pushing the priest towards the double doors leading from the kitchen, with a slap on the back. "Not time for the pearly gates just yet, so stop taking everything so literal."

On climbing the stairs to the roof, Father Peters pushed open the fire door, greeted by the imposing figure of Michael.

The archangel was in obvious pain, a blood-stained break

in his armour showed an obvious wound. It also appeared to hinder his movement as his attention went to Raphael laying out a motionless Simon on the gravel floor. With a raised hand, Michael moved to the recent arrivals. "Please, no need for alarm, for Simon will recover. He underwent a mind wipe necessary under the circumstances, for he has made his choice."

Father Peters knelt beside his friend, adjusting glasses for a better examination for himself.

"Why would he go through another wipe?" A curious D asked.

"His own decision," Raphael replied. She stepped back, giving the priest more room. "All knowledge about the Celestial Temple purged for everyone's protection."

"Wow, kid sacrificed his past for the team," D added as he lent over Father Peters to see the still unconscious Simon.

"And has refused the return of his wings, the consequence for his refusal to come back with us," Michael added.

D paced. "Damn Si, what are you thinking. It's not supposed to play out like this."

Confused, Raphael came to face D. "I don't understand."

D offered one of his usual smiles, if not somewhat strained. "Nothing..." He hesitated. "You know Raphael, you need a holiday down here, perhaps loosen those wings and live a little."

"Perhaps you should return with us and rehabilitated in the ways of the Celestial Temple again," Michael glared, "You appear to have gone native to these apes."

D avoided eye contact, retrieved his secpad and found something else to do away from the archangels.

Raphael's attention went back to Simon, stroking his face and trying to reassure the concerned Father Peters. "He will recover, Father, on my word as one healer to another."

"It's not Simon that concerns me Raphael but Lisa. She's gone missing and we found evidence to a disturbance downstairs. We fear someone has taken her again, and this time we have no clue to her whereabouts." Father Peter's attention moved to Michael. "Something has happened to her because of what happened today."

"No concern of the garrison. Do you not have authorities in helping in such matters?"

The Father removed his glasses with frantic haste to clean them on the pocket lining of his pants as he struggled with Michael's arrogance.

The tension within the group became broken by a slight groan.

Father Peters rushed to lift Simon's head, who sat up, rubbing at his forehead, still suffering discomfort from his ordeal.

Simon recognised the small group huddled around him. "How long has she been missing?"

"You heard our conversation?" The Father returned his glasses. "Soup still warm so twenty minutes if that."

"Then we need to start a search."

The Father pointed out the obvious. "But where to search is the question. There's a distinct lack of evidence to who has her. It won't be payback from Lewie, as the NEPD has him under tight surveillance since the garage incident."

"Perhaps your right Father, what we need is help from someone who has a unique talent in finding people."

D noticed all had gone quiet, glancing from the secpad to find all attention upon him. "What... what did I do?"

"It's not what you have done, D, but what you will do." Simon forced a smile through the nausea as he approached.

D forced a swallow, remaining pensive between each scrutinising stare. "I will not like what you're considering, will I?"

Simon took D's secpad and put his arm around his shoulder to walk him across the rooftop. "You will use this device of yours to narrow down Lisa's location. She is in danger of being hurt, if not killed, unless we can get to her." With a slight push, he shoved D in the stomach with the secpad to make his point important.

"I can't make that happen. She isn't dead or dying. Remember, I track the dead, not the living."

The expression Simon gave him made D take a step back, looking at the others for support, receiving none.

"I can't do that, do you realise how many rules I will have to break, tell him Michael."

The archangel remained silent.

"Look Simon, Fate doesn't enjoy being cheated, the repercussions with doing... well, you can't imagine."

Simon shook his head, turning to Father Peters. "You know I don't think it's because he's not allowed, but because he can't. His entire persona is a show, a conman in a flashy suit."

"Perhaps he doesn't have the smarts to do something this difficult," Father Peters offered with a glimmer of smugness that had D's nostrils flaring.

"Not thought of that, Father. Perhaps behind this facade of confidence and swagger is a small time wannabe playing out of his league."

D had a flush of anger as he ground on his perfect teeth. "Fine, but mark my words, there will be consequences for us all. No one cheats the reaper, no one." With that, he strode off, tapping away, muttering under his breath as he did.

"That was fun," Father Peters chuckled as he and Simon turned back to recognise the concern on both archangel's faces.

"What you're asking him to do is forbidden, it's not up to you to change Fate for your own personal gain."

"I've played this game to your rules since the beginning, Michael. So now I'm going by mine and if that means getting Lisa back safe, then I'm sure as hell going to do it."

"Michael is right, Simon. To spare one life, you must offer another," Raphael said.

"Lisa isn't dead and if D comes through with the information, she won't be because we will have saved her."

"What if her death is inevitable? You're upsetting the balance, a soul for a soul."

"Only if I fail," Simon answered. "Are you helping or not, Raphael?"

"This is for humans to resolve," Michael interrupted.

Father Peters grumbled. "Spoken like a true archangel."

Michael glared before returning his attention to Simon. "If it be the path you wish to follow, so be it. We shall take our leave."

"Do what you want," Simon offered, his answer filled with contempt as he strode to head for the entrance. "D, meet us downstairs when you have something." With that, Father Peters and Simon left.

"This will not end well, Michael," Raphael offered.

"If he continues following his human side, he's destined to make mistakes of the past and the consequences are already in motion. Let us hope he doesn't become consumed by his actions."

As Simon and Father Peters returned to the kitchen, the priest took a moment to survey the mess before them. "Where do we start?" He retrieved an overturned chair. "She put up quite a struggle." They deposited the largest fragments of broken plates into an empty box before continuing around the room.

Simon stood by the back door, examining something between his fingers. "What you got there, lad?" With no answer, Father Peters came to stand next to Simon, peering over the top of his glasses to what had his friend so enthralled.

"Someone has walked in, looks like birdseed." The Father grimaced. "You think whoever took Lisa brought the seed in with them."

Simon's lips twisted in thought.

Father Peters recognised a hint of doubt in his friend, including a flash of fear. "Hey, what is it, what's got you so rattled?"

"I... I don't know, it's nothing."

It was then D entered his appearance worst for wear. The stress etched his face as he sank into a chair, tossing the secpad onto the kitchen table.

"Any luck finding Lisa?" Father Peters asked.

"It's done and for all our futures, I hope you know what you're doing."

"D, I understand what you had to do, but it's for the greater good if it means bringing Lisa home safe." Simon retrieved the secpad and scrolled the page left open.

"I don't think you understand, Simon," D explained, watching as he read the details. "Father Peters has known Lisa the longest so would know if she would be okay allowing people getting hurt because of her, those she cares about the most."

"Which is why I'm doing this alone, not letting anybody else getting hurt. It will be a straight swap of my life for hers and that's the deal."

D threw his hands in the air, lurching from the chair to pace the floor. "It's not that easy, not with Fate. You can't pick who she takes, she's never cheated without consequences."

"So what do we do, let Lisa die?" Father Peters suggested.

"If it's her fated time, then yes we do."

"That's not acceptable D. I will not let her suffer because of something I could stop from happening."

Both D and Father Peters turned to meet Simon's determined gaze.

"And I do this alone."

The Father frowned as D shook his head in disappointment to Simon's determination.

"This place, it's where she's being held?" Simon pointed to the secpad.

D nodded. "That's the place or nearby. It isn't an exact science, maybe a block or two. It looks to be part of the old warehouse district, a group of cold storage and meat packing units, abandoned. You have less than forty-three minutes, and that's the best I can give you."

"Then I ask you for one more favour, Simon said."

D knew what that last favour meant as he rolled his eyes, sinking back in the chair with a heavy sigh.

CHAPTER TWELVE

Sacrifice of the Innocents

The re-materialisation was rough and uncontrolled, as they landed hard and thrown across a tiled floor, hitting the far side with bone cracking impact.

Simon was the first to his feet, scrambling to take in his surroundings.

The warehouse was vast, a cold storage stacked with used pallets and empty crates. Whilst a heavy layer of thick dust showed, no one had been here in years.

Simon realised D had not joined him, but a quick search found him sprawled, catatonic. Rolling him on to his side, a trail of blood trickled from his mouth and left eye as he responded with the slightest of groans. "You okay D, can you walk?"

D pushed away the help. "Bro... I can't even see, let alone go for a stroll." A spark of pain crossed his face. "I've done what you've ask of me, now you're on your own." The unkind smile showed he was in no mood to go any further. "Go play the hero. Save the girl." With the last of his strength, he pushed Simon.

"Lisa could be anywhere in this maze," Simon responded.

D wiped at the metallic taste of blood from his mouth, his soulless eyes struggling to focus. "I don't give a shit if you find her or not. Use angelic hearing, bat sonar or crazy ass mind tricks, I don't care. Just leave me here, I'm done with you all, I want to die in peace." His last action was pointing as he slid down the wall. "Don't think I missed the irony in my last sentence." With that, he was unconscious.

Simon checked for a pulse, finding it faint but steady. He dragged the unconscious body behind a stack of pallets. With hope to keep his friend safe until returning, if he ever did, but the priority was finding Lisa.

A roller mounted door resisted at first until opening onto a joining corridor stretching the entire length of the warehouse. It was late in the day and light from the overhead skylights was fading, casting deep shadows in the abandoned warehouse as Simon continued into the building. His concentration on an image of Lisa, a memory of their earlier days during his recovery, the long times spent together as she took care of him. Eyes closed tight, remembering as she sat on the side of his bed. With hair catching the light, offering the slimmest of infectious smiles that lit up her face. *Lisa, where are you?* Simon repeated the words until his attention caught a faint echo coming from the corridor. With his body tense, he focused on the distinctive sound, a sound of someone whistling as though they did not have a care in the world. He pushed on, cautious to stay close to the walls and cause as less noise as possible. On reaching a fork in the corridor, stopping to listen and hope to pick up on which direction to take. The only sounds were the ageing building and his breathing. So with reluctance he chose, hoping to have made the correct choice, making it only fifty yards before the corridor ended at a steel staircase descending to the lower levels. A quick glance over the railings showed a stairwell flooded in darkness, but for a faint glimmer of light at its deepest recess. Almost on cue, the faint whistling continued, taunting him. Everything so far was telling him not to continue, that it was a trap, but with caution he started his decent. As the stairs narrowed, all he could do was focus on the distant light. Once reaching the bottom, he found swing doors opened to a corridor. The walls were water damaged but lit with the red hue by emergency lighting. The limited light allowed Simon to navigate and continue, all senses continuing to tell him it's a trap with each step. He continued deeper into the recesses of the warehouse, passing abandoned offices running the length of a larger space. A quick search of the nearest found it empty, and he was about to check another when the whistling started again. Quickening his pace, Simon followed the haunting melody. A jolt of a memory forced him to stop, remembering where he had heard that same tune. It was during his convalescence on one of Jake's visits. The youngster had brought a small music box, made from dark green wood of crude construction. It had been an odd impulse buy at a local flea market in Sufferance by his mother. Jake had hoped its melody cheerful and would help in his recovery. Simon sought to remember until a name of recognition came back. "Ring a ring of roses," he whispered.

Ahead, the whistling stopped, replaced by the ominous sound of metal scraping metal.

Simon hurried his pace, all caution gone as he ran the final distance, finding the way blocked by a security door. Unlike the office doors, this one was solid plated steel and windowless. With little chance of knowing what awaited him beyond, Simon hesitated to grip the locking bar. Then taking a deep breath, trying to make no sound, he pulled on the bar and slid it back. Any chance of stealth evaporating as the door unlocked and opened with annoyance from rusted hinges. Inside, what greeted Simon was a stench of burning flesh and human waste.

The room offered little light but a pair of florescent ceiling strip lights at the far end. The furthest one, struggling to stay lit, casting long shadows into the corners. Grime and years of neglect stained the industrial tiles, which made the room cold.

Simon concluded it had been a cold storage unit and pressed on to continue his search. He glimpsed something suspended against the wall. A possible impending threat made him stay low, and to the shadows as he approached to investigate. A sickening tightness gripped his insides, recognising the obvious shape of a woman suspended semi naked by her arms. Her underwear not enough to hide the evidence of torture, as burns and cuts covered the full length of her bloodied body. A hemp sack concealed her identity, making recognition impossible to be sure, but her build and height matched Lisa.

Simon fell to his knees, pained by the thought he was too late. A wash of emotions swelled until forced past the dread, all caution to his safety no longer an issue as he moved forward.

It was then the room filled with laughter, a macabre threatening laughter.

Simon froze, spinning in search for who taunted him. "Who's there? Show yourself, you bastard."

The laughter continued.

Simon grew angry, frustrated. "Stop playing games and show yourself."

"For all your years, Simon, you never understood patience." The gravel filled voice appeared to be in the room, resonating against the confined walls.

"If you know me, then know what happens when I find you."

"That's your greeting for an old friend?" the voice responded.

Simon flexed his fists, fingernails biting palms as his attention came back to the captive woman, needing to know who she was.

"Take another step towards her and she dies. Even you, my angelic friend, are not fast enough to reach her before the rigged generator fries her from the inside out."

Simon sank back, eyes reddening with the sense of helplessness. "What have you done to her?"

Her torturer had branded her body with the same symbols Simon recognised from Carla's crime scene photos.

"Oh, we had fun together as she pleaded, not for herself but for her son. Please don't hurt him, she sobbed, so emotional I could cry, a selfless act in her last hours. But we both know what they say when the end comes, don't we, Simon? When the pain is immense, the fight gone and they have nothing else to give, then it's always me, me, and me."

Simon's stomach twisted. "Why are you doing this?"

"The reason is that I can, dear boy. It started as a hobby and found I had a unique talent, which grew into a successful career opportunity. Please understand I consider myself an artist of sorts, even though I'm my worst critic when I say it's become an art form of monumental creativity."

"If it's me you want, why put my friend through this horror."

"Because you must feel the loss as I once did, when you turned on me, Simon. We're good together, a partnership that could have done so much, but now you must suffer as I did, feel my pain."

Simon placed his head in his hands, fighting emotions, tears swelling with rage. "I don't understand."

"Oh, you will, you will." The tone became sinister. "Soon enough all will become clear because I miss our chats. Simon. I want us to go down memory lane again, remember the good old days, you and me, Butch and Sundance, what you say."

I'm so sorry, Lisa, so sorry. Simon was at a breaking point. He could but lay on the tiled floor, pulling his knees against his chest, continuing to sob. Time passed through stirring red-rimmed eyes as he watched with forlorn sadness the lifeless body.

Deep from the shadows, the voice broke the silence. "You still with us half-blood or are you happy to continue dribbling into the tiling?"

Simon remained silent.

"Do you remember our first? How much easier it was back then when nobody cared what we did on our blood thirsty adventures?"

"What are you talking about," Simon asked, rousing from forced solitude. "I don't know... our first what? You're making little sense."

"Our first hunt together. What was her name? Such an attractive little dark-haired thing, her name's on the tip of my tongue?"

Simon rolled back to his knees, running dirt covered hands through his hair.

"Beth... Bethany, no Elizabeth," continued the voice. "A beautiful African girl, as I remember. She mumbled scripture as the petty bitch assumed those pathetic words had any power. We had to shut her up by cutting her tongue out. Do you remember?"

"I'm not playing your games," Simon protested, trying to understand the tone of the one sided conversation.

"Then there was Malcolm who pissed his pants, screaming like a baby girl as we pealed his skin from his feet to knees. Like them all, he cracked and told us what we needed to know."

Simon stopped listening and calculated the distance to the suspended body.

Almost as though sensing his thoughts and intentions, his tormentor's tone turned agitated. "Tut tut their Skippy, do nothing you'll regret." As a warning, a spark of electricity sprang at the woman's feet, jolting the body in its restraints, to release a muffled scream before falling silent again.

Simon sat back, chewing his lip in building frustration.

"We're linked, you and me, always have been. For I know your mind, Simon. It's impossible to hide from me. I'm in that little pocket of your subconscious, an itch you can't scratch."

"You expect me to believe you're in my head. If that's true then you truly know my intentions and I can end us both here and now, what do you say?"

"Oh Simon, plenty of time for that, but first tell me how beautiful was Carla?"

Simon tensed to the mention of the name.

"You must remember, you fell from grace for her and lost your wings, and yet you watched her plead for her life as she cursed your name. Oh, the surprise on her face when she real-ised who had been cutting into her, torturing her the whole time. It was a moment I shall cherish forever, when the apprentice became the master."

Shock etched Simon's face at the sudden revelation, unable to breathe as his body convulsed. "You're lying!"

All around, sickening laughter filled the room. Then from the far corner came a scraping of metal.

Simon raised his head, catching the glimpse of someone entering the room.

The figure's robes resembled a priest, brown habit dragging the floor, the hood obscuring any chance of recognition.

Simon's focus never left his obvious tormentor. His mind drifting between reality and the images of Carla's last moments draped in his arms and the possibility of his involvement in her death.

The figure circled the room.

Simon stirred, sensing adrenalin flooding his system, a chance to confront the sadistic manipulator until fear stabbed his thoughts again of perhaps being too late.

On approaching the suspended captive, the figure checked each restraint with gloved hands.

The stricken woman tensing at the interaction, she released a muffled response from under the sackcloth hood.

Simon flinched, knowing she still lived, and maybe still had a chance.

The figure raised a hand in warning. "No, please stay where you are, my friend." The tone sounded strained. "Any thought to free her and I promise she will be dead before you get to your feet."

Simon did as instructed, releasing the tension in his body.

"That's better. Now please sit on your hands like an obedient puppy."

Simon pushed his hands under his legs, straightening his back, trying to stay comfortable under the circumstances. The coldness of the tiled floor sank into his tired legs and hands as he waited.

The robed figure turned, continuing the facade to their identity. "Now where were we? Oh yes, it's coming back. You made such a cute couple, such a pity the powers were too late to bench you, couldn't believe my luck finding a Chosen so vulnerable. We partied for hours, I relished in the fear coursing through her veins. Then looking upon those beautiful brown eyes of hers, pleading for it not to be true. Wow, it gives me goose bumps just thinking about it all."

Simon felt his strength evaporating, remaining crouched but feet away. The distance might as well be miles. He was helpless to intervene.

"But that's right, for you still don't remember the full facts. The powers stripped your memory, disgraced you, and sent you back to this cesspit."

"Who are you?" Simon asked through a strained voice.

The question went ignored as the figure continued. "I've studied the human brain and found it to be a limitless resource? With the correct manipulation opens a host to suggestion and like a computer never erased without destroying the drive. So no matter how you try to wipe that information, deep down those fragments are retrievable, you just need the right motivation."

A deep sense of unease washed over Simon as he shuffled in forced capitulation on the floor.

"Maybe we need to stimulate those lost memories somehow, relive the great old days with a little bloodletting." The figure's attention returned to the woman still suspended.

Simon sought to stay seated as he watched a blade rest under the concealed woman's chin.

A muffled scream emanated from the hood as she struggled, sensing what was occurring, pulling against the restraints, struggling to resist.

"I remember nothing before my decent and swear to you they have wiped all knowledge, everything."

"Not everything, Simon." The voice sounded angry and full of spite, but the knife remained at the woman's throat. "You forget I've seen what you've seen. Experienced what you've done, for we are the same Simon and capable of such magnificent things."

Simon watched horrified as the knife cut deep in one fluid motion.

The women convulsed as a dark red smear appeared where the knife pierced the hood as her body floundered. Her blood ran the curvature of her neck, soaking her skin until she hung motionless.

Simon cried out, watching the blood pool around her suspended feet. "She has nothing to do with us, she's innocent," he cried.

The figure paced the room, pointing the blood-smeared knife. "No one's innocent Simon, no one. The humans are tools in a war that has being raging for millennia and we do with them as we please."

Simon turned back to the lifeless victim, eyes welling.

The figure appeared to sense what Simon was thinking. "Her involvement here is to create my point."

"Why did she have to die?" Simon pleaded.

"Because she holds the key to a power over all, we are Gods in our own right, so why should we keep the balance? We are the masters of what this entire world offers if we wish to take it."

"But you killed Lisa, and she was nothing to you. You're telling me you did it because you can, showing me who has the power here?"

The robed figure returned to the woman's body. "Don't tell me you didn't enjoy watching her flounder, knowing she gasped for air in her last moments. That is the power we relish in taking, enjoying the moment of the kill."

Simon tried to understand what was happening, trying to get his emotions under control as he felt his own life was irrelevant. A surge of revenge ran through his mind as he readied himself, rising to one knee.

Laughter resonated again. "Poor, poor Simon, you don't see the enormous picture around you. Did you ever understand what those dreams meant?"

"Dreams, what dreams?"

"They were memories of your past life, Simon, whilst under my teaching. Join me and we will experience them again."

"No." Simon screamed, lunging forward.

The figure lashed out with the hilt of the knife, striking Simon across the temple, forcing him on his back, disoriented.

"Can't you handle the truth, that you're the reason for countless innocent deaths? Look… Look upon the face of your latest victim." Simon's tormentor grasped the back of his head, dragging him inches from the motionless body. All before removing the sack cloth to uncover the blooded features underneath, returning a soulless stare in judgement.

Simon struggled to look away, forcing his head to turn, but the grip was strong.

"Look upon her, search the eyes of the woman you tried to save, killed by your inactions."

With reluctance, Simon glanced at the dark-toned features of burnt cheek, flesh cut deep and bloodied. The woman's hair hung limp, hazel eyes continued to judge.

Simon stomach tightened from the sharp intake of breath, a pang of guilt and relief in not recognising her. Then turning, he sensed the grip diminishing but was unprepared to see the distinct smile from beneath the hood, lost to recount the times mesmerised by those pencil thin lips.

"Hello lover, missed me?" she said.

With the release of the grip, Simon fell backwards in surprised horror.

Lisa straightened to wipe the bladc down a robed sleeve before pulling on her hood to uncover her still bruised face. A tug at the hair grip let a mane of hair fall around her as she smiled. "I'm sure you have questions?"

Simon remained in shock, the words failing as he strained to speak.

"Okay," Lisa offered, her face creased into a frown. "Do you need more time to process?"

"You could say that," Simon answered, wiping his mouth with the back of hand.

"Well, it works like this. I'm not who you think I am. Think of it as a test drive of sorts. But have to say, I appreciate the simple girl next door look in a woman, tidy butt and perky rack." To prove her point, she pushed up her chest. "Then you always had an eye for the ladies, Simon." The entity that was Lisa smiled. "So much better than the overweight paediatrician I've been riding these past few months.... so booooring."

"What are you?"

"There are things best kept a secret Simon, but if you think hard, you might remember."

Simon was looking at Lisa, but that spark that made her so precious gone. Nothing but cold blackness lived behind her eyes.

Lisa knelt to face him. "So why so glum chum?"

"Is... she still alive?"

"In me, noggin, you mean. Yep, she's here shouting and screaming, don't know how I can hear myself think."

"Can I speak to her?" Simon asked with hesitation.

Lisa seemed bemused. "Why? Not sure she would want to talk to you, not after laying out all your dirty little secrets to her. If I remember, Carla had a pair of lungs on her too. Oh, she cursed you as you carved her up on the table."

Simon grabbed Lisa's arm. "What do you mean as I carved her?"

Lisa laughed aloud, pulling away. "Well, I was driving, but you did the carving." She twisted the knife in the air. Pity etched her face. "All this time you thought the powers recalled you because you were bumping uglies with your charge. That was bad enough, but the actual reason was having a demon riding your celestial arse."

Simon sank back.

"That glimmer of the human soul you grew for your charge was enough for me to infect. There's a reason they don't allow an angel to love, it starts such a chain of events."

Simon shook his head in disbelief. "I killed Carla?"

"You should have seen her face. Such a picture as you strapped her down as she screamed for her hero, her knight in shining armour, to come rescue her." Lisa stepped forward, lifting Simon's chin. "Simon, Simon, come and save me, she shouted. Then you pulled back the hood to show her that her hero was her torturer."

"I couldn't have done that to her, I loved her," Simon replied, reeling from knowledge.

"Yes, you did lover boy," Lisa smiled, tapping her temple with a finger. "You forget about that insignificant piece of me, so deep in your subconscious. Overtime, I manipulated that piece until it was time to take control."

"Samuel," Simon murmured now, understanding.

Lisa winked, taking a bow in response, relishing Simon's response. "Not as stupid as you appear."

"The park, I guess, was your idea, your way of communicating with me and letting me think I was talking to my subconscious."

"I like to call them waiting rooms whilst I'm driving, but the park was the best one I've created so far. Once having the soul strapped down in a room of their own making, they have a front-row seat whilst unable to interfere."

"Then what, you kill the host?"

"I'm not that barbaric, although it's fun watching them live with the repercussions of their actions, the blood on their hands. Like you now."

"So why choose me?" Simon asked.

"How could I pass up the opportunity to ride an angel? I jumped at the chance. Not every day an angel develops emotions to grow a soul of their own. Once connected, I had a direct conduit to the powers and the locations of the Chosen past, present, and future." Lisa's smile increased as she recognised doubt on the mention of the Chosen. "You know why Carla was so special." She crossed her arms. "For every generation three hear the word of God. They become seers or

Chosen and are valuable to both sides for their predictions and influence in future events. My task has been to uncover these predictions by using my unique talents. This resulted in our paths crossing because of the delicious Carla." With a smack of lips, Lisa licked the air. "Twenty years later, I'm tasked again in finding the next generation."

"And her, what's her connection to all this?" Simon asked, attention returning to the suspended woman.

"The piece of meat hanging is not one, she's a negligible play thing I picked up to make my point, but I'm digressing. There I was, hot on the trail of the third, coming across this bit of tail." Lisa pushed her hands down the length of her body. "But how my face went red discovering who the third..." she pointed the knife, her grin increasing. "Now, now, don't be thinking I will all go big-headed and blab my plans like a cheap Hollywood super villain?"

"Can you leave Lisa's body without hurting her?"

She considered the question. "If you so wish. Then where's the fun in that?

Simon attempted to come to terms to what was going on with his friend and Samuel's revelations.

"Later, I was considering a stroll down to the strip, and pimp her out to the dopers or gangers for a quick ride." She stood up to roll her hips. "I'm positive she would like that, but I'm not sure you would want her afterwards."

Simon edged forward. "Perhaps the plan was taking her back without you having time to hurt her."

Lisa flipped her head back, laughing until doubt crossed her face. "What could you do? There's not a weapon forged on this planet that can kill me you, idiot."

"No, not kill you, but one capable of making it unpleasant for you to stay in that body."

"What weapon could possible to do that...?"

Simon launched forward, his legs carrying him crashing into Lisa.

Both hit the ground hard, Lisa's knife slid across the floor out of her reach.

"Forgive me," Simon asked, raising his arm, gripping the Blade of Light.

"You think a knife can harm me," Lisa scoffed.

"Look closer," Simon glared.

Lisa's eyes opened wide, recognising the symbols etched its length.

Simon hoped the blade held enough celestial power for the task. Thrusting into her shoulder, resulting in an inhuman scream coming out of Lisa's mouth as Simon continued to twist, her body thrashing beneath him. She clawed at his face and neck, leaving bleeding gashes as he continued to hold her down, praying for it to work. It was a fight to keep his grip, applying further pressure on the blade, deeper into her shoulder until she became motionless. A quick check for a pulse found none, and so in panic he released his grip and took her head in his hand.

A thick black liquid trickled from her nose and corners of her mouth. Then her eyes blinked open as she braced her back, arching to release black smoke from her mouth and nose.

Simon flung himself off the bucking body as the darkening cloud circled above them.

In a last throw of anger, the dark entity lashed out until finding an escape through an air grate in the far wall.

As Simon rushed to check Lisa's pulse and found a steady rhythm. Then her eyes flickered open to share Simon's concerned smile.

Now released from her predicament, Lisa cried out. "Oh God, I was shouting but no one could hear mc." She embraced Simon. "I tried to control my body, but it was hopeless." A flash of pain from her shoulder made her pull away. Then she winced at seeing the suspended woman. "There was no way to stop myself. Oh, sweet Jesus... the knife was in my hand and I still..." she sobbed. She could not finish the sentence as she cradled against Simon's chest.

For the next few moments Simon held her, stroking her

hair as she sobbed.

Then she pulled away, tears staining her face.

"It's not over yet," he said.

Lisa sniffed back her tears, frowning. "What, I don't know what you mean?"

"Samuel is still a part of me, lingering in my dreams, and is the same entity that took control of your body. It's hard to explain, but part of him dwells in my subconscious. To be free of him, I must remove him for good. So trust me."

Lisa reeled, wincing from her damaged shoulder as she pushed herself up using her good arm. "It's all confusing, you ask for me to trust you when the fact is I can't trust myself with all that's happened."

With a tender kiss to her forehead, Simon stood back. "I have to do this." With those last words, he plunged the blade into his stomach, the pain excruciating as he gasped for breath.

Lisa sat up, hand over her mouth as he fell forward into her arms.

The sensation felt warm from deep within as Simon closed his eyes, surrendering to the blackness.

The draped curtains parted, allowing the slimmest of light from the fading grey evening as the room remained in deep shadow.

Simon awoke, taking comfort at being back in his own room, in the familiarity that the Refuge of Lost Souls had become his home. Forcing his wracked body from slumber, he sought to prop himself against the bed's headboard, gaining the slightest of relief. Not surprising, as his body had suffered immense stress, for every muscle protested at the slightest movement, including his bandaged stomach. A subconscious scratch of cheek found many a lost day of growth. "How long was I out this time?"

A figure broke from the comfort of the faded leather chair.

"Almost five days." D said. "You're lucky I found the two of you still alive and could get you back here for treatment, you both lost a lot of blood."

Simon ran his hand through his hair. "Hmm... that explains why my insides burn."

D approached, back to his usual immaculate signature of an expensive tailored suit, but an air of pensiveness replaced his arrogant swagger. "What can you recall, since rescuing the damsel in distress?"

Simon lent to retrieve the glass of water left on the side table, wincing from the tightness of his bandaged wound. The drink was an immediate relief to his dry throat as he sipped the contents before returning the glass. He pulled back the covers to swing his legs over the bed, movement still an effort. "Last I remember was stabbing myself." He fumbled at the bandages. "Please tell me it worked and I'm free of Samuel."

"It was a gut wound bro, you need rest, as very few people walk away from such an injury," D said.

"But I'm no ordinary person, isn't that what you kept telling me D?" Simon dismissed D's silent concern with a nod, changing the conversation. "How is Lisa?"

"On the outside she's fine, over the worst of the bruising and her tennis games shot for the foreseeable future, but she will heal. The emotional stuff is another matter, those are deep. Time will tell. The good Father has convinced her to take Jake back home to see his grandparents, and under the circumstance it's an excellent idea."

Simon's eyes narrowed, returning D's glance. "What does she remember?"

"It's patchy as she remembers parts of a heated argument with Sister Angela and hurting her shoulder, but not the details. She remembers darkness as though lost underwater, but nothing more, and if she does she's keeping to herself. What we know is that to survive demonic possession is almost unprecedented. The fact is, we might never know what she remembers and assume she doesn't for all our sakes. The priest

convinced her she's had a traumatic break, a temporary amnesia to what happened. So it's a waiting game."

"But that's not why you've waited for me to recover, tell me
what you want?"

The malice in Simon's voice made D's face tense. "Bro,
there's something we need to discuss, and it's important."

"What about the fact you've lied about Carla's death? Not
forgetting, not telling, I've had a demon riding shotgun in my
subconscious. Are you aware of the deplorable acts of violence I did, so tell me D why should I trust anything you have
to say?"

The atmosphere of the room grew tense.

D rubbed the back of his head before answering. "You're
right and I can't apologise enough. That been said, there's a
consequence to rescuing Lisa and saving her from that demon.
She should have died."

"Please, not this speech again D, isn't having Lisa back safe
enough. Guess I'm indebted to have survived, and then there's
beating the big bad. Hasn't anything we have done these recent weeks satisfied the powers?"

D paced the floor. "Like I said, you don't understand how
it works. You screwed Fate, and she's pissed and wants something in return."

"I offered myself and she saw fit to send me back." Simon
argued.

"Offering yourself doesn't make it right, you're not listening."

Simon stood to retrieve his trousers and continue to dress.
"It's over, we won, the end."

"By the maker, you're an idiot." D said with a shake of head.
"It's not over, but just beginning. The cardinal is down, but
not out. In fact, he's a bigger threat than ever. We can't afford
to underestimate him. Then there's Lewie, he and his minions
know you're here and will want something for the car park
renovation the Order undertook on your behalf."

"He can't hold us responsible for that. It was the bishop and his clerics?"

"He does and will," D rolled his eyes to Simon's reluctance to recognise the situation. "Also, you have an NEPD investigation gathering evidence of your involvement in the murders of several people over the past twenty years. That is not going away."

Simon sank back to the bed, shoulders dipping in release of a heavy sigh. "What should I do?"

"Run, hide, get out of dodge. But staying in Sufferance will put a target on your back, this place and all your friends." Recognising doubt, D sat down on next to Simon. "Are you up to this?"

The slightest touch to his bandages made Simon wince. "Well, there's the stiff pain, and the sensation to having a hot poker rammed through my gut."

"Out of interest, what made you consider using the blade, how did you know it would work?" D asked.

"I didn't, took a chance a celestial blade was enough to hurt Samuel and force him out. I had nothing else left." Simon answered, wincing.

D offered a sympathetic grimace and nod, watching as he struggled to pull on a T-shirt and finish getting dressed.

On the rooftop Father Peters smoked his much needed cigarette. The surrounding streets beyond coming alive with various colours in the dusk as the nightlife awoke.

"You need not hide in the shadows, you know," the Father offered.

From the entrance, a large shape detached to step out, moving to stand next to the priest.

"Are the additions to the building your idea?" he asked, pointing with the lit cigarette.

Situated around the rooftop were grotesque-looking gargoyles merged with the stonework, hunched in silent sentry over the street.

Michael flexed his retracted wings. "As too the hidden celestial glyphs situated around windows and doors, they're for your demonic protection and as a warning, but we cannot protect from the evils of man."

"Great, hope you're right." The priest's attention remained on Michael. "I never got to acknowledge your help for sending Raphael to tend to Simon's wounds, touch and go for a while, but he will recover. Thank you for Lisa too and hope she does not remember what happened to her."

"For your sakes, that is true. As requested, Lisa will not remember the hours leading up to her injury. Also, she is once again unaware of our existence and we would prefer it stayed that way," Michael answered.

"I understand, but she has seen and experienced an unimaginable trauma. She has always been a fighter and hides her genuine feelings well, but I'm worried for her." The Father's attention remained on the archangel. "We were lucky but fear not, your secrets safe, this I promise."

Michael's glare narrowed. "Don't make promises you can't guarantee, priest. The human minds, weak and the block temporary if pressed, make certain she does not force herself to remember. Those hidden memories are an itch we cannot allow her to scratch."

Father Peters caught Michael's agitation. "What of Simon, what happens now?"

"Simon has made his choice and regardless of the consequences."

"But according to D, he made that choice to save us and no thanks from you. You're hanging him out to dry over these ritual murders?"

"Our retrieval or neutralising of the blade was paramount to his mission here, nothing more."

"The kid is number one suspect in a situation he couldn't control, so there must be something you can do, a celestial intervention, anything."

The archangel passed over a carved wooden box, Enochian symbols daubed its lid. "Give him this as a parting gift of our gratitude, but we offer nothing else." Michael moved to the roof edge, appearing to ignore the priest's plea.

Father Peters felt his anger building. "Makes my blood boil how emotionless you dicks are, the kids innocent."

Michael turned to stare down the priest. "We leave emotions to the apes. It doesn't concern us what you think, we serve our Father's will."

"So that's it? You give him a shitty trinket box and we go our separate ways, hoping to never meet again."

"We won a battle, but the war continues. Who knows what Fate has written? But Simon made his intentions clear. He chose life on earth over the Celestial Temple and the protection that provides. He will have to live with the repercussions and what they bring."

The Father hesitated, the cigarette nestled the corner of his mouth. "What does that bloody mean?"

But Michael had gone, leaving the priest sensing an icy shiver, an uneasiness passing through him as though someone walked over his grave.

On returning to the kitchen it encouraged him to see Simon dressed, still appearing pale and his movement hindered by his obvious injuries. He sat with Jake, both deep in conversation about the youngster's latest library book open on the table.

At the sink, Lisa struggled to use the washing-up brush because of her arm still in a sling. On noticing him, she returned a thin smile, and in her frustration discarded the brush to dunk the used coffee cup in to the soapy water.

"Leave the washing for me to do later, come and sit down, lass."

"No Father, I need to keep busy if you don't mind," Lisa responded pulling on her sling.

Father Peters took a seat opposite Simon, sharing a nod of greeting. He then thumbed towards D, navigating his secpad by the main door.

Simon shrugged. "He's been like that since I got up, won't sit down, and kept reading his secpad."

"Hey Jake, can I talk to Simon for a moment? Perhaps you could show him your books later before bed, okay?"

The youngster's forehead wrinkled for confirmation as Simon nodded. "Let us have a quick chat and promise you can tell me about the book, okay." That seemed to appease him and his face burst into a smile before gathering the book, dismounting the chair to head through the doors for his room.

"Is something wrong, Father?" Simon inquired.

"Wanted to make certain you're okay," the Father queried, peering over his glasses.

"Fine, I guess, considering having a demon resident in my skull this whole time."

"And Lisa, how's she been with you. Have you spoken?"

"She kept her distance since I came downstairs, with no actual eye contact, but you can't blame her. D mentioned she had a few flashbacks and an odd unpleasant dream but no real details the past few days, I'm hoping the mind wipe holds. Guess we wait and see what happens with time."

"Do you remember anything?"

"Everything's a blur and hazy." Simon answered with a shrug. "Samuel mentioned the Chosen and their importance to both sides, same as what the archangels mentioned."

Father Peters considered his answer. "Because they predict future events like a prophet. It sounds impossible, but after these past weeks I don't know what to believe."

A flash of doubt crossed Simon's face.

"What is it?" the Father inquired.

"Samuel mentioned tracking a third."

"There's a third Chosen? What do we know?"

"Nothing concrete, but my bet is they are the key to whatever is happening. Still, it doesn't explain why he took Lisa or what her connection is to the Chosen."

Both turned to watch Lisa struggling to wash up, unaware of their scrutiny.

"Is there a possibility she is the third?" the Father suggested, turning back to Simon.

Simon shook his head, pushing over a small secpad. "Not sure. We found information on the other victims. What we've pasted together is they brutalised their bodies with what we now know is Enochian script. D got me the police reports detailing the actual script but have no way to decipher their meaning. I have no memory and the archangels won't help." He handed over the secpad.

Father Peters opened a highlighted document. "Have to admit, I too struggle to understand their meaning, can't D help?"

"He's no help at the moment, something has him flustered and he isn't making any sense these days."

"Well, I can sift through the files, perhaps see a pattern. There's a friend in the New York diocese that might help us with a translation." As he scrolled the device, he paused.

"Have you found something, Father?" Simon asked.

The Father highlighted a passage of text to show Simon. "It states the last victim was Helen Zimmerman, the names familiar. Lisa knows her from Jake's school, as her son is a classmate of Jakes."

"So there's a connection. But what does it mean?" Simon asked.

"Not sure. But that doesn't interest me. It says the school uses a psychologist and this Helen Zimmerman was also a private patient of the same doctor. She was being treated for night terrors."

Simon read the details for himself. "What could that mean?"

"Might be nothing, and as the patient files are confidential we can't be certain, perhaps it's a coincidence. It's just…"

"What is it, Father?" Simon queried, trying to see if he had found anything.

The priest glanced back to Lisa, lowering his voice. "A few weeks ago, Lisa became concerned about Jake acting out of character. She mentioned he was speaking with God. With everything else, I hadn't spoken to him and Lisa put it down

to an overzealous imagination and corruption from Sister Angela."

"You think Samuel took Lisa instead of Jake?"

The Father raised an eyebrow. "We better hope not."

"Father, are we expecting guests this evening?" The question came from Lisa turning from the sink as she dried her
hands on her piny.

Father Peters frowned. "Tonight, no, rather late for a visit
would have thought?"

"Bro we need to talk," D interrupted, trying to get Simon's
attention. He appeared agitated, glancing over his shoulder to
the kitchen windows.

Lisa leant against the sink, trying to recognise the recent
arrivals.

Outside, the yard lay shrouded in darkness until distinct
car headlights illuminated the entire rear of the building.

"Two cars have parked in the yard with full beams," Lisa
continued.

"Bro, I have to talk now, it's urgent."

Simon turned to D. "Can't it wait, D, was discussing something important?"

"This concerns all of us."

Both Father Peters and Simon watched D scurry out
through the double doors.

"What's his issue?" Father Peters asked.

Simon shrugged, rising from his seat, and was about to follow D when Lisa turned from the window again, adjusting her
bandaged arm. "Curious Father, they are out of the cars and
stood watching the building."

In that split second, the entire yard side erupted in a blaze
of automatic fire, scattering shards of masonry and glass fanning out in all directions.

Lisa covered her face and screamed before throwing herself
to the floor as Simon pulled the startled Father Peters out of
his chair and under the large oak kitchen table.

"Stay down, Father, and stay low," shouted Simon through

gritted teeth. A search for Lisa found her using the protection offered by the double sink. She continued to scream in terror as the kitchen disintegrated around her.

Father Peters shared Simon's concern, showing with a nod to be okay as Simon scrambled over his legs, using the table as cover to reach Lisa.

Red and orange tracers sped over their heads, ripping cupboards and kitchen equipment to shreds. The microwave exploded, and then the coffee peculator excreted its contents down the front of the worktop. The rest of kitchen fared no better as it disintegrated under the amount of rounds striking the far wall. Then no sooner had it started then an unnerving silence descended but for exposed wiring sparking in final throes of death.

Outside, Lilith discarded her empty ammunition clip, tossing it to one of the dark-suited men accompanying her. "Retrieve our brass, leave no evidence we were here." She took a last glance to the peppered stonework and shattered facade. A perfect white smile to a job accomplished as she returned to the luxury of her car.

Inside, minutes passed, gripped in fear.

"What in God's name just happened?" asked Father Peters, retrieving his glasses, lost in his haste to find cover.

"Is everyone okay, anyone hurt?" shouted Simon checking over Lisa who remained in the foetal position with her head tucked to her chest and flinched, sensing Simon's touch.

"Stay still. They could still be out there waiting," he whispered before staying below the shattered window frames, making for the kitchen door and finding a splintered space where it had been. Pressing his back against the wall, he peered around the door frame to discover the yard empty but for the trusty Ford still parked. "They've gone," he confirmed. "The yard is empty."

Father Peters was now consoling Lisa, her face pitted with glass cuts, but she appeared otherwise unscathed if shaken.

Lisa saw the devastation as she pulled away, her expression

a mask of distress.

"What's the matter, lass?" the Father asked, sharing her concern as she searched franticly.

"Jake… Jake, honey, where are you?" she shouted.

"Momma!" The response sounded weak and came from the hall.

"Oh dear God, no," Father Peters said as Lisa rushed from his arms to push open the double doors leading to the hall.

The once sturdy wooden panels had not stopped the barrage of rounds tearing through, peppering the surrounding staircase and hall.

As Lisa pushed on, she came to an immediate stop, covering her mouth at the scene before her.

The hall was littered with evidence of the attack and knelt amongst it was young Jake. His baby faced cheeks ashen white as he pressed an opened book to his chest. The dark blue book of Animals of Africa had two perforated holes in its cover. As the youngster saw his mother, he cried out again. "Momma, it hurts, my stomach hurts."

Stood beside Jake was D, unable to find the words as he saw Lisa.

"No, oh, God no," she cried, rushing to her son.

Simon and Father Peters entered the hall, the priest crossing himself, whispering a prayer as he pulled out his battered mobile to dial the emergency services.

Simon looked on in shock as Lisa cradled Jake in her arms. Traces of blood soaked his clothing as she stroked his face, singing a quiet lullaby as though he were sleeping.

"I'm sorry, Lisa, but it's time," said D.

Tears streamed her face, unconcerned about her unslung arm, ignoring her own pain as she cradled Jake. "No, no, they're not having him, not my little boy, no." She hugged him tighter, her tears soaking his cheek as she rocked him backwards and forwards.

Simon clutched D's arm, pulling him further into the hall. "Save him, do something D. We have to try," he shouted. "Offer them someone else, tell them to take me."

D removed his glasses, pulling away with a glare. "I can't, Fate has requested he died today."

Simon grabbed D's arm again, his anger clear. "Don't give me this bullshit, not with Jakes life in the balance."

"I warned you and today you pay Jake for Lisa."

"That's not fair; it's not supposed to finish like this, we're not losing Jake."

"Life isn't fair," D snapped. "When are you going to understand, Simon?"

"We retrieved and neutralised the blade. That counts for something with the powers. Please D, call in favours and heal him."

D was not listening as he went to Lisa and Jake.

"They not going to help," Father Peters interrupted.

Simon turned on the priest, eyes welling with emotion. "What do you mean?"

"Michael made it clear earlier that there'd be no further help from the archangels. You are on your own and it was your choosing."

Simon rubbed his face, a sense of helplessness as he watched D crouch to hold Lisa's hand.

"It is time," he whispered. "He's ready to leave."

Lisa, with an unusual calmness to D's touch, gave a reluctant swallow as she fought her tears. She leaned back to show Jakes motionless body, his eyes closed, mimicking sleep.

D raised a hand, placing it on the boy's head, closing his own eyes.

The scene passed in silence until Lisa released a breath, sensing a weight lifting to pass through her.

D stood back. "He has ascended."

With further tears, she continued to hug Jake. "I felt him go, I swear I did." With a wail of emotion, Lisa sobbed into the body of her little boy.

The others could but watch, holding back their own grief.

Simon returns in Redemption for the Dead, the next chapter of the Redemption series.

AFTERWORD

Congratulations, Reader, and thank you for reaching the end of this novel. Do hope you enjoyed the ongoing adventures of Simon and his friends and are looking forward to the next instalment.

Want to stay updated with latest news, please use the following links:

Facebook Page
    https://www.facebook.com/RedBS2020/
Website
    https://www.redemption-series.com/

Last, if you have time please leave a review to help other like-minded Readers find their next brilliant read.

Thank you again, dear reader, and hope to see you again, for Simon has many adventures ahead.

REDEMPTION SERIES

A disgraced angel's descent triggers a chain of prophecies in the escalating war between heaven and hell, beginning the end of days in near future dystopia America.

Redemption

Redemption For The Dead

Printed in Great Britain
by Amazon